SINFUL BARGAINS

SINFUL BARGAINS

SINS OF THE FATHER BOOK I

ZARA JADE ASTRID

Olive Press
PUBLISHING

Praise for Zara Jade Astrid

I need book two like yesterday. My soul is not at peace until I get answers!

— AUTHOR CHEYANNE KING

I picked this book up not knowing what to expect—and when I put it down, I was absolutely blown away.

— JESSIE HASSAN, LIBRARIAN

I couldn't put it down!

— AWARD-WINING AUTHOR ASHER FREND

If you're looking for something gripping and unforgettable, this is it.

— FRANKIE VASQUEZ, EDITOR

ISBN: 979-8-9987751-0-9 (EBOOK)

ISBN: 979-8-9987751-1-6 (PAPERBOOK)

Any references to historical events, real people, or real places are used fictionally. Names, characters, and places are products of the author's imagination.

Published by Olive Press Publishing, South Carolina, USA

Cover design by Modern Designs 139

Editing by Olive Press Publishing, LLC

First printing edition 2025.

www.publishingwitholivepress.com

A Note From The Author

Dear Reader,

Sinful Bargains is a dark mafia romance/coming of age story that explores themes of crime, violence, power struggles, and morally complex relationships. This novel contains mature content that may be distressing to some readers, including:

- Graphic violence and murder
- Mafia-related crime and organized crime elements
- Manipulation, betrayal, and psychological distress
- Toxic relationships and emotional conflicts
- Abusive and violent relationships

While this story delves into heavy topics of power, betrayal, and survival, please be advised that some themes may be triggering. Reader discretion is strongly advised.

This is a work of fiction, and while it is inspired by real-world criminal dynamics, it is not meant to glorify or romanticize violence or illegal activities. My goal is " to tell a compelling and emotional story that captures the consequences of the choices made by the characters.

Take care of yourself while reading, and thank you for embarking on this journey with me.

With love and respect,
   Zara Jade Astrid

For my FBI agent—don't worry, it's all fiction.

Playlist

1. Let The World Burn By Chris Grey
2. You Put A Spell On Me By Austin Giorgio
3. Earth Angel (Will You Be Mine) By The Penguins
4. Unchained Melody By The Righteous Brothers
5. Crazy By Patsy Cline, The Jordanaires
6. The Way You Look Tonight By Frank Sinatra
7. Jailhouse Rock By Elvis Presley
8. Can't Help Falling In Love By Elvis Presley
9. Oh, Pretty Woman By Roy Orbison
10. Dream Lover By Bobby Darin
11. It's A Man's, Man's, Man's World By James Brown & The Famous Flames
12. Only Love Can Hurt Like This By Paloma Faith

Contents

Chapter One

ADRIANA

December 1959

The gun in my hand fired, the deafening blast shocking everyone into silence. I watched as he slumped over the counter, his eyes frozen in shock. There was only one way out of this fight, and I had made the call tonight.

Antonio lay trembling on the kitchen floor, his chest heaving with shallow, frantic breaths at the sight before us. This should have ended long ago.

The gun fired again. Pulling the trigger on the revolver not once, but twice. Desperate to seal the job, once and for all. This time, William's massive frame crumpled to the freshly mopped tile, blood pooling around him. It didn't matter where it was pouring out of, only that it was coming out, and by the time someone found him, he'd be gone.

Time was slipping through my fingers. I had to get Antonio and me out of there—far away—before it was too late. Before someone found out what I'd done.

The rain pounded against the windshield of my blue, 1940 Chevrolet Special Deluxe, relentless and unforgiving, each drop a reminder of my desperation to get us as far away as possible.

My hands gripped the steering wheel so tightly that my knuckles went white. They still trembled with the faint, ironlike scent of blood—his blood—clinging to my nostrils.

In the back seat, my thirteen-year-old son, Antonio, sat motionless, staring out at the storm with wide, unblinking eyes. I wanted to tell him everything would be fine, to offer some comfort, but I couldn't bring myself to say it. I didn't know if we could ever move past what happened tonight. I wasn't sure I could ever forgive myself for shooting his father in front of him, leaving him for dead as we made a hasty exit.

The Staten Island ferry terminal loomed ahead, its massive silhouette casting a shadow over my thoughts. I couldn't shake the gnawing fear that sooner or later, someone would come looking for us. For me. And I would have to answer for my actions. In 1959, there was no time for women's rights, and in such a world, there would be no forgiveness for women who were expected to endure the wrath of their husbands in silence.

For years, I had walked around, learning to cover up my scars since nobody was brave enough to ask me who had inflicted the wounds. But I convinced myself that Staten Island, with its quiet streets and small-town charm, was the last place anyone would think to search for me when they found my husband, William, dead on the kitchen floor.

Still, despite my attempts to quiet the fear, it lingered in the back of my mind, like a whisper I couldn't escape. A part of me hoped the city would swallow me up, disappear into its depths, and force me to forget everything I was running from. As if it never happened. As if I never killed my husband.

My breath hitched as the weight of what I'd done crashed over me; just the sheer, recent memory terrified me to my core. The bruises on my ribs throbbed with each shaky breath, a constant reminder of why I had to rationalize my actions. But murder could never be justified. For years, I had endured his fists, his threats, and the way he mocked my tears. But tonight, I had fought back—and there was no taking it back now. I would have to die with the guilt of murdering my abuser, and that I had done so in front of our son.

"Do you think we're safe, Ma?" Antonio's voice shattered the heavy silence.

I caught his eyes in the rearview mirror and forced a nod, more for his sake than mine. "We will be," I promised, though my throat tightened around the lie.

I parked near the terminal and dug through my bag, counting the crumpled bills and coins I had grabbed in our frantic escape. My savings were a pitiful offering for what we needed: safety, a roof over our heads, and a future untainted by fear.

"Come on," I whispered, as if anyone would know our secret.

Antonio climbed out, clutching his backpack. We had left so suddenly that he only had time to grab the backpack he'd kept hidden in his closet—the one he'd prepared for the day we would finally escape his father's abusive grip. And that day had come. Just not in the way either one of us could ever imagine.

My gaze darted inside the terminal, scanning the few stragglers —a janitor, an older couple arguing softly, and a group of teenagers loitering by the vending machines. Harmless, I thought, though my heart refused to slow. I wasn't used to the feeling of having a man's blood on my hands. It was as though everyone else could see it on me, smell it on me. Like they knew what I had done, but they didn't find my actions justifiable.

But when my eyes locked on a man sitting in the far corner, my stomach dropped. He was staring at us. Oh fuck, he knew what I'd done. He was tall, broad-shouldered, and cloaked in a dark suit and tie. His sharp jawline and cold, calculating eyes seemed out of place among the ordinary travelers. And yet, he was watching us as if he knew our story. I turned away, urging Antonio closer to me. I couldn't afford to draw attention to myself right now. I had to act calm.

But as we boarded the ferry, my mind raced with questions.

Was he following us, or was I imagining things? Had someone

found William already? Either way, I couldn't shake the feeling that I might have stepped from one nightmare into another.

The city waited for us somewhere across the dark expanse of water—the town I was seeking solace and refuge in was the very town filled with secrets and power, ruled by men who wielded both like weapons. I would soon learn that safety had a price.

And sometimes, salvation came with chains of its own.

I felt the cold sting of the wind as I tightened my grip on Antonio's arm. The Staten Island ferry groaned as it pulled away from the terminal, the bright lights of the city shrinking into a shimmering blur behind us. I watched as New York City faded into the night.

I hunched over, pressing Antonio closer to my side. My eyes darted in every direction at each unfamiliar face, fear curling in my stomach like a coiled snake. I didn't dare let my guard down, not after tonight. And not anytime soon. I was a woman on the run, and I would have to get used to looking over my shoulder.

That was the choice I'd made. The price that I had to pay for our freedom.

Twenty minutes later, the ferry docked, and we scurried off down the sidewalk to a nearby hotel. The blinking sign hardly blinked anymore, but I pushed open the entrance door. The lobby of the rundown hotel reeked of damp wood and stale cigarette smoke. But it was all I could afford, so I forced myself to meet the clerk's eyes, slipping him the few bills I had stuffed in my bag.

"One room," I hesitated softly, my voice barely carrying over the ancient ceiling fan creaking overhead.

The man glanced at Antonio, then back at me, his face devoid of curiosity or sympathy. He handed me a single key attached to a worn leather fob. "Room 3A. Third floor, end of the hall," he muttered, returning to his crossword puzzle without waiting for my response.

I took Antonio's hand, pulling him toward the narrow staircase. My heart thudded with each step, the old wooden boards groaning beneath our weight. I hated how exposed we were, how every sound in this place seemed to echo like a gunshot. I was certain I'd never be able to get the sound of the revolver firing out of my mind. We quickly reached 3A and ushered ourselves inside.

The room was small—barely big enough for the single bed pushed against one wall, a battered chair by the window, and a chipped nightstand. Once pale yellow, the wallpaper was a peeling, stained memory of better days. I closed the door and locked it, dragging the chair and placing it under the knob for good measure. I turned to Antonio, sitting on the edge of the bed, his tiny shoulders slumped. I hated to see him so defeated. We hadn't said one word about what I'd done, or what he had seen, and I dreaded the day I'd have to acknowledge what had happened out loud.

"I know it's not much," I crouched before him, "but it's just for now. Tomorrow, we'll figure things out."

He nodded silently, his eyes heavy with exhaustion. He hadn't spoken much since we'd left, and I couldn't blame him.

He was only thirteen, thrust into a world of uncertainty with no warning.

"Why don't you get some sleep?" I suggested, brushing a stray lock of his dark brown, curly hair from his forehead. "You'll need your rest for tomorrow."

"Okay," he murmured, lying back against the lumpy mattress.

I tucked the thin blanket around him, trying to summon a smile I didn't feel. "I'll be right here, okay?"

He nodded again, his eyes fluttering shut.

I waited until his breathing evened out, then sank into the chair I'd placed before the door. My body ached from the weight of my fear, my mind racing with the impossible task ahead. Tomorrow, I would enroll Antonio in school. He needed stability, something normal to hold onto amidst all the chaos.

But finding work? That was a different battle. The world did not have a place for single mothers in 1959. I had spent my life being told what I could and couldn't do by society, always standing in my husband's shadow, confined to roles society deemed acceptable for a woman.

Secretary. Seamstress. Waitress.

If I were lucky, someone might take pity on me. But pity wouldn't feed Antonio. It wouldn't pay for a room or keep us hidden, either. I'd make it work, no matter what.

Because failure wasn't an option.

Chapter Two

JOEY

The ambiance of Vino e Pasta, an upscale Italian restaurant in Manhattan, was impeccable. The back room had been reserved for our group—the Giordano Crime Family. A large rectangular table draped in crisp, white linen was set with polished silverware. An endless spread of Italian dishes was laid out, with an unspoken promise of unlimited whiskey refills—an offer I planned to take full advantage of.

This family was all I had ever known, the only one I'd ever had. Tonight, we gathered to celebrate the newest members, Lee and Sal, two young guys I had taken under my wing. We were dressed in our sharpest suits. But Vincent's presence had a way of dimming even the brightest of occasions. He was the underboss, and someone I secretly despised.

"That DiSantis motherfucker is talking about asking for a bigger cut of the dock operations," Vincent announced to the table, his voice edged with irritation. He leaned back in his chair, whiskey glass in hand. "He told Hector his men are getting sick of busting their asses for peanuts while we rake in the real money. But they wouldn't be able to operate without us."

The men around the table nodded in agreement, a well-trained chorus of approval. Vincent thrived on that—loyalty without question. "I just don't like when guys in his position get ideas and think they can make demands."

DiSantis was using the docks to smuggle luxury goods—radios, televisions, artwork, antiques—high-ticket items that sold for more than double their worth. I had spoken to him myself, and he claimed Hector's cut was so steep he could barely afford to keep his operation running. DiSantis had a reputation for exaggeration, but I had a feeling he wasn't far off this time.

The trade-off worked in our favor. DiSantis gave us access to the unions, solidifying our control. At this point, we had more power than the mayor, which was why he was on the payroll, too. We weren't just running the docks. We were taking over every crevice of New York.

"I think we need to send a message," Vincent remarked, swirling the whiskey in his glass. "Take one of 'em out—that'll show DiSantis where his place is."

That would start a war.

I took a slow sip of my whiskey, letting the burn settle in my throat before speaking. "Or we bring them to the table. Hear what they gotta say. Meet them somewhere in the middle."

The room shifted. A few of the guys exchanged quick glances. Vincent's expression darkened, his eyes locking onto me like a predator sizing up its prey. "The fuck do you mean, bring 'em to the table?" he barked.

"DiSantis has given us more power than this family has ever had. Instead of making an enemy out of him, we put him in our pocket," I said. "We cut him a deal, let him sit at the table. That way, we control the whole operation—inside and out."

Silence settled over the table. Vincent leaned back, studying me with that cold, calculating look of his. Then, he tossed his head back and let out a sharp laugh. "I thought prison made men tougher—seems like it just made you scared. Don't wanna get your hands dirty anymore, Joey?"

A few of the guys chuckled under their breath. At the head of the table, the boss, Christopher, cleared his throat. The laughter died instantly. "I think Joey's got a point," he said. "If we take out DiSantis or his men, we start a war. We need long- term security if we're gonna keep growing. We infiltrate, not dominate. If we start shooting, the feds start looking. And that's how we get taken down."

Vincent scoffed, shaking his head. "We've never run things that way before. Why change now?" His voice was sharp, testing every limit. "We got where we are by being ruthless. Even the goddamn mayor is scared of us. If we start going soft, the cracks will show, and this whole thing comes down. We've always decided who stays in the game. If I wanted to be a businessman, I would've gone to school for it. Nobody in this room wants to be some Wall Street junkie. We stick to the code. No new rules."

Christopher leaned forward, resting his elbows on the table. "This isn't about going soft. It's about being smart. Playing the game smarter. The feds are getting smarter. Joey would know; he spent a decade locked away with them." He gestured towards me. "We're bigger than that now. We've got politicians in our pocket, judges who owe us favors. We're not just enforcers anymore— we're the ones pulling the strings."

Vincent sneered, shaking his head. "And you think DiSantis is worth all that? You're betting on a guy who's already looking for more. What happens when he gets too comfortable and starts thinking he's one of us?"

"Then we remind him who put him there. We give him just enough rope to tie a noose around his neck. He steps out of line, we pull it tight. But we don't need enemies while we're trying to take over. We need assets. And we certainly don't need a war."

The table was quiet, waiting for Vincent's response. He exhaled through his nose, picking up his whiskey. But he didn't respond. And while the rest of the table continued on, I knew this was far from over.

I stepped onto the Staten Island ferry and made my way to the railing, pulling a cigarette from my coat pocket. I hadn't had a smoke all day, and after the night I'd just had in Manhattan, I needed it. The city's noise and lights faded into the open water, a relief I hadn't realized I'd been craving.

But something—or someone—caught my attention.

A woman. Young, in her early thirties, with wide, haunting, dark eyes and dark black hair gliding down her back. She was stunning—impossible to miss, even if she wasn't acting like every sound and shadow could kill her. When the light hit her face just long enough for me to take her hardened features in, I noticed the yellow tint shining on her cheekbone. It made perfect sense why she looked ready to bolt at any moment, her arm protectively wrapped around the kid beside her.

Someone had put this woman through hell.

My eyes narrowed as I took a slow drag from my cigarette. I wasn't one to meddle. And yet, I couldn't help watching as she shifted anxiously, scanning the deck like a hunted animal. I'd seen looks like that—usually after someone had witnessed great horrors.

I exhaled a cloud of smoke and shook my head. Not my business. I descended the stairs, pushing my thoughts about her aside. Whoever she was running from didn't concern me. I had my own problems—ones that didn't involve strange women I saw on my way home, even if they were beautiful. I shoved my hands into my pockets and started the familiar walk home, yet her face was in the back of my mind, even when I tried to forget it.

I stepped through the front door of my shared home with my girlfriend, Renee. I tossed my keys on the counter and shrugged off my coat, hanging it on the hook by the door.

"Joey?" her voice called out.

"In here."

She appeared a moment later, wiping her hands on a kitchen towel. Renee was attractive in the understated, effortless way I had always noticed, but never dwelled on. Her light caramel hair fell loose around her shoulders, and her hazel eyes, so much like her father's, narrowed as she gave me a once-over. I had known Renee for most of my life, but it wasn't until after my release from Ricker's Island that our relationship evolved into something more. Renee was Vincent's daughter, and unfortunately, she was like him in many ways.

I had gone down for a ten-year sentence for extortion. Was I guilty of extortion? Yes. But had I been the one to commit the crime, that would put me behind bars for a decade? No. And yet, I kept my mouth shut. I bid my time. I successfully guided Paul in running my car wholesale business, raking in millions for the family. Only to be set free and have Vincent push me down the chain of command.

But I had done my time, and I'll be damned if I stood shoulder to shoulder with a bunch of amateurs doing grunt work. So that night at the speakeasy, The Wise Guy, when I saw Renee, I thought, what better way to get back at the man stripping me of my life's work than to defile his own daughter? Only his fucking daughter was just as bad as him, digging her long claws into my back in ways I only meant for her to do after one too many whiskey neats.

Now I was playing house with her. But it was working in my favor. Vincent couldn't bear his daughter being involved with a nobody, so he made me somebody. Somebody, I was always destined to be. A title I was always destined to carry. Capo.

"Long day?" she asked, stepping closer and brushing invisible lint off my suit.

"Not bad," I lied. "You didn't have to wait up."

In fact, I wish you hadn't waited up.

She shrugged, leaning back against the counter. "Couldn't sleep."

I studied her, noting how her jaw tensed and her gaze flickered briefly toward the living room. "Something happened while I was gone?"

Renee hesitated before shaking her head. "No. Just...Dad called this morning."

Of course, he did. I'd managed to escape him before he could stop me after that sit-down.

"What'd he want?"

"Same as always," Renee responded, but I noticed how she bit her lip, avoiding my intrusive gaze. "Making sure you're watching out for his precious daughter." Her words were edged with sarcasm, but the look in her eyes told me she wanted something more from me. Renee wanted me to take our relationship seriously.

I reached out, wrapping my hand around hers and gently squeezing it. "You tell him I'm good for it?"

Her lips curved faintly, but it didn't reach her eyes. "I told him. I don't think he will ever trust anyone with me—not even you."

I gave a low chuckle, releasing her hand and leaning back again. "Wouldn't either, if I were him."

Renee rolled her eyes. "Very funny, Joey. But I hope he didn't give you too much trouble at dinner tonight."

"Not too bad," I lied.

She studied me, her brows knitting together. "Something happened. You're tense."

I exhaled heavily and sank onto the couch. "It's hard getting everyone on the same page," I admitted. "But Christopher liked my idea. I just hope your father doesn't think I'm stepping on his toes. I'm just trying to show there are smarter ways to take control."

She nodded. "Well, he's always at home. He doesn't need to know everything you do."

"He'd find out," I cut in.

"But you've got good ideas."

When Renee disappeared down the hallway, my mind wandered back to the mysterious woman from the ferry. I wondered who she was and where she'd gone after the ferry docked. Little did I know my life was about to shift again, and the stranger from the ferry would soon be more than a thought.

Chapter Three

ADRIANA

January 1960

I felt the world's weight on my shoulders as I sat at the local diner, the place that became my new routine. It was the same one I'd visited yesterday, and the only real source of food I could provide for Antonio and me. The regulars spoke in low, hushed tones to one another. Their lives were no more complicated than a daily coffee, but to me, this place felt like the only semblance of normalcy I could latch onto. It was the only way I could keep Antonio fed, but I grew more anxious as I knew my secret stash of cash would run out soon.

Antonio sat quietly across from me in the booth, scribbling something in his notebook as music played from the jukebox. My heart ached for him; this move, this new life, was as foreign to him as it was to me. He had been through so much and had witnessed too much for a child his age.

I feared the guilt of what he'd had to witness would be something I could never get over. He had begged me to leave for years, but I always felt trapped.

That night, everything changed when the usual violence went from being directed toward me to Antonio. I knew I had to strike.

And I did. Now, there was no way ever to go back. I could hardly live with the guilt that I had waited for it to escalate to that moment before I left.

Antonio, despite having gone through just as much as I had been through, promised me he didn't hold any harboring feelings towards me. He knew I was in a hard place—leaving an abusive husband with a child was greatly frowned upon by society. This fact held me back from leaving—until the moment I had to step in to protect my son from the very abuse that had been inflicted on me for years.

I wasn't surprised to see the same few faces I'd seen the day prior sitting in the diner. I had realized, since being in Staten Island for a mere two days, that it was a small island where most of the residents seemed to be either related or knew someone who knew someone. I had always lived in small towns, but something was different about this place. And I couldn't quite place my finger on it.

One face, however, stood out among the rest that morning.

The man I had seen that night at the ferry terminal on my way into Staten Island. In the daylight, I could see him clearly. He looked sharp, lean, yet his broad shoulders stretched the fabric of his single-breasted coat. His face had an inherent allure to it—compelling blue eyes, a sharp jawline thrust forward, and the faint shadow of a beard that gave him an even more manly aura. He had an air of authority and the appearance of one who demanded instant obedience. He didn't seem like anyone you would walk up to and approach.

Yet, I wanted to get closer. He held himself in such high regard that he demanded everyone's attention without speaking. He was an important man, whatever it was he did. My intuition was quick to tell me this man was different. Mysterious, enigmatic. Still, there was something magnetic about him. Even from a distance, I could sense his presence, an invisible force tugging at the corners of my awareness.

"Two coffees, please," I said softly to the waitress as she approached our booth.

"Comin' right up."

Fear and anxiety knotted inside of me, an itch to blend in, but my stiff demeanor was making that impossible to accomplish. The locals had been kind enough, but I could sense their wariness regarding strangers. Particularly newcomers like myself. Maybe it was the air of mystery I carried with me—or the fact I'd walked into town with nothing more than the clothes on my back and a thirteen-year-old boy.

The diner's door opened again with a clatter of metal, followed by the heavy scent of gasoline and sawdust that usually marked a day's labor. A stocky man with broad shoulders walked in, his work boots scraping against the floor. He didn't notice me, but rather nodded to the waitress and asked her for a coffee in his thick New York accent. I saw him here yesterday morning. I couldn't remember his face, only how he walked in at 6:15 a.m., already smelling like he'd been working for hours.

Still, everyone in the diner this morning had been here the past two mornings. Except for the man from the ferry terminal sitting at the bar counter, sipping his coffee. I watched him finally shift slightly, his eyes darting briefly over towards the man who had entered. He met my hardened stare before returning to his coffee.

I felt the electricity of his gaze like a spark in the still air, and just as quickly, his attention faded, leaving me both intrigued and suspicious. I took a deep breath, trying to steady myself, but the anxiety was creeping up again. My chest felt so tight, like it might cave in. I hesitated, gathering my swirling thoughts before standing and walking toward him. My heart drummed against my ribcage, still struggling to heal.

"Are you following me?" My voice was low, but firm. I didn't want anyone to overhear us. "I recognize you from the ferry terminal. I don't want to make a scene here, but I'd like to know if someone sent you to follow me around."

The man's eyes met mine. He hesitated and blinked with bafflement, caught off guard by my directness. His eyes seemed to soften as he processed my words briefly. His gaze, the way it slowly raked over my features, caused me to shift nervously on my heels.

He cleared his throat, leaning back slightly in his chair. "I been here my whole life," he said. His accent was thick with a New York drawl, just like everyone else in this town. His gaze flickered to mine, studying me in a way that made me visibly squirm and want to crawl out of my skin. "Who did this to you?"

I instantly became wide awake. His words sliced through the air like cold water to the face, washing away the makeup I had strategically applied to cover up the bruise that had painted my skin a soft yellow shade. My heavy lashes flew up in surprise. The images of my husband, the gun in my hand, the blood on the freshly cleaned tile, came rushing back—my bold escape, the fear for myself and Antonio.

"I don't know what you're talking about," I muttered, my throat tight with emotion. "I'm just trying to get settled."

He scoffed, shaking his head before reaching for a napkin, scribbling an address on it. Without meeting my eyes, he slid it across the counter to me. "Go to the counter and tell them Joey sent you," he said quietly. I stared at the napkin for a moment, my mind racing. Was he offering to help me? But why? He didn't know me. What could he possibly see in me that would possess him to want to help me? "It's a small neighborhood. A lot of people know each other here," he explained, breaking the silence between us.

I looked up from the napkin, disoriented. "I figured as much."

I dared to look at him directly, but his eyes, dark and assessing, were almost too much to bear. "You'll learn who matters here soon enough," he added. I searched his eyes for clarity on that statement, but all I saw was the beautiful shade of ice blue.

As he got up to leave, he turned again, his voice soft as he whispered, "If you need anything, don't hesitate. Folks here aren't all friendly, but some know how to help. And everyone knows where to find me. Just say my name, and they'll know exactly who you're talking about."

His words, simple yet loaded, followed him out the door. I caught myself staring long after he had left. There was something about him—unsettling yet compelling. I couldn't quite decide what it was. But something told me our paths had only begun to intersect in ways that would change my life in more ways than one, far beyond anything I could ever imagine.

There was no time for second-guessing; I knew it was a risk — this new life was a risk. But it was one I had no choice but to take.

I hurried out of the diner and down the sidewalk, Antonio's pace matching my own. "Ma, who was that guy, and what did he want?" he asked.

I was too preoccupied to answer his questions. Instead, my eyes were locked ahead as I scanned the small corner store whose address matched the napkins. I opened the door, and the bell above rang, announcing our arrival. Behind the counter stood an older man in his sixties, wearing an apron over a weathered shirt. He glanced up at me with an expression that was impossible to read.

"Joey sent me here..." I said, my voice quivering. I wasn't sure what I was doing or what would come of this, but I was running out of options. And money.

The man studied me, then slightly nodded, still expressionless. "When can you start?"

I blinked, struggling to hide my confusion. "Start what?"

"Well, you came here for a cashier job, didn't you? I don't know why else he would have sent you." The man's voice was steady, like this was an everyday request. A surge of disbelief hit me. Joey—the man I barely knew—had just gotten me a job. I could hardly process what was happening.

"Today," I said quickly, almost too eagerly. "Now. Whenever." The man let out a low chuckle, his face softening slightly.

"How about tomorrow? I open at 7:00 a.m., but I'll need you here by 6:45 a.m."

Relief broke from my lips, the weight in my chest easing just a fraction. It wasn't much, but it was a start. I glanced back at Antonio, quietly watching near the door, and gave him a hopeful smile.

The next morning, I showed up at 6:45 a.m. on the dot. My first task was simple: make the best damn pot of coffee I could make. Mr. Davidson, the store owner, had shown me the correct ratio of coffee grounds to water—his instructions were straightforward and exact. He didn't ask me any questions, and he didn't probe into my past. He simply showed me what needed to be done, and I did it without hesitation. For the first time since I'd arrived on Staten Island, I felt like I might be okay.

Like clockwork, as soon as the clock struck 7:00 a.m. and Mr. Davidson unlocked the front doors to the corner store, the men began trickling into the store, one after another. Each of them inspected me, but I stuck to my list of to-dos. As they filed in, their quiet yet assertive demeanor marked them as something more than just working-class men. These were no ordinary customers. I didn't notice initially; I focused on ensuring the coffee was perfect, the shelves were stocked, and the floors were swept.

However, it became clear that these men were paying far too much attention to my presence than I'd appreciated.

Joey was among the men who walked into the corner store for their first cup of coffee that morning. After pouring his cup, he finally walked toward the counter where I stood as he took a sip. As he reached the counter, our eyes met. I felt my compo- sure under attack, and I couldn't hold his gaze for long. Something in his eyes unsettled me, luminous shadows pulling me into his orb.

"Good coffee," he said smoothly, breaking the silence and giving me the slightest hint of a smile.

"Thank you...Thank you for the job," I muttered hastily. "I don't know why you did it, but I appreciate it."

The last thing I wanted when I arrived on Staten Island was to be indebted to a man, but I couldn't deny the generosity in his actions. It felt like I was suddenly less alone in the world, a feeling

I hadn't expected after everything I'd been through. My eyes flickered over his shoulder at the men mingling at the coffee bar, staring my way and snickering to one another. Joey's eyes followed mine as he looked over his shoulder.

He leaned his body against the counter; his eyes clung to mine, analyzing my reactions, the way I squirmed under all the eyes suddenly pointing my way. "They like to look," he said with a barely perceptible nod toward the men eyeing me all morning, "but they know I sent you here. They won't step out of line. They know better."

I hesitated, wondering what exactly that meant. Still, before I could ask, Joey tipped his fedora in a casual salute and turned away, moving toward the door with the same silent command he'd entered with. The doorbell jingled softly as he exited, and I was left standing there, still processing.

Joey had made it clear—he was looking out for me. And I didn't know if I should be grateful or terrified.

Chapter Four

JOEY

I told myself to stay away from that mysterious woman, but she was everywhere. Maybe it was just the nature of a small neighborhood—you couldn't help but keep running into the same faces. Maybe it was because she was beautiful, and I'd never been good at resisting a pretty face. Either way, I couldn't help myself. I had to know who she was.

The images of her were burning a hole through my brain. She had an undeniable presence, and I had to know what had brought her to Staten Island. Her beauty was unquestionable, but it wasn't just her looks that caught my attention—it was how she had seemed to develop a strength and stamina that were at odds with the slenderness of her body.

But God, was she heavenly. It was the kind of beauty that made men like me pause.

I was no stranger to attracting attention; I commanded it in any room I entered. And I made sure of it. The feds had nicknamed me "The Shark," an alias that reflected my demeanor and ruthless ability to climb the ranks of the city's organized crime scene. I'd climbed the organization faster than anyone had expected, earning a fearsome reputation.

After serving a prison sentence for extortion, many thought

they'd seen the last of me—but I emerged from the shadows stronger, more focused, ready to take back what had been stolen from me.

But she reminded me of something I'd thought I'd buried. I recognized that look on her face. That desperation. It was like staring into a mirror. My own mother's struggle against my father flooded my mind when I looked into her deep brown eyes—full of the same silent plea for relief, for freedom I'd seen in my mother's eyes growing up.

The difference was that she had somehow seemed to escape with her son, something my mother had never managed. As I looked at her teenage son, tall with unruly, dark hair, I realized that it had transported me back to my own childhood. It touched a softer spot in me that I thought had long died out.

I knew enough about pain, about survival, to offer her something that could give her a shot at a fresh start. I was many things, but I was also a man who had seen enough to know when people were worth helping, and when they were just a lost cause. Something about her was worth helping.

I sat in a dimly lit bar at a corner booth, nursing a glass of whiskey, when Ben, the rogue cop on my payroll, approached and slid into the seat next to me. I didn't acknowledge him, but instead placed a small manila envelope on the bar counter.

"What's this?" he asked.

I finally acknowledged Ben as I sat back in my seat, taking up the space between us. "A woman's driver's license. Goes by the name Adriana Bianchi. I need everything you can dig up on her."

His eyebrows rose. "You understand I risk my job when I pass over this kind of information, right?" he retorted.

My mouth spread into a thin-lipped smile. "Your pockets are rewarded justly, so don't start your nonsense with me. You know I'm good for the money once you give me what I want."

Ben studied me and flashed a stern expression. "Always straight to the point, huh? Who is she, anyway?"

I shrugged, weighing his question. "That's your job to figure out. All I know is she's new around here, staying at that dump of a motel on Hawthorne Street. Showed up outta nowhere with a kid. I noticed her one night on the ferry, and then again at the diner. I felt sorry for her, so I got her a job working with Davidson at the corner store."

"If she's staying there, she doesn't seem like your usual...type of interest," he noted, which was precisely why I had to get her out of that dump as soon as possible. She didn't belong in a place like that.

"You know better than to ask too many questions," I warned, sipping my whiskey.

Ben leaned back in his chair, making himself comfortable. He took out the manila folder from his coat that he had tucked away and opened it to retrieve the driver's licenses inside, studying the photo of Adriana before he finally broke the silence. "This Davidson you mentioned—is that where you got this from?"

"I owe him a favor, and he's recovering from hip surgery. He could use the help around that place, and she needed a job. You just need to do your part and get me a report. Past records, who she's running from—if she's running at all. I want it airtight."

One corner of Ben's mouth twisted upward. "Fine. But this one's gonna cost you extra."

I leaned forward, my voice dropping as my expression was tight and strained. "Let me tell you how this works, Benny. You give me what I ask for, and you get paid. You don't, and you'll be running from someone, too. Clear?"

"Crystal." His brows flickered a little.

"Good," I uttered, pulling out an envelope and sliding it towards Ben. "That should get you started. Half up front, half when I have her life story in my hands."

Ben didn't hesitate to grab the envelope and secure it in his coat pocket, along with the other manila folder. "You really know how to sweet-talk a guy, don't you?"

"It's a gift." I smiled blandly. "Now get to work."

Ben rose from his seat, disappearing behind me as I finished my whiskey and headed home. But before I did the dreadful task of returning home, I had one stop to make.

Home was with Renee. It was never supposed to be this way. The math was simple—two lonely people, one too many drinks, and fate was sealed. It was supposed to be a one-time thing. Renee offered me her home. She was Vincent's daughter. The plan fell into my lap. I had never played house before, but surely it wouldn't be too hard.

Only Renee made it nearly impossible. She could smell the guilt of my intentions every time I walked through the front doors. But I was too close to throw in the cards. I had regained every ounce of respect Vincent had tried to take from me. I brought in the most profit out of everyone in the family, successfully funneling in millions of dollars while posing as an honest businessman at a car wholesale shop.

Even when the cops came for my throat, I had Benny on my side. I stuffed his pockets full of dirty money, and he led the NYPD on a wild goose chase, never once successfully pinning The Shark to the cross. I had more money than I knew what to do with, yet I was playing house with Renee and chess with Vincent.

All I had to do was hang on a little longer, and I would rise to the top—where I belonged—becoming untouchable to Vincent. I could live in my quiet little mansion, raking in the dough. And the best part of it all? Vincent would no longer control my life, and Renee would have to dig her claws into another man.

I walked through the doors of the lonely mansion I had purchased. It was waiting for me to come home—to leave Renee, to rise to the top, and to claim it like the underworld king I was. And it had a special design just for me.

I walked through the chilly foyer, rounded the corner, and stepped into the living room. My little secret stash of cash hidden in the beautiful wooden floor. I had to get my cut ready for the family meeting tomorrow night—20% to Christopher, the head of the family, and 10% to that bastard Vincent, the underboss.

But soon—soon, all of this would be mine.

I had spent my entire life dedicated to the mafia. I was recruited young, desperate to escape my violent home life. The streets of the Bronx were home to scary individuals. At the time, Christopher, now the boss of the family, caught me stealing from the convenience store one of his guys ran.

Instead of giving me a good beating, he took pity on me. I was starving for not only food, but guidance. Roaming the streets of New York City day and night. I don't know why he decided to take me under his wing, but I have always been grateful he did. He was the only father figure I had ever had—he and the other guys in the family had become the only family I had ever had besides my mother. They stepped in as father figures, brothers, and friends to me. Paul and Marco stepped up for the past ten years, visiting Rickers and meeting up with Ben to follow out my orders from behind bars.

I never wanted to put a label on my relationship with Renee, but she had labeled me her man after our first night together.

Renee plays innocent, like any good mafia princess should, but she's far from innocent. Her first husband and the father of her son, Giovanni, was slapped with a life sentence, and Renee couldn't let her boy grow up without a father. I never wanted to be a father. How could I be someone's father when my own was a piece of shit? And no matter how much I hated his fucking guts, I knew his blood ran through my veins. I was a lot of things, but I would never roll the dice and fuck up a kid the same way I'd been fucked up.

Renee loved the underworld just as much as I did. She idolized men like me. She loved that she was a mafia princess because of Vincent's street status, which is why she forced me to the top of the food chain—just so she could don the title of mafia wife. She wanted to be mafia royalty just as badly as I did.

But in this life, love doesn't exist. You hold your cards close to your chest and learn to play them right. What she thought was love was just a desire to claim me, pin me down, and attach herself to The Shark—the man they report about on the 5 o'clock news.

The man they print in the newspapers for "suspicious criminal activity."

But maybe I can hold out just long enough to make it all work out in the end.

Later that night, I sat on the sofa at home, slowly enjoying a cigar. I was lost in my thoughts when Renee walked in and sat at the other end of the sofa.

She eyed me intently. I could feel her gaze, but I wasn't ready to acknowledge it. "You were quiet during dinner. Is everything okay?"

"Just thinking," I remarked, blowing the smoke into the air and watching it curl and dissipate. Something I wish I could do in that very moment—disappear. If only for a second.

"About what?" she pressed, like I knew she would. I never felt like I was allowed my own thoughts around her—it was an unspoken rule that I had to reveal what was on my mind if I were in her presence. "Us?"

I finally acknowledged her, reluctantly, as I snapped, "Why does everything have to be about us, Renee?"

She boldly met my eyes. "Joey, what is going on with you? With us? I don't want to keep dancing around this. We've been...whatever this is, for months now. What are we?"

I leaned my head against the back of the sofa, staring up at the ceiling fan swirling above us. I suddenly noticed how tense my jaw was as my hand gave it a soft rub out of exasperation. Renee always made me feel tense. Something that was supposed to be simple between us had become so much more—so much more than I had ever bargained for. "I told you, I'm not big on labels. You knew that going into this with me."

"Don't give me that," she scoffed, her voice rising in volume. "You've been staying under my roof, around my kid, sleeping in my bed. What do you call that? I deserve an answer, Joey!"

The other thing about Renee is that she shared the same anger as her father—she had no emotional intelligence to stay quiet, to read the room, to not overreact.

What I was so desperate to say at that moment was survival. I just needed to play my cards right, and then I would be gone. I felt trapped. Suffocated. Vincent had already been giving me a hard time about staying in her home without marrying her—a sin that could hammer the last nail in my coffin.

My gaze was brutal and unfriendly, even though I hadn't intended it to be so. "Look, Renee. I care about you—always have. You've been good to me, better than I deserve, even. But what you want is for me to love you, and I don't know if I'm capable of that."

She glared at me with burning, reproachful eyes. "That's a cop-out, Joey, and you know it. You can love someone. You can love me. You just won't let yourself."

"Maybe you're right. But don't act like you have no reasons for keeping me around, either. It's not just me, Renee. I'm not the only one looking out for their own interests here."

I knew I had hit a nerve by the hurt look on her face. I didn't want to hurt her, but I was only trying to be honest for both of our sakes. "That's what you think this is? Some kind of arrangement? I'll have you know I'm no arrangement, Joseph Romano."

"I think we both know this is complicated," I confessed. The truth was, this was some sort of arrangement she'd constructed. And with her father's backing, my hands were tied.

"You want out?" she challenged me, her expression clouded in anger. Yes, I did. Of course, I did.

A shadow of annoyance crossed my face. "I didn't say that. But you and I both know if I wanted out, it wouldn't be that easy."

"No, it wouldn't," she said coldly before storming off and leaving me alone with my own thoughts again.

Just hold on a little longer.

Chapter Five

JOEY

I stepped into Davidson's corner store, and the bell above the door gave a soft chime as I walked in. Behind the counter, Davidson looked up from his ledger, his weathered face breaking into a knowing smile. "How's it going, Joey?" he greeted.

I flashed him a grin, resting my hands on the counter. "Got a meeting downstairs."

Davidson nodded, setting his pen down. "Business as usual."

"How's Adriana doing lately?" I asked out of curiosity. "Figured you might need some help around here after that hip surgery."

"Oh, she's a nice woman. Does everything I ask and keeps her head down. I like her," he said with a small chuckle. "Glad you sent her my way." The deep lines on his face creased as he grinned, a reminder of the years he'd put into this place.

Most people only saw an old man, a shopkeeper past his prime. But I knew better. Davidson had been a real player back in the day. During Prohibition, he'd turned this little store into a front, building the speakeasy downstairs and making a killing. As time wore him down, he passed the reins to the family, letting the operation run under new hands. Now, he watched from the sidelines—but his mind was still sharp, and nothing in this neighborhood happened without him knowing.

I gave him a nod. "Good. I'll see you after."

He simply smirked, stepping aside to let me through the back door where the real business took place.

I stepped into The Wise Guy to see Angela behind the counter. She was the only woman I knew who fit into this world like she was born for it—probably because she was. Every man in her family, from her brothers to her late husband, had been tied to the mafia. Angela had grown up around more wiseguys than anything else, and by now, she was just "one of us." No one questioned it.

DiSantis was already sitting in the back booth, waiting for me, but before I could head over, Angela called out, "Got a minute, Joey?"

I stopped at the bar, drumming my fingers against the counter. "What's up, Ang?"

"My Enzo's been running around with that new kid—Antonio." She slid a glass across to me. "I don't know where they came from or why they're here. And I don't know how much I can trust them. I met his mother down at the school, and she's nice. Mr. Davidson adores her. Do you know anything about her?"

Before I could answer, the door swung open, and in walked Lucy. Her sparkly gloves caught the low light as she strutted up to the counter, her heels clicking against the floor.

"Angela, darling, make me a dirty martini, will ya? I'm parched," she said, flashing that signature smirk before turning to me. "Hey, Joey."

"Lucy." I nodded, watching as she pulled off one glove with a slow, practiced motion.

She always had a way of making an entrance. Lucy was Christopher's daughter, a mafia princess in every sense of the word. On paper, she was the loyal wife of Hector, Christopher's consigliere, but I knew better. She was sneaking around with Ben, but she'd never admit it.

I picked up the whiskey Ang poured me, letting the burn settle before answering. "I'm still working on the details," I admitted. "But I think it's safe to let kids be kids."

She let out a small chuckle, shaking her head as if she knew better. I smirked, taking another sip before nodding toward DiSantis. "I'll check in later."

I slid into the booth across from DiSantis, my movements steady, deliberate.

"Joey! How's it going?" he greeted me, his face lighting up.

I didn't return the smile. "Vincent's not happy with you. You need to watch your back—watch what you're telling Hector."

The grin faded instantly, his shoulders tensing.

"I went to bat for you," I continued. "Told them you deserve a bigger cut, a seat at the table. Christopher backed me up. But if you take that seat, you'd better watch what you drink. Vincent doesn't take kindly to requests."

DiSantis exhaled sharply, drumming his fingers against the table. "I never meant to step on any toes, Joey. I just want what's fair. My guys are breaking their backs for a small payout."

I leaned back, my eyes steady on him. "Fair don't mean shit in this life. You know that."

He nodded slowly, swallowing hard.

"You'll get your seat, but you need to tread lightly. Don't give him a reason to think you're a problem."

He leaned in, lowering his voice. "Look, Joey, I get it. But my operation at the docks—it's making all of us money. The shipments are coming in smoothly, no hiccups, no heat. Luxury goods, artwork, electronics—you name it. We move it clean, we move it fast. We sell it for twice its worth. Hector takes his cut before I even see a dime. My guys are breaking their backs. I'm not asking for a handout, I'm asking for a fair slice of the pie."

"I hear you," I told him. "You've got my word. I'm going to make it happen because it will benefit us all."

It would benefit us all. Lately, I'd been stepping up, taking more risks, and making bigger moves. Some things couldn't always be settled with blood and broken bones—sometimes, you had to play it smart, treat it like a business.

Power wasn't just about fear; it was about control. And control meant knowing when to take and when to give. You couldn't bleed a man dry and expect him to keep working for you.

Sooner or later, that kind of greed came back to bite you.

Chapter Six

ADRIANA

The morning sunlight streamed through the thin curtains of our new home into the modest living room where I slept on the worn, floral-patterned couch. I stirred awake, my body aching slightly from the unforgiving cushions. It was far from luxury, but better than the hotel we'd left behind. And much better than the hell we'd escaped from.

I sat up, stretching my arms as my eyes wandered the small living room. The space was sparse but cozy, with cheap carpeting and walls painted a soft cream color. If you looked closely, you could find peeling paint throughout the house, but I told myself I'd repaint as soon as I got the extra money. All the furniture was second-hand.

The living room had a small wooden coffee table and a worn chair in the corner with a lamp next to it. A small kitchenette occupied one corner, its white cabinets hanging slightly crooked, but functional, nonetheless. There was a four-seater table tucked away in the corner of the kitchen where Antonio and I had been spending plenty of time enjoying home-cooked meals again.

My gaze shifted to the closed bedroom door behind which Antonio still slept—the past few weeks had taken a toll on both of us. We had wandered into Staten Island in the middle of a cold winter night, my wounds still healing.

But now, with spring on the horizon, my wounds had disappeared—though the memories still haunted me every second of my life. I wished I could offer him more than just a tiny rental house, but it was a start—and starts, I reminded myself, were often humble. It was Mr. Davidson's kindness that had made it all possible. I didn't know why he'd taken such a liking to Antonio and me, but I wasn't about to question it. His nephew's property was affordable, and the rent arrangement was flexible—just what I needed while trying to find my footing.

I pushed off the couch, determined to start my Saturday morning despite the corner store being closed on Saturdays and Sundays. This was partly due to how uncomfortable the couch was, and partly due to the insomnia I had been facing since that night.

I padded to the kitchen and began preparing coffee, which I had become quite exceptional at, considering it was my main job at the corner store—ensuring the coffee pot was hot, fresh, and never empty. The steam curled toward the ceiling as I poured it into a chipped mug and sat at the small, wobbly table nearby. I clutched the mug tightly, savoring the warmth and the peace and quiet of the morning—something I was not used to, but had grown fond of.

A soft knock at the front door startled me. I glanced at the clock on the wall—barely 7:30 a.m. Setting the mug down, I crept over to the door and peeked through the peephole.

"Mr. Davidson?" I asked, opening the door, relieved to see his soft smile and weathered shirt.

His silver hair was neatly combed, and a paper bag was in his hand. His kindness shown in the soft lines of his face. "Good morning, Adriana. Thought I'd stop by and bring a little something. Figured you might need it."

He handed me the bag. Inside were fresh eggs, a loaf of bread, and a small tin of butter.

"Thank you," I said. "You've already done so much for us. This is too much. You know you don't have to do this."

"Nonsense," he replied with a dismissive wave of his hand. "It's nothing. Besides, I remember how hard starting out can be. Only I didn't start out with a hungry teenage boy."

I stepped aside, letting him in. He surveyed the small space I had turned into a home, nodding approvingly. "Place is small, but you've put a nice touch to it," he said. "How's Antonio settling in?"

"He's doing okay," I replied, glancing at the closed bedroom door. "Better than I expected, to be honest."

"You've got a good boy there. He reminds me of my own son at that age," Mr. Davidson said with a fond smile. "Listen, if you need help with anything—"

"I know," I interrupted softly. "You've been so kind already. I can't thank you enough."

He smiled warmly and patted my shoulder before glancing at his watch. "I should get going. I'm meeting my son for coffee down at the diner. But remember, I'm just down the road if you need anything."

The paper bag in my hands felt heavier than it was, a physical manifestation of the hope I hadn't dared feel in so long. I set the groceries on the counter, then quietly checked on Antonio. He was still fast asleep, his dark curls spread across the pillow, his chest rising and falling steadily. I often wondered if he ever thought about that night. But I wasn't brave enough to ask him. I could only hope he was able to erase it from his memory. The rental wasn't much, and our situation was far from ideal, but it was ours. It was a place to start rebuilding.

As I prepared scrambled eggs with buttered toast, Antonio stumbled out of his bedroom, still half-asleep, his dark curls messy and tousled. I smiled and gently pushed a curl off his forehead as he peeked over my shoulder at the eggs sizzling in the pan. "Finally decided to wake up?" I laughed.

He yawned, rubbing his dark brown eyes. "I could smell it from my room."

I plated our food as he poured himself some coffee, and we sat down at the table together, enjoying our breakfast in peace.

Antonio was in the 8th grade, and despite being the new kid where everyone had already formed their own groups, he made two friends—Enzo and Michael. For the first time in my life, I managed to befriend their mothers, Angela and Lucy.

Angela was a widowed single mother of two—Val and Enzo. She had a fiery, free-spirited personality. The complete opposite of me, which only made me admire her more. She had a knack for wearing bold, colorful prints that turned heads wherever she went, though she never cared who was watching. She loved handing out crude remarks in her raspy New York accent, forcing a smile to appear on my face. Something that once felt almost sinful and forbidden was beginning to feel normal and organic. And despite how much perfume she drowned herself in, you could always smell the faint hint of cigarette smoke on her.

Lucy, on the other hand, was married with one child—Michael. She often joked that she couldn't handle having another because she didn't want to "ruin her figure" with a second pregnancy. Glamorous and attractive, Lucy had a way of commanding attention, and people naturally made her the center of any room she entered. She always dressed in formal attire and could make the best dirty martinis in all of Staten Island.

Lucy and Angela grew up together and lived on the same street on the other side of town, which was considered the "nicer" side of town—the side you would want to reside in. But they welcomed Antonio and me with open arms, which I was grateful for.

"Any big plans today?" I asked Antonio as we ate breakfast, the smell of coffee lingering between us. I sipped my mug and glanced at him over the rim.

He shrugged. "I was thinking about hanging out with Enzo

and Michael later." He then hesitated, his gaze flicking to mine. "Will you be okay here by yourself?"

I smiled, setting my mug down. "Of course I will. I'll drop you off and then run my errands. We're low on groceries."

He smirked. "I noticed. Yesterday, I caught you rationing milk in your tea."

"Desperate times," I said, grinning. "Anything specific you want me to grab from the store?"

"Yeah, ice cream."

"Your wish is my command."

He laughed. "So, you'll come pick me up after?"

"Of course."

After dropping him off with Enzo and Michael, I decided to make the most of my free time. I headed to the grocery store for a few necessities and Antonio's chocolate ice cream. Afterwards, I stopped by the dry cleaners to pick up a few items I'd meant to grab yesterday.

I felt a satisfying sense of accomplishment— until my car sputtered to a halt in the middle of the road. The nearest payphone was miles away, and Antonio was even farther. I was mentally preparing to start walking when a car pulled behind me. Relief washed over me—until I saw who stepped out of the driver's side. Joey.

I shouldn't have been surprised, but I was. It was beginning to feel like Joey was either my knight in shining armor or someone keeping a much closer eye on me than I appreciated.

He walked over confidently. "Looks like ya Chevy gave out on ya. Need a hand?"

I should say no. I should just walk a few miles up the road to the payphone and call someone. Anyone other than Joey. But the sun was beginning to set, and he was already here. And before I could protest, he tapped the car's hood and said, "Pop the hood, and I'll take a look at it for you." Like usual, he took it upon himself to help me from the karma being sent my way for the blood still lingering on my hands.

I hesitated as my fingers clenched around the wheel. My eyes flickered ahead at the sun beginning to hide behind the clouds, then back to him and that bright smile, and how he's casually leaning against the driver's side of my car like it was his. But I reached down and pulled the lever.

I had to force myself not to giggle as he practically skipped towards the hood of the car, only to pull it up, and a plume of hot steam hit his face, causing him to back away and cough. I bite back my laughter. It would be wrong to laugh at him when he was only trying to help me. I stepped out of the car, crossing my arms over my chest, as I observed him take a brief look at the engine.

"Radiator's shot," he said. "This thing's not going anywhere tonight."

"I'll call someone," I said.

I just wanted him to leave. He had been solving my problems and inserting himself into my life since I had landed on this island. I didn't need him to solve this problem, either. I was capable of walking to the payphone and calling someone. I had people who would come and help me. I didn't need Joey to always be the one. Nor did I want him to be.

He raised an eyebrow, leaning against the edge of the hood. "Closest payphone's miles up the road. And unless you've got a spare radiator in your backseat, you'll need a lot of help that Davidson can't provide."

I narrowed my eyes at him, suspicion clear in every line of my face.

He shrugged. "Let me help ya out."

"Why?"

He chuckled softly. "Why not?" "What do you suggest I do?"

"A guy I know runs a shop near here—Gino's. He'll tow it and fix it up for ya. He owes me a favor, anyway, so it'll be of no change to ya. But until it's fixed, I'll drive ya and your boy wherever you need to go."

I shifted on my heels. I didn't want to take him up on his offer. I wanted to flat-out refuse. But as my eyes glanced from the asphalt to his eyes, and back down, I couldn't say no to him. And I despised myself for how weak I was in his presence. Since I had moved to Staten Island, Joey had shown up when I had nobody, inserting himself into my life like he was always a part of it. The last thing I wanted was to be indebted to a man, yet despite my best efforts to decline his offer, I relented.

I let out a small, defeated sigh. "Fine."

He gestured towards his car, a 1959 Ferrari 400 Super America Series 1. Brand new and sparkling under the fluorescent street lamp. "Let's go. I'll call Gino when I get back home tonight."

As he drove, the silence in the car was thick. I felt his eyes glance at me every few seconds, but my eyes remained straight ahead. I couldn't help but notice he was going dangerously slow, likely to buy us more time. Something I didn't want.

"You didn't have to stop," I finally said, eliminating our awkward silence.

"I figured you could use the help."

"Why do you care so much?" I wanted to know. I needed to know why he cared so much about my life circumstances.

Our eyes met briefly before I turned away. "Sometimes, Adriana, people just do the right thing. And for nothing in return."

I felt myself relax against the back of the seat. I didn't trust Joey. Not yet. But I also had no reason not to trust him. And he had been so kind to me since I'd arrived on Staten Island.

Giving him the cold shoulder made no sense. He didn't have to help me get a job, a job that led me to getting the rental house. He didn't have to stop when my car broke down, but he chose to help.

Many cars passed me by, but he didn't.

Chapter Seven

ANTONIO

Ma had woken me up earlier that morning to tell me Joey would pick me up and drive me to and from school. She had already left with Mr. Davidson, who came by to take her to open the corner store.

When I heard the car horn beep outside, I grabbed my backpack and headed out the front door. I'd be lying if I said I wasn't thrilled to ride shotgun in a brand new Ferrari. It had a fresh, black paint job and cream interior seats. It was miles better than Mom's old, beat-up blue Chevrolet.

"How you liking school?' Joey asked me as I settled into the passenger seat.

"It's better than my old school," I told him.

"Where'd you guys move from again?" he asked as he drove slowly down the street. "Newark, right?"

"Yeah," I said, shifting uncomfortably in my seat.

The flashbacks crept in, threatening to overwhelm me, but I forced them down. Ma and I never talked about that night. I didn't know if we ever would. She'd been through enough with my father— taking every punch, every hit, every broken rib. I used to wonder why she stayed, why she put up with his wrath for so long. But that night, I stood up to him. A bold move. And Ma had no choice but to stand with me.

But now, neither of us could erase what happened. And talking about it? That wasn't an option, either.

"Yeah, change can be good sometimes," he said, nodding in agreement. "Staten Island's quiet. Safe. A good place for you and your ma."

"Yeah," I replied, giving a slight nod. "It's better with just the two of us. More peaceful. I like it this way."

"How old are you anyway, kid?" He smiled at me briefly before his eyes returned to the road.

"Almost fourteen," I told him. I would be fourteen in December, nine months away, but I could hardly wait.

"Fourteen?" He smirked. "Alright, young man. You gotta look out for your mother, then. Take care of her, you know? You're the man of the house now. She'll need you to step up."

Did he know about our past? Had Ma told him about that night we left?

"Do you have a family?" I asked him, curious to know who he was. He drove the nicest car in town and looked loaded in nice suits and fancy watches.

He chuckled. "Got some folks I look after, but it ain't the same. It's complicated. Now listen," he said, stopping the car in front of my school. "You need someone to watch your back at school, give you advice on handling bullies or any kind of life stuff, you come to me, alright? I know we just met, but we take care of each other in this neighborhood."

I nodded as I grabbed my backpack.

"Your mother's doing all this for you. Gotta appreciate that, even if it don't make sense yet," he told me. "Alright, kid. Go knock 'em dead. And if anyone gives you trouble, you tell 'em Joey's got your back, alright?"

"Joey, who?"

"Joey. Joey Romano." He winked. I stepped out of the car,

glancing back at Joey with a small, uncertain smile before heading into the school.

Who was this guy, and why was he so damn cool?

If I'm being honest, I was probably the happiest I'd ever been. For once, I didn't have to worry about my father hurting my mother or enduring his relentless abuse. I didn't have to see the aftermath—the shattered glass, the bruises, the blood, the lifeless look in Ma's eyes. I knew it would take a long time for her to heal from everything she'd been through, but she was starting to make progress. She smiled more. Laughed more.

But I knew she was still holding on to the "what ifs." Always scanning every room we entered. Always looking over her shoulder. What if they find us? What would happen then? But I'd never let anyone hurt her again. Even if the feds found us, I'd never let them tear us apart. She killed him to protect me. I was the man of the house now. And it was my responsibility to look after us.

So *I* would.

"Hey, Antonio," someone called from behind me.

I turned around and found myself face-to-face with Louis, a kid who hung out with Giovanni—my arch-nemesis since I set foot in Staten Island Middle School two weeks ago.

"Was that Joey who dropped you off just now?" he asked, a smirk creeping onto his face.

"Why you asking?" I puffed out my chest, crossed my arms, trying to assert my dominance.

"Oh, no reason. You know he's Giovanni's stepdad, right?"

No, I didn't know that. I'd just asked Joey if he had a family, and all he said was that he "took care of people" and that "it was complicated." Not a word about being Giovanni's stepfather.

"Do you ever mind your own business?" I asked him.

"You know what he does for a living, right?" Louis tested, his smirk never faltering. "He's in the mafia," Louis said. "So is Giovanni's grandfather. That's why Giovanni's untouchable."

Untouchable? Now that was comical.

Giovanni had been working my nerves so badly lately that it felt like a full-time job. I could barely hold myself back from beating the shit out of him. But he might catch me on a bad day if he kept pushing.

"Don't end up in the trunk," Louis added with a wink before walking off.

"What the hell was that about?" Enzo asked as he walked up to me.

"You know Louis and his bullshit," I said, brushing it off.

"What's he talking about? 'Don't end up in the trunk?'" Enzo pressed, raising an eyebrow.

"He's just trying to get a reaction out of me," I replied. "And he almost got one."

"Almost?" Enzo shot me a skeptical look. "Man, you looked ready to knock him out. I say we team up and knock his ass out once and for all."

"Trust me, it took everything I had to hold back," I admitted. "The guy's such a pain in the ass. But if I let him get to me, he wins. Because my mom would fucking kill me for getting into a fight at school."

Enzo shook his head. "I don't know how you do it. If someone said that to me, I'd lose my shit."

I smirked. "You've got to pick your battles, Enzo. Louis? He's not worth it. But Giovanni? If he pushes me one more time, he's getting everything he's asking for."

"Alright, man," Enzo said with a shrug. "Just don't end up suspended. Or worse, in the trunk, apparently."

I rolled my eyes. "Not happening. But if anyone's getting shoved in a trunk, it's the two of them."

We laughed as we started walking toward class. Enzo was a lot like me. He was the first friend I made when I arrived on Staten Island, and, honestly, he was probably the best friend I'd ever had.

"Where's Michael?" I asked Enzo, glancing around the hallway.

"Who knows? Probably off playing teacher's pet somewhere,

kissing up so he doesn't have to do homework or something."
Enzo shrugged.

The two of us were laughing when Michael strolled up next to us. "What's so funny?" he asked, squinting at us.

"Nothing, teacher's pet," Enzo said with a smirk, elbowing me in the ribs. I fell over, letting out a laugh I couldn't hold in.

"Teacher's pet? Really? Not this shit again."

"I mean..." I started, grinning.

"Let's be real, Michael," Enzo added, "you were definitely in there trying to earn extra credit. Again. The only kind of extra credit I want is with that new nurse we got. You know how many times I've been to the nurse's office this week? And it's only Tuesday."

I snickered.

Michael shook his head, smiling despite himself. "Okay, for the record, I was not kissing up to anyone. I was helping Mr. Richards fix the printer. It's not fair that the teachers are here to give us a good chance at a better life, and they barely have proper working equipment to do so."

Enzo dramatically moved his hands back and forth, mimicking Michael's rambling on.

Michael rolled his eyes. "And for the record, Mr. Richards said I was the most helpful student he's ever had. I've fixed the printer for him twice in a week."

"Oh, now he's bragging," I said, clutching my chest like I'd been offended.

Enzo pretended to wipe a tear from his eye. "We're so proud of you, Michael."

The three of us laughed, earning a few side-eyes from kids passing by in the hallway.

Michael was the second friend I made when I came to Staten Island, and Enzo introduced us. The two of them had been best friends since they were kids, practically since diapers. Michael differed greatly from Enzo and me, but he balanced us out. Michael was calm, collected, and serious, while we were hyper, impulsive, and always messing around. But every now and then, he'd crack a joke with us.

He had big dreams and the brains to back them up. As for me? I was just skating by, barely passing my classes with a C average. I didn't know where I wanted to go or what I wanted to be. The jokes masked the feelings I had inside—the anger, the sadness. It was easier to pretend I wasn't feeling those things. That I didn't close my eyes and watch my mother shoot my father dead, right in front of me. A secret I couldn't tell a soul. Every day I kept it locked away, it gnawed at me.

"You know, Louis did say something interesting," I told Michael and Enzo, trying to gauge their reactions. "He said Joey's in the mafia. I always thought the mafia was fake. Is that shit real?" I asked them, watching as they exchanged a knowing look—one that immediately gave them away. They knew something I didn't. "Hey! Don't leave me out of this!" I shot at them. "Is it real or fake?" I demanded.

Michael shrugged. "I mean, honestly, how would we know?"

"Yeah, it's not like anyone's confirmed it," Enzo added.

"But you know something, don't you?" I pressed. "Something I don't."

"No, we don't!" Michael said quickly, throwing a glance at Enzo.

Enzo shifted his weight. "Nobody's ever said to me the mafia is real. Now, whether or not I believe it's real or fake. Well, that's a different story."

"Well?" I asked, pushing him further. "Do you believe it's real or fake? And don't look at Michael!"

Enzo hesitated for a moment. "I think it's real."

I turned to Michael, my eyes narrowing. "Yeah, so do I," he added, confirming what I already suspected.

"And Joey? Do you think he's in the mafia?"

"Maybe if you didn't spend all your time flirting with Mia and laughing at Enzo's stupid jokes, you might find time actually to read the papers. That'll give you all the answers you need."

And just like that, I added one more thing to my to-do list—figuring out if the mafia was real.

Later that day, Joey and I sat on a bench at the park, just a short drive from my school. Joey was making an effort to ease the awkwardness between us. He'd brought me a cold can of soda when he picked me up, and now we sat side by side, watching kids toss a baseball back and forth. As people passed, they greeted him casually, as if he were another familiar face in the neighborhood. No one seemed intimidated by him.

If he were involved in the mafia, wouldn't they be scared of him?

He gestured towards the two young boys tossing the baseball back and forth, and asked me, "You into baseball, kid?"

"A little." I shrugged. "My mom doesn't let me play much, though. Says it's too dangerous. She says everything's too dangerous, now that I think of it."

"Dangerous?" He chuckled. "What's she think you're gonna do? Take a fastball to the head?"

I stifled my laugh and shrugged. "She worries about everything."

"Moms are like that. It's in the job description," he said, sipping from his soda can. "You got a team you root for?"

"I guess I like the Yankees." I shrugged. "I've never been to a game, though."

"Never?"

"Nope," I said, shaking my head.

"Huh. Well, that's gotta change," he declared with a nod.

"What do you mean?" I asked, arching my eyebrow.

"I mean," he said with a grin, "I'm takin' you to a Yankees game. Gotta fix this tragedy of yours. Every kid deserves to see a game, eat a hot dog, and complain about overpriced peanuts."

"I don't know if my mom will let me go." I frowned, knowing she was still too terrified that the feds would find us.

"Don't worry, kid. I'll handle your mom. Besides, this ain't just a game—it's a rite of passage. Trust me, you'll love it." He smiled widely.

"Really? You'd take me?" I asked, mirroring his smile. "Just like that?"

"Of course," he exclaimed. "What's the point of livin' this close to Yankee Stadium if you never step foot inside? How about this Saturday?"

"Yeah, okay!"

"Then it's a date," he said, patting his hand against my shoulder. "Just don't tell anyone I got a soft spot for kids, alright? I got a reputation to maintain."

"Your secret's safe with me." I grinned.

Surely, if Joey were truly who Louis said he was—a mafia gangster—he wouldn't be this nice to kids.

Chapter Eight

ADRIANA

I sat at the kitchen table with Angela and Lucy. Lucy had already made herself at home, fixing each of us one of her famous dirty martinis. She drank them like water, much like Angela's constant need for cigarettes. I preferred to keep things in moderation.

Her cigarette delicately held between her fingers, Angela leaned forward with a sly grin. "So, Adriana...I heard through the grapevine that Joey's been helping you and Antonio out while your car's in the shop."

Lucy grinned, sipping her martini. "That's awfully kind of him."

"Yeah," I said, trying to hide how flustered they were making me. "I guess it is nice of him to help out. I could take care of things on my own, but he insisted on helping me."

Angela exchanged a knowing look with Lucy. "Let me guess. He just happened to be there at the right moment, like some kind of brooding, Staten Island knight?"

"Oh, Adriana, let me rescue you from your car troubles with my strong, capable hands and ridiculously handsome good looks," Lucy said, her voice dripping with a mock tone.

I couldn't help but laugh. "You two are ridiculous. He offered to help because he was driving by, and the nearest pay phone was miles up the road."

"Did he happen to drive by, or was he keeping tabs?" Angela asked. "You know Joey has always had his ways with the ladies."

No, I don't know his way with the ladies. And I don't want to know.

Lucy smirked. "He probably saw you and thought, perfect, here's my chance to play the hero. He likes that kind of thing."

I crossed my arms, feigning innocence. "He's just being a gentleman."

"Oh, sweetie," Angela gushed, "of course he's a gentleman. They all are when they want something."

"Trust me, we've known Joey our entire lives." Lucy laughed. "Women fall for him all the time."

"Not me," I said back.

Angela eyed me, tilting her head like she wasn't buying my words. "No? Not even a little? Not even when he flashed that million-dollar smile your way? Oh, you know the one I'm talking about!"

I couldn't help but laugh. I didn't have a thing for Joey, and he sure as hell didn't have a thing for me. He was attractive. Charming, even. But that's where I drew the line.

Lucy smirked. "Joey doesn't help just anyone. He's picky, you know."

"Maybe he's just being polite," I said, trying desperately to maintain a straight face.

Angela laughed. "Joey? Polite?"

"Come on, Adriana. Be honest. You can tell us. We're your friends."

"There's nothing going on between us," I said, grinning despite myself.

"Liar." Angela grinned back.

"I'm not some homewrecker. I've been there, and I'd never do that to another woman," I said. I was vaguely aware that Joey had a girlfriend.

"Homewrecker?" Lucy scoffed. "Oh, please. You're the whole package, and Joey knows it."

"Joey's with Renee," I replied. I hadn't heard this from Joey himself, but from Mr. Davidson. He warned me to "watch out" —not for Joey, but for Renee. He said she could be "vengeful, vindictive," and I knew better than to cross a woman like that. Especially with the secret I was keeping.

"It's more of an arrangement than a relationship," Angela said.

"An arrangement?" Lucy echoed. "She's practically holding the man hostage."

"How do you two know all this?" I asked. I should stay out of his personal life, but it seemed only fair considering he continued to insert himself in my life.

"Because we know Joey—and Renee," Angela said. "And let me tell you, he doesn't love her."

I could hardly help the warmth that crept up my cheeks, nor could I shake the lingering thought of Joey. Did I really like him? Part of me resisted the idea, but another part couldn't deny that something about him drew me in. His sharp, confident, disarming smile was hard to ignore, especially how he'd smiled the day he'd helped me with my car.

I wasn't sure if I was ready to confront what those thoughts meant. It felt too complicated, and I wasn't looking for complications. But every time I caught myself thinking about him, I couldn't help but wonder if there was more to our interactions than just a gentleman's gesture.

Later that evening, as I was preparing dinner, I heard Joey's car pull into the carport. Moments later, the front door burst open, and Antonio ran inside, beaming with excitement. It was a joy I hadn't seen in so long, and it warmed my heart.

"Ma! Guess what? Joey's taking me to a Yankees game on Saturday!" he shouted towards me.

My eyes met Joey's, standing behind Antonio at the front door. "A Yankees game? You're taking him to a game?"

"Yeah," he shrugged, "figured the kid could use a little fun.

Don't worry, I got it all covered—tickets, snacks, the whole shebang."

"Joey, I don't know..." I said, crossing my arms tightly over my chest. The thought of Antonio being so far away in a large crowd made me uneasy. Anything could go wrong; by anything, I meant someone could recognize him, and our quiet, peaceful life would be blown. "He's never been to a stadium before. It's crowded—anything could happen."

"Ma, please! Joey said it's a rite of passage!"

"Go wash up for dinner. We'll talk about this later," I told Antonio. He hesitated, looking at me and then at Joey before marching towards his bedroom.

"Joey, I don't think this is a good idea. I mean, I hardly know you. I can't let my thirteen-year-old son go off to the city with a strange man that we hardly know." I sighed, turning my attention to Joey.

He leaned against the wall, a strikingly handsome figure in his crisp, navy suit paired with a white shirt and a neatly knotted tie. His dark hair was slicked back with pomade, faint streaks of gray just beginning to show. I knew it was wrong to think of him this way—let alone blatantly checking him out.

Joey exhaled sharply, pushing off the wall as he fixed his gaze on me. "Adriana, I get it—you don't know me. But people get to know each other by spending time together. Everyone knows who I am. Nobody is going to let me run off with your son. It's just a ballgame. I'll be with him the whole time—he'll be safe with me."

I wanted to trust Joey. And a big part of me felt like I could, but the other small part, the nagging voice of guilt in my head, was making it nearly impossible.

"Adriana, I'm not gonna let anything happen to him. The kid's gonna have the time of his life. You've got my word, and I don't go back on my word."

I hesitated, but I couldn't bring myself to ruin this for Antonio. He was so excited about the chance to go to a Yankees game. He needed to experience things that children his age experience.

"Look, I get it—you're protective. But you can't keep him in a bubble forever. He deserves this—a memory he'll never forget," Joey said with a smile. Oh, that smile. Angela and Lucy were right —it could make any woman weak. But I couldn't afford to be weak, especially not for a man like Joey.

"Why are you doing this, Joey? You barely know us," I said, searching his face for answers. "And don't you dare say it's because you want to get to know us. Because I'm not stupid and I know you want something else."

He tried to hold back the smirk threatening to break through. "You've got a good boy. Maybe I just see a little of myself in him. He loves the Yankees—I do, too. And let's not forget, you already trusted me enough to pick him up and bring him home while your car's in the shop. I'm not taking him far. Besides, anybody on the East Coast knows who Joey Romano is. I'm not a kidnapper, Adriana. I don't hurt women or kids."

I studied him, arms crossed, eyes narrowed, my lips pressed into a firm line. Everyone seemed to know who Joey Romano was —everyone but me. And my gut told me that men like him, like most men, only wanted one thing. He wasn't going to butter me up with a smooth smile and easy charm. I'd escaped one man already, and I'd be damned if I let another take advantage of me.

"If anything goes wrong—"

Joey's grin stretched wider than I'd ever seen. "Nothing's gonna go wrong. Scout's honor," he said, holding up three fingers in a mock salute, his tone light, almost teasing.

I smirked, arching an eyebrow at him. "Somehow, I doubt you were ever a Boy Scout."

Joey laughed softly, and I realized it was the first time I'd ever heard him laugh. Suddenly, I wanted to hear it again and again. "You got me there. But hey, trust me on this one, okay?"

"Okay," I reluctantly smiled, "but you'd better bring him back in one piece."

"One piece? You drive a hard bargain, Adriana." He smirked. I shook my head, a small laugh escaping my lips momentarily. Our eyes lingered a bit longer until Antonio emerged from his bedroom.

"So?" he asked with a grin. "What'd she say?"

"Be ready by 5:00 p.m. on Saturday," Joey announced, causing Antonio to wrap his arms around my waist and squeeze tightly.

Men like Joey Romano were trouble. Smooth talkers with easy smiles and sharp suits, the kind of men who took what they wanted. I'd already lived that once. I wasn't about to make the same mistake twice.

Chapter Nine

JOEY

Paul and I sat in a booth, the soft jazz filling the air as he swirled his drink, studying me intently. I took a slow drag from my cigarette, watching him over the smoke. "So, what's the deal with the new broad in town?"

"What broad?" I asked, raising an eyebrow. I knew what he was talking about, but I played dumb, anyway.

He smirked. "Don't play dumb, Joey. The one with the kid.

Adriana, right? I've seen her around. Quiet, keeping her head low, but she's got you acting like a damn bloodhound."

I shrugged, taking another drag from my cigarette. "It's nothing."

He let out a soft chuckle. "Joey, I've known you long enough to know when you're full of shit. You had Davidson dig up her license. And had Ben run a background check on her. That ain't nothing."

"Keep your voice down, Paul," I snapped at him, looking around, hoping nobody had heard us.

He grinned. "Relax. No one's listening. But seriously, what's her story?"

"I don't know yet," I told him. I didn't know yet, but I would soon. "I'm just trying to help her out. It's not what you're thinking. She's...different. That's all."

"Different?" He laughed. "Come on, Joey. Every pretty face looks different when you're bored with the one at home."

My eyes narrowed, and he raised his hands up in mock surrender. "Alright, alright. But seriously, you're playing with fire. As your friend, I'm just looking out for you. I think you should be worrying about avoiding Vincent and Renee's wrath rather than getting involved with Adriana. You're already skating on paper-thin ice."

I leaned back slowly, exhaling the smoke into the air between us. He had a point. But I wasn't getting involved with Adriana. I was helping her. "All I want to do is help her out," I said out loud. Not only to Paul, but also a reminder to myself.

"Help her out?" he scoffed. "Joey, we don't help people. Not unless there's something in it for us. You want something from this woman. And I think what you want from her will be your demise."

"It's not like that," I said. But I didn't fully believe myself, either.

"Look, brother," Paul said, shaking his head, "I'm saying this because I got your back. You're already in deep with Renee and Vincent. If Vincent gets wind that you're poking around some other woman, you're a dead man walking."

"Let me worry about Vincent," I snapped.

"Fine." He sighed. "Don't say I didn't warn you."

"I'll handle it, Paul." My eyes narrowed on him. "I always do."

"Yeah?" He grinned. "Well, I hope she's worth the heat you're about to bring down on yourself."

Paul downed the rest of his drink, leaning back against the leather sofa while I sat there, trying to figure out what the hell I was going to do. Paul was onto something, and I knew all too well how complicated my life had become lately.

Antonio reminded me too much of myself—young, scared, and carrying more weight on his shoulders than any boy should. I knew that feeling. I had lived it. And maybe helping him, making sure he had something better, was my way of fixing what I couldn't fix for myself.

And then there was Adriana. I wanted to help her because no one had ever helped my mother. No one had stepped in when we needed it most. I knew what it was like to watch someone you love struggle and to feel powerless to change it. Maybe this was my chance to do what no one ever did for us. To make things right—not just for them, but for the kid I used to be.

The background check I'd ordered on Adriana came back clean. "She's married," Ben told me as we sat at the bar, sipping our drinks.

"I figured as much," I remarked, unsurprised by the news. "You knew she was married?"

"Not entirely, but I wanted to be sure. I don't like surprises."

I paused, swirling my drink in thought. "I need you to do something else for me."

"Yeah?" Ben raised an eyebrow.

"I want you to find her husband. I don't care how you do it, but track him down. Make sure he's not trying to look for her. I need to know he's not about to show up at the wrong time." Not until I could come up with a plan to take care of him myself, without anyone ever knowing.

Ben nodded, his lips curling into a slight grin. "I can get that done for you. It'll take a little time, but I'll keep my eyes open. You sure about this?"

I leaned back, looking him square in the eye. "Yeah, I'm sure. And when you find him, I'll take care of the rest."

"You know I'll get it done, Joey."

I reached into my jacket pocket, pulled out an envelope thick with cash, and slid it across the bar to him. "Here's your payment upfront. Consider it a retainer. Get me what I need."

Ben tucked the envelope into his jacket. "You'll have your answers soon enough. Don't worry, Joey. I've got this."

I nodded, finishing my drink in one long gulp. "Good. Keep it quiet, though. No need for unnecessary attention."

I barely had the front door of the house shut before I heard the sharp click of Renee's heels against the floor. I exhaled through my nose, bracing myself.

"Where the hell have you been?"

She was already in front of me, arms crossed tight over her chest, nails digging into her arms, red lips pressed into a thin line.

I dropped my keys onto the side table and ran a hand through my hair, loosening it as the pomade gave way. "I was working. What is it this time?"

"Working?" she retorted. "Are you sure you weren't playing chauffeur?"

I debated lying. But I knew there was no way out of this. I didn't want to fight with her. But the thing about Renee was she liked to call the shots, and I had no choice but to bite my tongue and go along with it. "Her car is broken down. And she's got a kid, Renee. No family. Nobody to help her and the kid get anywhere."

Silence. Then a short, bitter laugh followed by the identical, sinister grin Vincent loved to plaster. It made my stomach turn. "You want me to believe you're helping her because she's a single mother without a family? Do you think I'm an idiot? You never help anyone unless it's a benefit for you!"

I clenched my jaw, and my nostrils flared. I had to hold back the urge to react. To bottle it up inside. "Are you saying I don't help people? I help people all the damn time, Renee!"

"Oh, really?" She took a step closer, tilting her head. "Is that supposed to be directed to me? You haven't helped me. I've helped you. You've used me."

"If I'm using you, get rid of me." I stepped closer, my eyes boring into hers.

She smirked, looking me dead in the eye. "Maybe I'll just have to tell my father what you're doing."

I stood frozen, locked in a stare-off that neither of us dared to break. A choice sat in front of me, one I didn't want to make. My jaw tightened as my hands moved on their own, reaching for her arms, gripping them just enough to steady the storm between us. It felt automatic—like muscle memory, like my body knew how to bandage the moment long enough for me to figure out my next move.

I let out a slow breath, forcing my voice to stay even. "I wasn't sneaking around. I was helping her out. That's all."

Renee scoffed, shaking her head. "I don't believe you."

My patience was running thin. I exhaled sharply, dragging a hand down my face. "Jesus, Renee, just drop it."

For a second, I thought she might. Her lips parted, hesitation flickering in her eyes. But then she tossed her hair over her shoulder, her expression hardening. "You're full of shit, Joey."

I didn't have the energy for this. Not tonight. Not ever.

I stepped past her and headed for the kitchen, ignoring how she stood there, fuming, waiting for me to turn back, to fight, to give her something to sink her teeth into.

She wanted a war. She lived for the fight. But there was nothing here worth fighting for. There never was.

I barely had time to enjoy the silence before I heard Renee's footsteps. Heavy footsteps. The sharp click of heels. Coming straight for me. "You don't get to just walk away from me, Joseph Romano!" Renee's voice was sharp, cutting through the room like a blade.

I didn't turn to face her just yet. Instead, I poured myself a drink. "Didn't realize I had to stand here and get screamed at to keep you happy."

She let out a cold, loud laugh, but there was nothing amusing about it. "You think I don't have the right to be pissed when my boyfriend—" she spat the word out, just to remind me of the title she gave me and made public to others. The title that sickened me to my fucking core. "—is sneaking around with some woman and her kid behind my back."

I turned, locking eyes with her finally. "I already told you—I was helping her. That's it. You want to twist that into something else, go ahead. I don't give a shit."

"Oh, you don't give a shit? Right. That's real comforting, Joey. I just don't get why you won't admit it."

I let out a humorless chuckle, shaking my head. "Admit what? That I gave someone a ride? That I made sure a woman and her son didn't have to walk home alone? That ain't cheating. That's basic decency. Something you wouldn't understand if it smacked you dead in the face!"

Her lips parted in mock offense, but I saw the way her jaw clenched, the way her hands curled into fists. She wasn't used to me pushing back. She wanted me to fold, to smooth things over. She wanted control. "You think I don't see right through you? You wanna be a hero, Joey? You wanna go play house with some broken little damsel and her son?" She laughed, bitter and cruel. "Go ahead."

The only house I was playing was with her. And I couldn't wait to watch the whole damn house burn to the ground.

I should've known better than to get involved. But there was something about Adriana that made me throw all caution out the window, like I was playing a game I didn't even understand. And I was a master chess player.

Helping her—driving her around, taking care of her kid, all that shit—felt like a distraction. A way to escape from everything that was slowly suffocating me. But now? Now it felt like I'd walked right into a fucking trap.

Renee was right—well, partially. I wasn't cheating on her, not in the way she thought. But this—whatever this was with Adriana —wasn't just helping someone out. It was more. More than I wanted to admit. More than I should've let happen. And if I wasn't careful, it was gonna ruin everything.

But the thing was, I was becoming careless.

Chapter Ten

ANTONIO

E nzo and I sat in my bedroom, finishing off the last of the cigarettes he'd stolen from his sister, Val. She wasn't allowed to smoke, either, so she couldn't tell on him without explaining why she had them in the first place. That little detail was starting to work in our favor. We sat in silence for a minute, the smoke lingering between us, before I flicked the butt of the cigarette into the ashtray I had stashed under my bed.

We both stood up, brushing the ash off our jeans, knowing we were running out of time. Ma had already started her usual routine of dragging me to St. Augustine of the Sacred Heart, and I had to meet her at Davidson's before she came looking for me.

I shoved my hands in my pockets, feeling the weight of the walk ahead. It was a long stretch, especially for a place I didn't care to go, but she insisted. I knew the reason. She was trying to repent for the sin of killing him. I couldn't bring myself to call him my father. A real father wouldn't hurt you. I knew that much.

We made our way out the door, the chill of winter in February biting at my skin. Enzo walked beside me, his pace matching mine as we headed toward Davidson's. I glanced at him, my mind drifting back to things I'd kept buried for too long.

"Do you still have dreams about your dad?" I asked.

Enzo didn't respond right away, but I could tell he was thinking it over. It wasn't the easiest question to answer. He didn't have to say it aloud for me to know. We both carried those ghosts with us.

Enzo had confessed to me once that after his dad was murdered, he was the first one to walk outside and find him lying in the yard. He said he hardly slept anymore, that he could never shake that last image of his father out of his mind. He'd wake up in cold sweats, nightmares clawing at him.

The difference between us was that Enzo loved his father— and his father loved him. From everything Enzo told me, his old man was a good guy, the kind who would've never hurt him. The kind who deserved better than some drive-by shooting in the early morning hours.

"Yeah, why?" Enzo asked, his bushy brows furrowing as he glanced at me.

I shrugged, trying to make it sound casual. "I've been having some difficulty sleeping lately. Just wondered if it ever gets better."

Enzo sighed, his hands stuffed deep into his pockets as we kept walking. "I'll let you know when it does." We fell into silence again, the chill biting as we walked in rhythm toward Davidson's.

Ma wasn't just afraid of the cops finding her and locking her away—she was terrified that even if she dodged the cops in this life, she'd pay for it in the next one. She'd always been devout, always believed that God would come in and make it alright if we prayed hard enough. And I hated that belief, because it didn't matter how hard we prayed. It didn't matter how much we hoped. No one was coming to save us. Not God. Not Father Delgato. No one.

At least I had Enzo. And he had me. He was the one person who truly understood me, the one who had my back no matter what. He didn't need to know the darkest secret I carried—that my mother killed my father—but he was the closest thing to family besides Ma that I had. He knew the surface of things, but not the truth. Not the whole story.

59

My father didn't die as a war hero, and I hated that my mother used that lie to paint him as someone he wasn't. It made him sound like a man with bravery, morals, and values. The truth was, he was a veteran, sure—but he was also a drunk with a gambling problem who took out all his frustrations on women and children. He wasn't a hero. He was a man who left scars, who left bruises that didn't just show on the skin, but were buried deep in the soul.

I spotted Joey right outside Davidson's, dressed sharply in his suit and fedora, casually puffing on a cigarette with Paul and Marco standing beside him. Paul gave him a nudge, pointing in our direction. Joey spun around, his voice booming with that thick New York accent. Sometimes I wondered if he even realized how cool he was.

"Ay! Look who it is!" he called out, his voice cutting through the air. I couldn't help but smile. Joey had this way of lighting up the room, this easy, carefree vibe. It made me wonder if he'd ever seen anything that could actually steal that smile from him.

"What do we got here?" Marco asked with a teasing grin.

"A bunch of troublemakers, by the looks of it, boss," Paul added, smirking.

I couldn't help it—my grin stretched wide. These guys were the coolest people I'd ever met, and I wanted to be just like them.

Before I could respond, the chime of the exit door rang behind Joey, and Ma stepped out. Her brows knit together, arms folding tight across her chest.

"Antonio," she called, her voice firm. Everyone's eyes shifted to her, but she didn't care. "We'll be late. Come on."

I let out a sigh, dragging my feet forward.

"Where you two heading off to?" Joey asked, flicking his cigarette to the curb.

Ma's head snapped in his direction, but before she could answer, I jumped in, hoping he'd feel sorry enough for me to take me with him—anywhere besides St. Augustine of the Sacred

Heart, where Ma could confess to a crime she had no choice but to commit.

"Confession," I muttered. "Second time this week." I shot Joey a look, silently pleading for an escape from another round of pointless prayers and penance.

"What do you have to confess about?" Joey chuckled, flicking his gaze past me to lock eyes with Ma.

I felt her tense beside me. Guilty. Of. Murder.

"Let's go before we're late," she said quickly, tugging my arm. I shot Joey a desperate look, mouthing a silent help. Lucky for me, he could read lips. What couldn't he do?

Joey smirked. "Why don't you let Paul give you a ride? He lives right by the church. And I'll take this little rascal to practice some baseball—he's gotta be ready for the Yankees game this weekend."

Ma hesitated, struggling with the decision. I could see the war playing out in her head. But I kept my eyes locked on hers, silently begging her to give me this out. I couldn't endure this new routine—the endless cycle of guilt and repentance, like she could pray away what had been done.

Paul stepped forward, pulling open the passenger door. "After you," he said smoothly, leaving no room for argument. These guys had a way of making you do exactly what they wanted without you even realizing it.

Ma sighed, rubbing her temples. "Fine. But only because I've been on my feet all day. I want him home in time for supper."

Joey straightened up and gave her a sharp salute. "Yes, ma'am."

Enzo and I snickered as Ma shook her head, pressing a quick kiss to my cheek before sliding into Paul's car.

Joey clapped me on the back, grinning. "Come on, kids. I'll drop you off at home, Enzo."

We climbed into his car and pulled away from Davidson's. Joey dropped Enzo off first before heading toward the baseball field. The familiar rhythm of tossing the ball back and forth settled my nerves, but I could feel Joey watching me, waiting for the right moment.

Eventually, we took a break, settling onto the park benches with our water bottles. I could tell by the way Joey was studying me that the question was coming—why I didn't want to go with Ma to church.

And I knew I had two choices—lie, or tell him the truth.

The thought of either one was enough to drive me insane. "What's on your mind, kid?"

I shrugged, fidgeting with my baseball glove. "Just some stuff. It's nothing." There we go, the lie. I guess I had trained myself well. Don't acknowledge. If you pretend long enough, you might start to believe the lies you tell yourself.

"Stuff, huh?" he asked. "Stuff's a big category."

I hesitated, staring at my glove. After a moment, I let out a sigh and glanced at him. "Do you go to church? Do you believe in God?"

He took a moment to answer. "I believe in karma. What goes around comes around. If there is a God, sometimes he doesn't deliver fast enough. Why?"

"So you believe if someone bad hurts you, they deserve whatever comes their way?" I asked him.

His eyes searched mine for answers. "How badly did they hurt someone?"

I sighed, shaking my head as if the act could knock the memories of the violence and blood out of my mind. "Badly."

"Then I believe whatever happens is justified."

"Even murder?" My eyes met his again.

His face nearly went white. "What are you not telling me? What's going on?"

"I can't tell you." I sighed, letting my head fall. My body rocked side to side in some strange effort to ease my mind. I felt his arm draped over my shoulders, and he pulled me into his side. There was something about the warmth he offered. Was this how a father was with their son?

"Look, kid. You've got a good thing going here. You've got your mom, you've got me—and hey, you're not bad at baseball, either."

I couldn't help but let out a chuckle. It didn't want to escape, but Joey just had this way about him. "You really think I'm good?"

"Better than good." He grinned. "We need to work on your swing, but with some practice, you'll be the next Joe DiMaggio."

I smiled widely. "Yeah, okay. As long as I get to marry someone like Marilyn Monroe."

He threw his head back, howling in laughter, and I couldn't help but mirror him when he did it.

"You and every guy with a pair of eyes," he teased. "But hey, if you can hit a ball like DiMaggio, maybe you'll have a shot. Just don't forget who taught you."

Chapter Eleven

ADRIANA

A ngela and I sat at the small dinner table in my cramped kitchen. Lucy was running late, as usual. Lucy always said she preferred to be "fashionably late," which somehow excused the fact that Angela and I had been waiting for her for half an hour now. Angela leaned across the table, wearing a mischievous grin.

"Have you ever been to a speakeasy before?" she asked.

"No, do they still exist?"

"Well, of course! And it's Friday night, so you should come with me to my speakeasy," Angela declared.

"Your speakeasy? What are you talking about?"

"I own one, it's called The Wise Guy. Have you ever gone into the supply closet at Davidson's during one of your shifts?"

"Yeah, plenty of times. Why?"

"That's where it's at. It's hidden, and you'd need a password to get in if you find the door. But lucky for you, I own the place. We can bring Michael, Enzo, and Antonio over to hang out at my place. Val can babysit while we're out, and it'll be fun," Angela said. "Plus, I think you could use a night out."

"I'm not sure if I should be impressed or concerned," I said, eyeing her.

She mentioned she'd owned a bar, but I had no idea she ran a speakeasy hidden in the same place I worked. But with Angela—bar, speakeasy—they were the same difference.

"Anyway, you, me, and Lucy are going tonight. You're coming, no arguments," she said with finality.

"I don't know, Angela," I said, anxiety gnawing at my chest. That familiar tightness began to consume my chest.

I had been struggling with nightmares, vivid horrors pulling me from sleep at all hours of the night. Each one felt like an omen, a reminder of the danger we were in, of how close we were to being discovered.

The thought of someone finding us paralyzed me with fear every day. I had become an award-winning actress, working my shift at Davidson's, being a mother to Antonio, and harboring a sinful secret that only Antonio and I knew.

But it was at night that the act slipped away. I was left with myself and the things I had done. Whether they were out of protection for my son or not, I had still done them. I had pulled the trigger, causing a man's death. An act that was still a crime, even if he were a bad man.

I paced the living room floor all hours of the night, trying to shake off the images, but they lingered, gnawing at my consciousness. Sometimes, my chest would tighten, and I'd break down, tears streaming down my face as I thought of what I'd lose if they found us.

What would happen to Antonio? What would happen to us?

The police would rip him from my arms, and the fear of that alone threatened to swallow me whole. The idea of Antonio being taken from me, of him being forced to live a life without me—I'd much rather die than face a life behind bars away from him.

I felt helpless, trapped in my own reality. I had no plan, no escape. All I knew was I had to keep going, keep hiding, keep pretending everything was okay—even when I was far from okay.

Father Delgado had told me, in that hushed voice behind the

confessional screen, that I should go to the police. That I should confess what I'd done—that I was the one who killed my husband.

But what did he expect?

I was sure the police already knew. When they found him dead in the kitchen, they would piece it together. They knew. They had to know. They had to be looking for me. It was only a matter of time before they found me.

I didn't need to go to the precinct to confess. I couldn't bring myself to face them. To turn myself in. Not when Antonio was finally starting to heal, finally starting to feel safe again after everything. I couldn't—I wouldn't—rip him from his new life. We'd arrived here, in the dead of winter, full of fear and desperation, and somehow, we'd survived. We'd rebuilt in mere weeks.

I'd take the sleepless nights. I'd take the nightmares. I'd carry this guilt with me every moment of my life if it meant keeping him safe. If it meant he could have the chance to be normal, to have the life he deserved. I would take it all to my grave. For Antonio, I would.

"Oh, come on! You've been cooped up too much. You deserve a night out, and this is the perfect night. Plus, Enzo has been begging for Antonio to spend the night."

I half smiled. "Antonio has been asking the same." "And Joey's going to be there," she said with a smirk. "Joey? How do you know he'll be there?"

"He's always there." She grinned.

He's always there?

She leaned back, grinning, "You're coming. And when you're sipping on the best Negronis you've ever had, you'll thank me later."

"Alright," I sighed, giving in, "I'll come. But only for you. I'm not going for any other reason. Except, maybe I could go for a Negroni."

Angela smirked, knowing she'd won, just as Lucy walked

through my front door. Angela could hardly contain the news when she saw Lucy. Anxiety still lingered, but the thought of seeing Joey, or having Joey see me, fueled me with a thrill I couldn't quite understand. I could hardly care about the Negronis. But I wanted to wear my best dress and have Joey admire me. Even though I knew I shouldn't. Even though I knew it was wrong.

The Wise Guy was unlike anything I'd ever seen. Amber-hued light bulbs lit an intimate glow across the room, while dark wood floors complemented leather couches and vintage decor scattered throughout. The music, a mix of Elvis Presley and Frank Sinatra, played softly in the background. The bar was stocked with premium liquor, and Angela served us Negronis in elegant vintage glassware.

The seating was minimal—a few round tables paired with leather couches, each accompanied by an antique lamp and a glass ashtray on the tabletop. A velvet curtain concealed a hidden VIP section in the back. Angela let me peek behind the curtain, where there was a singular poker table sitting in the center of the room.

The Wise Guy filled up quicker than I expected, though I didn't know what to expect. I stayed by the bar to keep Angela company as she mixed drinks for the guys coming in. My eyes flicked toward the door every time it opened, hoping the next person to walk through would be Joey. He finally strode in alongside Paul and Marco. Marco had a thing for Angela, but she wasn't the type of woman you could easily tie down.

Joey's eyes didn't take long to find mine, and his usual swagger faltered. His gaze followed me as I moved closer to Angela at the bar. My hair was styled in victory rolls, and I wore a navy knee-length dress paired with a bold, red lip. It was the first time in a long time I had felt this confident in myself. And a part of me wanted someone to notice. But not just anyone—Joey. I wanted Joey to notice me. This version of me. Not the one he was used to seeing.

He walked over, his eyes never leaving mine. As he drew closer, a smirk danced at the corner of his lips. "Well, well, well, look who decided to join us tonight," he said, his gaze sweeping over me. "You clean up nice, Adriana. Real nice."

I tried not to smile, but my efforts were a waste. "Is that supposed to be a compliment?"

"Do you take 'you're the best-looking woman in the room' as a compliment?" He grinned, glancing around the room quickly before his eyes returned to me. I could feel the heat rise to my cheeks, certain I was blushing beet red.

He let out a soft chuckle, stepping back but never breaking eye contact. "Enjoy yourself tonight. And if you need another drink—or someone to remind you how good you look—you know where to find me." He flashed that smile as he let Paul and Marco pull him off in the opposite direction.

His confident stride made it hard to look elsewhere. The way he moved, so sure of himself, seemed to command the entire room's attention. If I didn't know better, I'd think he owned the place because he seemed to own every room he walked into. I couldn't help but notice the way his shoulders tensed and relaxed with each step, how his eyes flicked back toward me as he took a seat in one of the booths. I shook myself out of the trance, trying to focus on Angela's conversation with Lucy. But Joey's smile echoed in my mind. He was so mysterious and intoxicating, it was hard not to pay attention to him.

The Wise Guy came to life as the hours ticked by, with soft music filling the smoke-laden room. Couples drifted to the small dance floor, their bodies swaying. I sat at the bar with Angela and Lucy, nursing my second Negroni of the night.

I felt Joey's presence before I even saw him. I had trained myself to feel anyone sneaking up behind me. Angela and Lucy's eyes widened in sync before darting to mine. Their expressions betrayed something—someone—fast approaching. And I knew it was him even without their bulging eyes trying to tell me so.

I whipped my head around, and there he was. Joey stood with

effortless charm, one hand tucked into his pocket, a smirk teasing the corner of his lips. His intense, blue eyes demanding that mine meet his.

He tilted his head towards the dance floor. "What do you say, one dance?"

Lucy nudged my arm. "Oh, go on. The man's practically begging. Don't make a man like him get on his knees for you."

"Why not? I think that would be very entertaining," Angela chimed in. "Adriana, make him sweat it out."

"One dance," I said, rising to my feet and smoothing out the creases in my dress.

Joey smirked, extending his hand. "That's all I need."

I slipped my hand into his, and he led me to the dance floor. As the soft strains of Earth Angel filled the room, he placed one hand on my waist, the other clasping mine with an easy air of confidence. We began to sway to the slow rhythm. Our movements felt natural, almost effortless, but the tension between us felt static. Every step, every brush of his fingers sent a shiver down my spine. Though I tried to act unaffected, I think he sensed it.

"I didn't take you for much of a dancer," I murmured, glancing up at him.

His smirk softened. "I'm full of surprises." The warmth of his hand on my waist lingered, his eyes never leaving mine. "You're good at this," he murmured, leaning in just enough for his breath to brush against my ear.

His low voice sent a shiver racing up my neck, and I tried to keep my composure. But it was becoming an internal battle that I knew I could not control if he continued to touch me with such purpose. Like he knew exactly what he was doing.

"Does that surprise you?" I asked him, arching a playful eyebrow.

"A little." He grinned. "Thought you might step on my toes just to prove a point."

"The night's still young," I smirked. "Don't take it off the table yet."

"You should let yourself have fun more often. It suits you," he said, his tone just as soft as his blue eyes. "You're different. You know that?"

"Different how?"

He tilted his head slightly, studying me. "You don't belong in a place like this. But at the same time, you fit so perfectly. Like you were supposed to be here all along."

The song played on, but I hardly heard it anymore. It was just the sound of his voice, the warmth of his touch, and the sense that we were the only two people in the world. His hand lingered at my waist for a fraction longer as the song ended before he let me go. His eyes stayed locked on mine, holding my gaze in a way that made it impossible to look away.

But I took a step back, my pulse racing. Joey just grinned—slow, satisfied, and entirely too confident—knowing exactly the effect he'd had on me.

The walk back to the bar felt like miles away. Every nerve in my body was on fire. A hot, electric pulse that made my heart hammer away in my chest. The feeling of Joey holding me so close lingered on my skin still, a sensation that shouldn't have felt so right. My mind kept telling me to stay away, to remind myself that this—whatever this was—was wrong. But I couldn't. I didn't want to.

There was something about being so near to him that made me feel safe.

Safe. The word echoed in my head, confusing me. No man had ever made me feel that way before. I'd spent years living in constant fear. But with Joey's arms around me, I felt shielded. Protected. I couldn't let myself get lost in it. I couldn't let myself need him. But God, the way he held me, the way he made the world outside feel so far away, was like a dream I wasn't sure I was ready to wake up from.

Angela and Lucy were waiting at the bar, their eyes locking onto me as I approached. My cheeks burned with heat. I was too bashful to meet their gaze, my nerves fluttering in my stomach. I kept my head down, avoiding their intrusive gazes, and slid onto the barstool.

"Jesus Christ, Adriana, what was going on out there?" Angela teased, her voice dripping an octave lower as she leaned on the bar.

I groaned. "It was just a dance."

But I knew it was no dance. It was the start of something that I should put a stop to. Only I wasn't sure I was strong enough to do it.

"Just a dance?" Lucy exclaimed, throwing up her hands. "Hector, better look at me like that next time I see him, or he's getting an earful!"

I rolled my eyes. "You're imagining things. Joey's just—"

"Not fooling anyone," Angela interrupted, smirking as she pointed a finger at me. "If a man looked at me like that, I'd lose all self-control right there on the dance floor. And someone would have to take over this bar for me!"

"A man does look at you like that," I shot back with a grin. "Marco!"

Angela wagged a finger at me, still chuckling. "Don't even try it. Marco doesn't smirk like he's got some secret he's hiding. He's obvious about it. Joey practically burned a hole through you with his eyes."

Lucy nodded vigorously, taking a sip of her drink. "It's true, babe. That wasn't just a dance; that was the start of a good love story. And tension. Not just any kind of tension, if you know what I mean."

I shook my head, laughing despite myself. "Or perhaps you both need to get your eyes checked."

"Oh, please," Angela said, leaning closer with a grin. "Just admit it—you liked it."

I stayed quiet, sipping my drink, refusing to give them the satisfaction. But as the music swirled around the room and I glanced at where Joey had been standing moments ago, I couldn't quite keep the smile off my face.

It was another secret that would only live in my head—I did

like it. I liked it a lot. I liked how his hungry eyes drank me in. How his hands held me as if he'd done it many times before. I liked it all.

More than I should.

More than I wanted to.

Chapter Twelve

JOEY

"If it isn't Mr. Smooth himself." Paul grinned slyly as I walked over to the table where he and Marco were still seated. "How have I known you my entire life and never once known you were a slow dancer?"

"Dancer?" Marco chuckled, swirling his whiskey neat in his glass. "Please. The guy was practically putting on a show out there."

I smirked, shaking my head in disbelief. "You two got nothing better to do than run your mouths?"

"Oh, we could mind our business, but where's the fun in that?" Paul's grin widened. "So, tell us, Joey. How are you going to explain to Renee you're willing to sign yourself over to Adriana?"

"Nah, don't rush him, Paul." Marco laughed. "He's still recovering from that look she gave him. I swear, if her eyes burned any hotter, we'd be sweeping up ashes off the floor right now."

"You're both idiots, you know that?" I said, though a hint of a grin tugged at the corner of my mouth. Who was I kidding? Adriana's piercing, dark brown eyes had captivated me since the first night I saw her on the Staten Island ferry. And I knew they'd continue to do so for the rest of my life.

"Explains why you looked like a cat that caught the canary when it was over," Pauly remarked, arching his eyebrow as a smug grin danced on his face.

"Adriana's got you wrapped around her finger, brother. Admit it," Marco teased, nudging my arm with a playful grin.

"Admit it?" I asked, leaning back against the leather booth, a smirk now visible on my lips. "The only thing I'll admit is that you two are idiots who don't know what the hell you're talking about."

"You're just a goner. But, hey! Don't worry! It happens to the best of us!" Paul exclaimed, holding up his ring finger.

"Exactly. Deny all you want, Joey. But trust me, the whole room could see it. You've got it bad," Marco teased. "You're confirming the gossip being passed around."

I took a long sip of my drink, trying to hide my smirk. "If I've got it bad, then what's your excuse for still sitting here single and running your mouth?"

"Ouch." Paul snickered, and the three of us burst into howling laughter.

"So, what's the plan for the rest of the night?" I asked, my gaze flickering to Adriana sitting beside Lucy at the bar.

She looked different tonight—dressed to the nines, radiating happiness, and carrying an ease I wasn't used to seeing from her. I liked this version of her, the one that felt untouchable by fear or worry. I'd do anything to protect her, to keep that light sparkling in her eyes.

Paul noticed my eyes on Adriana as he sat back, sipping his whiskey. "You sure you don't want to go back over there?" he teased me. "We can take care of things tonight."

Marco grinned knowingly. "Go ask her for a second dance. I could use some entertainment in here before I have to get back to a hard night's work."

I forced my gaze off Adriana. But only for a second.

Paul arched his eyebrow. "She's begging you to come over with that look she keeps giving you. And every man can see it. We got everything taken care of tonight. Don't worry."

Marco chuckled, elbowing me. "Come on! Do me a favor and go back over there. One of us deserves to get laid."

I shifted my weight, trying to tear my eyes away from Adriana in that navy dress that clung to her curves like it was made just for her. But it was damn near impossible. Paul wasn't wrong—every man in the room seemed to have noticed her. They always had.

She was beautiful, and anyone with a pair of eyes knew it. She caught my gaze more than once, each time offering a soft, sweet smile that sent a pulse of heat through me.

If it weren't for all the obstacles standing between us—Renee, Vincent—I'd already have made my move. But no matter how much I wanted to, I knew this wasn't the time. Our time would come, I knew that. But it wasn't tonight.

"If I don't know nothing, I know one damn thing—and that's this is going beyond helping her out," Paul smirked, eyebrows rose high, creasing his forehead.

"He ain't thinking about the dance anymore, Pauly. He's already one step ahead in his head." Marco grinned before nudging me. "Tell me I'm wrong."

I fought to keep the smirk off my face because Marco wasn't wrong. Hell, all I could think about was the way she smelled, her eyes looking into mine, and that navy dress pooling around her ankles. I could almost feel it—our bodies so close there'd be no room for air between us. "What the hell does it matter? Not like I can do anything about it tonight. She's beautiful, but I ain't no fool. If Vincent didn't take me out, Renee would poison me."

"Hmph," Marco grunted, a smirk tugging at the corner of his mouth as he finished off his whiskey. "I hate to be the bearer of bad news, but Renee's been poisoning you. Just hasn't given you enough to notice yet," he said, making a slow motion across his neck with his hand, followed by a sharp clicking sound.

Paul leaned forward. "Marco and I will cover for you. You know that."

"Got your back, brother," Marco said, draping his arm across my shoulders and pulling me playfully.

The offer hung in the air, but so did the consequences. One thing was clear: after tonight, nothing would ever make me look at Adriana the same way again. But the last thing I could do was drag her into my mess. She'd already been through enough.

I was stuck with Renee. I had no way out without starting a war in the family. I had put in the time, and I was too close to let it slip through my fingers.

"I know what I'm doing," I said, breaking my gaze from Adriana. As much as I didn't want to. I couldn't get swept up in her beauty.

"Sure, you do. Keep telling yourself that, Joey." Paul laughed.

"We'll see about that, won't we?" Marco challenged me.

Saying goodbye to Adriana was torture. Her gaze lingered on me, and mine stayed glued to hers, unwilling to look away. What the hell was happening to me? I couldn't make sense of it. I'd never loved a woman a day in my life—not even my own mother. I tried, but she'd never let me in.

She'd tainted me with a scar so deep, I wasn't sure I'd ever feel love for another human. The closest I'd ever come to it was with Paul and Marco. My brothers. Not by blood, but by choice. That's the only kind of love I knew. The kind you kill for. The kind you die for.

So why the hell did Adriana make my heart beat faster? She was beautiful, no doubt—damn near impossible to ignore that fact—but this? This had to be lust. It couldn't be anything else. Lust was one thing. I could control that. But if it was love...

If it was love? I didn't know what would happen then.

I needed to get out of here. "Nah, we have work to do tonight." I took one last glance at Adriana before vacating my seat, Paul and Marco following me. Once I'd crossed the threshold of The Wise Guy and hit the streets of Staten Island, I was no longer Joey. That guy was gone.

I was The Shark. And I smelled lies. Fear. And betrayal.

My fists ached from the last punch I'd landed—hard enough to crack bone—but I wasn't finished yet. I stood back, watching Nicky slump against the brick wall, his face a mess of blood and cuts. Nicky was an associate, desperate to climb the ladder. Hungry for power and street credibility. But he knew better. He knew better than to undermine me. Or he should have.

"You thought you could steal from me? You thought I wouldn't find out?" I squatted in front of him, grabbing his collar and forcing him to look at me. "You got balls. But not much else. Let me give you some advice, pal. You don't steal from the boss and live to tell the tale."

"Please...I-I didn't—"

A sharp crack echoed as I backhanded him, sending his head spinning. Blood splattered against the brick, the ground, and my fucking suit. I looked down, my nostrils flaring at the sight of it.

"Don't insult me," I growled. "You skimmed off your percent. You know you pay ten percent to the boss. Me. You thought you could keep the money? You thought you could get away with it? Outsmart me? You thought I wouldn't notice? You thought I wouldn't find out?"

I stood up, rolling my shoulders. My long coat shifted as I reached inside, fingers brushing the cold steel of my revolver. "You got two choices, pal. I make this quick, or I make this slow."

He whimpered, hands shaking as he fumbled for an answer. I already knew what it would be—tears, begging, swearing. It was a mistake. They always thought words would save them. These new kids were different. Weaker. You couldn't survive this life if you acted like that. The Shark didn't deal in mercy. He dealt in reminders. He sent messages.

I turned to Paul and Marco, standing behind me. "Break his hands," I ordered. "I've got to get this fucking idiot's blood off my new suit."

I began walking towards my car. I could hardly hear the screams coming from the alleyway with each step I took. I'd learned to tune it out. I turned around once I'd made it to my car, leaning against the hood. I lit a cigarette, watching as Paul and Marco went to work. The sound of crunching cartilage mixed with cries for help flooding my ears before I tuned it out again. No one was coming. Not in my town.

Business was business.

And The Shark always collected his debts.

Chapter Thirteen

ADRIANA

My mind drifted back to that night. The night with Joey at The Wise Guy. I caught myself smiling, a small, unguarded moment that felt foreign. When was the last time I smiled like that? It was strange because before that night, all my thoughts had been consumed with fear. Anxiety gnawed at me every time I let my mind wander back to the night I shot him. William. The memory had lived in my body like a sickness, a constant weight pressing down on my chest.

But Joey made me forget, even if only for a second.

Now, I sat in his passenger seat, the hum of the engine filling the silence between us. We hadn't said much since he picked me up from Davidson's. I told him the walk was only a mile ahead, but he refused, brushing off my protest as if I never had a say in the matter. Maybe I didn't. Maybe I liked it that way.

If I were being honest with myself, I wanted the alone time with him. Even if we hardly spoke. There was something about him—his presence, the way he carried himself, the way he existed in my space. And for the first time in a long time, I felt safe. And because of that, I just wanted to be around him.

I sat in the car outside his wholesale shop, waiting, my fingers smoothing over the fabric of my dress in a futile attempt to calm my nerves. My palms were damp, my pulse unsteady, and I couldn't even explain why. There was no reason for this nervous energy twisting inside me—at least none I was willing to admit out loud. I shifted in the passenger seat, trying to get comfortable, but it was useless.

That's when my gaze drifted to the backseat—and caught on something that made my breath hitch.

A duffel bag, unzipped just enough to reveal what was inside. Stacks of cash. Not a few crumpled bills, not a paycheck's worth —but bundles. Wrapped in rubber bands, thick and neatly packed.

My heart hammered against my ribs, a deep, insistent pulse that I couldn't ignore. Something was off—I felt it in my gut, that sharp instinct that had never steered me wrong. My mind raced, trying to piece it together, trying to make sense of why there was a duffel bag full of cash sitting in the backseat of his car.

Before I could process it, the driver's side door swung open, and Joey slid in beside me. I jumped, my breath hitching at the sudden intrusion. He let out a low chuckle, but the amusement in his eyes quickly faded as his brows pulled together, studying me. He noticed the shift.

"Good news," he said, "Gino almost got your car fixed."

I barely heard him. My gaze flickered back to the bag, then to him.

"What's with all the cash?"

He shifted into drive. "What cash?"

"The bag of cash in the back. It's got a lot of money in it, Joey."

He chuckled, the sound low and easy. "Oh, yeah. I'm just taking it to the bank once I drop you off."

My eyes flicked back to the duffel bag. "How much money is that?"

"Oh, I don't know." He shrugged, keeping his gaze fixed on the road ahead. "Just a few thousand. The business is making a good profit lately."

I wanted to believe him. God, I wanted to. It would be easier that way—to take his words at face value, to pretend there was nothing more to question. But I knew better. I'd spent years learning how to read a man, how to spot the lies hidden between his words. Joey wouldn't look at me. That was the first tell. The way his grip tightened just slightly on the wheel, the way he feigned an easy shrug—too practiced, too casual. He was lying. I could feel it like a weight in my gut, warning me. A duffel bag full of cash wasn't just business doing well. It was something else.

"Tell me the truth," I pressed. "Is this illegal money?"

He didn't answer right away. That was answer enough.

He reached for the pack of cigarettes on the dashboard, tapped one out, and lit it with one hand, never taking his eyes off the road. The flame flickered, catching the paper. Smoke curled around his lips as he exhaled slowly—too slowly, like he was buying time. Like he was choosing his words carefully.

"Adriana," he said finally, "the money's goin' where it needs to go. That's all you need to know."

His eyes flicked to mine, and I held his gaze, searching—for what? Clarity? Reasoning? A hint of reassurance that I was over-thinking? But he gave me nothing. Just an empty look and a finality that settled between us like a locked door.

"That's not an answer," I said, my pulse quickening.

He flicked the ashes out the window. "It's the only answer you're gettin'."

I watched him for a second longer, willing him to give me more, to say something—something that wouldn't make my stomach twist the way it was now. But silence filled the space between us. I turned away, staring out the window, my mind drifting away.

There had always been something off about this town. I felt it the moment I arrived. The way people watched without seeming to, the careful hush that seemed to settle over certain conversations. I remembered standing at the market checkout when my eyes caught a headline on a newspaper rack. Staten Island: A

Mafia Stronghold? The article claimed corruption ran deep—
right down to the mayor and the cops.

I had looked away then, refusing to let my mind go there.
Refusing to believe that I had escaped one hell just to land in
another. But now, sitting in Joey's car with a duffel bag full of cash
in the backseat and a non-answer hanging between us, I wasn't so
sure.

Chapter Fourteen

JOEY

Game day at Yankee Stadium meant fans everywhere, decked out in navy and white, the pinstripes showing up on jerseys, young and old. People clutched hot dogs, peanuts, and foam fingers like it was some kind of religion.

Antonio walked ahead of me, his head swinging left and right, taking it all in with these wide, curious eyes. It's like he's a kid again, not a kid who's had to grow up too fast. I keep an eye on him as we weave through the crowd of fans.

Part of me wished I could enjoy this the way he does, carefree and full of wonder. But I've been me for too long. Even here, with thousands of strangers screaming for the same team, a part of me is always on alert.

But then I catch his grin when we step out into the stands, the field stretching before us like something out of a dream. For a second, it's enough to make me forget who I am on the streets of New York.

Just as much as I liked Adriana, I liked Antonio, too. The two of them had entered my world, leaving a mark I never imagined possible.

When I looked at him, I saw myself. In him, I saw a chance to rewrite my own past, to reshape his future, even though I knew my own outcome was already set. This life had no redemption for my sins. But he could be spared with me by his side.

"Whoa! This place is huge!" His grin stretched ear to ear as he looked around.

I smirked. "Yeah, not bad, huh? You feel that energy? That's the sound of a city that loves its baseball." My hand clapped against his back as we stood side by side, taking in the sights before us. "You know, first game I saw was way back in '41— Yankees versus Red Sox. Place was so loud, I thought my ears would pop."

His eyes widened. "Did the Yankees win?"

"Of course, they won," I said, grinning. "You think DiMaggio would let the Sox walk away with it? Nah. And I wouldn't bother telling the story if they'd lost."

We made our way toward a vendor, the smell of peanuts and pretzels thick in the air. I grabbed a Yankees cap and a foam finger, handing them to Antonio.

"Here, put these on. Can't come to a game without gear—it's bad luck."

He didn't hesitate, sliding the cap onto his head. His excitement was contagious. "Oh, man, this is awesome. Thank you, Joey!"

"There you go." I nodded, satisfied. "Now you look the part. Let's get to our seats before we miss the first pitch."

Antonio and I settled into our seats near the third baseline, surrounded by fans shouting and cheering. I passed him a hot dog and soda as he balanced a bag of peanuts in his lap.

"Alright," I said, pointing toward the field, "here's the deal. You see the guy at the plate? That's Mickey Mantle—our star hitter. They call him the Commerce Comet. He's got one of the best swings in the league."

Antonio took a bite of his hot dog, studying Mantle. "He looks pretty calm for having, like, thousands of people staring at him. I think I'd be nervous if it were me out there. How do you think he does it?"

"That's the game, kid." I chuckled. "Pressure's part of it. You stay cool, keep your focus, and deliver when it counts. Kinda like life, ya know?"

Before he could answer, a loud crack split the air as the batter connects with a fastball, sending it deep into the outfield. The crowd leaped to its feet, a wave of cheers erupting all around us.

He jumps up, his eyes wide. "Is it gonna be a home run?"

I stand beside him, tracking the ball. "Nah, looks like a double. But still, that was a helluva hit!"

As the game continued, I explained plays and strategies while Antonio soaked it all in, nodding and asking questions like a kid seeing the world for the first time. During a break between innings, he leaned back in his seat with a huge grin. "This is so much better than watching it on TV."

"Told ya," I said, matching his smile. "Baseball's not just a sport—it's an experience. You don't just watch it—you feel it."

"Did you ever play when you were a kid?" he asked, glancing at me.

I hesitated for a moment, then shrugged. "Not as much as I wanted to. Life had other plans for me, ya know?" Other plans. Like climbing the ranks of organized crime before I was old enough to buy a game ticket.

Antonio didn't pick up on my meaning. Instead, he asked, "You think I could play someday?"

I turned to him, his eager face reminding me of something I couldn't quite place. I didn't fully understand why, but the kid felt like the son I'd never had. "Kid, you can do whatever you set your mind to. Let's start with your school's team; see where it takes you. I know Coach Artie pretty well."

His grin stretched wider. "That'd be cool."

The game's final inning came down to the wire, the Yankees clinching the win with a walk-off hit. The stadium exploded in celebration, and Antonio was on his feet, shouting alongside the fans.

"Now that's how you win a game!" I clapped, laughing at his sheer excitement.

"That was amazing!" He turned to me, his eyes shining. "Thanks for bringing me, Joey. This was probably the best day of my life."

I smiled, a rare feeling of contentment settling over me. I'd always despised the thought of being a family man—settling down, playing house, living by someone else's rules. It wasn't for me. But maybe I was wrong. "Anytime, kid. You deserved a day like this."

We joined the sea of fans streaming out of the stadium, Antonio holding onto his foam finger like a trophy. I rested a hand on his shoulder as we walked, feeling something close to pride as I watched him soaking up the moment.

I wasn't his father. I had no right to think of him like a son.

But damn, if it didn't feel that way lately. The way he looked up at me when I talked, the way he stuck close like he trusted me to keep him safe. It did something to me—something I didn't have a name for.

By the time we got back to Staten Island, it was late. I pulled into Adriana's carport, and before I even shut off the engine, Antonio bolted out of the passenger seat, rushing into the house with the energy only a kid could still have after a long day. He was still wearing his Yankees cap, clutching his foam finger like it was a treasure.

"Ma! You should've seen it!" he yelled as he burst through the front door. "The Yankees won, and it was the coolest thing ever!"

I followed him in, closing the door behind me. Adriana stood up from the couch, and a warm smile spread across her face. I noticed a pillow and blanket folded neatly on the sofa—a quiet reminder that she was giving Antonio the house's only bedroom.

The sight of it hit me in a way I couldn't quite explain. I wanted to fix that for her. I wanted to fix everything for her. And I would. I would fix everything for her in time. But right now, we both have to suffer just a little while longer.

"That's great, Antonio," she said.

"There was this huge crowd," he continued, his words spilling out in rapid-fire enthusiasm. "And we had these awesome seats! Joey taught me all this cool stuff about pitching and batting, and —Ma, they hit a walk-off! The whole stadium went wild!"

Adriana glanced at me briefly before focusing on him, her smile never wavering. "Sounds like you two had quite the time."

"It was the best, Ma! And look!" He tugged at his cap with pride. "Joey got me this!"

Her eyes shifted to me, softening a little. "You didn't have to do that, Joey."

I shrugged like it was nothing. "Kid needed some gear. Can't go to a game lookin' like a rookie."

Antonio beamed up at her. "Oh, and Joey said maybe I could try out for the school baseball team!"

Adriana's eyebrow arched as she turned her gaze back to me. "Did he now?"

I smirked, holding up my hands. "Don't give me that look. The kid's got potential. Just needs a little push in the right direction, that's all."

Her expression softened again, and she turned back to Antonio. "Well, if that's what you want, we'll talk about it."

"Thanks, Ma!" he said, his grin wide as ever.

I watched the two of them, something warm settling deep in my chest. Antonio's grin was unstoppable as he ran to his room, his foam finger bouncing in his hand.

The sound of his door shutting left the house quieter, and then it was just Adriana and me in the small living room. We hadn't been alone since I had dropped her off, after she had asked about the duffel bag full of money in the backseat.

She crossed her arms, leaning against the couch as she looked at me. I felt the weight of her gaze, steady, searching like she was trying to figure me out—or perhaps decide if I was worth trusting.

"He hasn't been this happy in a long time. Thank you for this, Joey. He's never going to forget it," she said softly.

I smiled, leaning against the doorframe, letting the weight of her words settle. "Kid's a good one. Just needs someone to remind him what being a kid's all about. I'm glad I could do that."

She crossed her arms tightly, her eyes flickering with hesitation. "I appreciate what you're doing, Joey. But I don't want him getting too attached. We've been through a lot, and—"

I raised a hand, cutting her off before she could finish. "Look, I get it. You're used to doin' everything on your own. I see it. But you don't have to—not all the time. I'm just tryin' to help the kid out. No strings attached."

Her shoulders sank slightly. I knew she wasn't ready to let go just yet. "It's not just about Antonio. I'm trying to protect him. And me. From—"

I stepped in again, softer this time. "From someone like me?"

"Joey..."

I nodded. "I get it. You've got every reason to keep your guard up. But I'm not here to mess anything up for you or Antonio. I just saw a kid who needed a day out, and thought I could give him that. No harm. No hidden agenda."

For a long moment, silence filled the room. She studied me. I held her gaze, refusing to flinch, letting her see I meant every word I said. She let out a soft sigh and nodded. "Okay. Thank you, Joey."

"Anytime." I nodded. I debated bringing it up the other day. I let out a sigh. "I'm sorry if I upset you the other day when you asked about the money."

"No, I overstepped. It's not my business," she cut in. "I don't want to know."

"All I meant was—" I began to try and explain myself, but she held up her hand, stopping me as she cut in again.

"Please, I don't want to know." Her words stopped me. "I didn't see anything. I don't know anything. I'd like to keep it that way. I don't need trouble."

Our eyes met, the silence stretching between us. I hesitated, my hand hovering over the doorknob, lingering longer than I should have. I forced a small smile and turned away, making myself leave.

She had every right to be cautious. Her life, Antonio's life, had clearly been through enough. She didn't need more chaos. And I sure as hell didn't want to be the person who brought it.

But there was something about that kid, and something about her, that made me stick around longer than I probably should. Antonio had started to remind me of a kid I never got to be— hopeful, full of wonder, still untouched by the darker things in life.

And Adriana was strong, no doubt about it, but something about her made me want to be strong for her—I wanted to take the weight off her shoulders and carry it for her.

I wasn't sure what I was doing here exactly. Perhaps it was just the guilt, trying to make up for all the bad I'd done. Whatever it was, I couldn't shake the feeling that, for once, I was in the right place—even if I wasn't sure I deserved to be.

Or understood it.

Chapter Fifteen

ANTONIO

L ife on Staten Island was better than it had ever been. After the Yankees game, I discovered a love for baseball. By the following Monday, I'd already made up my mind. I marched straight to Coach Artie and told him I wanted to try out for the team. There were just two problems.

First, tryouts were still a month away. Second, even if I made the team, the expenses that came with it were steep—way more than I could ask my mother to handle when she was already working so hard to keep us afloat.

So, I came up with the next best idea.

"A paperboy? Are you sure about this?" She adjusted her victory curls in the bathroom mirror, turning to me with a hand on her hip, skepticism written all over her face.

"Ma, I've got it. Just a bike and a bag. It's not like I'm working in a factory or something. It's a win-win situation for me."

"And how do you figure?" she asked, crossing her arms and giving me a pointed look.

"We need the money, right? And I'm the man of the house. So I have to help you out."

She sighed deeply, her scowl softening. She didn't want me to feel responsible, but she couldn't deny the truth. "You shouldn't have to worry about money, Antonio. That's my job. And if you do this, I want you to keep the money you make."

"Ma, you're already doing enough. Besides, it's not just about the money. This'll help me get on the school baseball team. Think about it—throwing newspapers all over town is great pitching practice. Who knows? It might make me the next Joe DiMaggio. Then you'll never have to work another day in your life again!"

There wasn't a baseball player alive better than DiMaggio, at least in my eyes. I didn't just admire his skills on the field; the fact that he once had Marilyn Monroe on his arm made me admire him more. I'd always had a thing for blondes ever since I saw Marilyn Monroe in The Seven Year Itch.

She sighed, shaking her head, but smiling this time. "Promise me you'll be careful, okay? And promise me you'll come right back when you're done. You can't be late for school."

I knew she was more worried about someone spotting me and blowing our cover. But cops were rarely seen on the streets of Staten Island—strange, yes. But maybe we'd just gotten lucky, ending up in a place so safe the police weren't even needed.

"I promise." I forced a grin, even though I didn't feel it.

The next morning, I stood in the alleyway behind the diner as Mr. Russo, a stocky man in his fifties with a cigar hanging from his mouth, leaned against a stack of newspapers. He handed me a canvas bag crammed full of neatly folded papers.

"You get these out by seven sharp, kid. No later. And don't even think about skipping a house. Last boy who tried that? Docked his pay. You got it?"

"Yes, sir. Got it." I nodded.

He smirked around his cigar. "Route's marked on the map in the bag. Lose that, and you're out."

"Yes, sir. I won't let you down," I promised.

He turned away, and I slung the heavy bag over my shoulder, hopped on my beat-up bicycle, and pushed off. The streets were deserted in the early morning, and I already liked that about the job. The air was crisp, and the world felt hushed like it was just waiting to wake up.

It was the best thing in the fucking world.

As I rode, my heart raced—not with nerves, but excitement. The real challenge came when I started tossing the papers, trying to land them as close to the front doors as possible. Sometimes, I nailed it perfectly, the paper smacking the door with a solid thud. That usually brought some groggy husband barging outside in his bathrobe, hollering at me. Those moments had me pedaling off like my life depended on it.

DiMaggio, watch out!

I stayed en route, hit every house, and finished the deliveries in record time. By the time I rode home, sweaty and grinning, I knew one thing for sure—the job was mine.

I burst through the front door, my breath coming in quick, sharp gasps. Ma was sitting at the kitchen table, her hands wrapped around a steaming cup of coffee. She looked up, eyebrows raised, as I leaned against the doorframe, still panting.

"Ma! I did it! Every paper delivered right on time!" I said, grinning from ear to ear.

She set her mug down, her expression softening into a proud smile. "Good. That's good, Antonio. I'm proud of you."

Mr. Russo paid me $12 a week to deliver fifty newspapers around the neighborhood, but I must've impressed him because he bumped me up to $15 after just one week. I could hardly believe it.

There was something oddly satisfying about being up before the rest of the town, hopping on my beat-up bike, and making those perfect throws to the front steps. By the time I got to the fortieth house, the sun would usually start to rise. One morning, the sunrise was so breathtaking that I had to stop for a moment to take it all in.

As I paused, I fished a paper out of my bag, planning my next toss. That's when a bold headline jumped out at me, demanding my attention.

Local Mafia Ties Alleged: Joey "The Shark" Romano released from Rikers After Decade in Prison.

Alleged mobster, Joey "The Shark" Romano, Staten Island resident and longtime associate of the infamous Giordano crime family, recently returned home following a ten-year prison sentence for extortion on mafia-related offenses. Sources suggest The Shark's return has reignited activity within the family's operations like never before, though authorities remain tight-lipped about any investigations.

A black-and-white photo of Joey stepping off the Staten Island ferry was plastered beside the article, leaving no doubt in my mind—it was him. Joey. The same Joey I thought I'd gotten to know—a mobster. Or so the paper claimed.

I flipped the paper over, my hands trembling, and skimmed through the rest of the article. Words like "organized crime," "violence," and "illegal activity" jumped off the page, painting a picture so dangerous it felt unreal. My breathing quickened as the realization hit me—this wasn't just any guy from the neighborhood. I clenched the paper tightly, my mind racing, a thousand questions forming, but no answers.

"Hey, kid! You planning to keep that paper, or should I come get it myself?"

The voice cut through my thoughts, sharp and startling. I turned quickly, my heart still pounding.

"Sorry! Uh, here you go!" I said, tossing the paper at his feet and speeding off.

Chapter Sixteen

ANTONIO

I walked down the hallway toward the exit, knowing Joey would be waiting for me. My mind had been consumed all day by that damn newspaper article. I could hardly focus on anything I learned, because all I could think about was what I had read—the confirmation that Joey was indeed a mafia gangster. Michael had told me weeks ago to check the papers, but I had brushed it off. Now, there was no way to pretend I hadn't seen it. That article made everything so painfully clear.

"Hey, paperboy!" Giovanni's voice rang out, dripping with his usual smugness. "How's the newspaper empire treating you today?"

I ignored him, keeping my eyes straight ahead. The last thing I wanted to deal with was Giovanni Accetta.

"Do you get a bonus for dodging barking dogs?" he called from behind, his small crew of sycophants laughing and egging him on.

"What happened? Why the long face?" he continued. "Did someone stiff you a nickel?"

I stopped right in front of the exit. I could walk out and ignore him, or I could turn around and face him. My feet made the decision before my brain could catch up. Without thinking, I marched through the hallway, straight toward Giovanni and his arrogant grin.

"You got anything better to do than run your mouth, or do you need me to help you shut it?" I spat, standing toe-to-toe with him.

He grinned, his eyes scanning me from head to toe. But I didn't flinch. My fists were clenched, and I was ready for whatever came next.

Giovanni raised an eyebrow. "What's the matter, paperboy?"

Luckily for Giovanni, Enzo appeared just in time, shoving himself between us before I could flatten that smug face of his with my fist.

"Whoa! That's enough of whatever the hell is going on here!" Enzo exclaimed, pushing his hand into my chest and forcing me to step back.

"Well, if it isn't Superman to the rescue," Giovanni sneered, eyeing Enzo.

"Oh, I'll show you Superman," Enzo growled, his stocky frame now pressed chest-to-chest with Giovanni.

"Hey!" Michael's voice rang out as he grabbed Enzo, pulling him back. "Cut it out!" Michael shouted at Enzo, his hands firm on Enzo's shoulders. Then, turning to Giovanni, he snapped, "And back off!"

Enzo didn't back down, still glaring at Giovanni. "You're not too bright, are you? You know what happens when you keep poking a bear? Let me tell you, you're not gonna like the results."

Michael yanked Enzo's shirt, trying to calm him down. "Knock it off. I'm not letting you guys fight. It's not happening."

But Enzo's fists were still clenched, his face twisted with fury. "I swear, Michael, one more word from this—"

"Listen, looks like you've got your hands full, Michael. Taking care of these two idiots," Giovanni interrupted with a smirk. "I'll let you handle it. I've got practice to get to. See ya later, paperboy!" He winked in my direction.

"I'd really like to know what the hell is wrong with you two!"

Michael snapped, frustration evident in his voice as he turned to us.

"Wrong with us?" Enzo roared, his voice echoing down the hallway.

I took a deep breath, exasperated, and mumbled, "Listen, I've gotta go. Joey's been waiting outside for a while now. I'll catch you guys tomorrow." Without waiting for a response, I hurried off, eager to get away from the mess we'd just created.

As soon as I got outside, I ran into the next mess.. Joey sat in the driver's seat, parked right in front of the school, his fingers tapping against the steering wheel in rhythm with the song playing. I slid into the passenger seat, doing my best to avoid making eye contact.

He turned the music down, his gaze moving to study the side of my face.

"How was your day, kid?" he asked, his voice casual.

"Not too bad," I muttered, my gaze fixed out the window. "You seem angry," he remarked, pulling the car out onto the street. I could see Giovanni's eyes locked on me from the baseball field.

"I'm fine," I said, my jaw clenched. I was anything but fine. I knew he didn't buy it, but luckily, he didn't press.

I pushed the encounter with Giovanni to the back of my mind, focusing on the more pressing matter at hand. I wanted to confront Joey, but my heart was pounding so hard I felt like I might pass out. The man sitting beside me—calm, almost gentle —didn't match the ruthless figure painted in the newspapers. But I had to know if the stories were true.

"Joey," I started, "can I ask you something?"

He glanced at me briefly, curiosity crossing his face before his eyes returned to the road. "Sure, kid. What's on your mind?"

I swallowed hard. "Did you really go to prison?"

He nodded without hesitation, like he'd been waiting for this question. "Yeah, I did."

"For how long?" I asked, even though I already knew the answer. I wanted to hear it from him.

"Ten years."

"Ten years?" I choked out. Yes, I'd read it in the papers, but to hear him confirm it nearly made me sick to my stomach. "That's forever, Joey."

He chuckled; the sound just as warm as it usually was. "It felt like forever at times."

I hesitated, but then the words tumbled out. "Why did you go? What did you do?"

His hands tightened on the wheel, and I felt the air shift. I thought he wouldn't answer. Then he sighed. "I made some bad choices," he admitted. "Got involved with the wrong crowd. Did things I'm not proud of."

"Like what?" My pulse quickened. Was this the moment he revealed who he truly was? Go on, say it. Tell me you're actually just a wise guy. A street guy. A gangster. A mobster. Whatever they called themselves.

He shifted in his seat. "You know what extortion is?"

I nodded. "Sort of. It's, like, taking money from people, right?" I only knew because the papers had spelled it out in grim detail: how Joey had tried to extort a small business owner, only to discover too late that the man was an undercover cop.

"That's right," he said. "I worked for people who didn't play by the rules, and I did what I thought I had to do. But when you break the rules, you have to deal with the consequences. For me, that meant prison."

"Who did you work for?" I asked.

His jaw tightened, and his eyes stayed fixed on the road. "That doesn't matter," he said.

Maybe he'd changed. He had to have changed. He couldn't be the monster they said he was. I knew Joey. I trusted Joey. I couldn't be wrong about this. The man I spent all my free time with—playing baseball, laughing, joking—could not be a gangster. Joey was the closest thing I had to a father. He wasn't a killer. He couldn't be.

The Joey I knew was always dressed sharp, driving the nicest car in town, because he owned the most successful wholesale shop on the East Coast. He was loved by everyone—family, friends, even strangers.

I saw the way people greeted him. They weren't afraid of him. I watched him help Mr. Davidson carry boxes into the corner store. I saw him help Mrs. Simpson across the street. He was there when Ma's car broke down, becoming our personal chauffeur without ever expecting a dime in return. He took me to my first Yankees game. He tapped his foot at red lights when Frank Sinatra came on the radio, turning it up just a little so he could whistle along.

This wasn't the man who made low-level gangsters disappear without a trace. This couldn't be the same Joey.

"You're not like them," I said softly, almost to myself.

He didn't respond right away, but I thought I saw the faintest hint of a smile at the corner of his lips. "I'd like to think so," he said.

"Were you scared?"

"Scared?" Joey repeated, a faint smirk tugging at his lips. "I don't know about scared. Not much gets to me like that. But I'll tell you one thing—it's not a place you'd wanna be, kid."

"You don't still do any of that stuff, do you?" My heart thudded as I forced the words out.

His gaze was steady. "No. Sometimes life throws you a second chance, and I'm trying to make the most of mine."

I wanted to believe him—so badly. Joey had been good to Ma and me. Better than anyone else had been in a long time. If he'd changed, it couldn't be for some scheme. Not to hurt us, like my pops had. The papers might say all kinds of things about Joey, but that didn't make it true. He didn't deserve my mistrust after everything he'd done for us.

"So," I started, "you're kinda like a baseball player who strikes out, but comes back to hit a home run."

Joey's grin broke through, warm and genuine. The one I was

used to. "I like the way you think, kid." He reached over and ruffled my curls, making me laugh.

"I think it's cool you're trying again," I said. I wanted to trust and believe he wouldn't let me down.

"Thanks, kid. That means a lot."

We both laughed, and the weight between us seemed to lift. I caught his smile as he leaned back in his seat, looking more relaxed. Like the Joey I know.

I had made a promise to myself after the night we'd escaped. I'd never let anyone hurt Ma again, no matter what. But Joey wasn't here to hurt us—he was here to help us. A man who'd made mistakes but turned his life around.

That's the Joey I chose to see.

That's the Joey I was going to believe in.

Chapter Seventeen

JOEY

I never saw myself as a liar, but I told lies to protect those around me, knowing the truth would tear them apart. There was no way in hell I could look Antonio in the eye and tell him who I was when he went to sleep.

I'd never sought validation before, but I wanted it from him —a kid I was starting to think of as my own, our bond growing by the day. It felt like looking at a younger version of myself, and I wasn't gonna tell him that I'd joined the Mafia, committed crimes without a second thought, and became so numb to it that I couldn't even recognize myself and The Shark as the same person.

At eighteen, after a childhood full of trauma, and finally finding a family, whether they were in the Mafia or not, it was family. The only family I had. The only one I knew. They told me there was one way in and one way out. That if I wanted to become a made man, I could never go back. I still felt the Virgin Mary burn in my palms, a blood pact, an oath. I was reborn.

At the time, it felt like the only thing I wanted.

Now, seventeen years later, sitting here with Antonio, I wasn't so sure I'd make the same choice if I could go back. But that was okay. I was a man, and a man had to live with his choices. But I would protect Antonio. I could rewrite my wrongs with him.

When Antonio and I walked through the front door after playing baseball at the park, the sound of *Elvis Presley's Jailhouse Rock* greeted us, spinning on the record player perched on the kitchen counter.

Adriana stood at the stove, stirring a pot of sauce while swaying to the beat. She sang along, her voice light and carefree, twirling between stirs. The scent of simmering pasta sauce filled the air, and I couldn't take my eyes off her. She was beautiful like this.

Antonio caught my gaze and snickered. I leaned against the doorframe, smirking at both of them before calling out, "Didn't know dinner came with a show."

Adriana spun on her heels, startled, the wooden spoon clutched in her hand like a weapon. Her wide eyes met mine, and her cheeks turned pink. "Joey!" she exclaimed as Antonio stifled a laugh beside me.

I grinned, folding my arms over my chest. "Don't stop now. I think you were just getting to the best part of the whole performance."

Truth be told, I just enjoyed watching her dance—the way she let herself go without a care in the world. How her hips swayed. My hands were nearly ready to leap forward to grab them.

"I thought I locked the door!" she said, her blush deepening.

I shrugged. "Guess you're starting to get comfortable. Don't worry—I don't mind surprise performances."

Antonio tossed his baseball glove onto the coffee table, still grinning. "Mom sings Elvis every time she cooks."

"Antonio!" Adriana groaned, her eyes darting toward him. "You weren't supposed to tell anyone that!"

I laughed, shaking my head. She held her hands over her beet-red cheeks, playing bashful. But I loved every second of this. "Don't be too hard on the kid. I think it's cute. And for the record, you've got a great voice."

She bit her lip, too flustered to respond, which only widened my grin.

"So, Joey, are you staying for dinner?" Antonio asked.

Adriana's eyes snapped toward him. "Antonio! Joey probably has plans—"

I cut her off, smirking. "Actually, I don't. If the chef doesn't mind, I'd love to stay."

Adriana sighed. "Fine. But don't expect me to dance while you eat." She tried to stifle the smile threatening to show. But I could see it. Even if it were faint. Even if I had to work harder to get a real smile from her. That was okay.

"No promises," I teased. "I might start requesting encores."

She turned back to the stove, but I caught the faint smile she was still trying to hide. "Sit down before I change my mind," she muttered.

Antonio practically flew to the table, pulling out a chair. "You're gonna love Ma's meatballs and sauce, Joey."

As I sat down beside him, I glanced back at Adriana and smiled. "I think I already love everything that goes on in this kitchen." She shook her head, her cheeks pink, but we both knew what I meant. I wanted to get lost in her, and there was no use in hiding it.

Adriana placed our plates in front of us, the hint of a smile still lingering. I looked at her and said quietly, "It's good to see you like this. Happy. Carefree. Smiling. I'm liking the new version of you."

She didn't say a word, but she didn't try to hide her smile this time, either. So that was a win enough for me.

The three of us sat around the small, cozy kitchen table; plates piled high with meatballs and the best homemade pasta sauce I'd ever tasted. A single candle flickered between us.

My attention was fixed on Adriana, though I tried to keep it subtle while Antonio carried most of the conversation. She wasn't immune to my gaze, either—I caught her stealing glances at me. Her unsuccessful attempts to suppress a smile didn't go unnoticed, either.

"And then Joey told Coach Artie I should bat third when I

get on the team, because I'm better at hitting fastballs than curve-balls," Antonio explained with a mouth full of food.

"Oh, did he now?"

I smirked, leaning back. "Hey, I just call it like I see it. The kid's got a good arm. All that practice delivering newspapers must've paid off."

Antonio beamed. "And it worked, Ma! I hit a double—and Joey said I could've gone for a triple if I pushed harder."

"I'm proud of you, Antonio."

"Every great player started somewhere," I said, nudging his arm with a grin. "We've got the next DiMaggio sitting right here."

Adriana turned back to me, a playful glint in her eye. "So, what are you now—his agent?"

I chuckled. "Nah, just his biggest cheerleader. But I'm telling you, the kid's got potential."

"See, Ma? Joey knows baseball!" Antonio said eagerly, glancing at her. She shook her head with a smile, avoiding my gaze—but I wasn't letting her off the hook that easily.

"This sauce and these meatballs?" I said, taking another bite. "Easily the best I've ever had."

"I told you, Joey!"

Adriana's cheeks turned pink again as she waved off the compliment. "Oh, it's nothing special. Maybe you two just worked up an appetite."

"Nah," I said, meeting her eyes. "This is one of those meals you remember and think about eating again. It's that good, Adriana. I'm a tough critic, trust me."

"You should come over for dinner more often, Joey!"

Adriana gave Antonio a mock-stern look. "Only if he brings dessert next time."

I laughed. "Done. I know just the spot for the best cannolis in all of Staten Island." Her lips curved into a reluctant smile.

After dinner, Antonio headed to his room to prepare for school the next day. Adriana walked me to my car parked in her carport, her arms folded across her chest. She stood close—so close that I could've reached out, grabbed her by the waist, and pulled her against me. Every instinct in me screamed to do just that, but I held back.

"Thanks for spending so much time with Antonio," she began, "and for talking to Coach Artie. He's been happier lately with you around." She shifted her weight anxiously.

I slid my hands into my pockets to keep myself grounded. "You've got a great boy, Adriana. I'm lucky you've let me spend time with him. It's been good for me, too."

Her lips curved into a small smile. "I appreciate it, but you don't have to go out of your way like this. I know you're a busy man."

My gaze locked on hers, and my voice dropped low. "I'm not too busy for you two."

Her weight shifted again. "Why? What are you getting out of this? I'm not going to sleep with you."

I stepped closer, the space between us shrinking. "Not everything has to be about getting something. If you think I'm that kind of guy, you're wrong. I don't want anything from you."

Her eyes flicked up to meet mine, confusion and hesitation battling in their depths. "I don't know what to think."

I moved in close enough to brush her arm with my fingers. "Then stop overthinking," I said. "You're allowed to let someone in. Whatever happened before me is over now."

She looked up at me, her guard still up, but I could see beneath it. Even if it were just a peek. She wanted to let me in.

"What if something goes wrong?" she whispered.

I smiled, tucking a loose strand of her hair behind her ear. "What if nothing does? You'll never know unless you give it a chance."

Her breathing hitched, her hands curling against her sides. "Joey..."

"You've been through hell, but you still wake up every day and do everything you can for your son. That's admirable. You deserve to let someone take care of you now, Adriana." I leaned closer, my voice dropping lower. "Tell me to back off, and I will. But I don't think you want that."

Her breath caught as her gaze softened. "No, I don't want that."

That was all I needed. I closed the distance between us, my hands finding her waist as I pulled her closer. Her palms pressed against my chest, but not to push me away. "Then stop fighting against this," I murmured. "Just let it happen. Whatever happens, happens."

I dipped my head, ready to claim her lips, but she stepped back, her arms wrapping around herself like armor.

"Joey, I can't," she said, shaking her head. Her voice wavered as her eyes darted away. "You're in a relationship. I can't be the other woman."

I sighed and nodded, creating distance between us. How could I forget? Renee.

Her gaze flicked toward me briefly, her voice soft. "Goodnight, Joey."

I studied her for a moment longer before getting into my car. "Goodnight, Adriana," I said.

As I drove away, I saw her lingering on the porch, her silhouette framed by the flickering carpool light. My grip on the wheel tightened. I'd wait as long as it took. She was meant for me. And I promised myself in that moment I'd do whatever it took for her to be mine.

Years ago, I'd asked Paul how he knew Florence was the one for him. A pretty girl from a good family ending up with Paul? Paul was a good guy. My best friend. My brother. But what he did, what we did when the city went to sleep, wasn't understood by many—only those of us who were wrapped up in the streets. He told me, "When you know, you know." I thought he was full of shit. I figured Florence must have been the greatest lay of his life.

But standing across from Adriana, I got it. I knew exactly what Paul meant. Because I didn't know shit about love, but suddenly, I wanted to learn. I wanted to be everything Adriana wanted, to figure out how to break through all the walls we had between us. But I had no damn idea how to make it happen yet.

What the hell was I thinking?

This was dangerous. The kind of thing that could ruin everything I'd built, every connection I had. But damn, the way she looked at me, the way she made me feel. Her and that kid.

It was like nothing else mattered.

Chapter Eighteen

JOEY

I met Ben at the diner in town. We sat in the back booth together, the one no one ever bothered us in. I slid him the cash for his next installment and leaned back against the cracked vinyl seat.

"What's the update?" I asked, not wasting any time.

Ben glanced at the wad of bills, then tucked it into his jacket pocket, smirking as he reached for the menu. "Not even gonna let me order something to drink first?"

"They know not to come over here unless I call them, and I'm not calling them unless you've got something to say." My voice was cold and flat, straight to the point.

He sighed, closing the menu with a snap. "You really know how to kill a mood, Joey."

"You're still alive, so start talking."

Ben's smirk faded as he gave me a long, annoyed look, but he knew better than to push too far. "Alright," he said. "It would appear Adriana's husband is being nursed back to health. The hospital staff I interviewed says he had a long road ahead, but he'd make a complete recovery."

That got my attention. I straightened up. "What the hell do you mean, nursed back to health? What happened to him?"

"Good question." Ben scratched at the stubble on his chin. "Turns out someone shot him. Took two hits: one to the shoulder, one to the abdomen. Shoulder's just a graze, but the abdomen? Let's just say he's one lucky bastard. The shooter was an amateur, though. Close, but no kill shot. Still, they meant it. There was intent behind those shots. Whoever did it didn't want him to live through it. Whoever did it thought they killed him."

The implication hit me like a brick. "You're saying it was Adriana."

Ben shrugged one shoulder. "Just a hunch. Everyone's innocent until proven guilty, I suppose."

I wanted to dismiss the thought, but it wasn't easy. Adriana didn't seem like the person who'd pull a trigger, but perhaps that was why she was always so jumpy. Perhaps she thought she'd finished the job and got it wrong. And if this guy recovered, she'd be right to think he'd come back angry. Real fucking angry. And ready to finish what she failed to. One thing this life has taught me is to make sure you finish the job if you go in for the kill.

Otherwise, it ends badly.

Real fucking bloody, too.

"Has he talked to the cops?" I asked.

Ben leaned in. "Not much. He's in the hospital still. Cops were called to the house when neighbors heard the shots. They found him bleeding out on the floor. Neighbor says a woman and a kid came running out scared, carrying bags, and took off in an old Chevy 150. They've patched him up, but since he woke up, he's been keeping his mouth shut while he recovers. Apparently, he's got a bad gambling problem, which might just save her in the end."

Ben watched me, amused at my silence. "It's a matter of time, Joey. He's going to talk, and he's going to tell them. And the cops over there in Newark? They aren't gonna let it slide. Especially not for a guy like him. She's in deep water. Unless..."

"Unless what?'

"Unless The Shark comes out to play and cleans up the murky waters." His eyes darkened. My jaw tightened. I'd never let anything happen to Adriana. "The question is, does she trust you enough to have you take care of what she failed to do?" Ben raised an eyebrow.

"She'll trust me," I said, though part of me wasn't so sure. "She doesn't have another choice."

Ben sat back, crossing his arms. "Fair enough. But you'd better move fast. It's only a matter of time before someone from Newark starts sniffing around in these waters."

I narrowed my eyes on him. "And that's where you come in, Benny. I need you to handle it."

He chuckled, shaking his head. "That's not my jurisdiction, Joey. I can't just walk into Newark and tell their cops to back off without them suspecting me of something. And if I go down, then we all go down."

I leaned in close enough to smell the stale coffee on his breath. "Make it your jurisdiction," I said, "if you know what's good for you."

Ben stared at me for a long moment, then nodded once. "Alright," he muttered. "I'll see what I can do."

"Good," I said, sitting back, my mind spinning. Adriana didn't realize how much trouble she was in—and now, neither did I.

The first thing on my agenda was Gino's. Quick. That car had to disappear, no questions asked. That part would be easy—almost too easy. But the real challenge? That would be prying that gun out of Adriana's palm. Because if anyone found it, it was over. And I couldn't let her go down.

What the hell was she thinking, carrying around something like that? She wasn't cut out for this. She wasn't like the rest of us —she was too good, too innocent. I had to make sure she didn't get dragged into my mess.

I couldn't let her pay the price for this. Adriana deserved more than that. She deserved to be free of all this. And if I had to risk everything to protect her, I would. No question. But first, I had to get that gun out of her hand. Because if anyone found it, no matter the reason, there would be no turning back. And I wasn't about to lose her over something I could control.

Gino's garage smelled like motor oil, gasoline, and cheap cigars. Gino stood under the hood of some old Cadillac, grease smeared up his arms, sweat glistening on his forehead. "Let me get you the keys to that Chevy you brought over," he muttered, wiping his hands on a rag.

"Nah. I've got another favor," I began, his eyes studying mine, confusion written all over his face. "That car has to disappear. Tonight."

He sucked his teeth, glancing toward the car. Adriana's car. The one that needed to be erased from existence. "You want it dumped?" Gino asked.

I shook my head. "No water, no fire. I need it crushed. I need it gone."

He let out a long breath, nodding. "Alright, alright. I'll take it to Mancini's yard, get it in the press before sunrise."

I walked up to him, close enough that I got dizzy from all the gasoline he was covered in. "No parts left over, no scrap sold off. This ain't about money. This is about cleaning up a prob- lem. You get rid of the whole fucking car like it never existed, or we'll have a big problem."

He nodded fast. "Yeah, Joey. I got it. No trail."

I studied him for a second, then pulled a thick wad of cash from my coat pocket and slapped it onto the workbench. "For your troubles."

I turned and walked out, leaving Gino with the car, the cash, and the weight of knowing that whatever was tied to that car was best left buried with it.

I leaned against a brand-new 1959 red Chevrolet Impala parked outside my wholesale car lot, its polished surface glinting under the afternoon sun. Paul strolled up, coffee in hand, his pinstriped suit looking sharp as always. His smirk widened as he caught sight of the car.

"Damn, new wheels? I like it, Joey!" he exclaimed, giving an approving nod.

"Nah, not mine. It's for Adriana."

The grin slid from his face as he cocked his head, one eyebrow arched. "Adriana?" he repeated, studying me like he was trying to solve a riddle.

"Yeah," I confirmed, fishing the keys from my pocket. "I need you to take it over to her place for me. I've got some business to handle."

The business? Plotting out how the hell I would confront Adriana.

Paul let out a low whistle. "Hold up. You're giving her a car? What the hell happened to Gino fixing hers up?"

"Her car's a death trap." I shrugged. "It's not safe for her or the kid."

That earned me another smirk, this one sharper, sizing me up. "Ah, I get it now. The knight in shining armor, swooping in to save the day, huh?"

"Knock it off, Paul. It's not like that," I said. On a normal day, that would have caused me to grin. Not today. Not with all the loose ends I had to tie up.

"Sure it's not," he shot back, his voice dripping with sarcasm. "Just a charitable act, out of the goodness of your heart, like the good, law-abiding citizen that we all know you to be. If that's the case, then I'm the fucking Pope."

He chuckled. "Come on! You don't hand out new rides to just anyone. This has everything to do with whatever is going on between you two. And I don't know why I'm not in on it. I'm your brother, you know I'll have you back."

I stared at him. "She's got a kid, Paul. That changes things."

He nodded, lips twitching like he was fighting back laughter.

"Ah, it's for the kid. Right. Has nothing to do with the fact that you can't stop thinking about her. I mean, half the town's noticed your car parked outside her place more nights the past few weeks. I've had people ask me if you lived there."

"You're out of line," I said. "What I do is nobody's business but mine. I don't need to explain myself to this town. This is my fucking town. I'll do what I please."

Paul held up his free hand, the other still gripping his coffee. "Okay, okay, no offense meant. Just saying—you're not exactly subtle." He paused, leaning closer as if to make his point.

"I'm just looking out for them, that's all."

"Of course you are," he said, unconvinced. "And next week? What's the plan—buying her a house? Maybe a ring while you're at it? Will I be the best man at the wedding? Godfather of your children?"

His words stung because they weren't far from the truth. A house, a ring, a life with Adriana and Antonio—those thoughts had been creeping into my mind more and more lately. But it wasn't that simple. I had Renee and Vincent breathing down my neck. If I didn't play my cards right, they'd play for me, and it wouldn't be a game I'd survive.

Adriana must have been holding onto the gun she thought she'd use to kill her husband. If the cops came looking for her, they could never find that gun. Not in her hands, not anywhere near her. But that didn't change the bigger problem. I still had to finish what she started. I had to take care of her husband. She'd tried to kill him, but she hadn't finished the job. I would. I had to. For her. For us.

There was no backing out now. If I were going to protect Adriana, if I was going to get her out of this mess, I had no choice. I couldn't let him live to hurt her again. And if that meant finishing the job myself, then so be it. I had enough blood on my hands; another man wouldn't keep me up at night.

Certainly not a man who had already put his hands on someone so precious.

"You done? Or do I need to find someone else to deliver it?" I barked.

Paul chuckled, raising his hands in mock surrender. "Relax, Joey. I'll take care of it." I tossed him the keys, not bothering to say thanks. I heard him laughing softly behind me as I headed to my car.

Chapter Nineteen

ADRIANA

I was tidying the kitchen after breakfast with Antonio when movement outside caught my attention. I spotted a car pulling into the carport through the living room window. My stomach knotted as I peeked through the blinds.

It was Paul.

Dressed sharply in a pinstriped suit, a toothpick dangling between his lips. He leaned casually against the hood of a brand-new Chevrolet. Before I could fully process what was happening, Antonio bolted to the front door and stepped outside, leaving me no choice but to follow.

"What's this, Paul?"

Paul's grin stretched wide. "This?" He tapped the car's hood with a knuckle. "This beauty is yours, Adriana."

My brow furrowed as confusion hit me like a freight train.

"Mine?" I repeated.

Paul straightened, arms open like he was showcasing the car on a game show. "Joey's orders. Said you needed something reliable, so here it is."

I crossed my arms. "No. Absolutely not. I didn't ask for a car."

Paul shrugged. "Doesn't matter. Joey's not really the 'wait

until you ask' kind of guy. He does what he wants, if you haven't noticed. He prefers to live by his own rules."

I scoffed. "Well, you can tell Joey I'm not taking it."

Paul smirked. "Sure, I'll let him know. But you know Joey— he doesn't take 'no' for an answer."

"This is too much, Paul! I can't accept it."

"Look, Adriana, I'm just the delivery guy," he said, dangling the keys in my direction. "You've got a problem with this? Take it up with Joey. I'm just following orders."

I shook my head, taking a step back. "I don't want or need his handouts."

Paul chuckled dryly, cocking an eyebrow. "You think this is some handout? Joey doesn't do handouts. Joey takes care of his family, and like it or not, you're family now."

"Family?" The word stuck in my throat. Family? What did that even mean? The way he said it sent chills down my spine because I had a feeling Joey's meaning of family wasn't the usual one.

Before I could ask further, Antonio darted toward the car, his face full of excitement. "Ma, it's so cool! Can I look inside?"

"Antonio—" I began, but Paul interrupted.

"See? The kid's got taste. What's the harm in checking it out?"

Antonio was already peering into the car windows, his hands cupped around his face to block the carport light.

"This isn't how normal people do things. You know that, right?" I muttered, shaking my head.

Paul let out a hearty laugh. "Joey's not exactly 'normal people.' You're in one of the least 'normal' places in all of New York."

I rubbed the bridge of my nose, letting out a breath I didn't know I was holding onto. "Fine. I'll talk to Joey. But don't think for a second I'm keeping this without saying my piece. He was supposed to get my car fixed, not buy a new one."

Paul's grin widened. "That's on you, Adriana." He sauntered to the driver's side, opened the door, and tossed the keys onto the dashboard before tipping his head toward me. "Oh, and Joey already paid for the insurance. You're covered." He winked and strolled off, whistling, hands tucked in his pockets as he disappeared down the sidewalk toward Davidson's.

I stood there, frozen, staring at the car. It was too much, too grand, too unexpected. This wasn't the kind of treatment I was used to—certainly not from a man. And I just knew it came with strings attached.

"Can we keep it, Ma? Please?" Antonio begged, his eyes wide with hope.

Joey was going to hear about this, no question about it.

Antonio huffed, crossing his arms when I didn't give a response. "It's ours. Joey took care of it. You heard Paul—he gave it to us because we need a car. What's the big deal?"

The big deal was that I had asked Joey to fix my car, not replace it. I had trusted him to handle it the way I wanted, but that was my first mistake. I should have known better. Men like Joey always had something else up their sleeve.

Antonio was already running his hand along the door handle, testing the grip, his excitement written all over his face. "Ma, come on, at least sit in it. Just once."

I sighed, knowing I was already losing this battle. The moment I hesitated, Antonio's face lit up, and he rushed around the back of the car, slipping into the passenger seat before I could say another word.

I slid into the driver's seat, the rich scent of new leather filling my nostrils as I wrapped my fingers around the wheel. My old Chevy could never compare to this—not in a million years. The engine purred to life with the turn of a key, smooth and powerful, nothing like the rattling, struggling sounds I was used to.

"This is the nicest car we've ever had." Antonio grinned.

I stole a glance at him as I pulled out onto the road, watching him beam out the window, soaking in the feeling of riding in something so pristine. My stomach twisted. This car was a statement—a message, a claim.

When we reached Angela's house, I parked along the curb,

barely putting the car in park before Antonio leaped out and bolted toward the front door. Angela opened it just as he cut past her, already on his way inside to find Enzo. Angela's gaze shifted to the car, her arms folding tightly over her chest. Her sharp eyes took in every inch of it before settling on me. She stepped forward, her brows knitting together.

"Is this," she pointed at the car, "what I think it is?"

I pressed my lips together and gave a single nod. Before Angela could say another word, Lucy, who lived right next door, sauntered over.

"Well, that's a mighty fine gift you were given, Adriana." She smirked, eyes flicking between me and the car. I clenched my jaw. That was exactly the problem.

"Lucy's right." Angela nodded along, arms crossed, as she studied me. The two of them stood in front of me like a united front. "It's only right that you take it for a little spin. You know, make Joey's money worth it and all."

"I did drive it over here," I shot back. "And now I'm driving it straight to his shop to confront him, because he promised to fix my car—not buy me a brand-new one."

Lucy smirked. "Mind if I tag along? I think you might be the first woman ever to tell Joey Romano no, and I'd love to see how that plays out."

"Well, I'm not letting him make decisions for me," I said firmly. "I've already had that happen and refuse to fall victim to it again."

Angela sighed, nodding. "You know what? I agree, Adriana. We're more than capable of making our own decisions."

"Well, perhaps you two are," Lucy said, tilting her head. "But personally? I'd love to sit back and let a man make all the decisions for me."

Angela snorted. "Hector doesn't do that for you?"

Lucy rolled her eyes. "Hector? That man is practically useless. Don't get me started." She exhaled dramatically before flashing me a grin. "And listen, I'm all for women's empowerment. But wouldn't it be empowering if you just kept the free car?"

"How would that be empowering?" I asked, narrowing my eyes at her.

Lucy shrugged. "Well, it's a free car with your name on it. You'd be a fool to give it back. If the man is so love-sick that he's handing out Chevy Impalas, you might as well keep it."

"He wants something from me," I stated firmly. "And I'm not giving it to him."

Angela smirked. "No, no—imagine this. He gifts you something, fully expecting something in return, and you just leave him in the dust. Literally. Now that's the best move yet."

I couldn't help but laugh at the two of them. "You two are so much help," I said, shaking my head as I walked toward the driver's seat.

Lucy pranced over, stopping by the window as I slid inside and started the engine. Leaning down, she smirked at me, resting her arms on the doorframe.

"Stay focused," she warned. "Don't get distracted by that little act he puts on. Reclaim your- self. Do it for me and my lack of self-control."

I chuckled as she stepped aside, shaking my head as I pulled out onto the road, heading straight for Joey's shop.

My pulse quickened as I pulled into his wholesale lot and spotted him leaning against the hood of his car, a cigarette dangling lazily from his fingers. He looked too smug for my liking, his eyes gleaming with amusement as I slammed my car door shut and stormed toward him, my heels clicking furiously against the pavement.

"Tell me that isn't for me," I shouted, pointing at the car behind me.

He took a long drag, exhaling the smoke, and then smirked. "It's not for you. It's for whoever lives on Blythe—the one with a kid and no car. Turns out it was better to buy you a new one than have Gino try to salvage that one you were driving."

I crossed my arms. "I can't take this."

Joey stood straighter, towering over me, and flicked his cigarette to the ground. "Well, it's a little late for that. The car's already in your name."

I was certain my glare could've melted steel. "Who do you think you are? You were supposed to help me fix my car, not buy me a new one. I don't need a man to make decisions for my son and me."

He shrugged, unfazed. "You've got things to do, Adriana. You don't need to break your back doing them."

"I don't want your handouts, Joey!" My voice rose as I tossed my hands in frustration.

He stepped closer, the scent of his cologne mingling with the faint trace of smoke. "Handouts? This isn't a handout. It's common sense. You need a car. I own a car wholesale shop. It was an easy fix. Don't let your pride get in the way."

I squared up to him, practically seething. "My pride is the only thing I've got left! I've been doing fine on my own—"

He cut me off. "No. You've been surviving. And that kid of yours deserves more than just surviving, so I thought I'd help you out."

That struck a nerve. I stared him down. "You don't know anything about what we need. I'm his mother. I know what he needs, and I'll get it for him."

His smirk returned as he leaned in. "I didn't know this was how you reacted when you were angry. It's going to be really hard to stay on my best behavior after this."

Before I could stop him, his hand brushed a strand of hair from my face. My breath caught, heat rushing to my cheeks despite my best efforts not to let it affect me. His touch disarmed me, and I hated how much I liked it at the moment.

"Stop it. I know what you're doing, Joey," I said.

His grin widened. "What am I doing? What's it doing to you? The same thing it's doing to me?"

I took a step back, my heart hammering away. He was onto

me, and I couldn't let that happen. It was too risky to let him in, even if some of me wanted to.

"I've got to go get Antonio," I said softly, trying to steady myself. Every fiber of my being wanted to stay, to feel his gaze, his touch, his presence. But I couldn't afford to lose myself to another man. I pushed my palms against his chest, forcing the space between us, and spun on my heel. Walking away felt like tearing myself in two.

Behind me, Joey chuckled low and deep, his voice carrying after me. "You're welcome for the car, Adriana."

I slid into the driver's seat, but I heard him say. "See you on the road, sweetheart! Oh, and you're welcome!" I clenched the steering wheel, heat rising in my cheeks, and drove out of the lot, leaving his smug grin in my rearview mirror.

After picking up Antonio, I pulled up to the carport, only to see a parked car already there. I parked on the street, my eyes narrowing as I recognized the driver. Renee stepped out, slamming her door and heading straight for us.

"What's she doing here, Ma?" Antonio asked, glancing at me.

"Go inside," I told him as we exited the car. My chest tightened as I approached her. "Renee? What—"

She cut me off. "Oh, don't even start. We need to talk."

"What's going on?" I asked, even though I already knew the answer. This was about Joey and the damn car.

"What's going on?" she repeated with a bitter laugh. "That's what I came to ask you. Why did Joey buy you a brand-new car?" My heart thudded painfully in my chest, but I kept my expression calm. "And don't lie to me," she snapped, her tone sharp as she stepped closer. "I know he's been here day after day. I know Paul, his little lapdog, delivered it. What I want to know is why."

"Renee, whatever you're thinking, it's not like that. Joey—he just—"

"Joey, just what?" she interrupted again. "Bought you a shiny new car out of the kindness of his heart? Joey doesn't do things like that for no reason. He never did anything like that for me.

You know who Joey really is, Adriana. He's not some saint, and you know it."

I felt my pulse quicken. Renee's words rang in my ears, but my mind was already spiraling out of control.

I thought back to that day at the grocery store, when I'd seen the newspaper headline at the checkout counter—Staten Island Riddled with Mafia Dealings. I had ignored it because, perhaps if I ignored it, then somehow it couldn't be true. But then there was the day I had seen that bag of cash in Joey's car.

Stacks of bills.

I'd told myself it wasn't my business, that maybe there was some logical explanation. He was a successful businessman, after all.

But now, as Renee stared at me, waiting for an answer, everything snapped into place.

Joey's money. Joey's power. The way people looked at him when they passed by, with recognition—respect. How he never really talked about what he did all day, only that he was "handling things." The expensive car. The expensive suits. My stomach twisted as I met Renee's eyes. The real question was— who had I gotten myself involved with?

"Are you sleeping with him?" Renee asked.

The question hit me like a slap. My eyes widened in shock. "What? No! Renee, it's nothing like that! This is about my son and me. I—I needed help. Joey was just—"

"Helping you? Please," she scoffed, her disbelief cutting deep.

"Joey doesn't help people. He rules this town with fear and manipulation. He doesn't help anyone but himself."

I stood straighter, refusing to let her push me into a corner. "Renee, I'm not interested in Joey. I would never get involved with a man who's in a relationship. He's just been kind. To Antonio and me. That's it."

"Kind?" She laughed. "Oh, spare me the act! You think I don't know Joey? You think I don't see what's happening? You show up out of nowhere, and Joey's bending over backward for you?"

"Don't put this on me, Renee," I shot back. "I didn't ask for any of this. Joey offered, and I didn't know what else to do. But it's not what you think. I swear."

She stared at me, her eyes blazing with anger. "Do you really think I'm buying this?" She shook her head, a bitter smile twisting her lips. "Joey doesn't change, Adriana. He'll get bored with you like he gets bored with everything. And when he does, you'll end up just like me."

Renee didn't wait for a response. She turned, her heels clicking against the pavement as she got into her car and slammed the door.

I stood there, hands clenched at my sides, my breath unsteady. Her words echoed in my head. I needed to distance myself from Joey—for my sake and Antonio's.

But I wasn't sure I was strong enough to resist him.

Chapter Twenty

JOEY

I sat on the couch, the weight of the day pressing down on me. Saying it had been a long day was an understatement. It was so late by the time I got home that Renee had already gone to bed. The house was still, and there was peace for what felt like the first time all day. But it didn't last. It never lasted.

Renee's bedroom door opened, and she appeared in the living room, her bathrobe loosely wrapped around her curvy frame. Her face darkened with anger the moment she saw me.

"Oh, you finally decided to come home?" she said.

I raised an eyebrow, too exhausted for games. "I live here. Last I checked, that's what people do, Renee."

"Live here?" she scoffed. "That's something coming from you. You sleep here for a few hours, eat here if I'm lucky enough to catch you, and drop your laundry off. But actually live here? That's a stretch, Joey."

She wasn't wrong. It didn't feel like living. It felt like another prison sentence, just with different walls.

"Renee," I said, exhaling sharply. "I really can't do this with you tonight."

Her voice cut through the quiet like a knife. "Fuck you, Joseph Romano! What's this I hear about you buying Adriana a car? I let it go when you started driving her kid all over town. I even let it go when half of Staten Island was whispering about your car parked outside her house all the time. But this? Buying her a car? Are you out of your damn mind?"

I stood, forcing myself to stay calm even as my temper rose. "She needed help. Her car was a piece of junk. Even Gino couldn't fix it. She's a single mother with no one to rely on, and she needed to get her kid where he needed to go. I helped her out. That's all there is to it."

"Is that right?" Renee's arms crossed, her eyes locking on mine. "And what have you ever done for me, Joey? What have you bought me? What have you done other than take from me?"

"Take from you?" I asked, the accusation hitting a nerve. "Don't twist this, Renee. I helped her because she needed it. She's got no one, Renee. No family. She's trying to survive on crumbs!"

Her laugh was cold and bitter. "And I guess I don't need anything, right? Funny how that works. I'm here, day in and day out, but somehow, Adriana walks in, and she gets the royal treatment when I've begged you for the bare minimum for months now! Do you even hear yourself right now?"

"This isn't about you," I snapped, running a hand down my face. "It's not some competition, Renee. She's been through hell, and I'm just trying to help her get back on her feet. That's all."

She closed the gap between us. "You keep saying it's just about helping her. But tell me, Joey, if that's all it is, why does it look like so much more? Why is everyone whispering, huh? Why do you keep defending her like you've got something to hide?"

"I don't have anything to hide," I said, though even I could hear the lie in my voice. She was breaking me down, and I wasn't a weak man. I was falling for Adriana.

She stepped back, shaking her head, her voice trembling now. "You don't even see it, do you? It's not about the car or the kid. It's about the fact that you'll never love me. You never did. And you know why? Because you're already in love—with her!"

"Renee, that's not—" I tried, but I couldn't even finish the lie.

"Oh, save it," she snapped, cutting me off. "I know the truth. I've known it for weeks, Joey. You'll never feel that way about me."

Her words hit harder than I thought they would. She was right, and I knew it. I never loved Renee. I wasn't built for love, or so I thought. But Adriana and Antonio had changed all that. They showed me what love could be—what it should be.

I sighed. "Renee, I don't want to hurt you."

Her laugh was hollow. "It's too late for that, Joey. Way too late." She pressed her lips in a thin line and spat, "But I get what I want."

I chuckled; I couldn't help but let the laugh out. After the day I'd had, and this was how it was going to end? "Are you blackmailing me?"

Her eyes said yes. Though she turned and walked away, leaving me alone in the quiet once more, the weight of her words pressing harder than anything else had that day.

Chapter Twenty-One

ANTONIO

I listened from the carport, watching Renee and Ma. I wasn't sure what Renee was capable of—I didn't know her like that. But I could tell she was pissed. And I had vowed to myself, a long time ago, that nobody else would hurt Ma ever again. If Renee so much as looked like she was going to cross a line, I'd step in.

Giovanni must have gotten his ways from someone, and looking at Renee now, I had a pretty good guess. It was the same kind of controlled fury I'd seen in Giovanni many times before.

But then she said, "You know who Joey really is, Adriana. He's not some saint, and you know it."

My heart dropped into my stomach.

Did Ma know? Did she not care? Or was she just finding this out?

Was Renee talking about what I'd seen in the papers—about the mafia, about Staten Island crawling with criminals and Joey leading the pack?

An uneasy feeling settled in my stomach. I had pushed those thoughts away. I had told myself that wasn't who Joey was. Joey had helped us, no questions asked. He was like a father to me.

But was any of it real? Or was I just seeing what I wanted to see?

Then Renee asked if Ma and Joey were sleeping together, and I wanted to burn my own ears off. My stomach twisted, bile creeping up my throat. I had to swallow it back down before I lost it right there.

That couldn't be true. They hardly spent any time alone together. But what if there was more? What if things were happening right in front of me that I hadn't noticed?

I felt ambushed. Who was lying?

I didn't know. But I needed to find out.

For Ma's sake. To protect her.

Ma came marching toward me, her lips pressed so tightly together they were white. She didn't slow as she passed; she just threw a sharp, "Come inside and wash up for dinner."

I knew better than to protest.

So I followed her in, keeping a few steps behind, watching the way her shoulders were stiff, her hands curled into fists at her sides. She was mad—really mad. This was supposed to be a fresh start for us. She stopped in the kitchen, hovering over the counter, her eyes squeezed shut as she took a few deep breaths.

"Are you okay?" I hesitated to ask.

Her eyes flicked open and landed on me. She forced a smile, but it didn't reach her eyes. "I'm fine." She nodded.

It was a lie. I knew it was a lie. She hadn't been fine in a long time.

I stood there, unsure of what to do next. The words were right there, pressing against my throat. Do you know who Joey really is? Do you care? Are you lying to protect me, or are you lying to yourself? There were too many pieces that didn't fit, too many questions with no answers.

But looking at Ma now—her jaw clenched, her fingers gripping the counter like it was the only thing keeping her upright—I knew now wasn't the time.

So I swallowed my questions.

For now.

Chapter Twenty-Two

ADRIANA

A knock at the door startled me. I hesitated, glancing toward it, debating whether to answer. Would there ever come a day when I don't flinch at every loud sound? I opened the door and found Joey standing there.

"Joey, what are you doing here?" I asked, folding my arms across my chest. I was relieved he wasn't a cop coming to arrest me for the murder of my husband, but I still didn't want to see him. Not now. Not after Renee had confronted me.

"I needed to see you. Can we talk?"

I soaked in all his charm. How he leaned against the door frame, his blue eyes begging me to let him in. I couldn't say no to him, and that was becoming a big problem. A sigh escaped my lips as I stepped back. We moved to the kitchen table, where I sat across from him, my arms still crossed.

"Renee came by earlier," I started, watching his reaction. "She did?" He blinked, caught off guard.

"She was upset," I continued, "convinced that something was going on between us. I told her she was wrong, but she didn't believe me. She's quite adamant that we're having an affair."

Joey's jaw tightened. "She said that to you? Jesus, I'm sorry,

Adriana. She had no right coming here, and I promise it won't happen again. I'll make sure of it."

I looked at him skeptically. "Joey, I don't want to be part of whatever mess is happening between you two."

"You're not," he said quickly.

I arched an eyebrow. "It doesn't feel that way. She said some awful things—about you, about me, and whatever story she's spun in her head about us."

Joey leaned forward, his gaze steady. "Adriana, trust me. You're not the problem." He reached across the table, his hand brushing mine. His touch sent a shiver down my spine. I hated that it did. I should've pulled away, but I couldn't. His touch paralyzed me. "She's not the one I care about," he said in a hushed tone. "She never has been."

I yanked my hand back, clutching it in my lap like it burned. "Don't say that, Joey. She's your girlfriend. You have history—she said so herself."

"History doesn't matter if there's no future," he replied. "And history is not the word I would use, but that doesn't matter."

I shook my head. "Joey, this isn't fair to her or to me. My life is messy enough without you making it worse. Whatever you're involved in, I don't want any part of it."

His hand hovered over the table, as if he wanted to reach for me again, but didn't. "I know things are complicated, Adriana. But ever since the ferry, I haven't been able to stop thinking about you—or Antonio. You both deserve better than the life you've been handed, and I want to do whatever I can to make it better for the two of you."

I clenched my fists in my lap, the pull of his words hitting too close to home. His charm and his intensity were dangerous, but so was my reaction to them.

"This has to stop," I said. "It isn't right. You know where this is headed."

"It's the truth. And you deserve the truth. I care about you, Adriana."

I stiffened. "Let's not forget, you're with Renee."

"For now," he admitted. "But not for long. You don't know the circumstances of our relationship. I need to end it. But I've got to do it cleanly, for both of our sakes. You don't need to do anything. Or worry about anything. Just sit back and let me handle it. I'll handle everything."

I shook my head again, resisting the pull I felt toward him. "You can't just show up here and expect me to fall into your arms. I have to think about Antonio. About his life. About our future. We're finally in a good place. I can't screw that up."

He nodded. "I don't expect anything, Adriana. I never expected anything from you. I just can't pretend anymore. I need you to know how I feel. It's hard for someone like me to even express this to you. But it's the truth. I care about you. More than I even understand."

I stared at the table, unsure if his confession made everything simpler or infinitely more complicated for us. I was almost certain it was the latter.

"That's not the only reason I came, though," he said. Our eyes met, and I searched his face, trying to read him, but he gave nothing away. "Where's the gun?"

The question knocked the air from my lungs. My fingers tightened around the arms of my chair. His question sent goosebumps crawling up my arms. The gun? How did he know about that? I swallowed hard. "What gun?" I murmured.

He sighed, the scent of cigar smoke lingering on his breath. Then, without warning, he grabbed the legs of my chair and pulled me closer. My knees brushed against his, and suddenly, I was trapped between his legs. His gaze held mine, and it was impossible to focus when he was this close. His fingers trailed up my legs—slow, deliberate—before settling on my thighs.

I should tell him to stop. I should push him away. But I couldn't.

"Where's. The. Gun?" he asked again, each word a slow, measured demand.

He knew. Somehow, he already knew.

"Sweetheart, I don't give a damn what you've done—or what you think you've done. I need that fucking gun." His eyes locked onto mine. Unrelenting. I felt cornered with those ice blue eyes piercing straight through me.

I frowned. "What do you mean, what I think I've done?"

He exhaled sharply, dragging a hand over his face before tugging at his bottom lip. His hesitation told me everything—whatever he was about to say, he didn't want to. "You didn't kill him," he said. "But I will."

My breath caught. Everything felt as though it came to a standstill. Frozen in place.

"I just need the gun," he continued. "Because if the feds come sniffing around and they find it? Adriana, sweetheart, you're going down. And I don't know if I'll be able to pull you out of it."

My pulse pounded in my ears. My body was hot. Burning with fear. Anxiety.

"I'm going to clean this up for you," he said, softer this time. "I told you—you don't need to worry about anything. I'll handle it."

I couldn't breathe. My chest tightened, my vision blurred, and the walls were closing in. I hadn't killed him? I didn't know what was worse—that I hadn't killed William, that the cops weren't coming because William would make sure to finish what I started himself, or that Joey knew and was willing to kill for me.

My fingers tangled in my hair as I shoved the chair back and shot to my feet. I paced the kitchen, hot tears streaming down my cheeks. My pulse pounded, my stomach twisted, and then—Joey's arms were around me, pulling me against him.

And just like that, I felt safe.

Safe. But not for long.

Because Joey would leave. He'd go home. Back to Renee. And William wouldn't stop until he found me. I couldn't tell Joey the truth. He couldn't protect me if he wasn't here, and I had to protect Antonio if—when—William came back.

Joey's voice cut through my thoughts. "Sweetheart, he can't hurt you. Just give me the gun, and I'll take care of it."

I swallowed hard, fighting the nausea curling in my gut. "I don't have it," I whispered, stepping back, slipping from the warmth of his embrace. "I tossed it into the water when we got onto the ferry."

A lie. But a good one.

Joey studied me, his eyes searching mine. And then—he nodded. He believed me. "Good," he said. His hands came up, cupping my face, his touch gentle. He pressed a soft kiss to my forehead. "That was a good move."

Tender. Safe. Just not for long.

Chapter Twenty-Three

ANTONIO

I had left while Ma was cooking dinner to grab my jersey from Coach Artie. I'd saved up enough money to get on the school baseball team, and now, it was finally real.

"There you go, number three." Coach Artie grinned, handing me the white and blue baseball jersey.

Ma might've been having an epiphany, but as far as I was concerned, life couldn't get any better. I had friends. We had a brand-new ride. I was on the baseball team.

Walking back home, clutching my jersey with a grin plastered on my face, I felt unstoppable. But that feeling came to a screeching halt when Giovanni's voice rang out behind me.

"Hey, paperboy! What number are you?"

I turned, already knowing I'd see that smug grin of his. But nothing—not even him—was going to ruin this for me.

"Number three," I said proudly.

"Number three," he repeated, laughing alongside his friends. Then, with an exaggerated motion, he turned to show me the back of his jersey—bold white lettering stitched over a dark blue background. Number one.

The smile faded off my face.

"It's just a number," I muttered.

Giovanni chuckled, shrugging. "Hey, that's the spirit! I'd tell myself that, too, if I were you!"

"Just because you're number one, doesn't mean you're going to be better than me. I'll show you it's just a number," I said through clenched teeth.

Giovanni smirked. "Yeah? How'd you get on the team, anyway? Don't you need money for that? What money do you have?"

"If you're nervous, I'm going to outshine you. You could just say that," I shot back.

His nostrils flared, his face flushed—I was getting under his skin, and that gave me all the satisfaction I needed.

Then he said it.

"Did you get on the team the same way your mother got that new ride?"

His little posse erupted into laughter. But I wasn't laughing.

I took off running—not away from him, but straight at him. Not my smartest move. I was smaller, and he had four guys backing him up. Five against one.

Before I could reach him, Louis—one of his friends—knocked me down. My back hit the pavement hard, the impact knocking the breath out of me. Before I could react, Louis's foot pressed into my chest, pinning me down.

Giovanni bent down, his face inches from mine. "I don't care what that mother of yours does with someone like Joey. But you stay in your lane—or else."

"Or else what?" I challenged.

"Or else you'll find out there are more powerful men than Joey Romano," he mocked.

My eyes bored into his, my jaw locked tight. "I don't need Joey to save me. I can handle you all by myself."

"Is that so?" He chuckled. "You look like you're doing a great job at that."

"Well, I'm a bit outnumbered." I sighed. "But don't think for a second that if it were just you and me, one of us would be going down—and it sure as hell wouldn't be me."

He smirked. "You can't fucking touch me. I'm un-fucking-touchable. You lay a hand on me, and you're fucking dead. My grandfather owns this city, and he'd come for you and your mother."

"Leave my mother out of this," I growled.

"I'll do whatever I want," he sneered.

I lay there, chest rising and falling, as the five of them walked off. Above me, the sky stretched out, pale and clouded. The air still carried a winter chill, even though we were heading into March.

I exhaled sharply and sat up, brushing dirt off my jersey. My mind swirled with Giovanni's words.

There are more powerful men than Joey Romano.

Chapter Twenty-Four

ADRIANA

A ntonio burst through the front door. "Hey, Ma. Hey, Joey," he said, his tone laced with suspicion. "What's going on?"

I forced a tight smile, suddenly very aware of how I must look right now. "Nothing. Joey was just leaving." My hand nudged Joey's arm, signaling for him to leave. The last thing I needed was for Antonio to know that his father was alive and coming for us.

Antonio didn't look convinced, his brown eyes darting between us. "Leaving? You two looked like you were in the middle of something. Did I interrupt?"

Joey chuckled. "Nah, kid. Just talking. You didn't interrupt anything. Your Ma was just upset about the day."

"Since you're here, why don't you stay for dinner?"

"Antonio—" I started, but he cut me off.

"C'mon, Joey. You've gotta eat, don't you?"

Joey smirked, glancing at me. Neither one of us knew what to do. "I don't know, kid. Your mom might not want me sticking around for dinner. I didn't bring dessert like I promised I would."

What a smooth talker.

"She doesn't care about dessert," Antonio said.

I sighed, shooting Joey a warning look. "Antonio, it's late.

Joey probably has other plans. Don't you?" I said, nudging his arm again.

But Antonio was relentless, turning back to Joey with the stubbornness only an innocent teenage boy could muster. "Then he can take care of them after dinner. Right, Joey?"

Joey shrugged, his grin smug. "If your mom's good with it, I don't mind staying."

"Fine," I sighed, moving towards the stove. "Let's just sit down and eat dinner."

Antonio grinned, plopping down at the table as Joey took his seat. "Paul says we're family now," Antonio declared. "And family eats dinner together. Might as well get used to Ma's cooking, Joey."

Joey ruffled Antonio's dark curls, his smirk softening. "Family, huh?" He glanced at me before turning back to Antonio with a nod. "Alright, kid. You're right about that. Let's eat."

The three of us sat around the kitchen table, the only sound the clink of forks against plates as we ate the homemade carbonara I'd prepared. The tension between Joey and me hung thick in the air. No one said a word—until Antonio broke the silence, his voice cutting through the quiet like a knife.

"Hey Joey, is the mafia real?"

The question hit me like a slap. My eyes widened in horror, and I nearly choked on my food. Joey froze mid-bite, his fork hovering in the air, his eyes flickering from me to Antonio.

"Antonio!" I snapped, lightly smacking his shoulder to get his attention. I was horrified at the word mafia leaving his lips.

He shrugged at me. "What? I saw it in the papers. They were talking about 'The Shark,' saying he's in the mafia."

Joey let out a low chuckle, the corners of his mouth quirking up as he twirled pasta onto his fork. "The Shark, huh? Sounds like a comic book villain. Guess the papers are getting creative these days."

Antonio wasn't laughing. His expression was dead serious as he leaned forward, staring at Joey. "Well, they made it sound serious. Said you were dangerous. Said you're involved in a lot of bad stuff. One article said you were a glorified serial killer."

I coughed on my food. "Antonio, that's enough! Please drop it and don't read any more of that crap."

I knew I was lying to him. But how could I explain the truth to him? It was too complicated, too dangerous. How could I tell him that, yes, the mafia was real? That, yes, Joey was involved? And yes, I was aware of it—and somehow, I'd let Joey into our lives despite knowing. And felt safer with Joey in our lives.

But Joey wasn't the monster the papers made him out to be. He wasn't some ruthless killer, running wild through Staten Island. He was respected, even admired, by the people around here. He was good-looking, charming, and kind. He'd done nothing but help us since we met him. I believed that Joey wasn't a threat to Antonio or me. We were safer with him than without him.

"But Joey, why do they call you 'The Shark'?" Antonio asked. "It's hard to ignore when I'm a paperboy, Ma."

Joey leaned back in his chair, a grin tugging at his lips. "Great question, kid. Do I look like I swim around, eating people for a living?"

But Antonio wasn't amused. "I'm not joking. They said you're some kind of big-deal gangster," he insisted. "Ma, did you know that?"

"Antonio, drop it," I pleaded. "Cut it out."

"I'm just asking!" Antonio shot back.

Joey let out a quiet sigh, setting his fork down. "Listen, kid. Those papers? They're all about telling stories that sell. A scary nickname like 'The Shark'? That's how they grab people's attention. I mean, look. It even caught your attention, and you know me. They've even tried to corrupt your mind into believing I'm a bad guy. Makes it more exciting than the truth, doesn't it? Mr. Russo makes good money selling copies with my face plastered on the front page."

"So you're saying it's not true?" Antonio pressed.

Joey gave him a soft, reassuring smile—the kind of smile that made me question every moral I thought I stood for. The only crime that smile was guilty of was holding my heart captive. "No, Antonio. I'm just a guy who runs a business and happens to play ball with you on weekends. That's all."

Antonio tilted his head, not willing to drop it, and I couldn't understand why. "But why would they write about you if it wasn't true? I just don't understand that. You make the papers at least once a week."

"Antonio, that's enough!" I cut in, my pleas slicing through the air like a slap.

Joey placed a hand on Antonio's shoulder. "People will say all kinds of things about you. Doesn't mean it's true. Look at me, kid." Joey's eyes poured into Antonio. "You know who I am. I'm Joey. You know me."

My conscience allowed me to see past the sparkle of his blue eyes. Joey and The Shark were the same person. And I could see it written all over his face.

Antonio nodded. "Yeah, I guess you're right."

"And while we're at it, how about you focus on baseball, school, and delivering newspapers instead of what's printed inside them." Joey chuckled, ruffling up Antonio's hair again.

"Sorry, Joey," Antonio mumbled.

Joey flashed that easy grin of his, the one that had charmed its way into both our lives. The very same smile that "The Shark" plastered for the newspapers. The same man, and yet I felt myself accepting every part of him—the good and the bad.

"Don't sweat it, kid. You're family now. You can always ask me anything—and I'll always tell you the truth."

It was how Joey said we're family now, like it wasn't even up for debate. His eyes flicked my way, holding mine for a second too long, as though he meant it just as much for me as for Anto- nio. And when a soft smile tugged at the corner of his mouth, my heart betrayed me—it melted. I didn't want to get caught up in his charm, but it was so effortless, so natural. So demanding. Joey pulled me in, no matter how hard I tried to resist.

I knew better than this. I had spent years with a man who used words and gestures to lure me in, only to use them against me later. But Joey didn't feel like a trap. He didn't feel like danger —not to me, anyway. I knew there were two sides to him. But I felt safer when he was near.

I glanced at Antonio, who had returned to eating his carbonara as if he had gotten the answers he was searching for. Joey had that effect—he could command respect with a single look or a few perfectly chosen words. If he was like this in my presence, I could only imagine who he was when he wasn't with us.

A part of me had been dormant for years, buried in fear and survival. That part came alive whenever Joey smiled at me or brushed his hand against mine. His eyes softened when they landed on me, like I was worth looking at. With him, I felt seen, even when I didn't want to be seen.

I realized then that I'd been staring at him too long, lost in my thoughts. Joey caught my gaze and held it, his smile soft but knowing, like he could see right through me. Like he could read my thoughts.

"Adriana," Joey said, his voice pulling me back to reality.

"Yes?" I replied too quickly, my voice higher than I intended. "We're good, right?"

I swallowed, forcing a smile. "Yeah, Joey. We're good."

Chapter Twenty-Five

JOEY

Antonio went to his room to prepare for bed, leaving Adriana and me alone in the kitchen. I leaned against the countertop, arms crossed over my chest, watching as she busied herself at the sink.

Her movements were quick and purposeful, almost too much —like she was trying to outrun something in her head. She had a long day. No doubt about it. I was sure she must be thinking of all sorts of things. I wanted to ease her pain. I wanted to take it all away.

I wasn't blind to the walls Adriana had built. They were solid and kept her upright in a way a lot of people couldn't manage after going through the hell she'd been through. But every once in a while—like now—I'd catch a crack in the foundation.

A hesitation in her hands as she scrubbed the plate. A glance that darted in my direction. That pleading look in her eyes, begging me to tear down the walls. And it made me wonder if I could be the person she didn't have to keep the walls up around.

I'd be a lying fool if I said I couldn't get used to this. In the small kitchen, she hummed Elvis Presley under her breath as she worked, the warm smell of garlic still hanging in the air. For a guy like me, this felt like everything I'd ever needed in this lifetime.

But that was the problem, wasn't it? I didn't do "good." My life wasn't built on clean edges or happy endings. It was deals in The Wise Guy and breaking bones in dark alleyways. It was lying and scheming. Even if the papers didn't always get the story right, the gist of it wasn't wrong.

The Shark.

They weren't exactly off the mark. The things I'd done weren't the kind of things a guy can just leave behind, no matter how much he wants to.

What the hell was I doing here? Pretending I could have something like this—a quiet dinner, a woman like Adriana looking at me like I was something other than the guy they printed stories about in the newspaper. A family.

Adriana wasn't the kind of woman you kept things casual with. She had this presence, this way of standing her ground even when it looked like the world was trying to knock her down. She didn't seem like the type to fall for sweet words. But I wasn't the only one feeling these feelings. Thinking up these thoughts. I caught how she melted into my touch. How her eyes lingered on mine.

I knew she was fighting something inside herself, the same way I was. And maybe that was what pulled me toward her—the shared feeling that we were both too used to running. Surviving in a cold, harsh world. But now—now, we were standing still in this cramped little kitchen, and I didn't want to run anymore. I didn't want to leave these walls. I didn't want to face the world outside of this kitchen.

"Adriana."

"I'm sorry about what Antonio said earlier. He didn't mean to cause trouble. He's just a kid," she said, her hands still busy scrubbing the dish with a little more force than necessary.

I shook my head, a faint smile tugging at my lips. "It's okay. He's just curious. He's just looking out for you."

Adriana let out a quiet sigh. "Yeah, well, he doesn't really understand what he's asking."

"You don't have to apologize," I reassured her, "Kids don't know any better. They only see what's right in front of them. A few recurring papers with my face slapped on it, calling me a monster, would worry any kid."

She paused, her movements slowing, before continuing in a more serious tone, "I just don't want him getting caught up in anything dangerous. He's been through enough." Her words were laced with something heavier now, something that hinted at more than just concern—like she was warning me.

With Adriana, I was just Joey. But out there, in the world beyond this cramped kitchen, I was the Shark. I couldn't live with myself if Antonio got caught up in any of my mess. I would never put him through what I went through as a kid—growing up too fast and seeing the darker side of life far too soon.

He deserved a real childhood without the skeletons hanging over his head, like they always had over mine. Adriana didn't need to worry. I'd be damned before I let any of it reach Antonio. He was better than that. They both were.

"You don't need to worry about Antonio when he's with me, Adriana," I told her.

Her eyes flickered up to meet mine, searching. "Joey, I know it's real. I know who you are."

"You don't need to know the other side of me, Adriana. What matters is who I really am. The man standing right here with you. That's the real me. You've got to trust me on that."

"What will happen if they find out you're hanging around here?" she asked.

I exhaled. "I won't answer that. It's not a weight you need to carry. But I can promise you, I've got it under control. And soon, it won't even be something we have to worry about," I said, trying to make her believe me, trying to ease the voice in her head.

"I don't want anything to happen to you on my account." She sighed.

I pushed myself off the counter, taking her hand gently in mine, turning off the water as I drew her toward me. Her body was tense, but I pulled her into my chest, my hands gently cupping her face, forcing her to look me in the eyes. "Don't worry about me. I can handle myself. What you need to focus on is taking care of you and Antonio. Everything else, I'll handle. Do you trust me to take care of it?"

She hesitated. But then her soft voice broke through the stillness. "I do trust you, Joey. More than I should. And that's what terrifies me."

A smile tugged at the corners of my lips as I stroked the side of her face with my thumb. "I'm just asking you to take a chance on me. I'm not going to let you down, sweetheart."

As bad as I wanted to claim Adriana's lips, the moment she stepped back, the distance between us grew. Unwanted.

"I'll walk you out," she said, her voice soft but final. I nodded, following her out of the house and into the carport. I didn't want to leave. I wanted to stay and keep her close, but I knew that wasn't an option for us.

"Promise me something?" I asked. Her eyes met mine, waiting for me to continue. "Promise me you aren't scared of me."

"I'm not scared of you, and that's what terrifies me." The truth hit me like a punch in the gut. I wanted to reach for her, pull her to me again. "What if someone hurts you? What will I do if I fall in love with you and they take you from me? I don't think I can allow that pain to seep into my life." Her eyes began to glisten under the flickering carport light.

I moved toward her, closing the distance between us until I could feel her breath on my skin. My hands found her hips, my eyes scanning her face. "If anything were to happen to me— even though it won't—you wouldn't be alone if it did. I'd make sure of that. You and Antonio would be taken care of. Marco and Paul will make sure you're safe. I've given the orders."

Her eyes widened. "What do you mean, 'taken care of'?"

"They're my brothers," I said, my gaze never leaving hers. "They're my family, Adriana. And they're yours, too. I've been in this life long enough to know that loyalty is the only thing that keeps you alive. They'll do it for me if I'm not here to protect you."

The shock in her face deepened. She pulled back, crossing her arms over her chest. "That's not exactly what I wanted to hear you say!"

"I know it's not what you wanted to hear," I admitted. "But I want you to know this—we look after family. We take care of family. And you and Antonio are family now. You don't ever have to worry about anything ever again. Not while I'm here, and not if something were to happen."

She turned away, running her hands over her dress, smoothing out creases that didn't exist. "Joey, I don't want anything to happen to you," she said, her voice threatening to break. "Especially because of me."

I reached down, my hand slipping into hers, holding it. "Nothing's going to happen. I promise you, sweetheart." I couldn't help but watch her, my gaze never straying. Adriana, standing just inches away, was a complication I hadn't ever planned on.

Nobody was going to come between us. Not Vincent. Not Renee. And damn sure not her husband.

I clenched my jaw at the thought of him, thinking he had any claim over her. The way he'd hurt her, scared her even in his absence, was something I could never forgive. He was a threat I intended to chase down and destroy.

I would be her protector. I would be the one to make sure no one dared step out of line with her again. I wasn't leaving her to fend for herself this time. Adriana didn't realize it yet, but I'd already made up my mind. She was under my protection, now and for the rest of our lives.

I would make sure her life was different from now on. A normal life. A safe life. A life she deserved. No more running. No more fearing what came next. No more looking over her shoulder. If anyone tried to take her from me, they'd have to go through me first. And they would never make it out alive.

I'd do whatever it took to make this work for us. Whatever it took to erase the scars of her past and carve out a future where we were all that mattered.

My face hovered just inches from hers. "I've never wanted anything as badly as I want you," I whispered. "And I'm going to make it all work out for us."

Chapter Twenty-Six

JOEY

I sat in the driveway, staring at the front door, but I couldn't bring myself to move. I didn't want to walk inside. I didn't want to see Renee. I didn't want to return to this—to my reality —after being with Adriana. Holding her. Comforting her. Feeling her body pressed against mine.

My fingers drummed against the steering wheel, to the soft hum of *Can't Help Falling in Love by Elvis* filling the car. One of Adriana's favorites. She was always swaying to his music, humming to his tunes. I closed my eyes, just for a second, picturing her. Wishing I could pack us up and disappear. Flee the country. Leave all of this behind.

But that wasn't a possibility. I forced my eyes to open. I killed the engine, forcing the thought of Adriana out of my head.

I barely had the front door shut before Renee's footsteps began down the hallway. "Where the hell have you been?" she snapped, arms crossed, eyes blazing with rage. Hatred.

"You went to her fucking house." My voice was sharp, cutting over hers. "What the fuck were you thinking, Renee?"

"I wanted to warn her who you really are! I wanted to look her in the eyes and see if she would lie!" she spat, stepping toward me. "Turns out she is a liar."

I towered over her, nostrils flared. "Watch your fucking mouth," I growled.

"Watch my mouth?" She bit out a bitter laugh. "The question is, where has yours been? I can only assume attached to hers! Do you think I'm just gonna sit back while you embarrass me?"

My hands curled into fists. Goddamn it. I despised her. "You don't know shit."

"Oh, really?" She stalked closer, her voice dripping with venom. "Then tell me. Tell me you weren't just in her driveway." I exhaled sharply, dragging a hand over my face. "Jesus fucking Christ, Renee. You don't give up, do you?"

She scoffed. "I don't even care that you were there. I expected you to run to her. What I care about is that you think I'm so fucking stupid that I would sit back and allow you to mock me! That you would insult my name! She's nobody in this place! I'm somebody, and you have the nerve to think you can insult me?!"

I snapped.

"You think this is some fucking game?" I roared. We were chest to chest now. "You don't know shit! You're enough to drive someone fucking insane! Do you want to talk about what's embarrassing? What's embarrassing is that you would still threaten to have your father put a hit on my back, even though I have made it so fucking clear I will never love you! I will never marry you!"

"You don't have a choice. You won't win this. You do what I say. You do what my father says. Or you'll be six feet under, and I'll stand right next to your casket, crying like a good little wife," she said with a sickening smile spread wide across her face.

I shook my head, rage simmering just beneath my skin. "Get your black dress on, then. Because Vincent will have to blow my fucking brains out, honey."

"You love her," she spat in a disgusted tone, her face twisted and sour. "Don't you? I want to hear you say it to my face." I didn't say anything. I didn't need to. My eyes gave me away. She let out a bitter laugh, shaking her head. "You son of a bitch!" she screamed, slapping her hands into my chest.

I turned away, grabbing my keys. My fingers gripped the doorknob, and I yanked it open, walking out without another word, taking in a deep inhale of the cool night air. Being in that house made me feel like someone was smothering me with a pillow. Insufferable.

I had never loved anyone in my life. But I loved Adriana. I couldn't say it out loud, but I felt it in every part of me. She was everything I'd never had—genuine, warm, resilient. A rare light in a world that had only ever been cold and ruthless to me. Unlike anyone I'd met in thirty-five years, Adriana wanted nothing from me. And that only made me want to give her everything. The whole damn world, if I could figure out a way to do it.

She didn't care about my reputation or the power that others feared. She was different—respectable, a woman who had carved her own path in a world ruled by men. I never thought I had it in me—to protect someone so fiercely, to be tender, to let someone in.

To want to be more than the man I saw in the mirror.

For the first time in my life, I could see a future beyond the violence and crime that had consumed me. Adriana never asked me to change. But for her, I wanted to. And that terrified me as much as it consumed me.

I drove down the road slowly, the windows down, letting the cool, spring night air slap against my face. It brought me back to life, kept me from suffocating. I pulled into the driveway—the house that I would soon call home. Not tonight. But soon, I'd turn off the engine and walk inside to Adriana's sweet kiss.

I stepped out, grabbing the duffel bag from the backseat. I had barely shut the door when headlights cut through the darkness, pulling into the driveway.

Marco.

I squinted as he climbed out, his face set in a hard line. "What happened?" I asked, cutting straight to the point.

He exhaled. "Dominic's been wearing a wire. Ben just got wind of it and tried to reach you, but he couldn't get hold of you."

My blood went ice cold. Then boiling hot.

"A fucking rat?" I roared, the sound tearing from my chest. "That's the last goddamn thing I want to deal with right now!"

"I know," Marco said. "I just needed to get your orders. Paul and I can take care of him."

I shoved the duffel bag into his chest. He caught it with a grunt. "Put it up," I ordered. "I'm handling this myself. And I don't need any fucking help."

I was already sliding back into the driver's seat, the engine growling to life.

The Shark was back. And he was coming straight for the head.

Dominic was an associate. A low-level, fucking nobody. A rat. A traitor. And a dead man walking. Fortunately, he wasn't hard to find. Unfortunately, he was sitting in The Wise Guy—wearing a goddamn wire—with cops on the other end, listening in on God knows what. I pushed through the doors, my jaw clenched so tight it ached.

"Joey!" Angela called out from behind the bar. "What can I get you?"

I barely heard her. I barely heard the jazz spilling from the speakers or the chatter and laughter of the packed speakeasy.

All I saw was him.

Dominic, laughing at something Sal said, completely fucking clueless that The Shark was circling. That his time was up. My fingers twitched toward the cold metal pressed against my ribs. If I didn't play this right, this place would turn into a bloodbath. And I hated a mess. I exhaled sharply, forcing my shoulders to relax.

"Whiskey," I muttered.

If I said too much, the feds would be all over this place. And if that happened, we all went down.

"Shark, hey, I wanted to talk to you—"

Dominic barely got the words out before Angela slid my whiskey across the bar. I cut him off with a sharp glance. "Let me have my drink first." I tossed it back in one go, the burn barely registering in my throat.

Then I stood, rolling my shoulders, forcing a smile that seemed unnatural. My gaze flicked to the mirror behind the liquor display—dark coat, sharp jaw, ice-cold eyes.

I didn't look like Joey. I didn't feel like Joey, either.

"You've been bringing in some serious cash," I said. "Paul's been talking you up. Christopher wants to meet with you tonight."

Dominic's face lit up like a fucking Christmas tree. Like the idiot I knew he was, he bought it. Because if you give a rat enough cheese, he'll take the bait every time. He grinned, all teeth, thinking he was about to become a made man.

No. He was about to become fish food at the bottom of the Bay.

"Let's go. I've been ordered to drive you."

I forced another smile. I let Dominic walk out first. I could've ended it right there—one clean shot to the back of the head, and he'd never see it coming. But I wanted him to see it coming. The drive to the dock was only five minutes, but the silence stretched between us, thick and suffocating. "I wasn't expecting this," Dominic said, grinning like a fool.

"Me either," I muttered, my eyes locked on the road. I pulled up to the loading dock, shifted into park, and killed the lights. That's when I turned to him. Confusion flickered across his face —just for a second—before realization set in. I drew my gun, leveling it at him. His hands shot up, his voice rising in panicked chants.

"Joey. Joey. Joey—"

But Joey wasn't here.

I yanked up his shirt. There it was—taped right to his chest.

A wire.

A fucking rat.

I ripped it off, then nudged the barrel of my gun between his ribs.

"Out," I mouthed. He hesitated. "Now," I mouthed.

He obeyed, stepping out onto the dock, his hands trembling at his sides. I stayed behind him, the gun pressed firmly against his back as we walked toward the edge.

"Joey, c'mon, let's talk—" he whined. I tossed the wire into the water, watching it sink to the bottom. My fist drove into his gut, cutting off whatever bullshit plea was about to spill from his mouth. He doubled over, gasping for air, but I wasn't done. My boot slammed into his ribs—once, twice, three times—each impact earning a pained wheeze. I crouched, grabbing him by the collar, yanking him up so we were face to face. His eyes were wide, desperate.

"You think I don't have guys everywhere?" I hissed. "You thought you could get one over on me? You wouldn't be the first. You sure as hell won't be the last. But you're about to pay the price, my friend."

"Joey, please. T-They don't know much—" he choked out.

Pathetic. These new guys didn't know the rules of the game. I let his collar go, stood back, and pointed the silencer towards his forehead. "You don't get to be a rat in my city."

Dominic's mouth opened—one last desperate attempt to beg —but the silencer coughed. His body went limp, eyes frozen in shock, a neat hole between them.

I straightened, tucking the gun back into my waistband. I exhaled, rolling my shoulders, and turned back toward the car.

One less problem.

Chapter Twenty-Seven

ADRIANA

D ays had passed since I'd last seen Joey, and I needed it to stay that way. The emotional rollercoaster he'd thrown me on had to end. Every day since I learned William wasn't dead, had been another day spent looking over my shoulder. That fear had settled into my bones. I carried the revolver in my purse and slept with it at night. It was becoming a part of me.

I untied my apron and hung it behind the counter at Davidson's. "See you tomorrow, Mr. Davidson," I said with a smile.

He looked up from the register, returning it. "See you, Adriana. Take care of that boy of yours."

The bell jingled as I stepped outside, slipping into the driver's seat of my car. The newness of it still lingered. I couldn't let myself enjoy it too much. But it was nice. *Dream Lover* drifted through the radio as I pulled onto the road, the afternoon sun warm against my skin. I pulled into the school parking lot, cut the engine off, and stepped outside. I adjusted my white cat-eye sunglasses and made my way toward the baseball field behind the school.

As I rounded the corner, I nearly collided with Renee. She stopped dead in her tracks. The last time we had come face to face was outside my home, when Joey bought me the car. Her glare was sharp, but I only smiled, brushing past her.

My smile widened when I spotted Antonio on the field beside Coach Artie as I walked over. "Ready?" I asked him.

Antonio nodded, but before he could take a step, Artie spoke. "Adriana, do you have a minute?"

My brows knit together as I glanced at Antonio. Artie held up a hand. "He's not in trouble. Nothing like that."

I handed Antonio the keys. "Go wait in the car." Antonio jogged off, leaving me alone with Artie. "What's going on?"

Artie shifted on his feet, kicking at the sandy baseball field with the toe of his shoe. "He's a great kid. I'm glad you let him join the team. He's got potential and the drive to get there. Between you and me, he's the *best* player out there."

I let out a soft laugh. "Well, thank you. Your secret's safe with me."

His eyes lingered on me a little longer than necessary. "You've done a *fantastic* job with him."

"Why, thank you," I said, smiling. "That's always nice to hear."

My gut knew exactly what this was. Exactly what was happening. A prickle of discomfort ran down my spine. I forced a polite chuckle, shifting my weight. "Well, Antonio's waiting, so..."

Artie nodded, still smiling. "Right, of course."

I spun on my heel, eager to escape the awkward situation as quick as possible. But before I could get too far, he called after me. "Adriana?"

I turned back to face him. He stood there, one hand clasped behind his neck, rubbing it as he squinted against the sun beaming down on him. "If you need anything..." He hesitated. "Just let me know."

I offered a small smile and nodded. "Thank you. I'll keep that in mind."

Without another word, I turned and headed straight for the car. Antonio was already in the passenger seat, the radio blaring. I reached over, turning it down a notch as I backed out and started toward Angela's.

"What did Coach Artie want?" Antonio asked, glancing at me as I drove.

"Oh, nothing," I said lightly. "He just wanted to say he's happy you joined the team and that you're doing great." I shot him a smile. "But I already knew that."

Antonio smirked, leaning back in his seat. "Well, yeah. I am pretty good."

I chuckled. "Oh, is that so?"

He smirked out the window, enjoying the quiet ride—until the music cut off, replaced by the sharp voice of a news anchor.

"*Another shooting in Manhattan earlier today. Witnesses reported a group of well-dressed men in ski masks, firing openly in the streets. No silencers were used, which points to one group in particular. One of the alleged New York crimes—*"

I quickly reached forward and shut off the radio, just as I pulled up to the curb outside Angela's.

Antonio shot me a suspicious look. "Why'd you turn it off?"

I kept my voice even. "Because you don't need to hear that. And honestly? I don't either."

His expression darkened. "Why? Because it's true?"

I sighed, turning in my seat to face him. "Antonio, we're not doing this again. You don't need to know everything happening in the world."

His jaw tightened. "This is the next city over. This is happening right in front of us."

I exhaled, gripping the steering wheel. "Sometimes it's best to stay out of things, Antonio." He flung the passenger door open and stepped out, heading straight for Angela's front door. I followed a few steps behind, my mind still tangled in the conversation we'd just had.

Inside, Angela was in the kitchen alongside Lucy. "Adriana!" Angela grinned as she spotted me.

I slid my sunglasses off, setting them on the counter before plopping into a chair at the kitchen table. "What's happened?" Lucy asked, narrowing her eyes.

"Where's your martinis when I need one?" I sighed.

Her eyes lit up, and she straightened. "Jesus, that can be arranged at the snap of a finger," she chirped. I chuckled, shaking my head as she got to work, carefully eyeballing the correct ratio of olive brine, vermouth, and vodka.

Angela, however, kept her focus on me. "What's going on?" she pressed.

I exhaled, rubbing my temple. "Well, Joey showed up at my house a few days ago and practically spilled his feelings for me. I've avoided him since. And today, when I picked up Antonio from practice, Coach Artie decided to subtly flirt with me."

Angela nearly choked. "Arthur? What on Earth did he say?"

"Hold on, you're getting ahead of things, Angela," Lucy cut in. "I want to hear what Joey said first."

I chuckled. "He's under the impression I should just wait around for him to figure out whatever it is he's got going on with Renee, and then, I suppose, we'll live happily ever after."

"And you don't want to?" Lucy asked, setting a martini in front of me before taking a seat.

I sighed, taking a long sip. "I want a nice man. A *good* man."

Angela raised an eyebrow. "*Artie* is a good man."

"I am *not* dating my son's baseball coach," I stated firmly. "I don't need a man right now."

"I hate to be the one to ask this," Lucy chimed in beside me, swirling her drink, "but what fun are good guys?"

"Don't listen to Lucy," Angela said, waving a dismissive hand.

"We've got each other. We don't need a man to make things happen."

Lucy rolled her eyes dramatically. "Oh, Christ, *girl power* again?" She took a long sip of her martini.

Angela smirked. "You literally chased Hector out of the house yesterday morning. Maybe consider your *own* love life before handing out advice to Adriana, who is perfectly fine without a man."

Lucy giggled, raising her glass. "She's right. My love life is a *train wreck*. Don't listen to me."

I shook my head, taking another sip of my drink. "Well, at least you're self-aware."

"Self-awareness is *key*, darling," Lucy said, clinking her martini glass against mine. "Not that it stops me from making terrible decisions."

Angela rolled her eyes. "That's the understatement of the year."

"At least my love life is *interesting*. Unlike some people at this table." Lucy grinned and side-eyed Angela.

Angela scoffed. "Excuse me?"

"Don't think I haven't noticed Marco's car parked out front every Saturday night," Lucy smirked.

Angela sipped her martini, completely unfazed. "This is about Adriana."

"*Sure it is*," Lucy mouthed before turning back to me. "Anyway—back to Artie. What exactly did he say?"

"He was *terribly* shy," I began. "He usually is," Lucy cut in.

"It was the way he looked at me. The energy he exuded. And then, when I walked away," I sighed, shaking my head, "he told me if I ever *needed* anything to let him know."

Angela shrugged. "Well, he's just being a good guy. Arthur *is* a good one."

Lucy scoffed, swirling her drink. "Arthur is a *man*, Angela. And we *all* know no man in this town does anything for free. I don't care how *good* they seem."

Angela frowned, considering. "Well...how did he say it?"

"There was just...an *emphasis* on *anything*," I admitted. "*Ohhh.*" Angela sighed, eyes widening in realization.

Lucy smirked into her martini glass, nodding knowingly. "I could have told you that, and I wasn't even there. But you know what? I think Artie would be *good* for you. You should let me set you up on a date."

"Absolutely not," I said immediately.

"Why not?" Lucy pouted dramatically. "Once Joey finds out, he'll *lose* his mind."

Angela tilted her head, considering. "That *could* be entertaining."

"My love life is *not* your entertainment," I shot back.

But the idea of making Joey jealous lingered in my mind, and it tugged at something inside me.

Chapter Twenty-Eight

ANTONIO

I had spent days trapped in my own head, questions circling like vultures. Was Joey really in the mafia?

And if he was—did Ma know? Or was she too caught up in his swagger to see him for who he really was?

No matter how hard I tried to piece it together, the answers slipped through my fingers, leaving me with nothing but a pounding headache and more questions. But I couldn't let it go. Not until I knew the truth.

I stood inside Mr. Russo's small newspaper shop, waiting to head out on my morning paper route. The air smelled faintly of newsprint and fresh coffee, as it did every morning. Behind the counter, Mr. Russo was busy sorting through stacks of newspapers, organizing them for everyone's routes.

I shuffled my feet, my nerves getting the better of me. The question I'd been dying to ask was burning a hole in my brain, but part of me wondered if I should keep it to myself. The longer I waited, the more the silence suffocated me. As I fidgeted with a newspaper, I finally asked, "Mr. Russo, can I ask you something?"

He didn't even look up from what he was doing, stacking and sorting the morning papers with practiced efficiency. "You can, but make it quick. I've got things to do, and you've got papers to deliver."

I swallowed hard, my nerves threatening to choke me. "Do you think the mafia is real?"

That got his attention. He paused mid-motion, his hands still on the papers, and turned to glare at me. His eyes narrowed as they locked onto mine. "What kind of question is that? Where you gettin' these ideas from, kid?"

I shrugged. "I dunno. I just hear stuff, you know. People talk. Plus, it's always on the front page of the papers."

He snorted and shook his head. "No. Ain't no mafia. Just a bunch of shit people tell to scare kids like you into behaving. Now, hand me that stack of newspapers," he said, nodding toward the pile at the end of the counter.

I grabbed the stack and brought it over, but the question still burned in the back of my mind. I couldn't let it go. "Then why do people call Joey *The Shark*? They say he's—"

"Enough!" he snapped, cutting me off. His voice was sharper now, clearly angry. "Joey's just a guy trying to live his life. He's brought Staten Island to the height it's at right now! You're Italian! This is stereotypical hate being plastered by those who don't want men like Joey to succeed! People like to run their mouths when they don't know nothin'. Joey's the best goddamn thing Staten Island's ever seen, you hear me?"

"But the papers—"

He pointed a finger at me. "Stop reading the goddamn papers, Antonio. Half of it's lies, the other half's trouble. You'd do well to leave it alone, you hear me, boy? You deliver the damn papers—you don't read 'em! That ain't your job! They got proofreaders in the city! You're a paperboy, so deliver the papers! It takes me long enough to pack them up for you!"

Frustration boiled inside me, but I didn't dare show it. I just wanted to understand why everyone acted like this. The papers and the news claimed there was a mafia, but everyone I knew who might be connected swore it wasn't real. Why did people clam up or get angry when you said the word "mafia" in this town?

"But why can't we talk about it? If it's not real, then—"

Mr. Russo leaned onto the counter. "Kid, there are things you don't stick your nose into. Things that ain't your business. Joey's a good man, and that's all you need to know. Now, if I hear you bring this up again, we're gonna have a problem. I'll have to dock your pay or, worse, fire you. And you're a damn good paperboy. I don't wanna do that, but you keep pushing, and you'll leave me no choice. You got it?"

I nodded reluctantly, knowing this wasn't the end for me. "Yeah. I got it."

I slung the bag of newspapers over my shoulder, adjusting the weight as Mr. Russo straightened up and muttered to himself, loud enough for me to hear, "Kids these days. I tell ya."

I didn't respond. I just pushed open the door and stepped out into the smug morning air. But as I hopped onto my bike, I knew one thing for sure—this was far from over. Someone was going to have to explain why the newspapers were printing this. After that talk with Mr. Russo, I wished I'd just let it go. All the mafia rumors, the questions—perhaps were better left alone. But I couldn't help myself. Curiosity got the better of me, and I started asking a few of the neighbors on my paper route. Just questions here and there, nothing serious—or so I thought.

That morning seemed like any other. The streets were quiet, the air crisp despite it being springtime, and my basket weighed down with newspapers. Then, out of nowhere, a car rolled up beside me, its tires crunching softly against the pavement.

I glanced over—and my stomach dropped. Vincent "Lucky" Accetta.

Oh, fuck.

Everything in me screamed to pedal faster, to bolt and put as much distance as possible between me and the man staring out from the car window. But what was the point? You don't outrun someone like Vincent Accetta. I knew that much from the papers alone. They called him "Lucky" for a reason—he was a walking miracle, having survived not one, but five assassination attempts.

I gripped the handlebars of my bike tighter, trying not to let my nerves show. My instincts told me one thing for sure: I was in hot water. Boiling fucking water.

"Hey, kid," he said with a smile that didn't hold a trace of sincerity. It was fake—like the smile a predator might give before pouncing.

"Uh...hi?" I barely managed to get the word out; my throat felt like it had closed up entirely.

"You got a minute?" he asked casually, like we were old friends.

I looked around, hoping someone—anyone—might be in earshot. But the street was empty, and even if someone was nearby, I doubted anyone would dare cross Vincent "Lucky" Accetta. I gripped the handlebars of my bike tightly. "I—I gotta finish my route. Papers don't deliver themselves, sir. Mr. Russo will dock my pay if I don't finish on time."

"It'll just take a second."

I hesitated. My heart thumping like it wanted to escape my chest, but I nodded and reluctantly wheeled my bike to the curb. He stepped out of the car in his nice, tailored suit and polished shoes, starkly contrasting my worn trousers and sneakers. He looked powerful. Dangerous. And someone you didn't want to mess with.

Before I could think better of it, the words tumbled out of my mouth. "Look, I don't know anything about anything. If this is about something I said, I'm sorry. I didn't mean—"

Vincent raised a hand, cutting me off mid-ramble. "Relax," he said. "If I wanted trouble, we wouldn't be talking."

I swallowed hard and nodded. "Yes, sir."

"Word around town is you've been asking questions," he continued, "about things that don't concern you. About people who don't like being talked about."

"I wasn't trying to cause any problems!" I blurted out the

words, spilling over each other in my panic. "I just—people talk, and I got curious. I swear, I'll stop. I'll keep my mouth shut, sir."

His eyes narrowed, and something dark gleamed behind them. They reminded me of my father's eyes—cold, calculating, and full of a darkness you didn't argue with. I felt small under his gaze, like a mouse caught by a hawk. "That's smart," he said. "Curiosity can get people hurt, Antonio. You don't want to end up in over your head, do you?"

I shook my head so hard I thought it might fall off. "No, sir. I swear, it won't happen again. I'll forget all about it. I'll forget I even heard the word 'mafia.'"

He chuckled then, but it wasn't a friendly laugh. It was low and cold, like a predator's sound before it strikes. "Good. That's what I like to hear."

He pulled a cigarette from his pocket and lit it, taking his time with the first drag. I could tell he was enjoying how scared I was. Then he exhaled, his eyes on me the entire time. "But—" he started, pausing, "I got a question for you now."

I tightened my grip on the bike, my palms damp with sweat. "Yes, sir?"

"What's going on with your mother and Joey?"

The question hit me like a brick. I blinked, completely taken aback. "My ma and Joey?"

Oh, fuck.

His voice turned sharp, cutting through the air like a knife. "Don't play stupid with me, kid. If you don't want trouble coming your way—or your mother's—you'll tell me what's going on between her and Joey. Or you'll leave me no choice."

Panic washed over me, cold and smothering. My mother was all I had, and I knew I couldn't let anything happen to her. I stammered out the words, desperate to make him believe me. "Nothing! I swear, sir! Joey's just been helping us out, that's all! My mother wouldn't get involved with someone like Joey—no offense, sir! She doesn't want any trouble. Please, I'm begging you—"

He cut me off with a wave. "Calm down. I'm not gonna do anything to you or your mother. Just as long as you do me a favor."

I nodded so quickly it felt like my head might spin. "Yes, sir. Anything, sir. Whatever you need."

"Good," he said, flicking the ash from his cigarette. "Now, go finish your papers, keep quiet, and stay out of grown folks' business."

I nodded again. "Yes, sir. Of course."

His next words sent a shiver down my spine. "This afternoon. The park near your house. You come alone. Don't tell anyone about this."

I didn't hesitate. "Yes, sir. I'll be there, sir."

He flashed me a grin before slipping into the driver's seat of his car. The engine roared to life, a low, menacing growl that sent a chill down my spine. I stood frozen on the curb as the car disappeared down the street, my heart hammering in my chest.

What the hell had I just gotten myself into?

My mind raced with fear and a thousand unanswered questions. Why couldn't I have kept my mouth shut? Why did I have to go poking around, asking things I had no business asking? Now it wasn't just me I had to worry about—what if something happened to my mother because of my own stupidity?

The weight of it all crashed down on me like a ton of bricks.

And the worst part? I couldn't tell anyone. Not a soul. I couldn't risk it. The thought of what Vincent might do if I opened my mouth was enough to keep me silent.

I was fucked. Completely and utterly fucked.

I STOOD ANXIOUSLY AT THE EDGE OF THE PARK, watching for Vincent. My heart pounded in my chest. I saw his car pull into view. He rolled down the window and gave a casual wave, like we knew each other, his fingers signaling me to get in.

I froze. The last thing I wanted to do was climb into that car, but I knew better than to defy him. I didn't make the rules—Vincent did, and everyone knew the consequences when you didn't follow them. The newspaper articles I'd read were full of stories that made your blood run cold. Those who resisted didn't just disappear; they just ended up in the headlines. The thought of becoming another gruesome tale forced my feet into motion.

"Get in the car, kid," he barked. I hesitated before opening the passenger side door and slipping into the seat. I couldn't shake the gnawing feeling in my gut, wishing I had told someone what had happened—how Vincent and I were alone in his car—but I hadn't dared speak. Fear kept me silent.

The moment he started the car, the air thickened with the scent of cigarette smoke. He lit one, taking a long drag before glancing at me sideways. The pack of cigarettes landed in my lap, along with a lighter.

"I'm not allowed to, sir," I muttered.

He chuckled, an unsettling smirk curling at the corner of his mouth. "But you do it anyway, don't you?"

How did he know that? Was he watching me? The thought sent a cold shiver down my spine.

"Go ahead," he encouraged, his tone more a command than an offer.

I grabbed a cigarette, lit it with the lighter, and returned it to him. I inhaled the smoke, hoping it would calm the anxiety coursing through my body.

"How close are you to Joey?" "Close," I replied.

"Do you see him as a father figure?" "I guess you could say that."

Vincent smirked, but it wasn't a playful one. The kind of smirk made me nervous like he knew something I didn't—and I was about to find out.

"I wanted to answer the questions you've been dying to know," he said, "The mafia? It's real."

The words hit me like a punch. I thought I wanted that

confirmation until I was sitting face to face with Vincent, and now I wished I were as blind as everyone else in this godforsaken town. I blinked, my mind scrambling to process what he was saying. I glanced out the window, inhaling a long drag of the cigarette to calm myself. "You mean—"

He cut me off before I could finish. "It means things around Joey are a lot deeper than he's letting on. This life *always* catches up to you. You know why they call me Lucky? 'Cause I've been lucky enough for it not to catch up to me, but most guys aren't as lucky."

Vincent exhaled a puff of smoke between us. "You want to know how it all works, huh?" His voice lowered. "Let me break it down for you, kid. It's a game of chess—a game you'll *never* escape alive."

The papers had made it sound like the mafia was just a group of criminals wreaking havoc in the streets of Staten Island, but they never talked about how it actually worked. They never explained why it functioned the way it did.

"What are you saying?" I asked, gathering the courage to speak.

Vincent smirked at me—the kind of smirk that crawled under my skin, sending a chill through me. "I'm saying there's one way in and one way out. You've read the stories in the papers, haven't you? I'm sure Joey tells you he's just a hard-working businessman who owns a car wholesale lot—and he is. But that's not all he does, kid. Whether he admits it to you or not, Joey is in the mafia. And he's what we call a capo. You know what that is?"

I shook my head. "No, sir."

"Caporegime," he corrected. "Capo for short. In simple terms, a lieutenant. Which means Joey runs his own crew. And under him? You've got Marco and Paul—what we refer to as his soldiers. They're the ones doing the *real* work. The jobs. The collections. The muscle. The heavy lifting. The stuff you don't read about in the papers." He took a slow drag of his cigarette.

"And beneath them, you've got low-level associates trying to prove they're worthy of moving up the ranks."

My mind was spinning. "Wait, so Joey's in charge of people?" I couldn't help but ask. It was hard to wrap my head around.

What I meant was—Joey, the guy I thought I knew, the one who had been helping us, the guy who took me to a Yankees game, helped me get on the baseball team, and swore up and down he wasn't involved in the mafia—wasn't just *in* the mafia. He was a key player, a capo, giving orders for some of the most vile, heinous crimes I could barely begin to understand. Crimes like murder, kidnapping, gambling, prostitution, and drugs.

Paul and Marco? The same guys who'd fixed the lights that flickered in our house, who'd repaired the electrical unit that sparked, and the guys who'd delivered a brand new car to my mother—they weren't just good guys doing favors. They were carrying out Joey's orders—violent, ruthless commands. They were the ones cleaning up the murders he committed. They were the ones beating people up in back alleys.

The realization hit me like a cold slap, shattering everything I thought I knew about Joey. He wasn't just a businessman, but a criminal mastermind, pulling the strings behind the scenes. And I was sitting there, stunned, realizing I'd been living in the middle of this world without even knowing it. Everything I'd trusted, everything I'd believed in, was all a lie.

"He runs his crew, but he answers to the underboss—which, in this case, is *me*," Vincent explained. "The underboss answers to the boss, Christopher. Alongside Christopher and me is the consigliere, Hector. It's a chain of command, kid, and we all play our part in it."

I couldn't wrap my head around it. Christopher—Michael's grandfather? The sweet old man who always smiled and handed us five bucks when he saw us. He was the boss? And Hector—Michael's father—he was in on it, too? Then there was Michael, one of my best friends, swearing up and down that he didn't know anything. That had to be bullshit. If Michael was lying, then Enzo had to be lying, too. And if that was the case, how much of my new life had been wrapped in lies?

"So, you run things? You're higher up than Joey?" I asked, trying to piece the puzzle together.

"That's right. I'm the underboss. Think of me as the one who keeps the whole operation running smoothly—the planning, the enforcement, the business. Joey's got his reputation and connections, but I'm the one making sure it all stays in line."

"So, it's all organized?" I said, half to him, half to myself. The realization hit like a punch to the gut—an organized crime family operating right out in the open. Right under my nose.

He smirked. "You could say that. We call it la cosa nostra." The pride in his voice was unmistakable. "Play the game right, and you get everything—control, money, respect. That's what it's all about."

Greed.

He paused before adding, "Joey's part of this life, yeah, but he has his own way of handling things. And I disagree with how he's been running the show lately."

"If you're the underboss, can't you stop him?" I asked before realizing I might regret saying it.

He chuckled, a dark, knowing laugh. "We've got something called le regole—the rules. Break them, and there's a price to pay, whatever the boss decides. Joey hasn't crossed the line *yet*. But I see it coming. The money, the streets, the power—it's all connected, and Joey's no saint. Doesn't matter how smooth he talks or how soft he acts around you. He'll make decisions you can't even begin to imagine when push comes to shove. And I'm going to be the one to catch him." He turned to me, grinning, rolling the cigarette between his fingers. "I need you to keep an eye on Joey. All the time. Let me know what he's up to."

My eyebrows shot up. "How am I supposed to do that? I'm just a kid, sir."

Without a word, he pulled the car into park next to a sleek, brand-new Chevrolet Corvette and tossed me the keys. "Those are yours now. I want you to sneak out, follow Joey in this car, and report back to me. *Easy*."

"Wait, you want me to spy on him?" My heart raced as I stared at the keys in my hand.

"That's right," he said. "I need to know everything—where he goes, who he meets. And listen closely, kid—I also want to know if things between him and your mother get serious. You got that?"

I tightened my grip on the keys and glanced out the window at the car. "And you really think I can do this?"

Vincent leaned back in his seat. "Oh, I'm betting on it."

His eyes and smile felt like they were sizing me up, like he already knew what I could do before I realized it myself. "You're smart," he said. "Follow him without him catching on, and you'll earn some serious street cred. You've got a front-row seat to everything, Antonio. Just make sure you give me the details, yeah? And believe me—there's more money to be made than what's sitting in the driver's seat of that car."

Money? A new car? It felt like a trap wrapped in an opportunity, but I couldn't ignore the temptation.

"Okay, I'll do it," I said, the words feeling heavy as they left my mouth.

Chapter Twenty-Nine

ADRIANA

I had agreed to let Lucy and Angela set me up with Artie for *one* date. If you could *even* call it a date. It was just coffee at the local diner on Saturday morning. Hardly my idea of a date, but then again, I wasn't *exactly* an expert on dating.

Artie *was* a *nice* guy. Tall, thin, with a sweet smile. There was nothing mysterious about him. No duffle bag in his backseat filled with anything but baseball equipment. No questionable business dealings. No extravagant brand-new car he could gift me. He was a modest man. *A kind man.* The kind of man you were supposed to picture when you closed your eyes and imagined a future.

With Artie, I could see it clearly—simple, secure, predictable. No complications. No shady late-night disappearances. I wouldn't see his name in the papers. Wouldn't spot his smirk on the front page at the grocery store checkout. In fact, Artie didn't even smirk—he smiled. He laughed from his chest. He gave himself away easily, with no secrets lurking behind his eyes.

The worst thing he'd ever done was run a stop sign because he was late for work.

"It wasn't a complete stop," he confessed from across the booth, a friendly smile on his face.

I chuckled. "Wow, you're a *real* daredevil."

He laughed, then told me the sad story of how he'd lost his wife to the influenza outbreak in '56. After a pause, he asked about my husband. The one I thought I'd killed. The one coming back to collect. And when he did, I'd be ready.

"Oh, well," I murmured, shifting uncomfortably as I fidgeted with the handle of my coffee mug. "He died."

Artie's expression softened. "I'm sorry, Adriana," he said, reaching across the table to caress my hand. His touch was gentle, kind.

But it wasn't Joey. He wasn't Joey. And the entire time, all I could do was compare him to Joey—and hate myself for it.

Artie's thumb brushed over my knuckles, a small gesture of comfort. I should've felt something, but instead, all I felt was the heavy weight of comparison pressing down on me like a sickening vice.

I pulled my hand back, wrapping it around my coffee mug. "Thank you," I said, offering a tight-lipped smile.

He hesitated, then leaned back against the booth. "Must've been hard," he said gently. "Losing him."

I swallowed, forcing myself to nod. "Yeah," I murmured.

Harder than you know.

Artie studied me for a moment, his kind eyes searching my face. "You don't talk about him much, do you?"

No, because I can't. Because talking about my husband meant unraveling a truth I couldn't afford to let slip. Because every word out of my mouth had to be carefully measured, carefully controlled.

I forced a chuckle, shaking my head. "It's too hard to relive, I suppose."

Artie nodded. He stirred his coffee before speaking again.

"You know," he said, glancing up at me, "I get it. Not wanting to talk about it. Some losses just sit too deep in you."

I swallowed, forcing myself to hold his gaze. "Yeah," I said.

He exhaled through his nose, a wry smile tugging at the corner of his mouth. "After my Elena passed, people kept telling me to move on. Like grief had some kind of expiration date." He let out a short chuckle, shaking his head. "But you never really move on, do you? You just learn how to carry it."

I forced a small smile. "Yeah. You carry it."

Artie's eyes softened. "I hope you've had people to help you with that."

My grip tightened around my coffee mug. *Help?* Now that was a loaded word. The only thing I had was the weight of my own choices, pressing down on me like a debt I couldn't even begin to understand—because Joey was a hitman I never hired.

The thought made my stomach turn. Jesus. I was no better than Joey. In fact, I could be worse.

Chapter Thirty

JOEY

I sat behind my desk in my office, a cigar smoldering in the ashtray beside me. I flipped through the stack of invoices in front of me. Some were real, detailing legitimate repairs, oil changes, and tire replacements. Others? Not so much. I skimmed one from *Gino's Auto Supply*—a cover for a weapons shipment that had come in last week. Another from *West End Supply* disguised a cash transfer meant for a payoff. My fingers lingered over an invoice for a '58 Cadillac, a routine service on paper, but in reality, the car had been stripped for parts after its owner met an unfortunate end. I sighed, tapping the edge of the paper against the desk before tossing it onto the "*handled*" pile.

A knock on the door pulled me from my thoughts. "Yeah?" I called out.

The door creaked open, and Sal walked in. "Got a problem."

I took a long drag of my cigar before stubbing it out. "What is it?"

Sal sighed, raking a hand through his hair. "It's not bad. Not too bad, at least. It's just about the job you gave me—keeping an eye on Adriana."

My jaw tensed. "What the fuck are you talking about? Spit it out," I snapped.

He hesitated. "She's safe," he started.

I slammed my palms onto the desk and pushed myself to my feet. "You're starting to piss me off, Sal. Get to the fucking point."

He exhaled sharply, eyes flicking to the invoices scattered across my desk before finally meeting my stare. "She's seeing someone."

My pulse spiked. My fingers curled into fists. "*Who?*" Sal shifted on his feet. "Arthur."

I blinked, my mind scrambling for recognition. "Arthur?" I repeated slowly. "Coach Artie?"

Sal just nodded.

I stared at him, my pulse roaring in my ears.

You've gotta be fucking kidding me.

The air in the room grew thick, *suffocating*, as I let Sal's words sink in. *Coach Artie.* The last person I'd ever expected her to be with. I ran my hand over my face, trying to suppress the mountain of emotions consuming me. "Artie? You sure about this?" I muttered, barely able to believe what I was hearing.

Sal shifted uncomfortably. "Yeah, he just dropped her off. He took her for a coffee down at the diner."

I gritted my teeth. I could already feel the anger bubbling up. She was mine to protect, and now Artie—*Coach fucking Artie*—was worming his way into her life. Another obstacle I was going to have to tackle.

As Sal left, I stood there, my hands gripping the edge of the desk, fury and frustration swirling within me. I wasn't going to let anyone take her from me.

The bell above the shop door jingled as I stepped out. My mind was clouded with the image of Artie and the anger that had settled deep in my gut, knowing he was taking Adriana out for a fucking coffee. I gripped the wheel, heading towards Adriana's place, the familiar route doing nothing to calm the fire raging in my chest.

As I approached her door, I hesitated for a moment, but

knocked anyway. She opened the door, her smile warm but cautious. "Joey? Hi."

"Can I come in?" I asked. She hesitated for just a second before stepping aside, letting me pass. The door clicked shut behind us. "Where's Antonio?" I asked, scanning the room.

"With Enzo and Michael," she said, her eyes studying me, as if trying to figure out why I was here.

I nodded, exhaling the breath I hadn't realized I'd been holding. My gaze drifted, trailing up the soft curve of her legs to the delicate pink dress hugging her waist *just* right. She looked *perfect*. Too perfect for a night spent with anyone besides me. "You look beautiful," I murmured.

She glanced down, smoothing her hands over the fabric. "Thank you."

Silence settled between us. I could dance around it, pretend this was just a friendly visit. "How was the date?" I finally asked, watching her closely.

Her eyes locked onto mine. "How'd you know about it?"

I let out a slow breath, tilting my head slightly. "It's a small town, Adriana. People talk. And I hear *everything*."

She didn't respond right away; she just stood there, rocking back on her heels, her fingers twisting at the fabric of her dress. The air settling between us was thick enough you could cut it with a knife. I took a step closer. "So? How was the date?"

"It was fine," she finally said.

"Fine," I repeated, letting the word hang between us.

She lifted a shoulder in a small shrug. "Artie's a good man."

I scoffed, shaking my head. "Yeah? That what you're looking for? A good man like Artie?"

"Seems like a smart idea." I let out a dry laugh, stepping even closer until there was barely any space left between us. She held her ground, tilting her chin up at me. "And why does it matter to you, Joey?"

"You know why," I said.

She crossed her arms, her eyes searching mine, challenging me. "No, Joey. I don't know why. So why don't you say it?"

I could feel the words clawing their way up my throat.

I reached up, brushing a knuckle along her jaw, slow and deliberate. "Because the second I say it, I can't take it back."

"I think you should go," she whispered.

I leaned in, my lips just a breath away from hers. I could feel her breath against my lips. Her eyes never leaving mine. "Tell me to leave like you mean it," I murmured.

Silence. Crickets.

I smirked, closing the small gap between us, my lips capturing hers in a slow kiss. My hands found her waist, pulling her against me, her body molding to mine like she belonged there.

Chapter Thirty-One

ADRIANA

The smoky, amber interior of The Wise Guy had an intimate charm, its soft lighting and smooth jazz blending with the low hum of conversation. I sat on a barstool, the cool leather pressing against the backs of my thighs as Lucy adjusted her leopard print scarf beside me. Angela worked the bar, moving with a natural ease that suited her perfectly. I took a small sip of my martini, savoring the tartness that danced on my tongue while my thoughts drifted.

Joey.

It had been days since he'd kissed me, but I could still feel his soft lips pressed against mine.

Angela leaned against the counter, her cigarette dangling between her fingers as her sharp gaze cut through my daydream. "Alright, spill it, Adriana. What's the story with you and Joey? I see the way he's been eyeing you since he walked in here."

I felt heat rise to my cheeks, embarrassment pooling as I tried to find the right words.

Lucy smirked, fiddling with the straw in her glass. "The man's been undressing you with his eyes. It's practically a strip show in here."

I tried to laugh it off, swirling the rim of my martini glass with a practiced detachment, but my heart betrayed me with its quickened pace. "There's nothing to tell," I said, though I didn't sound convinced.

Angela's expression sharpened into a knowing smirk. "When a woman says *'nothing,'* it's always *something*. And judging by that guilty face of yours, it's a *big* something."

Lucy nudged my arm, teasing. "Unless you want me to start guessing—'cause I will."

My heart leaped at the memory, and despite my best efforts, the warmth in my cheeks deepened. I sighed, giving in as I recalled Joey's lips brushing against mine days ago. "He kissed me," I admitted.

Angela flung her arms up with triumphant exuberance. "I know it! Didn't I say this was gonna happen, Lucy? Didn't I? I told ya she'd go on that date and then they'd kiss!"

Lucy's grin widened. "You did! So," she said, turning back to me, "how was it? I've heard he's a great kisser with that bad boy charm all wrapped up in a three-piece suit. Don't hold back on us. We need *all* the details!"

I laughed, covering my face with one hand. "He's a good kisser." Lucy squealed so loudly you could hear her over all the talking and music.

Angela's knowing smirk returned, sharp enough to cut glass. "Is that *all* that happened?"

"Of course!" I said. "He's still with Renee. I shouldn't have even let him kiss me in the first place."

Angela's mischievous grin returned, lighting up her face. "Are you two just gonna play coy forever?"

"It was just a little peck. It's not that serious, and it won't be happening again."

"A peck?" Lucy repeated with raised eyebrows, sipping from her glass. "Adriana, if you've got any sense, you'll kiss that man again—and this time, make sure he never forgets it. Coming from someone who knows Renee—screw her."

"Uh-oh! Trouble is fast approaching. I repeat, a tall, dark, blue-eyed man with sinful desires to take Adriana into the VIP is fast approaching—everyone act normal," Angela said in an exaggerated announcer voice, her grin wicked.

Lucy and I giggled. My pulse quickened before I even looked up. Joey strode to the bar with his signature confident gait, a smile curling his lips. His presence pulled every ounce of air out of the room. And when his eyes found mine, it felt like the rest of the world blurred into nothing.

"Ladies." He nodded to Angela and Lucy, his voice smooth and warm, before his attention snapped back to me like a magnet. "Mind if I steal you for a dance?"

Angela leaned against the bar with a playful smirk. "Do you practice this act of yours in the mirror, Joey?"

"Yeah, do we get next on the dance card, or is Adriana the only lucky one tonight?" Lucy added, crossing her arms. "Hector would sooner find himself dead than dance with me."

Joey didn't take his eyes off me as he grinned, brushing off their teasing. "Very funny, you two. What do you say, Adriana?"

My heart skipped at the sound of my name leaving his lips. There was no use fighting it. My legs felt like jelly, but I managed to stand as he offered his hand. I smoothed the front of my dress, trying to focus on anything other than the heat coursing through my body.

As we headed for the dance floor, Angela called after us, "Joey, don't step on her toes. She just got those shoes yesterday." "And don't forget Joey—we're watchin'!" Lucy chimed in. "No funny business on the dance floor. Hands where we can
see 'em!"

Joey glanced over his shoulder with a mock-serious expression. "You two got jokes tonight."

Once we were on the dance floor, I leaned in to whisper, "You know they're going to talk about this all night, right?"

His laugh was low and rich, sending a pleasant shiver down my spine. "Let 'em. Long as I get the dance, they can say whatever they want. *Anyone* can say what they want. You're all I care about."

He pulled me into position, one hand slipping to the small of my back, the other holding mine firmly. The warmth of his touch made my stomach flip. His proximity felt dangerous and safe all at once. I tried to keep my focus on the rhythm of the music, but Joey made me forget where I was entirely. His eyes locked on mine, softening as they searched my face. I wondered if he could feel how my heart raced against his chest.

"Relax," he murmured. "It's just a dance. I won't kiss you in front of everyone. Only in private."

His words sent a jolt through me, electrifying every nerve ending in my body. My breath caught in my chest, and I forgot how to move, my feet stuttering against the rhythm of the music. Joey's grip on my waist tightened, steadying me, and his lips quirked into the faintest of smirks, as if he knew exactly the havoc he was stirring inside me.

I tried to focus on the dance—the swish of my dress and the press of my shoes against the polished floor—but Joey was all I could feel and see. His presence consumed me, radiating so much confidence, as though he knew how much control he wielded over me in these moments. I had carefully built walls around myself, walls that were meant to protect my deepest secrets. But Joey didn't just break through them—he demolished them without hesitation.

My mind screamed at me to snap out of it. But his thumb brushed against my hand, silencing every logical thought I had.

I glanced up, meeting his gaze. His eyes locked onto mine. The music, the other people, and Angela and Lucy's watchful teasing faded into the background. It was just us, a pull that felt impossible to resist.

The steady movement of the dance floor did little to calm the turmoil inside me. His hand on my back was both grounding and incendiary, like he could sense every part of me I wanted to keep hidden. I felt exposed—like Joey saw through every wall I'd built and still wanted to be close.

"You're quiet," he murmured, tilting his head, as though studying me. A slow, knowing grin tugged at his lips. "Still thinking about kissing me?"

I let out a small laugh, shaking my head. "You're *awfully* sure of yourself, aren't you?"

He smirked, his grip tightening at my waist. "Am I wrong?"

I met his gaze, my pulse quickening. "I'm not answering that."

Joey chuckled, his fingers tracing idle circles against my back. He leaned in, his lips brushing just above my ear. "You look beautiful right now. I wish you could see yourself through my eyes."

A shiver ran down my spine at his words, the low rasp of his voice making it impossible to think straight.

Despite my mind trying to warn me, I couldn't deny how right this felt—how alive I felt. For the first time in years, something other than fear and uncertainty was swirling in my chest. Joey's confidence, unpredictability, and unwavering gaze scared me, but it also made me feel seen. Wanted. Desired. And safe. And I wanted to feel this way for as long as I could remember.

I knew I was in trouble. This moment wasn't just a dance; it was the start of something much bigger—and whether it would save or destroy me, I had no idea. But I couldn't stop until I found out.

The dance floor was bathed in warm, golden light that softened the edges of the speakeasy, making everything seem like a dream. *Earth Angel* played softly through the room, its melody wrapping around us like a secret. I wasn't sure if it was just a coincidence or if Angela had something to do with it.

"I'm beginning to think this may just be our song," Joey said, his voice low and teasing as we swayed to the music.

"It's just a coincidence," I told him.

He chuckled. "Had a feeling you'd say that," he murmured,

pulling me just a fraction closer. "You can't give in too quickly, can you?"

I didn't respond, I just smirked. I was hanging onto my self-composure by a single thread. He didn't need to know that, though.

As Joey's arms circled me, I relaxed in a way I hadn't in years. The strength in his hold, the steady way he moved like nothing could touch us.

His chuckle reverberated in my chest, and I glanced up at him, catching the faintest trace of mischief displayed on his face. It was hard to deny how this—*us*—felt like fate, no matter how much my rational mind wanted to resist.

"You know, you looked too good sitting over here. Like something out of a dream," Joey murmured into my hair as we swayed to the soft rhythm of the music. His voice was low and rough, making my pulse hammer. "I'd cross a hundred rooms just to get a minute with you."

His words sent a warmth curling through me, but his next ones nearly stole my breath. "I've been thinking about that kiss. Your lips. Will you let me kiss you again?"

"You're going to make this complicated," I said softly, more to myself than him.

He brushed a strand of hair from my face with a touch so gentle, it felt intimate. His eyes locked onto mine, as if he had all the time in the world to convince me. "This feels simple to me. It doesn't feel complicated at all."

I swallowed hard, his words settling heavy in my chest. I was stronger than this. I had walked through hell and survived. But as I swayed in Joey's arms, I felt the ground beneath me shift. Joey made me believe in something I thought I'd lost forever: *hope*. When he touched me, he knew every wall I had built and how to slip past it.

As his thumb brushed against my cheek and his eyes bore into mine, I knew the truth. I wasn't losing myself to Joey. I'd already lost myself to him. And as much as I feared it, as much as I wanted to pull away and keep my world neatly contained, there was no denying our fate.

I was falling for him. Falling fast, falling hard—and I wasn't sure there was a way to stop.

Chapter Thirty-Two

JOEY

The room was alive, brimming with energy as the *Jailhouse Rock* brass blared. Adriana's laughter rang clear, the sweetest melody cutting through the place. I still felt the softness of her hand in mine, the lingering warmth from the slow dance we had just shared. Her eyes bright as she brushed a loose strand of hair behind her ear.

She tilted her head at me, mischief sparking in her eyes, and before I could object, she grabbed my hand again, pulling me toward the middle of the floor. "C'mon, Joey," she said, her voice teasing over the music. "This is one of my favorites!"

She was already moving, her dress swirling as her hips rocked with effortless rhythm. I wasn't much for dancing— never had been before her—but I'd become a dancer to see that smile on her face. She lit up under those amber lights, her smile brighter than the whole goddamn room. I had daydreamed of gripping her hips as she swayed after watching her do it as she stood at the stove. But now, I didn't have to imagine. It had come true. She twirled around me, the two of us laughing like we didn't have a care in the world.

She threw her arms up, spinning with wild abandon, and I grabbed her by the waist and dipped her low. Her gasp turned into laughter, her hands gripping my arms for balance as her face tilted to meet mine. Her lips parted, breathless, and I forgot about everything. Everyone.

The song ended, and I set her back on her feet. She stumbled a little, still laughing, her hand clutching at my chest as she steadied herself. My body was on fire from her touch.

I didn't expect her to grab my hand. She started walking off the dance floor, weaving through the crowd like she'd just made a decision she wasn't about to question. And I sure as hell wasn't going to question her, either. Whatever was about to happen, she'd made her move, and there wasn't a damn thing in the world that could drag me away from her now.

"Hey, we're heading out," Adriana announced to Lucy and Angela.

Lucy raised an eyebrow. "*Wait*—you two are leaving together?"

"Yeah. He's giving me a ride home." She paused before adding, "I'll swing by in the morning to pick up Antonio, if that's okay."

Angela chimed in, "No problem at all!" Lucy glanced at Adriana with a look that said she'd have questions later, but she let it go for now.

I gave Marco and Paul a quick nod as Adriana slid her arm around mine, her touch sending an electric current straight to my chest. They both smirked. I couldn't even pretend to care. I pushed the door open and motioned for Adriana to step through first.

"Ladies first," I said, my voice smooth despite the pounding in my chest. She turned her head, her lips curving into a soft smile before she slipped past me. Once again, her arm found mine as if it belonged there. I opened the passenger door for her, holding out a hand as she eased into the seat.

I rounded to the driver's side, got in, and started the engine.

Her actions inside The Wise Guy—the way she'd danced with me, the way she'd touched my arm, the way she'd decided, without a word, that I was *hers* tonight—they were still messing with me. I wasn't used to feeling like this, completely thrown off my axis because of a woman. But here I was. I could barely focus or breathe right with her this close. I reached over and grabbed her hand, my fingers closing around hers like it was instinct. Her hand was so small, so warm, wrapped tightly in mine.

I backed out of the parking lot and started down the quiet street toward her house. The city lights produced soft glows through the windows. I could see her soft smile playing across her lips from the corner of my eye. Her perfume lingered in my car like a ghost I didn't want to let go of.

My grip on her hand tightened, and I stole quick glances at her instead of keeping my eyes on the road. I wasn't usually this guy. I knew how to play it cool and keep my emotions in check, but with her? All of that was thrown out the window. She was making me lose my goddamn mind. It took every ounce of restraint I had not to pull the car over, reach for her, and do everything I'd imagined since she stepped into my arms tonight. This woman had me wrapped around her finger. And I didn't care. I also didn't give a damn who knew anymore.

I pulled into her carport, putting the car in park. It was quiet except for the soft tick of the cooling engine. She walked ahead, her silhouette flashing against the porch light. I hung back on the steps, unsure if I was supposed to follow her in or wait like some fool with my heart already on a platter. She turned around, a smirk tugging at her lips, making my gut clench.

"Well, are you coming inside?" she teased, one eyebrow arching like she knew exactly what I was thinking.

I lunged forward, bolting into the house after her, slamming the door behind me. We stood in the cramped living room, not even a foot apart now, just breathing each other in. Her eyes were dark—sinful.

"Are you going to kiss me? Or do I have to kiss you?" she asked with another smirk, her confidence quickening my pulse.

My instincts kicked in before my mind could. "Who are you

tonight?" But she didn't shy away. She just stood there, staring at me like I was already hers. And funny enough, I was. All hers. I took a step closer, my hands cupping her face, tilting it toward me. And then I leaned in, slow at first, trying to savor it. My lips brushed against hers, intending to keep it soft, tender, controlled. But the second I felt her tongue dance against mine, all my self-control unraveled like a loose thread.

It wasn't a kiss; it was a collision. Needy, hungry, desperate. Her hands gripped the sides of my coat, tugging me closer, urging me on. Every sharp tug, every soft sound she made against my mouth—it pushed me further, set every nerve on fire. I wanted her. I wanted her more than I'd ever wanted anything in my life.

Every second that urged on began to blur the lines between restraint and pure desire. Her fingers slipped beneath my coat, pulling it off my shoulders and letting it fall to the floor. My heart was pounding in my chest. Her body pressed against mine, as if closing the distance would burn away whatever hesitancy we had left.

I backed her up until the back of her legs hit the edge of the couch. She pulled away just enough to let us breathe, her lips swollen from the kiss. A satisfied smirk danced at the corners of her mouth. My body was thrumming. I moved in closer, not willing to let go of her lips, tilting my head to kiss her again— but then she stopped me.

Her hand pressed against my chest, and my mind short-circuited. I had one thought, and one thought only: to strip us both of every layer until we were bare and tangled up together on the couch. I wanted to lose myself in her, to forget everything else. Because nothing mattered other than her.

"Wait," she said. "What is it?"

"I can't go any further than this, Joey," she said. "We've gone too far already."

I stood there for a moment, stunned, the heat between us still burning as my body begged for more. But her words hit me like a splash of cold water, and the haze of desire started to clear, leaving me with nothing but the reality of the situation. The silence between us stretched long, every beat of my heart echoing in my chest as I forced myself to step back.

"Okay," I muttered, running a hand through my slicked-back hair, trying to regain some semblance of control. My desire was raw, every nerve frayed, but I respected her words—she wasn't ready. We'd gone too far. I grabbed my coat off the floor and slid it back on.

I could have argued and tried to convince her to cross that line with me, but I knew she was a puzzle, and if I tried to force the pieces together too fast, I'd miss the beauty of figuring us out. She could do almost anything to me, push every limit we set, and I'd let her. Because even if it drove me wild, I didn't mind being in her control.

Chapter Thirty-Three
ANTONIO

Enzo, Michael, and I sat in Enzo's bedroom, the tension in the air so thick it could be cut with a knife. I hadn't been talking to them much. In fact, I'd been avoiding them like the plague. I'd been trapped in a nightmare—just a few hours of sleep, delivering papers at dawn, school, baseball practice, and then back to being a puppet for the cruelest gangster to ever walk the streets of Staten Island. He owned me. Fear kept me silent. I didn't care what happened to me, but I cared about what happened to Ma—and that's exactly what he used against me.

Ma had dropped me off with Enzo and Michael so she could go out with Angela. At least, that's what she told me. I could only hope it was the truth. She'd become quite the liar. Then again, I suppose killing a man will do that to you.

Michael kept nervously fidgeting with a bottle cap from his empty Coke while Enzo's eyes drilled into me. My body stiffened as I sat on the floor, my back rigid. Enzo broke the silence first. "What's going on with you, Antonio? You've been acting strange for *days* now."

I glanced at both of them—my *so-called* best friends. "Yeah, maybe that's because I don't want to be here. But hey, my mom thinks I need to be babysat by Val, so here I am," I hissed.

Enzo raised an eyebrow. "Did we do something wrong?" Michael glanced at me. "Yeah, what's going on?"

I couldn't hold it back anymore; the truth spilled like bitter poison. "Oh, I don't know, Michael. Maybe it's because I learned my two best friends are lying bastards."

Enzo snapped. "What the hell are you talking about?" He sprang to his feet, his temper flaring like always.

I shifted my gaze to Michael. "Michael, when were you planning to tell me that your dad and grandfather are mobsters?"

The question hung in the air, and Michael's face twisted in confusion. "What?" he choked out.

"When I asked if the mafia was real, you both acted like you didn't know a damn thing about it! Lied straight to my face." My voice grew louder, sharper. I stood up and faced him, my fists clenched at my sides. "You thought you could lie to my face like that and then think we could remain best friends? I had to dig myself because neither of you could be honest with me! So thanks a lot for that!"

The words echoed in my head even as I shouted them out loud. They never meant for it to go this far, but it was too late now. The damage had been done. My fate had been sealed.

"We don't know anything, you asshole! No one in my family sits me down and says, 'Yes, we're in the mafia.' Do I have suspicions? Sure. But I've got no proof, and I don't want any part of it. Why do you think I work my ass off in school? Because I want as far away from this fucked up place as I can be!" Michael's voice rang out. He never got angry. For the first time, I saw his nostrils flare, his face flush red with rage. And I felt bad for him. It made sense. I couldn't imagine what it was like to be born into a family like this. He had two choices—become just like them or carve out a different path for himself. He was choosing the latter.

"You should have just told me the truth when I asked," I shot back. "Because if you'd been honest, I wouldn't have gone digging, looking for answers. Asking people around town if the mafia is real. And maybe Vincent wouldn't have caught me on my paper route and pulled me into this shit."

Michael's face fell, the red now white, like all the blood had drained from him. "Wait, what? Are you saying you're roped into some mafia shit now? Is that what you're telling us?"

"Yeah, Michael, I am roped into some mafia shit! And I blame the two of you for it. Maybe it wouldn't have gotten this far if you'd just told me the truth."

"That's bullshit, Antonio! Don't put this on us. You're the most relentless fucking person I know, you would have never let this rest!" Michael's voice made my ears ring.

Enzo raised his voice above ours, trying to maintain order. "The two of you need to chill the fuck out before Val hears and reports this back to our moms!"

"Maybe she needs to hear! Someone's going to have to help him get out of the shit this idiot's put himself in!" Michael roared.

I looked straight at Michael, jaw tight, nostrils flared, fist clenched. "Don't call granddaddy and your pops now, Michael! That ship has sailed! I've been blackmailed to do whatever Vincent says, or I'll be the next one found in someone's trunk."

"Antonio, don't be stupid. You can't get involved in this type of shit. You don't understand, there's no clean way to leave once you enter. This shit isn't a game," Enzo said. "Look at what happened to my pops!"

"Your pops was in the mafia?" I asked him, in shock.

"That doesn't matter," Enzo said. "You can't get mixed up in this kind of shit."

"It's too late! I won't let another person hurt my ma again! If I've got to do this to keep her safe, then I will. I promised myself that a long time ago," I fumed.

Enzo let out a long sigh. "Well, I won't let you do it alone."
"What are you talking about?" I asked.

"You're my best friend. I'm not letting you do this alone."

Enzo's gaze locked onto Michael's, not letting up. Michael tossed his head back with a deep, frustrated sigh.

"You've got to be kidding me! Did anyone listen when I said I wanted *nothing* to do with the mafia?" he snapped.

"Don't be a dick, Michael. He's our friend," Enzo shot back.

"I may be a dick, but at least I know this is going to end badly," Michael retorted.

"And you can live with that? Knowing it and still letting him take orders from Vincent alone?" Enzo challenged.

Michael groaned, rubbing a hand over his face. "Don't say I didn't warn you when this shit goes south."

I felt warmth flood over me—a little hope amidst the mess I was in—but it was faint. I wasn't convinced that they could help, but at least I wasn't alone.

Enzo slipped back into the bedroom, locking the door behind him. Michael and I stood by the windowsill, waiting for the all-clear.

"I told Val we were going to sleep, so we're good. We sneak out, handle this, and get back before our moms are home," he said.

Michael shot him a skeptical look, one eyebrow raised. "Bold plan. You sure Val's not smarter than that?"

Enzo let out a laugh. "Please. You can't think this is the first time I've snuck out of the house, Michael. And Val couldn't care less what we do, she's too busy sucking face with Sal."

The three of us snuck out of Enzo's bedroom window. The adrenaline kicked in as we walked down the sidewalk to the park. I unlocked the car door and slid into the driver's seat. Enzo's voice cut through the quiet of the night. "Holy shit! This is your ride? And you don't even have a driver's license? Okay, I think I'd have said yes to Vincent, too."

"Shut up. This is no time for joking about serious shit like this," Michael hissed.

Enzo just shrugged. "Maybe I wasn't joking, Michael. And just for that, I call shotgun."

Enzo nearly knocked Michael over in his rush to claim the

passenger seat. Michael, dragging his feet, slid into the back and settled in the middle. He leaned forward, wedging himself between Enzo and me. "Do you even know how to drive this thing?" he asked me.

"Yes, Michael, I know how to drive this thing," I mocked.

Enzo snorted next to me. "I know where they're at," he added with a sly grin.

"Yeah? And where would that be?" I asked, backing out slowly.

"Davidson's," he said, looking smug like he had all the answers to whatever questions I was about to ask.

"Davidson's? What're they doing at Davidson's?" I asked. Davidson's corner store was closed at this hour; I knew that much.

Enzo leaned back in his seat with a grin. "Davidson's isn't just a corner store, *genius*. My mom owns the place downstairs."

My brow furrowed. "What place downstairs? Are you fucking with me right now?"

"She owns a speakeasy called *The Wise Guy*. It's under Davidson's. You have to know the right door," he told me.

"This town just keeps getting weirder and weirder," I muttered. "But wait, is your mom in on all this, too?" Enzo's smile faded, and he fidgeted around in the seat, which told me everything I needed to know.

————

WE SAT IN THE PARKED CAR ACROSS THE STREET FROM Davidson's, scoping the place out. The shadows made sure the car remained hidden from view, but even in the dark, the flickering glow from the store's sign illuminated everything around us like some kind of strange reminder that nothing here would ever be simple. Enzo was right. Davidson's turned into something more after hours. Which made me question Mr. Davidson's involvement. I thought he was just a fragile old man, but now I questioned everything and everyone I thought I knew in this fucking place.

Enzo had gone quiet now, slurping soda from a glass bottle, while Michael leaned against the headrest, chewing and smacking on Tootsie Rolls. It was taking everything in me not to lose it at all from the slurping and smacking the two of them were doing.

Enzo leaned back against the seat, scanning the crowd milling about outside Davidsons. "It's a lot busier than I expected."

"Yeah, your mom's got one hell of an operation going on here," I said, glancing sideways at him. "How the hell do the cops not get involved in this?" Enzo looked away, fidgeting around again. He knew something, and I was going to pry it from him. "Don't you dare keep any more secrets from me!"

"I think a lot of the cops are crooked, Antonio," Enzo mumbled. My eyes bulged out of my fucking head at that small revelation.

"It's true," Michael said through his smacking. "Ben's always at my place. What's strange is it's never when my pops is home."

Enzo's neck whipped around so hard I thought he would give himself whiplash. "Your ma is fucking a dirty cop!?"

"I prefer not to ask questions," Michael mumbled. "Yeah, that's for sure," I hissed.

The car fell silent again except for their relentless fucking slurping and smacking. I watched people come and go. Joey's Ferrari was parked out front. I saw his fedora before I saw him.

One hand holding the fedora, and the other wrapped around Ma like they were starring in their own private show. Only they weren't, because I was sitting front row to my worst fucking nightmare.

"Holy shit, it's Joey!" Enzo choked out through his slurping, jabbing a finger in his direction.

"And that's your ma!" Michael chimed in, practically climbing over the seat to get a better look.

My stomach tightened. *No way. No fucking way.* I leaned forward, narrowing my eyes as Joey helped her into his car. The puzzle pieces clicking together in my mind in that very second, my mother disappeared into his passenger seat, and he nearly tripped trying to rush over to the driver's seat. Vincent had me spying on Joey to confirm what he already knew. Joey was seeing my mother while he was still dating his daughter. And I knew a guy like Vincent wouldn't let that one go very easily.

"What now?" Enzo hissed, glancing at me nervously as we watched Joey back out of the parking lot.

I didn't take my eyes off the car as it pulled into the street. I knew exactly where he was headed. I wasn't a fucking idiot. "We follow him," I said, already reaching for the keys in the ignition.

"Oh, yeah, fantastic plan," Michael muttered, sinking back into the seat with an exaggerated sigh. "Because tailing a mobster always ends well. I fucking told you, Enzo, this would end bad! *But no*, nobody ever listened to Michael."

Joey pulled into my carport like he fucking owned it.

I parked a few houses down from mine. I watched the two of them disappear through the front door from a distance, my stomach twisting into knots. Bile creeping up my throat. I might have been only thirteen, but I wasn't clueless. I knew what it usually meant when a man and a woman were left alone like that.

"This feels wrong," Enzo whispered, shifting uncomfortably in the seat.

"We need to tell my grandfather or my father," Michael urged.

My jaw tightened, and I gripped the steering wheel hard enough that my knuckles turned white. My eyes stayed locked on the house, waiting for Joey to emerge. *He didn't.*

The silence stretched until Michael finally spoke up again. "We can't just sit here. If we wait too long, they might see us."

"You're right," I said. "*We* don't do anything. I'll figure this out. *Alone.*"

"Antonio—" Enzo started to plead.

"This isn't your problem, Enzo," I cut him off. "It's mine." This was my problem. Mine alone. Between Joey and me.

Man to man.

I had to protect Ma. She'd spent her whole life protecting me. I'll never forget the look in my pops' eyes when he came for me—cold, cruel, and full of rage. His hands reached out, and I could feel the chill before he touched me.

She'd pulled the trigger before I even registered what was happening. Her hand held my wrist so tightly, it left a bruise. I looked over my shoulder as we stepped out of the front door and watched as he slumped to the floor, blood pooling beneath him. I looked at her then, really looked at her—the trembling in her hands as she gripped the steering wheel, the tears she didn't bother to wipe away. She did that for me. She saved me because she loved me.

Now it was my turn.

I wasn't going to let Joey pull her into his world. No matter how charming he played it or how much he "meant well." She didn't deserve to get tangled up in another man's violence. If keeping her out of this meant playing nice with Joey, fine. If it meant being Vincent's errand boy for life, so be it. If it meant joining the damn mafia before I even had my driver's license, I'd do it without hesitation. *Whatever it took.*

Because I owed her that much.

Chapter Thirty-Four

ANTONIO

I pulled up to Vincent's house, parking my bike against the curb before dropping my empty delivery bag beside it. My routine had become second nature—deliver all the papers in record time, then stop by Vincent's place to check in. So far, Joey had done nothing notable.

As I stepped through the front door, I immediately noticed the tension in the room. Vincent stood in the dining area, locked in a heated back-and-forth with Hector. Their voices were low, but sharp. The moment they spotted me, the conversation came to an abrupt halt.

"You've got the fucking kid running errands for you now?" Hector hissed, his glare flicking between Vincent and me.

"Should I come back?" I asked, already feeling like I'd walked in on something I wasn't supposed to hear.

"Stay," Vincent ordered, his tone leaving no room for argument.

I did as I was told, sinking onto the couch, but I could still hear them whispering from the next room. Something about their hushed voices set my nerves on edge. I'd seen Hector before, in passing, when I hung out with Michael, but never like this. Seeing him here, going back and forth with Vincent, stirred something uneasy in my gut. Hector was part of the mafia—that much I knew. But there was something about this encounter that felt off.

I heard Hector's low, clipped voice carry through the room. "I've worked too damn hard for this title. Christopher's talking about bringing him in. So we're going to have to put a hit on him."

A hit? On who?

"I put him away for ten fucking years, and now he walks out like he owns the streets I bled for," Hector muttered.

That confirmed who. *Joey.*

Hector stormed past me, slamming the front door so hard the walls seemed to rattle. I kept my expression blank as Vincent strode over, lowering himself onto the sofa across from me. "What do you got for me, kid?" he asked.

I shrugged. "Nothing. Joey doesn't do much—just smokes and sits around with his friends."

Vincent studied me for a moment, then tilted his head. "What about your mother and Joey?"

I kept my face neutral. "Haven't seen anything," I lied.

His gaze lingered on me, and I could only hope he couldn't see straight through me. He didn't respond right away. He just kept watching me. The silence stretched, making my pulse kick up a notch.

"You're a smart kid," he finally said. "You know what happens to people who keep secrets from me, don't you?"

I swallowed hard, forcing myself to hold his gaze. "I don't got any secrets."

Vincent let out a slow exhale, then leaned back against the couch. "Good," he said, but the way he said it sent a shiver down my spine. "Keep your eyes on Joey. If he so much as breathes wrong, I wanna know about it."

I nodded, standing up. "Got it."

As I turned to leave, Vincent's voice stopped me in my tracks.

"Oh, and kid?"

I glanced back over my shoulder.

"Just remember what happens if I catch you lying."

I forced a nod and walked out, my gut twisting the whole way. I'd never pedaled faster than I did that day.

Chapter Thirty-Five
ANTONIO

Balancing Vincent, school, baseball, and delivering papers was enough to drive me to the brink of insanity, but I couldn't stop.

Baseball was my only escape. It gave me purpose, a joy I couldn't find anywhere else. It was the one thing that kept me sane. Being on the school team made me feel like I finally belonged somewhere. My whole life, I had felt out of place, like I didn't fit in anywhere. But since moving to Staten Island and stepping onto that field, I felt like I had found my place.

I was so lost in my own head that I didn't notice Giovanni walking up behind me until it was too late. "Hey, paperboy! Catch this!" His voice echoed from behind me.

I spun around just in time to see the baseball hurtling toward me. Before I could react, the ball slammed into the upper part of my cheekbone. The pain radiated from the impact, sharp and unforgiving. I staggered back, clutching my face, and a few gasps sounded from the guys nearby, but they didn't dare step forward. Except for Enzo and Michael. They always had my back.

"Antonio!" Enzo's voice rang out as he and Michael sprinted toward me.

"What the fuck, you little shit!" Enzo shouted, his face twisted with rage as he turned on Giovanni. "I'll fucking kill you!"

Giovanni didn't even flinch. Instead, he smirked, that smug, condescending look he always wore like a second skin. "You don't have the guts, Lorenzo," he hissed, crossing his arms. "It's not in your bloodline to survive. *Look at what happened to your father.*"

Enzo froze for half a second, but that pause was enough to scare me. His brown eyes turned black. Michael and I moved on instinct, grabbing him before he could lunge at Giovanni.

"Let me go!" Enzo snarled, straining against our grip. "I'll rip his throat out!"

"Enzo, stop!" I said. I could feel my pulse pounding in my ears. My cheek was throbbing, and I could feel it begin to swell. It didn't help that Enzo was strong and stocky; right now, rage made it almost impossible to hold him back.

"Don't stoop to his level," Michael said, his jaw clenched. He tightened his grip on Enzo's arm, glaring daggers at Giovanni. "You want to get suspended and kicked off the team? He's not worth it."

Giovanni chuckled. "That's right. Listen to your little babysitters, Lorenzo. Wouldn't want to end up like your old man, now would you?"

Enzo roared, pushing harder against us, but I wasn't about to let Giovanni bait him into his own demise. The sting in my cheek was a reminder of the constant garbage we had to deal with because of Giovanni. "Giovanni," I said. My hand dropped from my face as I stepped toward him. "I swear to God, if you ever try something like that again—"

"What? You'll tell your daddy?" Giovanni interrupted, laughing. "Oh, wait—your dad's dead too, isn't he? Or is he?" I surged forward, but Michael caught my arm before I could swing.

"Not you too, Antonio," Michael growled. "He's trying to get under your skin. Don't let him win."

My vision blurred with red. But then I glanced at Enzo, whose chest heaved as he glared at Giovanni like he wanted to tear him apart. And I remembered. Enzo didn't just hate Giovanni because he was a bully. Giovanni had crossed a line no one should ever cross. His day would come, and I'd make damn sure I was the one to give it to him.

"That's enough, Giovanni," Michael begged.

Giovanni looked between us, his smirk still dancing along his lips, as he shrugged. "Fine," he said. "Enjoy the bruise, paperboy."

As soon as Giovanni walked away, Michael and Enzo stood side by side, their gazes fixed on me and the shiner appearing on my cheekbone.

Michael sighed, rubbing the back of his neck as he looked at me. "Shit, Antonio. You alright?"

I rolled my jaw, testing the ache in my face. It throbbed like hell, but I wasn't about to let them see how much it hurt. "I'm fine."

Enzo wasn't buying it. His fists were clenched so tight his knuckles had turned white, his whole body vibrating with barely contained rage. "I should go after him," he muttered, shifting his weight like he was ready to bolt. I grabbed his arm before he could take a step. Michael clapped a hand on my shoulder. "Come on, let's get some ice on that before Coach Artie sees."

I let them lead me off the field, but as we walked, I could still feel Giovanni's smirk burning into the back of my head. His day would come. Sooner rather than later.

Coach Artie stormed over before we even made it to the dugout, his expression thunderous as he took one look at my cheek. "What happened?" he demanded, his eyes flicking between me, Michael, and Enzo.

I hesitated for half a second before blurting out the best lie I could come up with, "Enzo accidentally tossed the ball, and it hit me in my face."

Michael's head snapped toward me in disbelief, while Enzo, who had been bristling with rage just seconds ago, suddenly froze. His face contorted into a mixture of shock and confusion.

Coach Artie frowned. "Enzo?"

Enzo glanced at me and then back at Coach Artie, letting out a sharp breath and muttered, "Yeah. My bad. You know I got this bad arm."

Michael pressed his lips together, trying not to laugh, while Coach Artie just shook his head. "Watch your aim next time, Enzo. Antonio, you're done for the day. Go home and get some ice on that."

"I'm fine, coach," I tried, but he wasn't having it.

"Not up for debate. You're done for the day," he said firmly. As he walked towards the field, Michael leaned in, smirking.

"Enzo and his bad arm?"

Enzo grumbled under his breath. "Next time, I'll make sure my damn bad arm gets Giovanni's face instead."

When I walked into the house and dropped my backpack near the door, I spotted Ma standing by the stove, swaying to the *Elvis* vinyl spinning in the living room, a wooden spoon in hand as she stirred the pot. She turned mid-spin, her smile fading the second her eyes landed on mine. The spoon clattered onto the counter as she rushed over, her hands instantly cupping my face.

"What happened to you?" she gasped, eyes locked on the bruise blooming across my cheek. Her fingers brushing the tender skin, as if her touch could make it disappear.

"It's nothing, Ma," I muttered, slipping out of her grasp and heading toward the fridge. "I'll ice it. It'll be fine in a few days."

"Nothing?" she repeated, following close behind. Her arms were crossed now. "What happened, Antonio?"

I grabbed a bag of frozen peas and pressed them to my face, wincing at the cold. "It's nothing," I said again. "I had baseball practice, okay? The ball hit me in the face. It happens."

She was silent for a moment, and I dared to glance over at her. Her sharp, brown eyes scanned my face like she was trying to read between my lies. "It was an accident?" she asked.

"Yeah, Ma," I lied. "A bad throw. I wasn't paying attention, and it clipped me. That's all."

She wasn't buying it. I could feel her gaze boring into the side of my face, but I kept my focus on the bag of peas like it was the most interesting thing in the world.

"Antonio," she said. "If someone hurt you—if this wasn't an accident—you need to tell me."

I turned to her, trying to force a half-smile despite the throbbing in my cheek. "It was practice, Ma. A bad throw."

She reached out and ran her fingers through my hair. "Alright," she said. "But if I find out you're lying to me, Antonio, we're going to have a problem."

There was no way I was going to admit that Giovanni did this on purpose. The moment Ma found out, she'd fly into a rage and march straight over to confront Renee. And I just couldn't imagine what the repercussions of that would be at this rate.

Chapter Thirty-Six

ANTONIO

I finished my paper route, the early spring air cool against my face. Half of it was swollen and bruised in ugly shades of purple and yellow. I ignored the dull ache as I rode up to Vincent's place, dropping my bike at the curb.

The front door was cracked open slightly. But as I reached for the handle, a voice stopped me in my tracks.

A *woman's* voice.

Not just any woman. *Renee.*

My jaw tightened. The last thing I wanted was to see her, not after what her son had done to me. I turned on my heel. But then I heard her say, "You should've done something about Joey the *second* he got out. He's *insufferable,* and I don't know how long I can keep up this act. We are practically at each other's throats."

"You'll stay until I have what I need. Joey will slip up—it's only a matter of time. And when he does, I'll take care of him."

Renee huffed, but there was a pause before she spoke again. "He's not going to feed me any information. He's practically never home. Can't you do something about the fact that he's *embarrassing* me by flaunting Adriana in my face? "

"The more he believes he's untouchable, the *sloppier* he gets. And when that happens, I'll have *exactly* what I need. Adriana is the best thing to happen. She doesn't even know she's going to be the reason he unravels. She's making the job easier for me."

My heart pounded so hard I could feel it in my throat. My hands were clammy as I turned away from the door, my pulse thrumming in my ears. Renee wasn't just playing the part of Joey's girlfriend—she was out for him, and he had *no* idea.

I backed away slowly, careful not to make a sound, but my chest felt tight. The second I reached my bike, fear overtook me. I jumped on, my hands shaking as I gripped the handlebars, and pedaled as fast as possible.

Joey needed to know. But telling him meant revealing that I had been listening. And if Vincent found out, I didn't even want to think about what he'd do.

By the time I reached home, my mind was still racing. Every word Renee had said echoed in my head, twisting into something worse each time I replayed it. I felt like a ghost moving through the hallways that day at school. The usual noise of lockers slamming and kids shouting felt distant from everything I was going through.

"You look like hell," Enzo said, nudging me in the ribs. "Thanks," I muttered, too tired to come up with a better

response. "Really appreciate the concern, Enzo."

"I'm serious, you need to rest," he pressed, narrowing his eyes. "How much sleep are you even getting? Let me come help. I could drive for you."

"I told you," I said, shaking my head, "this is between Joey and me."

"How's that going for you, by the way?" Enzo asked, raising an eyebrow.

Before I could answer, Giovanni stormed toward me. "Hey, paperboy!" he shouted, loud enough to draw attention. I kept walking, hoping he'd lose interest. "Hey!" he barked, shoving me in the chest. My steps faltered, but I steadied myself. His glare pinned me in place as the hallway buzzed with whispers and stares. "If I say something, you answer me."

"Not in the mood," I muttered.

"You're going to tell Mia you're not taking her to the dance," Giovanni demanded, stepping closer.

"What?" I asked, confused.

"She's going with me," he snarled. His breath hit my face as he leaned in, daring me to challenge him.

"She asked me," I said. "I didn't beg her or force her. She made her choice."

"Well, now she's un-choosing you," Giovanni hissed. He stepped closer, but Enzo moved in as well. Giovanni scoffed and shoved him aside. "Back off, chihuahua."

"She's not your property, Giovanni," I said. "She wants to go with me, and that's what's going to happen."

"You've got balls, paperboy," Giovanni said, his lips curling into a smirk. "Who do you think you are? Some big shot? You show up out of nowhere, steal Mia from me, buy your way onto the baseball team—and don't even get me started on that mother of yours."

My world narrowed. All I could hear was the dull roar of blood flooding my eardrums.

"What did you *just* say?" I asked.

"You heard me." He grinned. "She's many things, isn't she? A whore, for starters. The only way she can put food on the table is by spreading her legs for Joey."

The punch landed before I even realized I'd thrown it. Giovanni's head snapped back, his body crumpling to the cold floor. He lay there, stunned, as the crowd around us fell silent.

Nobody talks about my mother. Not ever.

Chapter Thirty-Seven

ADRIANA

Renee and I sat across from each other in the school office. Across the desk, Principal Clayton flipped through the incident report. "From what I gathered, both of your sons were involved in a fight earlier today," she began. "And from what I've been told, it seems the argument was over a girl."

A girl? I frowned, glancing at Antonio slouched in the chair beside me.

Renee's voice cut through the tension like a knife. "My son looks like he was assaulted."

Mine did, too. But supposedly from a foul ball at practice, not a fist. I stiffened. "Let's not point fingers, Renee," I said. "I'm sure both are at fault here. There's clearly more to this story."

Principal Clayton raised a hand before Renee could snap back. "The girl's name is Mia. She was also very upset about the fight, and has been sent home for the day." She glanced between Antonio and Giovanni, who both kept their eyes on the floor.

"Mia's been close with Giovanni for a *long* time, and now your son suddenly thinks he has a right to interfere? I tell you, the apple doesn't fall far from the tree, does it?"

I forced a tight smile. "Mia isn't anyone's property, Renee. I know this may be difficult for you to comprehend, but people aren't property."

Her eyes narrowed. "I'm sorry. Are you defending your son for beating up my son? Do you support violence? He's had feelings for Mia longer than your kid has even *noticed* her!"

"I'm not excusing the fight, but I won't stand for the way you're talking about *my* son," I said. "He knows better than to resort to violence. *Your* son must have started this, because as you said, the apple doesn't fall far from the tree."

"Enough," Principal Clayton interrupted. "We're here to resolve this, not make it worse. This fight isn't just about a girl or even about their differences—it's about how we, as parents, choose to address what happens next. Your sons need to learn how to manage conflicts without resorting to physical confrontation."

Renee folded her arms, letting out a long sigh. "I'm not trying to make this personal. It's just that I know my son, and I *know* how much Mia means to him."

"I understand how he feels," I said. "But Antonio has just as much right to his emotions as anyone else. And Mia's free to make her own choices about who she wants to spend time with. And just as people aren't property, people can also choose to love who they want."

Renee's lips pressed into a thin line, and neither of us spoke. It was clear that this wasn't about Antonio and Giovanni anymore. This was about Joey—her staking her claim on him, while he had already staked his claim on me.

Principal Clayton's voice interrupted my thoughts. "The best way to resolve this might be for them to simply apologize. Of course, Antonio is suspended, but an apology could be a good starting point."

Antonio leaned back in his chair, a smirk tugging at the corner of his lips. "Sorry, but I'm not apologizing to him, Principal Clayton. Though I'd love to hear his apology."

"Antonio," I said, smacking his arm, "stop it. *Apologize*. Right now."

But he didn't budge. His gaze locked with mine, defiance burning bright in his dark eyes. "No," he said. "I'm not apologizing to him. He can cry it out."

The words sent a chill through me. This wasn't my Antonio. "That's fine, Principal Clayton," Renee cut in, standing and clutching both her purse and Giovanni's arm. Her voice was smooth and condescending, every word calculated. "I understand boys raised without a father develop these *tendencies*. But don't worry. Giovanni's grandfather and *stepfather* will have a talk with him. You won't have to worry about my son behaving this way again."

She punctuated her remark with a bright, almost sickening smile directed at me before sweeping past, the sound of her heels sharp against the tile floor. My jaw tightened, and heat rose in my chest. I dug my nails into the palm of my hand. I glanced at Antonio, his shoulders squared and his jaw tight. There was no trace of guilt or remorse in his expression—just raw, unfiltered rage.

As we left the office, the silence between us felt suffocating. Antonio shoved his hands into his pockets as he strode down the hallways. I watched him walk ahead of me. It wasn't just the fight that worried me now—it was the anger simmering beneath the surface. We finally reached the car, getting in. "Do you have *any* idea what kind of trouble you've caused? Getting into a fight over some girl? And then refusing to apologize?" I asked him. My head turned to him as he slouched in the passenger seat without a care in the world.

He ran a hand through his dark, messy hair. "Ma, it wasn't like that. I—I didn't want to fight him. He pushed me. And then—"

I cut him off. "I don't care what happened! You don't resolve things with violence. That's not who you are, Antonio. You know this. This isn't the way to handle things. You don't fight over a girl."

"You don't get it! You don't know how he acts—what he says! What I'm going through!" he shouted.

If Giovanni was anything like Renee, he was arrogant, insufferable, and smug enough to push Antonio over the edge. But none of that justified what had happened. You can't justify violence.

"Antonio," I started, my gaze fixed ahead. I had never wanted to talk about that night, but no matter how hard I tried, it kept coming back. "Is this about what happened that night?"

"What?" he choked out. "No! You can't seriously think I learned to punch people just because you learned how to kill a man in self-defense."

My eyebrows furrowed. "You're grounded," I said, feeling the tears threatening to spill over. I put the car in reverse and backed out.

"What?" he shouted. "Grounded for what?"

I slammed the brakes. "For starters, punching someone. Violence isn't justified, and I won't have you growing up thinking it is!"

This had to stop now. What I had done was wrong. What Antonio had witnessed—or thought he had witnessed—was a terrible thing, but Joey was going to handle it. I couldn't let Antonio think that he could grow up and take his anger out on others, just because he believed I had killed his father.

His brows knitted together. "I know you told Joey."

"I'm an adult, Antonio," I said, my voice tight as I drove down the street. "I don't need your permission to do things." I parked under the carport, and the two of us got out, meeting at the hood. "I don't know what's gotten into you, but maybe some time grounded and suspended from school, working at Davidson's, will do you some good."

His mouth gaped open for a moment. "This place has changed you!"

"Yeah?" I said, walking past him. "Well, it seems it's changed you, too." And then I couldn't hold in the hot tears any longer. They spilled down my face. Hot and unforgiving.

Chapter Thirty-Eight

JOEY

"Joey, hi," she greeted, her words rushed. Clipped. "Now's not really a great time."

She moved to block the door, but I stepped past her into the house, not letting it deter me. "I heard what happened," I said. "I came as fast as I could."

Her sigh was heavy, her shoulders sinking for a moment before she brushed her hands over her dress, smoothing out imaginary creases. "I don't know what got into him," she admitted, shaking her head like she couldn't believe it herself. "He's going to learn his lesson, especially with all that free time now that he's suspended and grounded."

I frowned, stepping into the kitchen as the faint smell of dinner simmering on the stove filled the room. She was still in her apron, her fingers gripping the counter for support. "What happened? What did he tell you?" I asked.

"He didn't tell me much." She sighed. "It was over some girl named Mia," she continued. "Renee claims Giovanni has had a thing for her for a while now, and is acting like Antonio just stepped in and took her. I don't know."

I stepped closer, resting my hand on the back of one of the chairs. "Antonio's a good kid. I'll talk to him. Don't worry."

"Renee was awful, Joey," she continued. "She was attacking Antonio, left and right. It was completely uncalled for—just because of whatever she thinks is going on between us."

I stepped closer, closing the distance between us. My hands gripped her arms, my eyes locked on hers. "I'm sorry. I'll take care of Renee. But Antonio's just a kid, Adriana. It's tough for a boy his age."

Adriana backed up, pushing me away, her palms landing on the counter. Her head dropped, strands of hair falling into her face as she spoke again, "Principal Clayton asked him to apologize, Joey. And you know what he did? He *refused*. Flat out *refused*. Then Renee made a comment—how boys without dads develop these sorts of *tendencies*." Her gaze shot up, burning into mine. "Antonio needs someone who can teach him how to deal with all of this. How to be a man. Or at least how to start becoming one. It'll be over my dead body that my son is out there acting like some hooligan."

I stepped forward again. "I'll talk to him—man to man. And I'll deal with Renee, too." My hand rested on hers as I lifted my other hand to tilt her chin upward. Her eyes met mine. "You've done an amazing job raising him," I said. "You're the best mother I've ever seen. But sometimes, a boy just needs someone other than their mother—someone who can show him what it means to handle things the right way. Let me help you with this one."

Adriana's lips parted, like she wanted to protest, but instead, she sighed. Her shoulders sagged, a small nod following. "Thank you, Joey. I'm glad you're here for him."

I drove Antonio to the park to toss the baseball around. He was quiet the entire ride, staring out the window. Even as we passed the ball back and forth, he barely said a word. His black eye wasn't from a bad catch. I knew that much. Antonio was a good player; he wouldn't have missed a foul ball like that. No, this had been deliberate—someone had meant to hurt him. And I had a pretty good idea who. "Alright, kid. We need to talk," I said, breaking the silence that had stretched too long.

I caught the ball mid-air, holding it instead of throwing it back. "I heard about what went down today," I began. "You and Giovanni getting into it over a girl? I want to know what happened. What's going on with you, with you and Giovanni?" He looked at me, but his body language gave him away. His shoulders tensed; his gaze shifted uncomfortably.

"It wasn't like I planned it. I just—I don't know. He pushed me," Antonio confessed. "Then he pushed Enzo. He was in my face. He was out of line. He's been trying to get under my skin since I got to that school. And *today* was my breaking point."

"I respect you for standing your ground. But fighting doesn't fix anything, especially not over some girl. Mia isn't worth all this trouble, trust me. Take it from me." I winked at him, letting the teasing note slip in. That worked; a smirk tugged at the corners of his mouth, though he tried to hide it by looking down, kicking a rock at his feet.

"She asked me to the school dance," he admitted, his grin widening. "I didn't even ask her, Joey. She asked *me*. He was mad because she chose *me*."

That got a chuckle out of me. "Listen, kid. You know I'd do anything for you. You're like a son to me." I watched him study me as I continued, "I see so much in you that reminds me of when I was your age. Actually, when I was your age, I had this kid, Tony, always getting under my skin, pushing my buttons. He and I went at it every chance we got. I remember one day, I just had enough, so I went up to him and gave him a lesson he wouldn't forget."

"What did you do?"

I exhaled, shaking my head, more at myself than him. "I waited for him to come outside when nobody was around and I beat him up," I admitted. "Thought I'd finally earned some respect. But looking back, all I earned was regret. You know the difference between you and me?"

He didn't say anything, waiting for me to answer.

"My old man was a real dirtbag. But my mother never left him. I used to secretly pray she'd wake me up one day and we'd disappear, but that day never happened. One night, though, he picked the wrong fight." The memory was still painful, even after twenty years had passed. "When he died, my mother wasn't the same. She turned into him." I paused, the memories biting at me. "I tell you this because I learned violence was the way to handle things at a very young age. I've been there, kid. I don't want to see you make the same mistakes I did."

I reached out, pulling Antonio into a one-armed hug.

"I hit him because he talked about Ma..." he admitted. "That's the truth."

"What do you mean?" I scowled. "What did he say about your mother?"

His eyes were burning with anger. "He told the school about you two. He called her a whore, that that's why you've been helping us." I paused, speechless for a moment. My vision went red before he cut in. "What's really going on between the two of you?"

I sighed, shifting on my feet. "Well," I started, kicking a rock with the tip of my shoe, "I love your mother. And I love you, too," I said, my gaze steady as I met his eyes. That was the first time I'd admitted something like this out loud. It felt like a foreign language on my tongue. "There are a few things that need to fall into place before I can be with her, but you have my word—I'm going to make it happen."

He frowned, still pressing. "What has to fall into place?"

I let out a soft chuckle. "Just trust that I've got it covered. I love her, and I'd never do anything to hurt her." I paused. "Now, what really happened to your face?" I asked him.

"Baseball practice," he muttered. "A foul ball clipped me in the face."

"Come on, kid," I said, nudging him. "You don't gotta lie to me. I got your back."

"Giovanni threw it at my face when I wasn't paying attention," he confessed. "But I guess we're fair. Please don't say anything to him."

"You know what?" I began, "Some of us were born to lead. You're a leader. Giovanni sees it. He knows it. And it probably eats him alive. That's what all this boils down to. You'll face a lot worse than Giovanni in your lifetime. *Trust me.* Save all that hostile energy for when it really counts."

"What are you saying?" he asked me.

"This stays between us," I said, gripping his shoulder, eyeing him. "You don't let nobody put their hands on you or someone you love." I broke the serious moment with a grin. "And I thought I told you if *anyone* messes with you, just tell 'em you know Joey Romano, and they don't want me to come straighten 'em out."

He let out a chuckle, which was all the satisfaction I needed. "Now come on, let's get back to this game so you can really mess with Giovanni's head when you're the next *Joe DiMaggio*, sporting his crush on your arm because you're the best damn baseball player on that team. And that's why Mia asked you to take her to the dance, and not him. Is she pretty, by the way?"

Antonio flashed a smug grin and nodded. I matched his expression. "That's my boy!"

Chapter Thirty-Nine

JOEY

I hesitated at the door, my fingers tightening around the knob. I didn't want to be here. But there was no avoiding Renee—not when she was waiting for me like a predator ready to pounce. I had managed to avoid her for days, but I knew I had to face her. She was curled up on the couch, legs crossed, a cigarette burning between her fingers. The moment I shut the door behind me, her eyes snapped to mine, burning with rage that matched my own.

"How lovely," she sneered, exhaling smoke. "You've penciled me in between playing dad to a delinquent and fucking his mother."

My jaw clenched. "Watch your *fucking* mouth. And stop trying to get inside Adriana's head, putting on your best goddamn performance in front of Principal Clayton."

Renee chuckled, shaking her head. She rose off the couch. "You know, I hate you. I didn't know it was possible to hate someone like I hate you," she said as she stood across from me.

I took a step closer, towering over her. "Then we've got something in common."

She smirked. "There will be no better satisfaction than the day my father puts a bullet in your head for the way you've treated me."

"A bullet in the head would be more pleasant than being held hostage by you," I tested back. My hands curled into fists at my sides, every muscle in my body wound taut with rage. I hated this woman. Hated the way she twisted the knife in my back, how she reveled in my misery just to feel like she had some kind of power over me.

I couldn't stand another second trapped in her presence. Not in this house, not in her life, not under Vincent's fucking thumb. I didn't give a damn what walking away meant for me—whether it was a death sentence or not. At this rate, I'd rather shine shoes on a street corner than stick around just to take Vincent's spot.

"Renee, this is over."

"You don't get to tell me when something begins or ends," she challenged. "My father—"

"Fuck your father," I snapped. "Him taking me out would be doing me a favor at this rate."

"You think you have a say in this? A choice?" She chuckled. "Of course not." I leaned in. "But I've got nothing left to lose."

I spun on my heels, gripping the door and yanking it wide open. "You're going to regret this!" I heard her call out. But I slammed the door behind me.

I didn't live by regrets. Regret was for men who thought they had a way out, for men who believed they could've made different choices and ended up somewhere better. I knew better. I'd done enough bad that if I let regret settle in, it would be a slow suicide —one I wasn't willing to entertain.

But as I walked out that door, I became very aware that maybe, I'd regret telling her that Vincent would be doing me a favor if he took me out. That wasn't just reckless—it was an invitation. And Vincent wasn't the kind of man to turn down an invitation like that.

The thought settled in my gut like a lead weight as I climbed into my car and started towards *The Wise Guy*. I needed a stiff drink. I parked and stepped out of the car, straightening my coat as I walked inside, already craving the burn of whiskey on my throat.

When I walked through, I took a seat at the bar across from Angela, who gave me a smile. She poured up a whiskey for me and slid it over. "How's it going?" she asked me.

I chuckled, taking a long sip of my drink, letting the burn settle in my chest before setting the glass down. "I broke it off with Renee."

Angela raised an eyebrow, leaning against the bar with a knowing smirk. "No shit? About time."

I let out a breath, shaking my head. "Yeah, well, let's see how long I live to talk about it."

She snorted, pouring herself a drink and clinking her glass against mine. "Did you tell Adriana?"

"Jesus, I'm not that much of a desperate *fuck*, Angela." I chuckled, shaking my head.

Angela arched an eyebrow, swirling the liquor in her glass. "Are you sure about that?" she teased.

I smirked, leaning back against the bar. "Well," I pretended to think it over, "*depends*. Does she talk about me to you?"

Angela let out a laugh, shaking her head. "You should know I don't give away secrets."

I tapped my fingers against the bar, eyeing her. "Come on, just a little hint?"

Angela rolled her eyes. "You really are desperate."

I chuckled, rubbing a hand down my face. "*Ohhh*." I sighed dramatically. "What am I going to do?"

"Hmph," Angela mused, tilting her glass. "Good question. What *are* you going to do?"

I shot her a look. "I was asking for advice." She smirked. "You think I'm good at advice?" "Great point." I laughed, shaking my head.

"But," Angela leaned in slightly, "if it were *me*, I'd ask her on a date. To start."

I nodded slowly, rolling the thought around in my head. "Because I can't keep watching this cat-and-mouse game you two have going," she added, exasperated. "It's exhausting."

Chapter Forty

ANTONIO

I was certain of one thing. I was a pawn in a game I didn't know the rules to.

I was running around doing Vincent's spying, convinced Joey was the problem. I let myself believe Joey was the enemy, the one tearing this family apart. But I was wrong. This was a game without instructions, but all I'd managed to piece together was that Vincent and Hector had been the ones who put Joey in prison. Renee was insane and working alongside her dad to somehow take Joey out. And I'd been roped into the entire thing.

I stood there as I swept the floor at Davidson's, which was just more dirty work. When I heard the door chime and saw the way her face lit up, I knew exactly who had walked in before I even turned around.

Joey. She didn't smile like that for anyone else.

He leaned against the counter like he owned the place, his eyes locked on hers. And I felt something settle inside me. Maybe this wasn't so bad, after all. Joey had been more of a father to me than my own ever was. And I'd never seen Ma this happy before. That's all I ever wanted for her.

"Morning, Joey!" I called from across the store.

He turned, flashing me a grin as he made his way over. Even

now, it was impossible not to admire him. The gold watch, the tailored suit, the fedora tilted just right—he was cool without even trying. I still wanted to be like him. Just like him.

Which meant I had to end this thing with Vincent. Before it ended me.

Or worse—before it ended, Joey.

"How's it going, kid?" he asked, pouring him a cup of coffee. "It's shit," I muttered, sweeping the floor. "Ma's got me doing all her dirty work just because of this suspension."

Joey chuckled as he took a sip of his coffee. "Yeah, well, if she hears you cursing, you'll be working for free even longer."

"Take me with you," I begged. "I swear I'll behave. Just get me out of here."

Joey looked thoughtful for a moment before shrugging. "Yeah, okay. I'll have to ask your mom first."

———

ROMANO WHOLESALE.

Not a very creative name on Joey's part, but I'd read in the papers that it was the most successful car wholesaler's shop on the East Coast. So he must be doing something right. Joey's office was fit for a king. A high-back, leather chair perched behind a large wooden desk with a chandelier hanging above. A small bar cart was in the corner.

Joey gestured toward the chair behind his desk. "Sit there," he said. I sank into the chair without a second thought, glancing around the room with wide-eyed fascination. Joey walked toward the window, cracking it open and lighting a cigarette as the faint scent of smoke filled his office.

"This is what it feels like to be you." I grinned, leaning back in the chair. He laughed and exhaled the smoke out of the crack in the window. "Can I have one, too?" I asked, nodding at the cigarette dangling from Joey's fingers.

Joey raised an eyebrow, tapping the ash into the small glass tray. "Not a chance, kid." He took another drag. "And I don't want to find out you been smoking. It's a bad habit."

"Then why do you smoke?" I asked him.

Before he could reply, there was a knock at his office door, followed by Sal poking his head through, asking Joey to step outside.

"Be right back, kid," Joey told me. "Make yourself comfortable."

My eyes drifted over Joey's desk—just a mess of invoices, listings, and contracts. Paperwork. Nothing out of the ordinary. Nothing interesting. My fingers brushed against the top drawer, and I cracked it open just enough to peek inside.

Bullets. Cash. And a gun.

My stomach twisted into a knot. The office door swung open, and Joey stepped in.

Shit. Caught red-handed.

My pulse thundered in my ears as I shoved the drawer shut—too loud. Too obvious. Joey's eyes locked onto mine, then dropped to my hand, still lingering on the drawer. He didn't say a word, just took a slow step forward. I forced myself to sit back in the chair, straightening under his stare. I braced myself for whatever happened next. But Joey just reached down, pulled the drawer open, and grabbed the gun like it was nothing. He slid it into his waistband, then nodded toward the door. "Let's go."

I hesitated, my heart still hammering. But I followed. We drove in silence, my mind racing with worst-case scenarios. Had I just crossed a line? But when we pulled into the empty dock, Joey did something I wasn't expecting.

He got out, rummaged through a garbage can, and pulled out an empty soda can. Then he placed it a few feet ahead of us, lining it up just right. I took in a sharp inhale as he turned back to me. "Come here," he said, pulling the gun from his waistband and holding it out to me.

The realization hit me like a hard slap across the face. He wasn't going to hurt me. He was going to teach me how to shoot.

Joey raised a finger as I stepped closer. "This *never* happened," he said, wagging a finger at me, trying to make his point clear. "Your mother would kill both of us if she ever found out about this, and we're both destined for a long life, kid." His serious facade quickly washed away in exchange for a smirk.

I grinned. "Of course not! I'll just tell her you worked me like a slave, and I never want her to let you take me anywhere again." I laughed.

Joey chuckled, too, but the tone in his voice became more serious as he raised it carefully, positioning it with precision. He held it with ease, like it was second nature to him. "It's a powerful thing, Antonio. Holding a gun. You don't realize what you're capable of until your finger is on that trigger." He smirked, handing the gun to me. "You got one shot. So you better make it count, kid. You never play around with guns. Don't ever mess with one unless you *absolutely* have to. And if you ever have to use it? It's because your mother's in danger, and I'm not around. That's the only time."

I swallowed, my fingers wrapping around the cold metal. He stood beside me, helping me line up the gun and adjust my aim. "Like this," he instructed, his hand steady on my arm. "Now, pull the trigger. And *don't* miss." His breath was hot against my ear.

For a second, I thought about Ma—what she must have felt, holding a gun in her hands. The weight of it. The power it yielded. But then I thought about *that* night.

And I pulled the trigger.

The familiar, sharp pop rang out. "*Oh, fuck,*" I exhaled, my pulse slamming against my ribs. But my arms stayed steady, the gun firm in my grip. Adrenaline surged through me. I'd never felt anything like it before.

Joey stood beside me as I lowered my arm, his arms crossed over his chest, head cocked to the side. Admiration lit up his face. Like a proud father watching his son. "How'd that feel?" he asked.

"Incredible!" I shouted, a wide grin stretching across my face. I looked down at the gun. There was something intoxicating about holding that gun, feeling the cool metal against my finger-tips. The adrenaline coursing through me was like a drug, addictive. My body responded in ways I couldn't fully explain; every nerve in my body had been set on fire.

It shouldn't feel this good. I shouldn't be enjoying this. My mind screamed at me to give it back, to walk away and forget about it. But there was a yearning I couldn't deny myself forever. I loved it more than I should have. I could taste the power, the control. It wasn't just the gun—it was the threat it carried, the fear it invoked, the sheer fucking power it yielded.

Joey took the gun back, tucking it back into his pants. "It's not a toy. You need to know when to use it and when not to."

"Yeah, yeah, I get it," I said, looking down at my empty hand still vibrating from the shot I fired.

"This shit is real. You don't mess with it unless you have to. *One shot, Antonio. One shot. That's all you get. So you always make it count.*"

Joey and I sat on the dock, cracking open boiled peanuts and washing them down with glass-bottled Coca-Cola. We drank as many as we could before I lined up the empties for target prac-tice. Eventually, we headed back to his shop, where he gave me the grand tour—not that I really needed one. I already knew everyone who worked there: Sal, Paul, Marco, Tommy. They greeted me like I belonged, like I was one of them.

Being suspended and grounded didn't feel like a punishment. That day, it felt like the best damn thing that had ever happened to me.

Chapter Forty-One

ADRIANA

"A date?" Lucy practically choked on her martini, eyes wide with disbelief.

I pressed my lips together to keep from laughing and nodded.

"No, I need *every* single detail," she demanded, setting her glass down with a dramatic flourish.

I finally let my laughter slip free. "Well, I was working my shift, and he came in," I started, watching as Lucy leaned in closer. "And he told me he had finally ended things with Renee—*officially*. Then he said he wanted to take me out."

Lucy's eyes sparkled. "And what were his *exact* words?"

I smirked, shaking my head. "He said, 'I want you to be ready by six tomorrow night, because I'm taking you out.'"

Lucy gasped and clutched Angela's arm. "He didn't even ask her, Angela! He *told* her!"

Angela grinned, clinking her glass against Lucy's. "I just like that you've got him running around town like some love-struck fool."

"I do *not* have him running around—" I started, but Lucy cut me off.

"Oh, *please*," Lucy began. "I've known Joey for twenty years, and in that entire time, he's never been so enamored by someone.

Joey, who wouldn't settle down if his life depended on it. *Literally.* And you've walked in here, strung him along, and put some sort of spell on him."

Angela laughed. "She has put a spell on him, hasn't she? And it's about damn time."

I shook my head, my face warm. Lucy waved a hand. "Okay, but what are you going to wear?"

Angela's eyes lit up. "Oh, we're picking out her outfit." "You two are worse than teenagers sometimes." Angela smirked. "And you love us for it. Don't you?"

I sighed, but couldn't fight the smile that tugged at my lips.

That night at dinner, Antonio and I sat down to eat, the clinking of forks against plates filling the quiet space between us. I watched him for a moment, taking in the familiar features that made my heart ache with love—the wild curls of his brown hair that always seemed to have a mind of their own, the deep brown of his eyes that held a sharpness beyond his years, the sun-kissed warmth of his skin, and the freckles scattered across the bridge of his nose like tiny constellations. He was growing up too fast.

"What did you do with Joey today?" I finally asked, breaking the silence.

"*Oh,*" he said, reaching for his glass and taking a sip of water. "He worked me like a *dog*, Ma. You should probably not let me go back. It's practically child labor in his shop. I'd do better sweeping and stocking down at Davidson's."

I chuckled, shaking my head. "Hmm..." I hummed. "Did you learn your lesson?"

"Oh, absolutely," he said without hesitation.

"Good," I said, twirling my fork into the pasta I had made for dinner. I hesitated for a second before speaking again. "I wanted to talk to you about something."

"Yeah?" he said, looking up, waiting for me to continue. "Well, I thought I'd go into the city with Joey tomorrow night," I said carefully, watching his face for any sort of reaction. Antonio only shrugged and kept eating. "Yeah, okay. You should do that,

Ma. You deserve to be happy, and if Joey makes you happy, I'm cool with that."

I blinked, surprised by his easy acceptance. "Are you sure?"

He nodded, swallowing a bite of food. "Yeah, Ma. I already knew something was going on between you two."

"Oh, you did now?" I arched my brow.

He grinned, leaning back in his chair. "I'm almost an adult. I know *things*."

I laughed, shaking my head. He really thought he was grown. But as I looked at him—the sharpness of his jawline that hadn't been there a year ago, the confidence in his expression—I realized that in some ways, he was. And I couldn't help but be proud of the young man he was becoming.

"Just go easy on him." Antonio grinned, popping a bite of pasta into his mouth. "Joey's softer than he looks."

"Somehow, I highly doubt that," I said, raising a skeptical brow.

Antonio smirked. "Oh, and he's got the biggest, most sickening crush on you."

"He told you that?"

"Not exactly," he admitted with a shrug. "But I'm practically a man, Ma. I can tell."

I narrowed my eyes playfully. "Oh yeah? And how's that?"

Antonio grinned. "Do you see how he looks at you? I noticed it the day you stormed up to him at the diner."

I laughed. "No, I think I just scared him half to death. He probably thought I was some crazy woman and took pity on me because of it."

"Well, that too," he quipped, flashing a mischievous grin. "Which is why I said *go easy on him*."

I shook my head, still chuckling at the thought of Joey's bewildered face when I'd confronted him at the diner. "I'll keep that in mind," I said, sipping my wine.

"I'll probably just stay over at Enzo's," Antonio said.

"Michael's coming over too. I'll ride my bike back home in the afternoon, if that's okay."

"Sure," I said with a smile.

In Joey's presence, I didn't feel timid or small. And I had been desperate to reclaim that power. That day when I'd brought Joey back here and kissed him, watching how Joey's chest rose and fell as he stood across from me, let me know just how much power I held in my hands. His lips begged me to keep going, to fall into his trap and give him a part of myself I was guarding. I could tell by the look in his eyes that I had shaken something loose in him. I had reclaimed my power in the wake of that kiss and felt like I was becoming everything I wanted to become.

Chapter Forty-Two

JOEY

I had been losing my mind. Not sleepy. Just fucking lovesick for Adriana. Desperate for her lips, her touch, her scent. It was like a fever that wouldn't break, a thirst I could quench. I couldn't rest until I had her.

Luckily for me, the day had come.

I stood in my office, arms crossed, half-listening as Sal droned on about the invoices we'd sent out. "We're getting some complaints," he said, shifting on his feet. "It's raising eyebrows."

The inflated invoices. The extra cash we skimmed off businesses under our protection. Standard shit, nothing new. But if people were starting to talk, it could mean trouble.

I exhaled through my nose, rubbing my jaw as I leaned back against my desk. "Who's talking?"

"A couple of shop owners over in Brooklyn."

The moment I tried to think about handling business, my mind went right back to her. *Adriana*. She had taken over every inch of my brain, leaving no room for anything else. I checked my watch. I had a meeting with the florist before I picked her up.

"Handle it for me," I told Sal. He nodded, understanding what that meant. I grabbed my fedora and headed for the door.

I felt untouchable. Walking through my wholesale business in a brand-new, tailored, pinstripe suit, I adjusted my cufflinks, smoothing down the fabric as I strolled past my guys. Confidence dripped off me like cologne. I tipped my fedora onto my head, slid into my car, and pulled out slowly. The window was down, letting in the fresh spring air. Sinatra hummed through my speakers, my fingers drumming against the car door.

I pulled up to *La Rosa d'Italia*, the local flower shop tucked neatly between the diner and the shoe shiner. Through the large glass window, I spotted Rosa, the sweet old woman who had owned the place for as long as I could remember. She was hard at work, arranging flowers into beautiful arrangements.

I killed the engine and stepped out, the bell above the door jingling as I walked inside. Rosa looked up, her face lighting up as I stepped inside.

"Joey!" she beamed, walking around the counter with open arms. Her hands, small and soft, cupped my face like she'd done for the past twenty years.

I bent down, hugging her gently. "How you doing, Rosa?"

"Better now that I see you," she said, patting my cheek.

"What brings you in, dear?"

"I need some flowers. For someone special."

Rosa's eyes twinkled. "Oh? Well, do you know what sort of flowers she likes?"

"I don't," I admitted, running a hand down my tie. "But she needs something perfect."

"Well, tell me about her." Rosa grinned.

"Oh," I grinned like a child on Christmas, "she's strong. Resilient. Beautiful. She's perfect, Rosa."

Rosa tilted her head, thinking for a moment before her face lit up. "Oh, I know just the thing!" She patted my arm before shuffling off towards the back of the store. A moment later, she returned, holding a delicate lotus plant in both hands.

I raised a brow. "A lotus?"

She nodded, smiling. "The lotus is a symbol of rebirth and

growth. It rises from the mud, untouched by the dirt, blooming into something beautiful. Just like your special someone."

I looked down at the flower, the weight of her words settling deep in my chest. Rebirth. Growth. Adriana had been through hell, but she was still standing. Still fighting.

Yeah. This was the one.

Just as I stepped back into the beautiful spring air, the sun beating down on me, Renee came whipping into the parking lot like a bat out of hell, tires screeching as she jerked her car into park.

I exhaled, feeling the irritation flood my senses, but forced myself to remain calm as I placed the lotus carefully on the passenger seat and slid into the driver's side. I had barely reached for the gear shift when I saw her in my rearview mirror—standing directly behind my car, arms crossed, making damn sure I wasn't going anywhere.

I tossed my head back against the seat and let out a long, slow groan. She really knew how to ruin anything good for me.

Pushing the door open, I climbed out and stalked toward her. "You're not very bright, standing behind my car, Renee. What, are you asking to get run over?"

She let out a sharp, humorless hiss. "You wouldn't dare." She was right—I wouldn't. But still.

I pulled a cigarette from my pocket, lighting it up. "Are you gonna move anytime soon, or are you just trying to put on a show for the whole damn town?" I asked, taking a slow drag.

Renee's eyes burned into me as she crossed her arms tighter, hip cocked, lips pressed into a tight line. "In a hurry to take my replacement on a date? You couldn't wait to get rid of me, could you?"

I stared at her, saying nothing. It wasn't her business what I did. I let the silence stretch between us, inhaling deeply before blowing the smoke out slowly.

"You don't have anything to say for yourself?" she scoffed, shaking her head in disbelief.

No. I didn't.

I had always wanted my spot as boss of the family. Christopher was about to make me underboss before I got locked away for a decade, and then Vincent succeeded me. Renee didn't just hate me. She hated that I wouldn't bend for her. That she couldn't own me, control me, or manipulate me into submission. If she couldn't have me, she damn sure wasn't gonna stand by and watch me give myself to someone else.

Well, maybe she ought to close her fucking eyes—because I was about to give Adriana a hell of a lot more than a lotus plant and a pearl necklace.

I was so deep in my own head that I barely noticed Renee yelling. It was almost impressive, the way I had mastered dissociation in this life. I only snapped back when I felt her fists pounding against my chest. I let her get it out of her system, then calmly flicked my cigarette onto the pavement, stepped back, and slid into the driver's seat.

"You will fucking pay for this!" she shrieked, her voice shaking with fury as I threw the car into reverse.

She slammed her palms against the hood as I pulled away, her rage disappearing in my rearview mirror.

But I didn't look back.

I would pay for pissing her and Vincent off. But please let it be after tonight.

Chapter Forty-Three

ADRIANA

J oey stepped through the door, his tailored suit hugging his frame like it was made for him—and I was sure it was. In one hand, he carried a white lotus plant, its delicate petals untouched, and in the other, a small velvet box.

His eyes softened the moment they found me, and I knew I wasn't doing a thing to hide the longing in my own gaze. He always looked good, but knowing he wore this suit for me made him look even better—irresistible, even.

"You look perfect," he murmured. His eyes lingered on mine, and my heart flipped in response.

"Thank you," I said, my cheeks flushing under his steady gaze. "You look handsome. You might put the rest of the world to shame tonight."

A flicker of a grin tugged at the corner of his mouth as he stepped closer, his eyes drinking me in. "With you on my arm, they'll never stop looking, sweetheart."

Heat curled low in my stomach, but I held his gaze, matching his grin with one of my own.

He placed the lotus on the kitchen counter beside us, his fingers lingering on the petals. "Rosa picked this out for you down at the flower shop," he said. "She says the lotus is a symbol of growth. Apparently, when it rises from the mud, it comes out untouched by the dirt. Still beautiful. Still strong." His crystal eyes flickered back to mine. "Like you."

My heart stumbled over itself. I swallowed, reaching out to brush my fingers over the smooth petals. "You sure about that?" I asked.

Joey tilted his head, stepping even closer. "Never been more sure of anything in *all* my life."

My eyes studied him. He held up the velvet box. "I got you something else, too."

A slow smile tugged at my lips. I wasn't used to being spoiled, to having someone go out of their way just to give me something beautiful. But I had a feeling this kind of treatment would become second nature with Joey. I'd be lying if I said that didn't excite me.

With a man like him, I had a feeling gifts weren't just about luxury—they were about *possession. Protection.* A silent way of saying *you're mine.*

"Oh?" I tilted my head, my gaze flicking to the box in his hand. "What is it?"

His lips curved into a knowing smirk. "Turn around," he instructed.

I spun on my heels, lifting my hair to clear the nape of my neck. I felt the brush of his knuckles against my skin. His body pressed closer—close enough that his heat seeped into me. I was sure that was intentional, yet I couldn't bring myself to care.

I let my hair fall, my fingers trailing over the cool pearls now resting against my skin. A smirk played at my lips as I turned to meet his gaze.

"Beautiful," he hummed. His eyes roamed over me, and I couldn't help but shiver under his approval. It was almost like he was photographing me in his memory, so he'd never forget this moment.

"I love it," I admitted, letting my fingers trace the delicate strand. "Thank you."

"No need to thank me," he said, smirking as he stepped closer, erasing the last bit of space between us. "It suits you— classy and beautiful, just like you."

His words sent a warm rush through me. I met his gaze, my chest tightening at the intensity in his eyes. I leaned in, pressing a soft kiss to his cheek. His skin was warm beneath my lips, his scent —smoke and cologne—wrapping around me, dangerous and addictive.

I knew if we didn't leave now, we wouldn't leave at all. I grabbed his hand, lacing my fingers through his, and tugged him toward the door. "Come on," I said, forcing a teasing smile. "If we don't leave now, we never will."

This was our second time on the Staten Island ferry. This time, I wasn't running away from anywhere. I was heading to Manhattan with him. And this time, I wasn't afraid. I wasn't thinking about anything other than this moment with him. The beauty of the ferry at nighttime struck me in a way it never had before—the dark water glistening under the moonlight, the city calling in the distance with its lights shimmering.

"It's beautiful tonight," I murmured, half to myself and half to Joey.

"Yeah," he agreed, but he wasn't looking at the skyline—he was looking at me. "Sure is."

A smile tugged at my lips as I recalled, "Do you remember that night I saw you here?"

"I remember." His eyes met mine, his hand pressing against my own. "But I don't like to think about that version of you." He exhaled, his gaze searching mine. "Look at you now. The woman you were that night—she's just a shadow of who you are today. They're not even the same person."

I wanted to kiss him so badly. The need surged through me, fierce and overwhelming, shutting out every other thought in my mind. Every word he said, every glance my way, every smile that tugged on his lips pulled me closer to the edge of no return. And I didn't care if anyone saw. I didn't care what they thought of it. I wanted him to kiss me. My eyes linger on him—on the curve of his mouth, the way the moonlight softened his features, the intensity in his eyes that seemed to hold only me. His hand brushed mine, and I nearly forgot how to breathe. Every nerve in my body went taut, waiting, aching for more.

The ferry's horn blared in the distance, snapping me back to reality. My eyes fluttered towards the glittery skyline of New York City ahead of us.

Chapter Forty-Four
ADRIANA

Joey hailed a cab, and we sped through the streets until we reached the Theatre on 44th Street, where Look After Lulu lit up the marquee. "A Broadway show?" I asked, barely able to contain my excitement.

"Only the best for you," he said, a soft smile tugging at his lips. He stood on the curb, helping me out of the back of the cab. I pushed aside the nagging thought about how he never bothered to pay the driver, and how the cab driver didn't even expect it. It was a detail I couldn't ignore, yet I chose to. I silenced that voice in my head, refusing to see him for anything other than the man standing right in front of me—the one whose presence consumed my every thought.

He led the way into the building, as everyone we passed greeted him like he was some sort of celebrity, as if he were JFK himself. We settled into the plush, front-row seats. Out of the corner of my eye, I caught Joey watching me instead of the show.

"Watch the show, Joey," I whispered, nudging him with my elbow.

"I am," he replied, his gaze steady on me. Heat crept into my cheeks as I turned my attention back to the performance.

I hadn't taken the time to appreciate the beauty of New York

City when I first arrived that night. I was too consumed by fear, too broken to notice much. But tonight, I saw it all—Times Square in all its glitz and glamour. I noticed how people stepped aside as we walked hand in hand. Men tipped their hats to him, and women glanced our way.

In this world, Joey was someone—powerful, untouchable.

But in that moment, with my arm wrapped around his, I felt more powerful than I'd ever felt before.

"Thank you. Tonight has been incredible," I said, turning to face him as we strolled down the sidewalk. He gave me a soft smile before he stopped in front of a sparkling sign that read, *21 Club.*

One of Manhattan's finest restaurants.

The doorman opened the door for us, and the waitress guided us to our seats without so much as a second glance. He didn't need to say a word—they knew who he was. And I knew it, too. Joey pulled out my chair for me, and I settled into the plush seat, catching a faint whiff of his aftershave as he leaned close. It made me dizzy. Hungry.

The way the waiter treated him, with such admiration and respect, would've made even the Queen of England jealous.

Oh, Joey was a charmer. He could charm the pants off a snake, and I had no doubt that tonight, I'd be his next victim.

"You know if you're going to pull out all the stops on the first date, you're setting the bar very high for yourself," I told him.

He chuckled, his grin widening. "Sweetheart, this is the first date. Not the last."

I smirked, arching a brow. "Confident, are we?"

Joey leaned in slightly, his fingertips brushing my leg. "Just stating the facts." His touch burned through the fabric of my dress, lingering and making me lightheaded.

Joey knew exactly who he was and what he was capable of. I searched for signs of the danger I had learned to expect in powerful men, but they didn't exist in Joey.

At least, not this version of Joey. The one he only revealed to me.

Chapter Forty-Five

JOEY

I walked Adriana up to her front door. Every step I took came with a silent prayer for an invite inside.

She turned the key and stepped inside, leaving me lingering on the front steps like a hopeful fool. She looked back at me over her shoulder, a teasing smile curving her lips, her dark eyes smoldering with desire.

I knew that look—it was the one I'd been silently praying for since we pulled into the driveway.

I didn't waste time. I didn't hesitate. I stepped inside and slammed the door shut behind me. The small amount of restraint I had was now gone, shredded to pieces by the look she'd given me. I grabbed her face, my fingers threading with the hairs at her nape, tilting her head back. My lips hovered inches from hers, torn between tasting the sweetness of her mouth and desperate to taste every other part of her.

Conflicted. Desperate. Needy. Things I was not used to feeling were the only feelings consuming me. I clung to the last shred of control I had left in me. Slow and soft, or hard and rough —I couldn't decide.

Adriana's breath hitched as she stared up at me, her lips parted, and that was all the confirmation I needed. My chest heaved, my hands tightening in her hair as I forced myself to speak instead of letting instinct take over completely.

"Sweetheart." Her name rolled off my tongue like a prayer. "Tell me to stop."

But she didn't. Instead, she closed the distance between us, her mouth finding mine in a kiss so consuming it knocked what little control I had straight out of me. Her hands gripped the lapels of my jacket, pulling me so close I could feel the world tilt on its axis. My lips trailed from her mouth to her jaw, then down her neck. I didn't just want to feel her body.

I wanted her soul.

The weight of that realization slowed me, making me pull back just a bit. My forehead resting against hers as we both caught our breath. I stared into her eyes, needing her to steady me.

"Are you sure?" My voice was rough, almost desperate. If she had any second thoughts, now was the time. Because there would be no going back after this.

"I'm sure."

"Turn around," I said.

Before the words had a chance to sink in, I took matters into my own hands, gripping her hips and spinning her to face away from me. I swept her hair to one side, exposing the smooth curve of her neck. I couldn't help but smile as I watched goosebumps appear across her skin.

I unclasped the pearl necklace, placing it on the kitchen counter beside us. My fingers traced the line of her collarbone, drawing a shiver from her before I leaned in to press a tender kiss there. She sighed softly, her hand rising to cup the side of my face. My fingers moved to her zipper, sliding it down slowly. I stepped back, needing to see this moment unfold in real time. The dress slipped from her frame, pooling around her ankles.

And what a fucking sight.

"Adriana," I breathed out. She turned, meeting my darkened gaze, her eyes mirroring the same desire pooling in mine. Her hands reached for me, pulling me closer.

"I want you so bad, Joey," she breathed. Before I could fully process my actions, she was laid back on the couch beneath me. My mouth trailed down her bare, taut skin, tasting every inch of her, my hunger insatiable for her.

My hands parted her thighs as I settled between them. She arched her back with a sharp gasp when my hot mouth attached to her aching core, the sound only driving me to consume her entirely. One hand gripped the edge of the couch, the other tangled in my hair, once neatly styled but now a wild mess.

I didn't stop. I couldn't stop until I felt her body trembling, her breath uneven, her chest rising and falling in jagged motions. Her skin became flushed, her moans spilled out in a symphony that was just for my ears. She was unraveling before me, and the sheer sight of her in the aftermath of that first orgasm brought a satisfied smirk to my lips. She lay there, chest heaving, trying to come down from the high I had given her. And I knew she was mine. *Only mine.*

"I love you," I said.

Her eyes met mine, and she smiled at me. "I love you, too."

A grin tugged at my lips. "Yeah? This is what I had to do for you to say it?" I teased as I moved between her trembling thighs. "You could've just told me. I would've done it the first time I'd seen you."

The sound of her laughter rang out like music to my ears. "But you didn't love me then."

I shook my head, brushing my lips against her neck. "That's where you're wrong," I murmured, my fingers skimming down her body. "I've loved you since the moment I saw you. And I've wanted you long before I even knew you existed." Her hands gripped my shoulders, her fingers digging in as my touch teased her.

I kissed her lips again. "Are you ready for me? Because after this, you'll never belong to anyone else. You'll be mine. *Forever.*" Her body trembled under my touch, her eyes rolling back as I pushed my fingers further into her, refusing to relent. "I want you to say it," I demanded. "Tell me you're mine."

Her head fell back, her cry of release filling the room. "Yes!" she shouted. "I'm yours!"

I smirked as I pulled my fingers from her slick core. The second I felt her wrap around me, I knew I had given her my soul. There was no going back now. She owned me, heart and soul, and I'd never be the same after this. Adriana would be my undoing, and I'd gladly let her.

Her arms and legs wrapped around me, pulling me in closer, urging me to keep going. Even if I wanted to let myself go, I couldn't—not yet. The way her body responded to mine, the way she held onto me, it was almost too much to bear.

But fuck, did it feel damn good.

The sight beneath me only confirmed what I already knew—this was where she was meant to be. Beneath me, and me above her, the two of us so close we couldn't get any closer. I didn't want this to ever end. My hand gripped her face, guiding her gaze to mine. Her brown eyes met mine, glazed over. Her lips parted as I drove into her relentlessly, each thrust sending us further and further into our high. This wasn't just passion—it was a deliberate breaking, a shattering of any walls left between us. And I planned to do it again and again, for the rest of our lives.

Her nails dug into the skin of my back, marking me as hers. Her breath came in ragged gasps, her body trembling beneath me. Then I felt it—the way she clenched around me. She cried out, her voice rising like a hymn to the heavens.

A second later, I let go, my world shattering into stars. My head dropped to the curve of her neck, resting there as I struggled to catch my breath. Her scent clung to me, and I welcomed it.

I wanted to freeze time—her body pressed against mine. We were as close as two souls could be, and yet it wasn't close enough. I never wanted to let go.

As I lay there, still breathing heavily, Adriana was cradled in my arms, like she was made for me. I wanted her more than I had ever wanted anything else in my lifetime. She was mine now. I didn't care about the repercussions. I was already far too gone to even try to care.

Everything before this night felt like it belonged to another lifetime. Now, all I could think about was her. She had me for as long as Vincent would let me live. I'd let her drag me to hell if it meant she was by my side. But I would never let her go now.

Chapter Forty-Six

ANTONIO

I stood in front of Vincent's door, my stomach knotted so tight it felt like I might be sick. The cool morning air did nothing to stop the sweat gathering at the nape of my neck, and my pulse hammered against my ribs. I wasn't one to usually cry, but my eyes burned anyway.

I'd spent days talking myself up to this moment. Telling myself I could do it. That I would do it. I was going to tell Vincent I was done—I couldn't do this anymore. But saying it in my head was one thing. Saying it to his face was something else entirely.

Before I could knock, the door swung open. Vincent stood there. "You gonna stand there all day, or are you coming inside?" he snapped.

I flinched, my breath catching in my throat. This was it. No turning back now. Forcing my legs to move, I stepped inside. The door slammed shut behind me, the sound making me cringe.

"Sit down," Vincent ordered. I obeyed, sinking onto the couch, my fingers digging into my knees as I tried to keep still.

He stared me down, waiting, probably enjoying how I squirmed under his gaze. "Well?"

I swallowed hard. "I don't have anything to report, sir."
"Nothing to report?" His voice rose in a thunderous roar.

"You practically live with the man, and you got nothing?"

My palms slicked with sweat, my mind scrambling for something—anything—that would get me out of this. "He doesn't do
anything," I stammered. "I would tell you if I had something, but
all he does is drive around town and smoke cigarettes with Paul
and Marco."

Vincent's jaw tensed. "Do you understand what's at stake
here?"

My throat tightened. My mouth went dry. I nodded. My life
was at stake.

He exhaled sharply, shaking his head. "I don't think you do."

He stood slowly, and I shrank back into the couch. My body
went rigid as he loomed over me, his presence suffocating. And
then he pulled out the revolver. The barrel leveled straight at my
face. My hands shot up instinctively, trembling in the air. I
squeezed my eyes shut, bracing for the blow I'd never live to feel.
"At what point were you going to mention that Joey works with
the feds?" he shouted.

"I—I don't know anything about that! I swear!" I choked out.
My hands shook as I held them up, desperation seeping into every
word. "I'd tell you if I did!"

"You don't walk until I say so," he growled. "Matter of fact,
when I say jump, you don't ask how high. You just fucking jump.
Or the next time you come here empty-handed, you *won't* leave."

My chest rose and fell in sharp, panicked breaths. Slowly, I
cracked one eye open, watching as he lowered the gun.

"Understand?" he asked.

I managed a shaky nod, still unable to find my voice.

"Good." He jerked his chin toward the door. "Get the hell
out of here."

I didn't need to be told twice. I pushed myself up so fast I
nearly tripped, stumbling over my own feet as I bolted for the

door. I barely got it open before I was outside, leaping onto my bike. My legs burned as I pedaled, my heart slamming against my ribs.

At this rate, if I didn't end up a big-time baseball player—or get myself killed by Vincent before I turned fourteen—I'd be a damn professional cyclist with all the pedaling I'd been doing.

Chapter Forty-Seven
JOEY

I t had been a week since I'd taken Adriana on that date. A week since I'd made love to her. And I couldn't help but think it was the best damn week of my life. We were two grown adults, but in love like two school kids. Vincent hadn't put a bullet in me, so I guess luck was on my side. But honestly, I didn't care either way—I'd risk my life to be with Adriana. I needed Adriana like lungs need air. Without her, I feared I'd just fall apart. When I look at her, I see our future. She sees me for who I am. And I see her for who she is. She doesn't care about what people say I am. Because with her, I can show her who I've always wanted to be.

I'm done paying my debt with my soul; whatever that meant, I'd live with it. Adriana's been through hell, and I'm no saint, but I'd sell my soul to the devil just to have her. I would be her peace. And she would be mine.

She sat across from me in the booth. *The Wise Guy* was filled to the brim, but it felt like it was just her and me. Her navy, tea-length dress hugged her waist, the pearls I'd gifted her resting around her neck. I couldn't take my eyes off her, couldn't stop thinking about just before this, when I had her in my office. And I'd have her every day after this.

"Do you like it?" I asked, motioning to the bottle of Chianti on the table. She nodded, her lips curving into a smile.

"It's really good," she said, taking another sip.

I'd spent my whole life doing what other people told me. Following the rules I didn't make up. But she was the only light in this lifetime. I'd burn down the world if I had to, taking everyone out in my path just to be with her.

"Joey, there's something on my mind lately," she said. "What is it?"

"I don't want Antonio to ever be a part of that part of your life." Her eyes locked onto mine.

"I would never let that happen. I don't want any of my kids to live the life I've lived. I've seen enough of what this world does to people. To families. I swore, long ago, that if I ever had a family, my kids would have everything I didn't. I want them to have something better than I ever had. I will do whatever it takes, Adriana. Whatever it takes to give them that life. I won't let them fall into this mess I'm stuck in. Not if I can help it."

I meant every word of that promise. I refused to let it continue. My sins die with me. I've seen too many people get swallowed whole by this world, their lives destroyed. But not my kids. I'll break every rule and do whatever it takes, just to make sure they don't get pulled into the same darkness. They deserve a future I can't even begin to imagine for myself—a life free of fear, free of bloodshed. That's the future I'll give them.

Adriana had walked over to the bar to talk to Lucy and Angela. She glowed with happiness, her laughter spilling over the music. "Joey," Paul said, snapping me out of my thoughts. I hadn't even realized he had slipped into the booth where Adriana had previously been sitting.

I glanced at him, his eyes focused on his fingers as they fidgeted on top of the table. He never fidgeted. Something was off. "What's going on?" I asked.

"Hector just told me," he started, but the words seemed like they were physically hard to get out, "that they called a sit-down with the boss. You and Christopher in Manhattan."

A sit-down with Christopher wasn't a conversation. It wasn't a friendly check-in. A sit-down meant decisions were made behind closed doors—decisions that were final. Sometimes you walked in and never walked out.

My eyes narrowed. "When?"

"Tomorrow night," Paul said. I knew it had to have been Vincent's idea to have Paul deliver the news to me—for my best friend to deliver the news, I may have twenty-four hours left alive.

I couldn't pretend I wasn't afraid. Only a fool isn't scared of what happens when Vincent decides you're no longer useful. But I wasn't going to run. Not from Vincent, not from my choices. If they were going to take me out, they'd have to look me in the eye when they did it. If tomorrow were the end, at least I'd have the satisfaction of knowing I lived for something, even if it was just for a little while.

"Paul, promise me something?" His eyes met mine. He knew what I was about to ask, even before I asked it. "Promise me you'll take care of Adriana and Antonio if I don't return."

Paul wasn't the emotional type—not any more than I was—but there was something in his expression I hadn't seen in all the years we'd run the streets side by side. It was pain. The lives we'd chosen, the men we'd become—there was no outrunning any of it.

"You know I'm good for it, Joey," he said. "Good," I said, "that's all I needed to hear."

Paul's lips twitched in a faint, grim smile. "Don't make me keep that promise, yeah?"

"You won't have to, if I can help it," I smirked.

But we both knew how this could end. Every sinner has their day. We could only hope mine wasn't tomorrow night.

Chapter Forty-Eight
ADRIANA

Joey parked in front of an estate, cutting the engine off. I tilted my head, confusion dancing in my eyes. "Where are we?" I asked.

He grinned widely, stepping out of the car. I followed, meeting him at the hood. He reached out, taking my hand in mine. "Come on," he said, leading me up the pathway. He pulled a set of keys from his pocket.

"Joey," I whispered. "What's going on?"

He squeezed my hand, turning the key and twisting the knob, pushing the door wide open. He turned to me, a smile plastered all over his face. "Ladies first," he said, stepping aside so I could walk in first.

I crossed the threshold of the house, my eyes scanning the grand foyer. The ceilings were high, the floors marble, and a sweeping staircase with iron railings leading upstairs. Crystal and brass chandeliers hung throughout the downstairs. The place was completely empty—no furniture in sight. And I knew what was happening before I even asked him.

"What is this, Joey?" I asked anyway.

He bridged the gap between us, slipping an arm around my

waist. "It's ours," he said. "Our house. For you. For Antonio. For us. It's supposed to be a fresh start for all of us."

My hand flew to my gaping mouth, tears pooling in my eyes. "I told you I'd take care of you, didn't I? I meant every word, Adriana. I'll *always* take care of you."

He bent down, scooping me up in his arms. My feet left the ground, and my arms wrapped around him. Our laughter echoed off the walls. "It's perfect," I said.

He set me down, his hand finding mine as he tugged me toward the living room. It was huge. Velvet curtains hung, parting to reveal the backyard. I rushed to the window, my gaze fixed on the lush view. I couldn't wrap my head around the fact that this was mine. *Ours.*

"Let me show you the best part," Joey murmured. He stood behind me, his hands gripping my hips as his lips grazed the exposed part of my neck. He guided me forward like this until we reached the kitchen. He spun me around, and I draped my arms over his shoulders, our lips meeting again.

"You know, most people get engaged, get married, buy a house, and have babies." I grinned against his lips.

He smirked, pulling me closer, his voice rough against my lips. "We're not most people, Adriana. We make our own damn rules."

There was something powerful about those words. *We make our own rules.* I knew Joey lived by his own code, but now, so did I.

I tugged his lips back down to meet mine. My tongue slipped between his lips to taste him.

"You like that?" He chuckled, his forehead resting against mine. "You want to make your own damn rules? Feel powerful, like you're in control?"

Yeah, starting now.

My fingers trailed down his body, and his eyes darkened the lower I went. I flashed an innocent smile, batting my lashes as I undid his trousers. "Adriana," he murmured. "What are you doing?"

"You know what I'm doing."

I pushed his trousers down, watching as they fell to the cool marble floor beneath us. I followed them down, sinking to my knees. I held all the control, and I could see in his glazed eyes that he was aware of this, as well.

He sucked in a sharp breath as I wrapped my fingers around the base of him, guiding him into my mouth and pumping my hand up and down his shaft. My eyes never left his as I took him in, inch by inch, savoring the feeling of him growing harder against my tongue.

I loved watching him let his guard crumble to the floor. Just for me. He let out a low groan, his body falling back against the kitchen counter.

Our kitchen counter.

"Oh fuck," he rasped. Tears pooled at the corners of my eyes, blurring the already hazy world around me. His hand tangled in my hair, using it as leverage, pushing my head back and forth, a brutal, intoxicating rhythm against the hard length of him. My hands dug into the muscles of his thighs.

His eyes locked onto mine, the distance between us shrinking to practically nothing. His breath came out hot and ragged. He was so close I could smell his musky scent. A desperate, aching hunger pulsed low in my belly. I pushed myself up from the marble floor, untangling myself from the fabric of my dress. A smirk danced along my lips as I saw him braced against the counter, knuckles white where his fingers gripped the cool surface, muscles in his forearms straining. His eyes, once blue, were now full of lust and desire—they burned straight through me.

He moved before I could even process my next move. His hand reached out, the back of his fingers brushing against the nape of my neck, pulling my body closer until my lips met his.

Our tongues tangled in a hungry, desperate dance. A moan escaped from deep within my chest, lost within our kiss.

His arms lifted me, placing me on the countertop. His hands

gripped my hips, and he dropped to his knees. My head fell back, a sigh escaping my lips as his hot breath fanned against my inner thigh, where his stubble brushed against my skin.

His mouth latched onto me, claiming my slick core as his own. My legs threatened to tighten around his head. My hands flew out, desperate for stability, reaching for something solid as he lapped at my core. I tugged at the back of his head, pressing him even closer, feeling the pull in the pit of my stomach. A cry, half-pleasure, half-surrender, tore out from my throat.

He rose to his feet, leaving me no chance to recover. His hands nudged my legs apart, making way for him. Before I could process anything, we were connected with a single thrust forward. His hand cradled my breast, finding my nipple, tugging it between his teeth. My hand found its way to the back of his head, clinging to him in any way possible. His thrusts were so unforgiving. As if this was the last time he would ever have the chance to make love to me.

"Joey!" I yelped, the sound torn from my throat as the tightening in the pit of my stomach heightened. It was the prelude to the storm, the gathering of an orgasm that threatened to shatter me. My fingers clenched onto the cool surface beneath me.

He didn't hear me. He didn't falter. He didn't pull back. He just kept going, the rhythm of his movements frantic, his hand firm on my lower back, urging me closer. Harder. Faster. Each thrust was sharp. Deliberate. I could feel the muscles in his back contract with each surge forward. A wave of pure, Earth-shattering bliss ripped through my body. I cried out again, spilling over the cold, hard counter.

I reached for him, my hand finding the rough stubble of his jaw. I pulled his face towards mine, forcing his eyes—dilated and dark with lust—to meet mine. His lips were on mine. Not gentle, not tentative, but possessive. Demanding. His mouth moved against mine, sucking, claiming, pulling me into him.

"I love you," he murmured, his breath mingling with mine. His body, damp and glistening with sweat, was pressed against me. "Tell me," he demanded. "Tell me, Adriana." He wanted to hear it, to witness the effect he had on me, to claim the words that were struggling to escape my lips.

I tried, but my vocal cords were useless. His hips surged forward, sharp and insistent thrusts that stole my breath away. I watched as a smirk curled at his lips. His thumb found its way between us, teasing and tormenting my heat. My head fell back, my eyes rolling back.

All I could do was silently praise God for this man.

"I love you!" I shouted, the words escaping my lips, free from the confines of my throat. "I love you!" I shouted again.

I felt the warmth of his release fill me. His body collapsed against mine as my arms wrapped around him, holding him close. Tight.

"What a great way to break in the new counters." His chuckle rumbled against my chest. He lifted his head, his eyes locking with mine, meeting the smile that stretched across my face.

"Welcome home, honey," I teased.

"Is this the kind of greeting I'll be getting when I come home every day?" he asked, his hands helping me off the counter.

We gathered our clothes and got dressed, settling into his car. We lingered in the silence outside, just gazing upon the place we would call home. I waited for him to pull out of the driveway, but he didn't move, didn't reverse. His eyes met mine, and he reached across the console, his hand gripping mine.

"I need to tell you something," he said. "And I need you to listen to me." A chill ran through me as I nodded, waiting. "Tomorrow night, I've got a meeting," he began, pausing as though the words pained him. "I don't know how it's going to end. But everything I have left—it's yours. Paul and Marco will come by after and show you where the money's stashed. They'll look after you. I made sure of it."

I hadn't noticed the tears spilling down my face until he stopped speaking, and my sobs were all that could be heard, his head dipping low like he couldn't bear to look at me. "What do you mean if something happens to you?" I choked.

His eyes lifted, locking onto mine. That knowing look shattered me. I couldn't believe this. I should have known the day would come. They would take him from me. "No," I sobbed. "No, Joey. They can't take you from me."

He reached for me, cupping my face in his palms. I clung to his shirt, desperate to keep him tethered to me. *Tangible. Present. Alive.*

"We can run," I begged.

He pressed his lips to my forehead, his breath warm, but his words ice cold. "No, we can't."

"Then I won't let you go!" I protested.

He sighed, shaking his head. "I'm just preparing you for the worst-case scenario," he said.

"You're saying that because you know it's going to happen!" I cried out.

He sighed, tugging his lower lip between his teeth. "I love you," he said, his voice threatening to break. "I've never known love before you. And if I have to go—whether tomorrow or fifty years from now—I'll die a happy man, because of you."

Chapter Forty-Nine

JOEY

I adjusted the cuffs of my shirt, my fingertips betraying me by their slight tremor. I straightened my jacket, glancing in the mirror once more. If tonight went sideways, I wanted to look like a man. My heartbeat drummed against my ribcage, a reminder that I was still breathing. For now, at least.

Was this the end of the road for me? The thought curled in the pit of my stomach.

No.

I can't write my own fate. It's not in my hands anymore. And thinking like that could get a guy killed faster than any bullet.

The gun strapped beneath my waistband felt heavier tonight. I didn't intend to use it tonight; that would be suicide. But in a world of strict rules, carrying it wasn't an option—it was insurance. I always swore I'd never beg for my life or go out like some rat huddled up in a corner.

But it was time.

I reached for the small gold cross hanging from a thin chain around my neck, rubbing it between my thumb and forefinger.

It felt like the only anchor left. I kissed it and slipped it back under my shirt. I wasn't a God-fearing man on most days. But today wasn't most days.

Staten Island felt colder tonight despite it being summertime. The world looked different when you weren't sure you'd still be part of it by sunrise. If tonight were my last night, I would go down in my best suit, with my memories of Adriana still fresh in my mind. I would die standing for everything I believed in. That's what real men do.

Once I arrived at the warehouse where the meeting was taking place, Hector was waiting for me outside. His expression was cold. Detached. "I'll need your gun," he said.

I slipped the weapon from the waistband of my pants and handed it over. He took it as his gaze locked on mine. There wasn't a hint of malice in his eyes, but that didn't stop the stray thought that crossed my mind.

What if Hector used my own gun against me the second I walked through those doors?

I pushed the thought aside, forcing my shoulders to stay square. It's amazing how you notice your own breath—how in tune you become with your body—when you're unsure if it'll still be breathing in the next few minutes.

Hector opened the doors, and I stepped inside.

As soon as I saw who was waiting for me, my pulse spiked. It wasn't just Christopher. Vincent sat next to him, his jaw clenched like he was daring me to slip up. Marco sat next to Vincent. But it was Paul, sitting stiffly at the far end of the table, who caught my attention. He couldn't even look me in the eyes.

Paul was the closest thing to a brother I'd ever had. We both knew the stakes of this game. If I were being set up for a fall, they would force Paul to pull the trigger—the weight of killing me rested on his shoulders. And if he didn't, then they'd take us both down.

I'd already told him he couldn't go down for me. He had too much to lose, and I wasn't going to let him throw his life away for mine. That's how this life worked. He was the only brother I ever had, and if the cards fell that way, I could live with him doing what he needed to do to survive. I'd rather it be him than Vincent.

Christopher was seated at the head of the table, watching me. I could feel the weight of every pair of eyes in the room. I stopped in the middle of the floor, standing tall despite the tension curling in my gut, and waited for my fate to be delivered.

"Joey, why don't you sit down?" Christopher said, gesturing to the chair opposite him.

Even Vincent's head snapped toward him, his brows furrowed like he couldn't believe what he was hearing. And honestly, neither could I. That was the last thing I expected—a polite invitation to take a seat at the table.

But I didn't hesitate. I didn't question his authority. That'd be signing my own death certificate. I moved forward and lowered myself into the chair across from him, keeping my expression steady despite the knot forming in my chest.

"I've been informed you're working with law enforcement," Christopher began. "I could have placed the hit as soon as I heard the news, but I *couldn't* believe it. I wanted to hear it from your own mouth."

"I'm not working with law enforcement," I admitted, but Vincent cut me off before I could finish.

"He's a lying piece of garbage! Kill him and get it over with!" he barked, full of pure rage. The same rage his daughter possessed.

Christopher didn't even look at him. "Sit down, or I'll have you removed," he warned. I smirked inwardly to myself, watching Vincent lower back into his seat like a dog with its tail tucked between its legs.

"Law enforcement works for me on occasion," I said. "NYPD Detective Benjamin Hudson—he's someone I met when I was at Rikers. He did me a solid back then, and we've kept in touch since I've been out."

I knew I'd sealed my fate. I'd just confessed to something no one in this room could forgive, but I'd rather go down telling the truth than let Vincent write my story for me.

"What exactly does this cop help you with?" Christopher asked.

"Intel, background checks—he keeps an eye on things from the inside and lets me know if the feds are sniffing around any of our business deals," I said. "But he'll do anything I tell him to." Vincent leaned forward. "We can't bend the rules for him, Christopher. He's broken rule five—no involvement with law enforcement. If we let this slide, we might as well burn this family to the ground. How can we be sure this cop won't flip

and take Joey down, dragging all of us with him?"

Christopher turned his gaze back to me. "How do you know he won't betray you?"

I met his eyes, refusing to flinch. "How do you know anyone won't betray you?" I shot back.

The tables could always turn, and I was ready to face that. "I don't know if he'd turn on me," I admitted, "but I've known Ben for ten years, and he's proven his loyalty over and over. He's led the NYPD on wild goose chases, making them think they could nail us, only to destroy any evidence they managed to gather. He's the reason we're still standing."

"Do you think I should kill you, Joey?" Christopher asked calmly.

"I don't think that's my call to make. But I understand if you have to pull the trigger," I replied. "I broke rule number five, knowing full well what I was doing. I twisted it to fit my own moral code—convinced myself I was doing what was best for this family. But I realize now that's not my place. I don't make the rules. I obey them. And when I break them, there's a price to pay. I've always known that. This is my family. The only one I've ever known. So, if you have to kill me, I understand. My only request is to let me stand, and I want Paul to do it."

I heard Paul exhale, a breath he must've been holding for far too long. I knew he didn't want to do it—but there was no way in hell I'd give Vincent the satisfaction.

No one spoke. The silence in the room was almost deafening.

"I want to meet the cop," Christopher finally said.

"I can bring him to you," I offered, grasping at the chance to stay alive.

"I know where to find him," Vincent interrupted. "Kill this rat, and I'll bring the cop to you by tomorrow morning."

Christopher didn't even glance Vincent's way. "When can you make it happen?" he asked me.

"Tomorrow," I said. *One more day to be alive.* I couldn't do that to Adriana—return only to leave her wondering if I'd come back alive again. "Paul will have him delivered to you."

Christopher nodded. "You're leaving here tonight, Joey. Rule number five will have exceptions."

"*Exceptions?*" Vincent snarled. "You'd make exceptions for this dirtbag?"

Christopher's gaze snapped to Vincent. "Rule number two," he said. "Respect the boss. Any disrespect will not be tolerated."

Vincent's face twisted with anger, but he said nothing. But it was just this: a noise sounded outside. Hector whipped his head toward the source, gun drawn. He threw the doors open, scanning for the threat. Around me, everyone had their guns loaded and raised, ready for action—except me. My hands were empty. That's what I meant about guns being insurance: a necessity to stay alive.

"Get me out of here, Hector!" Christopher barked. Hector and Vincent sprang into action, escorting him out while the others moved to secure the perimeter.

Somehow, my life had been spared. I spotted my gun, which Hector had left behind, and tucked it into the waistband of my pants. Marco and Paul rushed out, leaving me standing alone. But nothing could scare me more than what I'd already survived in that room.

Chapter Fifty

JOEY

I parked outside Ben's house, the driver's side window rolled down as I took a slow drag from my cigarette.

A moment later, the front door swung open, and Ben walked out, straightening the collar of his crisp button-down. "Decided to get dressed up?" I teased, smirking as he approached.

Ben shot me a look as he slid into the passenger seat. "Aren't you the one who said if you're gonna be killed, make sure you go down in your Sunday best?"

I let out a low chuckle. "Yeah, guess I did say that." I flicked ash out the window before glancing at him. "Then again, maybe you were hoping Lucy would be there. Just a piece of advice—don't let him in on that dirty little secret you're harboring. You know, the fact that you've been screwing his daughter for years now."

Ben let out an amused snort, shaking his head. "You know what? I think you're in the wrong profession. With all this warmth and wisdom, you would've made a wonderful psychiatrist." I scoffed, pressing my foot to the gas as we pulled onto the road. "Never thought you'd be the one chauffeuring me to my potential execution," he muttered as I drove toward Christopher's house.

"Need some advice from someone who *hasn't* been executed yet?" I shot him a glance. "It's all in how you think. You tell yourself you're gonna make it out alive—you probably will."

"Hmph," Ben grunted. "Are we talking manifestation here? Because if that's the case, I'm manifesting myself a bulletproof vest."

"Now *that's* the spirit, Benny!" I teased, giving his shoulder a shove. "Come on, show me a smile. First impressions mean a lot to the boss." He tried to stifle a grin, but that one got him. He let out a chuckle, shaking his head.

To be honest, I had no idea if either of us would be walking out of that house today. But I sure as hell wasn't gonna tell *him* that.

I pulled up in front of Christopher's estate as Ben and I got out of the car. We made our way to the front door and knocked. Christopher opened it almost immediately. His mouth didn't move, but the cold, calculating look in his eyes said everything we needed to know. He turned and led us through the house. We followed him out to the back patio, where he settled into a chair and began lighting a cigar, the smoke curling up into the hot air.

He studied Ben with a hard, calculating stare, as though he could see through him—strip away the layers and find the truth beneath.

"So tell me, officer—can you be trusted?" he asked.

Ben leaned back in his chair, his eyes never leaving Christopher's. "My badge might not mean much to you, but it can open just about any door you need it to. It gets me information others can't touch. And I've been doing business with Joey for a decade —I've made no mistakes. So, yes, I can be trusted."

"Joey trusts you, but that doesn't mean shit to me," Christopher spat. "I'm not concerned with what's been. I'm concerned with what's coming. This family's built on trust and loyalty, and I don't need someone who thinks they can play both sides."

"Well, that's great. Because I stand right where you need me to. I've been walking the line for years, and I've never crossed it.

Not a single time. I'm trustworthy because I know where my loyalties lie."

Christopher exhaled a cloud of smoke. "How am I supposed to believe that? You were supposed to be loyal to your badge, but you've done nothing but the opposite. How do I know you won't turn on us, too?"

Ben leaned forward, resting his forearms on the table. "You don't. You don't know, just like I don't know if you'll decide tomorrow that I'm more of a liability than an asset. Trust is a gamble. But what you do know is my track record. Ten years, not a single misstep. Not one reason for Joey—or anyone—to doubt me. I don't play both sides."

Christopher's eyes flickered between Ben and me before settling back on him. "Well, I suppose you've got a point. But just know this—one mistake, and there's no coming back. You fuck up, *even once,* and you're dead."

Ben nodded. "As I should be."

Christopher took a slow drag of his cigar. "And when I call for you, you come. No questions. You don't work for Joey—you work for the *Giordano Crime Family.*"

I'd seen this conversation play out a hundred times before—loyalty being measured like it was something that could be weighed on a scale. Christopher was testing Ben, pushing him, but I already knew the outcome. Ben wouldn't crack; he was made of steel.

I'd spent a decade trusting Ben, relying on him to walk the tightrope between law and lawlessness without falling. But Christopher didn't know Ben like I did. Ben wasn't just some disposable errand boy. He was a necessary piece of the puzzle.

Times were changing, and the rules had to change with them. When I rose to my rightful rank, I'd be the one to make that happen. But for now, Ben and I had been given a second chance. We were too valuable to be disposed of—at least for now.

Chapter Fifty-One
JOEY

When Ben gave me the signal that William had crossed over into Staten Island, a surge of venom coursed through me. Coiled and ready to strike. Paul and Marco intercepted him and spun him a story, claiming they knew exactly where Adriana was hiding after he'd gone around, asking if anyone knew where he could find her. They promised to take him right to her. He followed without question right into the trap I had waiting. Now, he was mine. And I was waiting and ready in the warehouse.

I stood, flexing my hands in black leather gloves, the seams stretching over my knuckles. My gaze locked on William, slumped and tied to a chair, his face a swollen mess from the *"conversation"* we'd had earlier. A thin line of blood trickled from his temple, staining the collar of his sweat-drenched shirt. "You made your choice, William," I said. "No one puts their hands on Adriana and gets away with it. *No one.*"

He strained against the ropes, attempting to free himself. A bitter smile tugged at his bloodied lips. "You'd kill me over her?" he sneered. "Hate to tell you, but she's just a stupid—"

I struck before the word could poison the air, my fist connecting with his cheek. His head whipped to the side, blood spraying across the ground below him in dark, jagged streaks.

"You're not very smart, are you?" I growled. "I don't let things go easily—not when the people I care about get hurt."

He coughed, spitting blood, then smirked again. "You think you're some kind of hero? You can't save a whore! She's always needed saving. You'll find out—"

The words hit like a slap, and I froze, my jaw tightening until it ached. I reached into my waistband and drew my small revolver.

"I'm afraid I can't let this go," I murmured, more to myself than to him. "I thought maybe I'd take the high road—let you walk if you signed the papers. But some stains only come out when you cut them out. Some messes don't go away on their own. They need cleaning up."

William's eyes narrowed. "You don't scare me," he spat.

A cold smile crept across my face. "Good," I said, tilting my head. "It's more satisfying when you don't see it coming."

I pressed the muzzle against his knee and pulled the trigger. The crack of the gunshot echoed, followed by his anguished screams. He thrashed against the chair, his cries ricocheting into the air.

"That's for Adriana's tears," I said, stepping back.

William gasped, his face twisted in agony as blood soaked his pants and pooled beneath the chair. His chest heaved, eyes wide with terror, as I lifted the gun again, this time aiming for his chest. I crouched, bringing myself to his eye level. His breaths were shallow, broken by the weight of pain and fear. "When you meet the devil," I said, tapping the barrel against his sternum, "tell him *Joey 'The Shark' Romano* sends his regards."

I didn't wait for a response. I stood back and fired again, a deafening crack shattering the air. I unloaded every round into his body. I straightened, rolling my shoulders as if shaking off the weight of what had just played out before me. I'll live with it.

Whatever weight it adds to my conscience, I'll carry it. Some people need saving, and some people need burying.

Paul and Marco took care of the mess. Ben would handle the

rest—the falsified papers, the cover-up. William would disappear from the records, leaving Adriana a widow.

But not for long.

Adriana was always meant to be mine. I wouldn't stop—not until the day she shared my last name. And that day was fast approaching.

Chapter Fifty-Two
ADRIANA

Our home was alive with laughter, the sound of clinking glasses and jazz music drifting through the air. I stood in the center of it all, wrapped in the warmth of Joey's arms. It still felt unreal—the ring on my finger, the weight of my new last name. *Romano*. It seemed like a big responsibility. I was his wife now. We were so incredibly happy, despite the road we had to take to get here.

I glanced at him from the corner of my eye, taking in the way he leaned against the kitchen countertop, talking with Paul and Marco, a whiskey in one hand and a cigar in the other. His black suit was unbuttoned at the collar, his sleeves rolled up just enough to reveal the veins in his forearms. He looked handsome, but more than that, he looked at peace. Like the war inside him had finally quit. Whatever had happened in the last few days had worked out in his favor. And I could tell by how carefree he had become since the night he had returned, waking me up with his tender kiss. I thought he wouldn't return, but he had. He had returned and made me his wife.

Adriana Romano.

It had a nice ring to it. It commanded attention. Respect.

Authority. Marrying Joey was like marrying the president. Except that Joey only ruled New York City.

"To the bride and groom!" Paul called out, and the room erupted in cheers.

Joey smirked, lifting his glass as he pulled me closer to his side. "To my beautiful wife," he said in his gruff voice. "And to all of you who actually showed up to celebrate with us!" And then laughter erupted, filling every corner of our home. *Ours.* Everything was ours now. And I liked that. "It was about damn time I made her my wife," Joey continued, his hand squeezing my waist. "Now drink, eat, and for the love of God, somebody put on some good music before Marco starts singing for us again."

"Hey! In another life, I was meant to be a famous singer! Sinatra wouldn't have known what to do had I been his competition," Marco teased as the room burst into laughter.

Joey tugged me into his arms, his chest pressed against mine. His grin wide and his eyes pouring into me. "I haven't got to dance with my wife tonight."

He swayed us to the music, his arms held me so tight, like he never wanted to let go of me. His lips brushed against my ear, sending a shiver down my spine. "You sure you wanna be stuck with me, Mrs. Romano?" he murmured into my ear.

I tilted my head up to meet his gaze, my heart swelling at the way he looked at me—like I was the best thing that had ever happened to him. "I'd want it no other way, Mr. Romano."

His lips found mine, kissing me like we had all the time in the world. Because we did. The room erupted into cheers and whistles, but he just waved them off without breaking the kiss, which caused a laugh to flow out against his lips. I had finally gotten everything I'd always wanted. And more.

———

THE SECOND THE BEDROOM DOOR SHUT, HIS ARMS

snaked around me. "You happy?" he asked, his eyes searching mine.

I smiled, running my fingertips along his tie. "Happiest I've ever been."

His lips brushed against mine. "Good. Because this is just the beginning, sweetheart. Just you. Me. And Antonio."

And as he kissed me again, I knew—with absolute certainty—that I was exactly where I was meant to be.

Joey's lips lingered against mine. His hands moved to my waist, pulling me deeper into him as if he needed to feel every inch of me. My fingers tangled in his hair as his lips trailed from my mouth to my jaw, then lower to the curve of my neck. "But right now, it's just about us," he murmured, his voice rough.

"Just us, huh?" I whispered, a smirk dancing on my lips.

His hands slid down, gripping my hips as he lifted me. I wrapped my legs around his waist, gasping as my back met the cool wood of the bedroom door. His lips were everywhere—along my throat, my collarbone.

He pulled back just enough to meet my gaze. His eyes softened, a slow smirk tugging at his lips. "You married me today, Adriana. And now there's only one more thing we have to do."

I smiled, brushing my fingers along his jaw. "And what would that be, Mr. Romano?" I teased.

His hand came up to cup my face. "I've been waiting all night to take you. I want to get this dress off of you. *Now*." And to think I had spent so long surviving, so long being afraid of men. I leaned in, kissing him, my fingers trailing down his chest. "So, what are you waiting for?" I whispered. "I want you just as badly."

A low growl rumbled in his throat before he carried me across the room, laying me down on the bed. He hovered over me, brushing my hair back, his lips tracing every inch of my face before he whispered, "I can't believe you're mine, Adriana."

And as his hands moved over me, as his touch sent heat

swirling through my veins, I knew—no matter what happened next, no matter the world we lived in—I was safe with him.

I was home. He was home.

Joey's lips moved over mine. Every touch, every whisper of his breath against my skin sent pure hot lava coursing through me. I wanted so badly to be claimed by Joey, over and over again, for as long as I lived. He hovered above me, one hand bracing himself beside my head, the other dipped lower. My hands slide over his broad shoulders, pulling him closer. "I just want you, Joey. No more waiting." His fingers began their torture, pushing in and out of my slick, eager core. I was so desperate to feel him deep inside me.

A smirk tugged at his lips. "You have me, Adriana," he murmured. "You've always had me."

I gasped as his fingers pushed deeper. Every kiss, every graze of his skin against mine, left me burning for more. He wasn't just taking me—he was worshipping me. Like I was something he'd never expected to have, but would never let go of now that he did. His mouth worked down my body, so slowly, my skin sizzled. My hips thrust up, desperate for him. And when he latched onto my burning core, his beard pressed against my inner thighs, and his tongue licking and lapping like he was a starved man, I knew it was my undoing. But I wanted so desperately to be undone by him.

"Joey," I panted, but he gripped my thighs tighter and dove deeper, his tongue working pure magic on me. My fingers threaded through his hair as I rode out my high. His lips were on mine, his cock filling me inch by inch. His body was slick against mine. His teeth dug into my neck, and his body crashed into mine.

Everything else failed to exist. It was us against the world. It always has been. It always would be.

Because lying in Joey Romano's arms, I was safe. I was his. He was mine. And nothing in the world could take this from us.

Chapter Fifty-Three

ANTONIO

I had been lying about being sick for a week now. Well, partly lying. I had been sick, just not in the way Ma thought.

The nausea wasn't from a virus. It was from the memory that refused to let go of me, sinking its claws into my mind like a nightmare I couldn't wake up from. The gunshots still rang in my ears, forcing me to wake up in cold sweats. My stomach twisted every time I thought about it, every time I saw his face, his hands—so steady, so sure of what he was doing—pulling the trigger like it meant absolutely nothing.

I had followed Joey back to the warehouse, convinced he might need saving. But he didn't. He hadn't come here to fight for his life—he had come here to end someone else's.

The man I had spent *months* believing my mother had killed. I should have looked away. I should have shut my eyes,

turned, and run. But I didn't. I couldn't. My body was frozen, and all I could do was watch as Joey used him for target practice.

I wasn't sad that he was dead. In my mind, he had been dead for months. But what unsettled me, what made my stomach twist and caused me to vomit, was knowing my mother had never killed him in the first place. She had known he was alive all this time. And she had sent Joey to finish the job.

And the worst part of it all was that I remembered something. When Giovanni threw that baseball at me. He had said something that didn't sit right, something my gut had told me was important. Something my insides kept screaming to dig deeper into. I had ignored it. Refused to acknowledge it. But now, the pieces had finally fallen into place. And I had no choice but to confront it.

"What? You'll tell your daddy?" he teased. *"Oh, wait—your dad's dead, too, isn't he? Or is he?"*

I had cornered Giovanni in the boys' locker room. "What the fuck do you want, paperboy?" he growled, changing out of his baseball jersey.

"How'd you know?" I asked.

He scowled, looking at me like I had five heads. "Know what? How'd I know what? That you're a fucking moron? That's pretty easy. Anyone with a single brain cell could figure that out."

"No, you asshole. I'm talking about—" I paused, checking to see if anyone was listening. The coast was clear. "I'm talking about how you knew what my mother did."

He stared past me before letting out a single chuckle, his eyes locking onto mine. "Because, as it turns out, we're both just lurking in the shadows. We're both just watching. Listening. To a lot of shit we shouldn't be."

My body nearly went limp. The last thing I wanted was to have anything in common with Giovanni Accetta. "What are you talking about?"

"Oh, I don't know." He sighed. "You're the idiot who thought it would be wise to work for my grandfather. He's my own flesh and blood, and you couldn't pay me enough to work for him."

"I don't work for him," I said. "Work isn't the word I would choose. It's more like blackmail. Manipulation."

He chuckled again. "I could have told you that was bound to happen. But then again, I suspected someone like you would tie yourself to someone like my grandfather. What I didn't expect was that you'd spy on Joey. Once I figured that out, I couldn't believe it. I heard him say Adriana was in trouble. He said she thought she'd killed your father, but it turns out she didn't, and now he was coming to finish what she started. But we both know Joey—both sides of him—don't we?" His eyes tested me, looking straight through me.

My jaw clenched tighter than tight, nearly grinding my teeth down. "He finished the job," I told him.

He shook his head. "I'm no fucking fortune teller, but I could have told you he was going to finish the job *months* ago. I'm surprised it took him this long."

We sat in silence, just sizing each other up.

"What do you want from me?" he asked. "You wanted to know how I knew all this? Because that's all. And if that's all you wanted, could you move along and never speak to me again?"

"That's not all I wanted," I breathed out. I tossed my backpack around to my chest, dug my hand through it, and pulled out the same revolver my mother had used when she thought she'd killed him. The same revolver she'd forgotten all about because she was trapped in Joey's spell. Giovanni backed up, his hands flying up as his back pressed against the lockers. "I wanted your help."

"Well, put the fuckin' gun down, you moron!" he shouted.

I put it back in the backpack. "I think we've got something in common."

"What the hell would that be?" he spat.

"Joey hurt your mother. And now mine is unrecognizable since he came into our lives. I thought it was for the good. I thought Joey was the best thing to happen to us. But my mother employed him to kill for her. She's not that kind of person. He's fooled me into believing he's two different people. I think he's fooled her, too," I told him.

"So you want my help with killing Joey?" Giovanni muttered. I had promised to protect Ma. I thought I'd done so. I had encouraged her to be with Joey because I wanted her to be happy.

But in the process of falling for Joey, she'd turned into someone unrecognizable at the hands of him. And I had to be the one to save her from herself.

Even if it meant destroying *everything*.

It wasn't that he'd killed my biological father so brutally. It was that he'd moved my mother into a huge house and brain-washed her into believing the best way out was violence. The very thing that she reprimanded and grounded me for because of Giovanni, and yet here she is, okay with Joey murdering for her. I had justified it when I thought she'd done it in self- defense, but this was premeditated. And she had helped Joey do it, even if she hadn't been the one to pull the trigger.

Chapter Fifty-Four
ANTONIO

Two Days Later

My bedroom door cracked open. I tossed myself back into bed, yanking the blankets up to my chest before Ma's voice called out. "Antonio?" I forced myself to sound weak. "Hey, Ma."

She stepped inside, her brows knitting as she reached out to press her palm against my forehead. I held still, letting her check for a fever she wouldn't find. "You feel warm. You still not feeling well?"

I shrugged, looking away. "Just tired."

The door creaked open behind us, and my muscles tensed as Joey stepped inside. He stood in the doorway, arms crossed, brow raised. "So, the kid's a faker, huh?" My throat went dry, but I forced a weak laugh, ignoring the bitter taste it left behind.

"He's warm, Joey," Ma said.

"I'm fine. I just need some rest," I muttered. "I'm going to go to bed. The two of you go out. I'm fine."

"Rosa's downstairs if you need anything," she said, brushing a strand of my hair from my forehead. I gave her a fake, weak nod before she pressed a kiss to my forehead and then slipped out, shutting the door behind her.

Sneaking out of my bed, downstairs, and out of the house without Rosa knowing was almost too easy. Rosa was busy cleaning—putting fresh flowers everywhere, fixing the garden Ma had started. She was humming an old tune under her breath, lost in her own world, which made it easy for me to slip past her.

Giovanni was waiting outside for me when I slipped out. I yanked open the door and slid into the passenger seat, barely getting settled before he slammed his foot against the gas. My forehead almost bounced against the dashboard. Luckily, I had my seatbelt on. I was sure that was done on purpose by the way he snickered next to me.

"Jesus fucking Christ!" I snapped, gripping the door handle. "Are you trying to kill me before we even get there?"

Giovanni snickered, his hands loose on the wheel. "What? You had your seatbelt on, didn't ya?"

"Listen, asshole, don't pull anything stupid," I growled, taking the gun out of my waistband and putting it on the floorboard.

"Chill out," he muttered. "I was just practicing for later." "Yeah, well, practice on your own time," I shot back.

"Where'd you get this car from, anyway?" I asked as he coasted down the street toward Davidson's.

"I told my grandfather I needed it to pick up a girl," he said. I let out a snicker. "It wasn't a lie. I did before I came to get you. *Mia, in fact.*"

I side-eyed him. "You know, after this is all done, it's going to be nice going back to hating your fucking guts."

"Oh, I know," he said back. "Tomorrow, I'll wake up hating you again. And it's really all I look forward to." We pulled up outside Davidson's, and he glanced over at me. "Last chance to back out, paperboy."

I shook my head. "If you're a pussy, just say so." "Fuck you!" he spat.

I let out a breath and leaned my head back against the seat. "I still can't believe I'm stuck here with you. Out of all the people in the world, why did it have to be you?"

"You're the one who came to me for help, *remember*?" He turned to face me, raising an eyebrow. "So, really, this is just an equal exchange of suffering for both of us."

I sighed, rubbing my temples. "Jesus. I should've just tried to take Joey out myself."

"Yeah, because that would've gone well," he snarled.

I exhaled and glanced back toward Davidson's. Joey's car was parked outside. People came and went as they always did, but we still had no sign of Joey. And every passing minute made my pulse drum faster.

I had never been in such a blind rage in my life. This was supposed to be our fresh start. We had escaped. We'd come to Staten Island for a new beginning. But so far, I'd been blackmailed by a mafia boss, my mother had fallen in love with one, and every person in this town seemed to have some mafia connection. You couldn't even trust the cops—half of them were on the payroll. Not to mention, I'd had a gun shoved in my face by a psychotic gangster, and my mother had let Joey kill for her.

This had to end.

And I would be the one to put a stop to it. Taking Joey out would make it all go away. We'd pack up and leave this mess behind—find somewhere far from the mafia. A place where we could finally start fresh. And just like Ma had kept her secrets, I wouldn't tell her what I'd done. Some things were better left locked away.

Chapter Fifty-Five
ADRIANA

J oey pulled me in close, his arm wrapping around my waist, the smell of his expensive cologne clinging to my dress. "You ready?" he murmured, his lips brushing over my ear.

I looked up at him, at the grin playing on his lips. I laced my fingers with his and squeezed. "I've never been more ready." The Wise Guy was alive. Smoke curling through the air, glasses clinking, and jazz buzzing. It was our world—our people. I belonged here.

"There they are! The newlyweds!" Angela called out from behind the bar.

Soon, I was being pulled into hugs, kisses pressed to my cheeks, and hands tugging me into a seat at her announcement. Joey sat beside me, his arm slung around my chair, his fingers tracing circles along my shoulder.

"You two look disgustingly in love," Marco teased, raising his glass before taking a long sip of whiskey.

Joey smirked, pulling me against his side. "Jealousy is a disease with no cure, brother."

"There's nothing better than the single life," Marco shot back. "But I'll drink to the fact that you finally found a woman *crazy* enough to marry you."

The table erupted into laughter.

"Don't let Angela hear that." Joey winked, clinking his glass against Marco's.

Joey leaned in, his lips ghosting over my ear. "Dance with me, sweetheart." He stood before I could say yes, his hand extending toward me. My hand slipped into his, and he led me to the dance floor. Joey pulled me close, his arms wrapped around my waist, and my fingers curled behind his neck. His forehead pressed against mine as we moved, his breath warm against my skin. His hands tightened around me. "There's not a single thing in this world I want more than you, sweetheart. And you're stuck with me now."

I exhaled a soft laugh, brushing my fingers against the back of his neck. "Good, I wouldn't want it any other way."

Joey's grip on me tightened as he pulled me closer, his breath warm against my ear. "You know, I've never been so sure of anything in my entire life. You're it for me, sweetheart."

My heart skipped a beat as I gazed up at him, my fingers brushing against his cheek. "I feel the same way," I whispered.

He smiled softly. "I don't know what I'd do without you, and I don't ever plan on finding out."

I leaned in, my lips brushing against his, and whispered, "Good, because I wouldn't let you."

His chuckle rumbled against my chest, and he pulled me even closer, his lips curving into a mischievous smile. "Is that so? You think you can keep me locked down, sweetheart?"

I met his gaze, grinning. "Oh, I don't just think it—I know it."

He raised an eyebrow, his smirk widening. "You could hold me hostage for the rest of my days, and I'd still say thank you."

I laughed softly, my fingers tracing the edge of his collar. "Careful what you wish for," I teased. "You might find yourself tied up in more ways than one."

His grin softened, his hand brushing against the small of my back. "You've got a willing and eager prisoner."

"I think I'm ready to leave," I whispered in his ear.

His eyes softened, a dangerous smirk pulling at his lips. "Right now?"

"Yes," I said. "Right now, Joey." I pressed my lips against his. When we pulled apart, I smiled against his lips. "I'm dying to make love to my *husband*," I breathed, a playful grin tugging at my lips.

He chuckled low in his throat. "Then let's get out of here."

He took my hand, and we started for the door. Just as we reached the exit and the humid night air slapped our skin, the sudden screech of tires echoed in the street outside. The hairs on the back of my neck stood up. I turned my head, just in time to see an all-black car pulling up to the curb, its engine revving menacingly. It came to a halt, and a masked figure emerged from the passenger seat, holding a gun out of the window. I barely had time to react when the man raised his arm, aiming a gun directly at Joey.

"Joey!" I screamed, but the words barely left my lips before the sharp crack of a gunshot split the night in half. He collapsed against me, his weight pushing me backward as I tried to catch him. My hands shook as I pressed against the wound in his chest, the blood soaking through my fingers.

The sound of my pulse drowned out everything. I could hear the distant roar of the car driving off, but all I could focus on was Joey.

I knew someone would take him from me, but I didn't think it would happen so soon.

Chapter Fifty-Six
ANTONIO

A cold sweat trickled down the back of my neck. My grip on the gun tightened, fingers almost numb, as if the weapon had become part of me—something I could control, something I could wield.

The memory of Joey's voice rang through my head, clear as day: *"One shot, Antonio. One shot. That's all you got. So you always make it count."* The words echoed in my ears as I lifted the gun to the window.

One shot. That's all I've got. That's all I needed.

Joey stepped further into the street, oblivious to the threat that was inches away from his life. My finger twitched on the trigger. The gun in my hand felt like it had always belonged there. I squeezed the trigger, aiming straight for the heart that didn't seem to exist in his chest.

Joey had been taken down. And by the person he would have least expected. But for some reason, as the echoes of the shot faded away, all I could feel was the weight of my choices. The invisible blood on my hands.

One shot. One shot.

And I had taken it. And now I had to live with the stain of Joey's demise on my hands.

Giovanni glanced over at me, eyes narrowing. "So, how's it feel? You feel like a big man now?"

I shot him a sidelong glance, rolling my eyes. "What do you think? Maybe you should stay focused on your job before we get tracked down by every mobster in this town."

The truth was, I didn't feel any better. I thought this was going to solve the rage. An eye for an eye. But now all I felt was guilt.

He smirked, leaning back in his seat. "You've got the whole 'cold-blooded killer' vibe going on now."

I looked out of the window, and the reflection, in a black ski mask, was looking back at me. Every inch of innocence I thought I had left had just been stripped. "Let's just focus on getting rid of the gun, okay?"

He chuckled. "Oh, I'm sorry, did I hit a nerve? You know, I think you should go down as 'Most Likely to Commit Murder' in the yearbook. What do you think?"

I shot him a look. "If you keep this up, Giovanni, I might just go down as 'Most Likely to Commit Back-to-Back Murder.'"

He raised an eyebrow. "How the hell are we getting rid of this gun?"

I glanced out the window, trying to ignore the tension building in my chest. "I'll toss it out once you hit the right speed."

Giovanni's neck snapped to face me, eyes wide. "What? Are you out of your mind? That's the worst idea I've ever heard! You'd do better just walking into a police station and turning yourself in."

"Just drive," I said.

"I'm just saying, you could've at least left a note for the cops. 'Dear Officer, I killed Joey. It was a family thing. Love, Antonio.'"

"Press the fucking gas!" I shouted at him.

He rolled his eyes, grip tightening on the wheel as he began to rev. "I can't believe I'm still in this car with you. And, if you get caught, you're by yourself."

I gripped the revolver, my fingers trembling as I dangled it out of the window. I let it slip from my hand, watching it fall into the darkness. I closed my eyes, silently praying it would shatter into a million pieces. But I couldn't bring myself to turn around, to see if it had landed or if the damage was done. I just focused on the road ahead, heart pounding, hoping the past would stay buried.

Chapter Fifty-Seven

JOEY

By the time I saw the car, it was too late. The blacked-out windows, the engine purring. It was too late when I recognized it, too late when I saw the figure lean out from the passenger side. I heard the sound before I even felt the impact.

A gunshot.

The searing pain that shot through my chest made everything go white. It jerked me back, knocking the air straight out of my lungs. I could feel the heat of the blood rushing out of me, soaking through my shirt. This wasn't good. Adriana's scream reached me like it was underwater. I couldn't hear anything but the thumping of my own heartbeat pounding in my ears. I wanted to say something, anything, but the words caught in my throat.

Adriana's hands pressed against the wound in my chest, but it wasn't enough. I could already feel it—the blood draining, the weakness spreading like a wildfire through my veins. I glanced at her face, her eyes wide with horror, her lips trembling as she cried out my name. But I could hardly hear her. I wanted to reassure her. I wanted to tell her I was fine, that everything was going to be okay.

"*I'm okay*," I mouthed, hoping she could read lips tonight. I needed her to believe it, even if I didn't.

I could feel Adriana's palms pressing against my chest, holding me in place. It felt like I'd left my body, watching everything unfold from somewhere far away. People poured out of The Wise Guy, their faces twisted in fear, towering over me. Their mouths moved, their shouts urgent—but I couldn't hear a goddamn thing. Just static. A relentless, buzzing noise drowning everything else out. But it was getting harder to focus. The edges of my vision were blurred.

Paul and Marco rushed toward us. I felt hands beneath me, lifting me, and dragging me into the backseat of Marco's car. The movement made my head spin. Adriana was still holding on to me, her grip so tight I thought her fingers would break through my skin. I could see Marco in the driver's seat, speeding through the streets, glancing over his shoulder every few seconds. I wanted to slap him, tell him to keep his damn eyes on the road, but I didn't have the strength. Paul and Adriana were shouting at each other—Paul was probably telling her to calm down, but she was hysterical. I wanted to tell her the same, but I couldn't get the words out. And I knew she wouldn't listen, anyway—not with my blood smeared up her arms, drying in streaks.

I was sure the only thing keeping me alive was Adriana's touch. I didn't know what would happen when they separated us.

I felt the car come to a standstill. Paul and Marco rushed out, yanking open the doors and lifting me from the backseat. A few nurses ran forward, shouting as they helped me onto a stretcher. The fluorescent lights were so bright I had to clamp my eyes shut. I felt them rip off my tie and force the buttons on my shirt to reveal the wound, then a sharp sting in my arm, an ice-like sensation crawling through my veins.

And then, there was nothing but silence.

Chapter Fifty-Eight
ADRIANA

I sat in the sterile waiting room, my head in my hands, rocking back and forth in silent prayer. The smell of antiseptic stung my nose, mixing with the lingering scent of Joey's blood on my dress. It had dried stiff against the fabric. I couldn't get the image out of my head—the way he stumbled, the way his body crumpled to the pavement, the way his blood pooled beneath him.

Joey wasn't a saint. He had done terrible things. Things I had chosen not to think about. Things I had turned a blind eye to. But I couldn't live without him.

Paul and Marco paced in front of me like caged animals, their fists clenched, shirts still smeared with Joey's blood. The double doors swung open, and a doctor emerged, pulling down his surgical mask. I bolted upright, jumping out of my chair.

"He's stable," the doctor announced. "We managed to remove the bullet. He's lucky to have been brought in so quickly. But he's got a long recovery ahead of him."

My knees buckled as I collapsed into the chair behind me. A strangled sob tore from my throat, pressing my hands over my face. Paul sank into the seat next to me. "He's gonna pull through, Adriana," he muttered, wrapping me in a side hug. "But whoever did this won't get away with it."

Marco's jaw was tight as he stood across from us. "They'll regret the day they ever crossed Joey Romano."

A month ago, the thought would have terrified me. A month ago, I might have begged them not to retaliate, not to spill more blood. But now I felt nothing. No remorse. No hesitation. Whoever was brave enough to try to take out Joey had a bullseye on their back.

"Let me take you home and get you cleaned up," Marco said gently. "Paul will stay here, and you can come back after, but you need to get out of that dress."

I glanced down at the bloodstains. He was right—I needed to get it off, but there was something else gnawing at me. *Antonio.* I had to tell him what had happened before someone else did.

My heart clenched. *Oh God.* This was going to *destroy* him.

Marco guided me through the hospital corridors. I felt numb, almost like I was floating. Everyone I passed stared at me in horror as they looked at the sight of my dress, and I didn't blame them. This was horrific.

Marco opened the passenger door for me. I hesitated for just a moment before sliding into the seat. My eyes drifted to the backseat, where Joey had sat just a few hours ago. The faint, dried blood was still there, staining the upholstery. A shiver ran down my spine as the memory hit me—how quickly everything had spiraled out of control.

"Marco," I whispered, my voice trembling, "I need to tell Antonio. He has to know."

Marco closed the door softly, his face hardening. "Do you need me to stay and help you?"

I nodded quietly as I sat in the passenger seat, the steady hum of the engine lulling me into a strange kind of daze. The weight of what had just happened was still suffocating me. As we pulled into the driveway, I felt a cold chill settle deep in my bones.

I stepped out of the car, my legs shaky as I walked toward the front door. When I opened it, I saw Rosa standing in the kitchen, her back to me. She spun around, expecting to find Joey walking in beside me. Instead, her eyes landed on me— bloodstained, disheveled, and broken.

Her face drained of color as she rushed toward me. "Adriana," she whispered. Her hands moved over me, checking for any wounds. I was fine—*physically*. But Joey wasn't. I collapsed into her arms. The tears came, thick and fast, flooding down my cheeks. The horror of it. She held me tighter, murmuring comforting words I couldn't make out through my sobs.

I needed to tell Antonio. I had to. But how could I? How could I break his world with this?

I let Rosa guide me upstairs, helping me out of the bloody dress. As I stood under the warm spray of the shower, I closed my eyes, trying to wash the blood away—trying to wash the guilt and the terror out of my soul. But I knew I couldn't. That stain was there to stay.

Marco was waiting downstairs, his silence a stark contrast to the whirlwind of thoughts spinning in my head. He didn't ask questions, didn't say a word. Just waited for me to be ready. Our eyes met, and Marco silently followed me up the stairs. I hesitated as I reached Antonio's door; the weight of what I was about to say consumed me. I didn't want to do this. But I had no choice. I couldn't let him find out any other way.

I raised my hand and tapped on the door before cracking it open just enough to see Antonio sitting on the bed. His eyes met mine instantly, brows furrowing in confusion as he took in Marco's presence behind me.

"Antonio," I said softly.

"Yeah?" He sounded calm, but I could see the concern in his eyes.

I stepped inside, Marco following, and stood there for a moment, unsure how to begin. "We need to talk to you," Marco said. He sat down on a chair across from Antonio.

I slowly made my way to the bed, sitting next to Antonio. The truth was a weight I couldn't avoid anymore, but I was terrified of how he'd react.

"Joey," I started, my voice faltering. I paused, not knowing how to go on. "Joey was almost killed tonight."

His face twisted in confusion, and I could see the tension ripple through him. "What are you talking about?" He leaned forward, brow furrowed in disbelief. "He's alive?"

I nodded, trying to steady my voice as I reached out to gently caress his back. "Yeah, he's going to be okay."

Marco spoke up. "Don't worry, Antonio," he said. "Whoever did this won't get away with it. They can't hide when the entire state is looking for them."

But Antonio didn't seem to hear Marco. He stood up abruptly, his eyes wide with a mix of panic and disbelief. His breath quickened, and without a word, he rushed to the bathroom just a few feet away. The sound of him retching echoed in the silence that followed.

I stared at the door, my chest tightening. This was a nightmare. How had it come to this? I thought we had escaped it all, but somehow, the violence had followed us.

I could hear Antonio's harsh breathing, and the sound of him gagging was enough to make my stomach churn. I closed my eyes, wishing I could take all of this away from him. But I knew I couldn't. The reality of it—of what had happened and what was still to come—was crashing down on all of us.

I glanced at Marco, who looked just as helpless as I felt. It wasn't supposed to be like this.

Chapter Fifty-Nine
ANTONIO

I couldn't leave my bedroom. I wouldn't leave until I figured out how to undo everything I'd done.

Because now, the entire state of New York was hunting for the shooter—and it was me. The kid in the room next door.

Enzo and Michael hesitated at the door before slowly stepping inside. I couldn't even look at them. I felt numb, like I was trapped in some twisted dream. Only it wasn't a dream. It was real, a reality I'd created in a fit of rage.

"Hey," Enzo said, walking over to the chair across from me and sitting down. Michael took a seat on the bed next to me.

"You okay?" Michael asked softly.

I didn't respond. I couldn't. But I couldn't keep this secret anymore. My voice was barely a whisper when I spoke. "I shot him." Both of them froze, their eyes wide with disbelief. I could barely believe it myself.

"Are you on something?" Michael asked, looking concerned. "I'm serious," I said, finally meeting his gaze. "I shot him." "Why the *hell* would you do that?" Enzo growled.

"I saw him kill my father," I said. "I thought it was the only way to end this...*all of it*. He's turned my mother into someone else. I know she had a hand in having him take my father out. I trusted Joey. I've been spying on him for weeks and haven't seen anything worth reporting. But because of that, Vincent threatened to kill *me*. I followed him that night, and I saw *everything*." The two of them exchanged looks, both at a loss for words.

"You should have told us," Michael said. "Who helped you?" Enzo asked.

"Why is that your first question?" Michael shot back, glaring at Enzo.

"It's a valid question," Enzo replied, his gaze steady on Michael.

"Giovanni," I admitted. "He has a vendetta against Joey over what happened with Renee. But the thing is, Renee was set up to date Joey so Vincent could catch him doing something he shouldn't, and take him out."

"That's fucked up," Michael muttered under his breath.

"I can't believe you had Giovanni help you," Enzo remarked in disbelief.

"What is wrong with you?" Michael snapped, turning to Enzo.

"I'm his best friend!" Enzo shot back. "He should have come to me."

"No!" Michael practically yelled. "He should have gone to someone with *real* power! This could've been over long ago—without all this bloodshed."

"Well, it's too late now." I sighed, running a hand through my hair. "Who knows what they'll do when they find out it's me?"

Enzo's eyes narrowed. "What did you do with the gun?" "I got rid of it," I said, trying to sound confident.

"So you're good." Enzo shrugged.

"*Good*?" Michael barked. "He's far from good. You should tell Joey."

"That's stupid! Don't listen to Michael!" Enzo interjected quickly.

"We could go to my grandfather," Michael suggested next. "No," I said, shaking my head. "That's not an option."

"What kind of friend are you?" Enzo muttered, glaring at Michael.

"A good one! They're not going to kill a kid! If he explains what happened, they'll understand!" Michael shot back.

"And to think, for someone as smart as you, turns out you're just book smart," Enzo remarked. "There's always a black sheep in the family, I guess."

"The two of you aren't helping," I muttered, rubbing my temples in frustration.

"Well, you can't just go on with your life like nothing happened," Michael declared.

"I know that," I replied.

Nothing would ever be the same again. If I knew anything at all, it was that. The consequences of everything that had happened—everything I had done—were already too far beyond my control. I couldn't undo it. No matter how hard I tried to fix it, I couldn't go back and erase what had been set in motion. Now it was all just some long, drawn-out waiting game.

Chapter Sixty

ADRIANA

Every day without Joey felt like a slow, suffocating torture. I'd turn the TV on, and there it was—another update. And of course, they had to throw in that atrocious nickname, *The Shark*. It made my stomach churn every time.

Flowers arrived daily, from people I barely knew, their sympathy plastered on cards. People could say what they wanted about Joey, but the truth was, he was a loved and respected man. He'd built something in this city that couldn't be undone, and everyone respected him because of who he was. You'd think the mayor had been shot, for Christ's sake.

I couldn't walk out the door without some stranger trying to offer their condolences or stare at me like I was a spectacle. I just wanted to vanish into the background, to keep my family together and find some sort of normalcy again, but how could I? "Hey, honey," I said, gently fluffing up Antonio's hair as I passed by him.

"Hey, Ma," he mumbled, barely looking up as he nibbled on his toast.

I sat down at the table, my hand reaching to caress his shoulder. "Listen, I'm going down to the hospital to visit Joey. Do you want to come with me?"

"No," he replied. "No, I don't think I can do it. I'm not ready to face him yet."

I nodded. "I get it, sweetheart. And Joey will understand, too. But I just want you to know he's doing better. He's going to get through this and come home. It'll be like he was never gone. And most importantly, I need you to remember that we're safe."

"Yeah," he nodded, "yeah, we're safe, Ma."

"I love you," I whispered, brushing my fingers along the side of his face, hoping to offer some sort of comfort.

"Love you, too, Ma," he muttered. It hurt to see Antonio so broken. He barely left his room, barely ate, and hardly spoke.

———

WALKING INTO THE HOSPITAL ROOM, I STOPPED IN THE doorway, taking in the sight of Joey. He was propped up in bed, wearing a hospital gown instead of his usual crisp suit. It was strange seeing him like this, so vulnerable. Without a suit and a fedora.

"Wow, look at you, sitting up," I said.

"Hey, sweetheart." Joey smiled when he saw me. I walked over, leaning down to kiss him, and he mumbled against my lips, "I missed you."

"We miss you, too," I whispered back, my heart aching just seeing him like this.

"Where's my boy?" he asked, glancing past me, as if Antonio would walk in any moment.

"He couldn't come." I sighed. "He says he can't see you like this. He's been taking it hard."

"You tell him I'm fine?" Joey asked.

"I didn't tell him you're fine," I replied. "I told him you're getting better and that you'll be home soon."

"I'm fine," Joey insisted. "I want them to send me home."

"Joey, don't give them a hard time." I frowned.

"I've been trying to tell him all day he's gotta stay until they say he's well enough to leave," Paul finally spoke up from the chair in the corner of the room.

"I'm well enough," Joey shot back.

"You're lucky you're not a vegetable," Paul retorted as he stood and walked toward the door. "Anyways, I'll be downstairs drinking coffee. Leave you two alone. Anything you want while I'm down there?"

"Yeah, the discharge papers," Joey said. "Joey!" I hissed.

Paul grinned, poking his head back in. "You said extended stay? I'll see what I can do!" And with that, he left, closing the door behind him.

"You look beautiful," Joey said softly, gently caressing my face. "How are you doing?"

"I'm fine," I replied, but it didn't feel true. "I just miss you, that's all."

"Well, I'll be home as soon as I can get out of here." Joey grinned.

I smirked, rolling my eyes. "I know you will." I chuckled softly. "You know, I can't even go to the supermarket now without someone asking how you're doing. Everyone's been so worried about you."

"What about Antonio? What's going on with him?"

"I don't know." I sighed. "He doesn't leave his room much."
"If I could get out of here, I'd go talk to him," Joey said. "Let him know I'm fine. It's nothing to worry about."

Chapter Sixty-One
ANTONIO

I sat on the couch, frozen in place. The only sound I could hear was the relentless, fucking drumming in my ears. Ma was helping Rosa sort through the flower arrangements we'd been sent —the house looked like Rosa's old flower shop. Every person in the state of New York had sent something. Even the goddamn mayor. I couldn't even turn on the TV without seeing it—every reporter, from The Sun to The Times, covering the story.

I couldn't escape the blood on my hands.

I had one shot. And I had failed. Now I was fucked.

I watched as Rosa swung the front door wide open. Joey was sandwiched between Paul and Marco as they helped him inside. "They didn't give him a wheelchair?" Ma asked.

"I'm gonna get it from the car," Paul said. "The asshole won't listen."

"I've got legs. I can walk. I'm not being pushed around in a fucking wheelchair. Donate it to someone who needs it," Joey growled. "I'm fine."

"You just spent weeks in the hospital. You're not fine," Ma shot back.

Joey managed a smile as he looked at me. "Hey, kid." I just stared at him, like a ghost that had come back to life. "Don't worry," he said. "I'll be good as new in no time." Paul and Marco helped lower him onto the couch. "I've got it," he growled at them.

Ma pushed them aside, towering over Joey. "Joseph Romano, you don't *got it*," she told him, her hip cocked to the side.

"They said he's a terrible patient." Marco nudged Ma, smirking. She chuckled, plopping down beside Joey as she combed her fingers through his hair. "If he gives you a hard time, let me know. I'll come by and straighten his ass out for you."

"You'd do good to go home," Joey smirked at him. My eyes shifted behind Joey as Ben stepped in—the NYPD cop gone rogue—*Joey's newest sidekick.*

"How many fucking lives does this guy have?" he teased, making Paul and Marco laugh. Ben walked over, smiling and greeting me. But I couldn't speak. I couldn't move.

"Ben, Joey needs rest," Ma told him.

"I'm fine," Joey told her. "I've been resting up in that hospital bed so long I damn near lost my mind."

"Joey, you just got home," Ma snapped at him.

"Someone tried to take me out, Adriana." That sentence made goosebumps creep up my arms.

They say when you live with someone, you can't hide who you are. Joey couldn't hide who he was. He spoke in a strange code, one I had learned to translate in my mind. One Ma could translate in hers, too. I'd watched her say it back to him at times, their words layered with meaning only they understood. But I had begun to decode it. "Marco and Paul are handling everything. You need to focus on healing." Ma's eyes bored into his.

Joey shook his head. "I can't sit here while there's a target on my back. I won't let anyone in this family walk around with one, either."

She cupped his face, forcing him to look at her. "You almost died, Joseph. You think I give a damn about anything else right now? You're still here. That's all that matters to any of us."

Marco and Paul helped Joey off the couch, the four of them

disappearing into Joey's office. Once they were finally gone, I stood up and made my way to the door.

"Antonio," Ma called from behind me. She was already walking toward me. I turned just as she pulled me into a hug, her hands cupping my face.

"He's going to be okay. They'll find out who did this to him. I don't want you to worry about any of this."

That was exactly why I couldn't stop worrying.

Chapter Sixty-Two

JOEY

I couldn't sleep. Every time I closed my eyes, I was back outside The Wise Guy. Adriana's lips on mine, her whispered words —*I just want to go home and make love to my husband.* The warmth of her breath still lingered in my mind, taunting me. It had been a perfect moment. And then—

The flash of headlights. The squeal of tires. The glint of metal.

I woke with my breath ragged, my pulse pounding against my skull. My body ached, a sharp pain digging into my side where the bullet had torn through me. I sat up slowly, wincing, rubbing a hand down my face. I couldn't stop replaying it. Over and over, like a broken record. I could see the gun, but I couldn't see the face behind it. That was the part that was eating me alive. Someone had tried to kill me. Someone who knew exactly where I'd be.

I swung my legs over the edge of the bed, pushing myself to my feet, biting back the groan of pain as I limped toward the window. The estate was quiet. I clenched my jaw, my hands curling into fists. I'd spent my whole life surviving, clawing my way out of the gutter, making damn sure no one ever got the best of me. And yet, someone had. Someone had gotten close enough to put a bullet through me.

I couldn't let it go. Not until I knew who. Not until I put them in the ground.

I pressed a hand to my side, the bandages rough against my fingertips. The pain barely registered. The rage burned hotter. I'd find them. And when I did, I'd make damn sure they regretted not finishing the job. Because anyone with any sense would know you've got one shot, so you always make it count.

Chapter Sixty-Three

ANTONIO

I hadn't slept in what felt like an eternity. And at this rate, I didn't think I would ever get any rest. Every time I tried to close my eyes, I saw Joey stepping out of that exit door. I saw my own hands gripping the gun. I heard his words echo in my head— *One shot, Antonio. One shot. That's all you got. So you always make it count.*

I had made it count. But not enough.

Joey was alive. And he wouldn't rest until he found out who tried to kill him. Little did he know the person was his son in the room down the hallway from him. Right under his nose the entire time. It was only a matter of time. Joey wasn't the kind of man to let things go. He'd dig and dig until he found the truth. And when he did...

I'd be dead.

I stormed into the boys' locker room, shoving the newspaper against Giovanni's chest. He scowled, snatching it from my hands and glancing down at the bold headline.

Could the shooter expect The Shark to be out for blood?

"We've got a problem," I said.

He chuckled, shaking his head. "No, *you* have a problem."

Smirking, he shoved the newspaper back at me. "Now get the fuck out of my way."

I grabbed his arm, spinning him around. "You were the driver! That makes you part of this!"

His jaw tightened. "And I did my fucking job. I got us the fuck out of there." He stepped in close, eyes burning into mine. "You had one job, and you fucked it up."

"If I go down, so do you," I shot back.

Giovanni grinned. "Joey would expect this from me. But you?" He tilted his head. "Imagine what he'll do when he finds out his brand-new son was behind the whole thing." He shoved me hard against the lockers. But I didn't move. I stood there, my mind racing, trying to figure out what the fuck I was going to do.

I had made a mistake. And there was no way to take it back. Every day, he was getting better. Stronger. But also more obsessive —more unhinged in his desperate search for the person who shot him. Living under the same roof with him had become suffocating. But I was sure that was just the guilt talking.

———

Joey's head poked through my bedroom door, startling me. "Hey, kid."

"Hey, Joey." I snapped my head up as he slipped inside, closing the door behind him.

The walls felt like they were closing in. Just the two of us. *Trapped.* I hadn't even noticed I'd been pacing until then. Joey sat at the edge of my bed, and I forced myself to join him. "I wanted to apologize," he began. "For everything that's happened these last few weeks."

"It's okay," I cut in.

He exhaled, running a hand over his jaw. "I just want you to know—I'm getting better. I'll be back to myself in no time. We'll be back to how we were before you know it. Tossing the baseball in the new backyard and getting you all ready to be the next big Yankee star, with me front row."

Then came the smirk. My stomach twisted. What the fuck had I done?

"I feel terrible that you've had to go through all this," Joey said, wrapping an arm around my shoulders and pulling me closer. I wanted to resist, but I was exhausted—in every way a person could be. My body slumped, and my head dropped.

"Did you figure out who did it?" I dared to ask.

His grip on me tightened. "Ben's working on it," he said.

My eyes snapped to his, searching for any hint of suspicion. But there was none. He didn't suspect me. Which could only mean he suspected someone else. And that meant someone else would die because of me. "What are you going to do to them?"

Joey sighed, shaking his head. "That's not important."

A sob tore through me before I could stop it. I collapsed forward, burying my face in my hands. Joey tugged me closer, holding me against him. But it felt wrong. Wrong to want his comfort. Wrong to let him give it. And wrong to know I was guilty while someone else would soon pay the price.

Chapter Sixty-Four
JOEY

I sat at my desk, my whiskey glass sat half-empty, the amber liquid swirling as I took slow sips. I looked over at the office door when I heard the tap that broke the silence. The door creaked open, and Ben slipped in. "What is it?" I asked.

I watched him cross the room like he was stepping over landmines, a manila folder tucked under his arm. "I got something for you," he said.

"Do you know who did it?" He didn't say anything. Just stood there, staring at me like he was trying to figure out how to break a man in half without touching him. Then, he placed a folder on my desk. There was a thud when it hit my desk, letting me know something was inside. My eyes met Ben's again, searching for answers.

"It's all in there," he told me. "You need to see it for yourself." Something cold curled in my stomach. Ben paused at the door, his hand gripping the doorknob as he looked over his shoulder at me. "Once you open that, there's no going back."

The door clicked shut behind him. I sat there, staring at the folder. The room was too quiet. The walls felt too close. For weeks, I'd been trying to drag the truth into the light. And now, it was right in front of me. Staring me dead in the eyes. But I wasn't sure if I wanted to know. I forced myself to face the truth. I knew I'd never rest until I reached the end.

So I flipped the folder open, stuck my hand inside, and pulled out a revolver. I'd never seen it before. I didn't know who it belonged to. But there was another envelope inside. It was registered. And the second I read the name William Bianchi, my world tilted. Nothing in the fucking world could have prepared me for that. Because Adriana couldn't have done it. She was with me. William couldn't have done it because I killed him. That meant it could only be one other person.

Antonio Romano. My son.

Chapter Sixty-Five

ANTONIO

The second I stepped through the front doors, I knew something was wrong. Joey was standing in the middle of the living room, hands in his pockets. Still as a fucking statue. Like the calm before the storm. A predator waiting for the right moment to pounce. "Where's Ma?" I asked, shrugging off my backpack. I dropped it by the front door and shoved my hands in my pockets. I had already begun to sweat profusely.

Joey tilted his head, his eyes never leaving mine. "She's gone over to visit Angela and Lucy."

I nodded, but the air in the room was suffocating. He knew. He fucking knew what I'd done. I could see it in his eyes. He was peeling back my skin, seeing straight through me. I could hear my heartbeat pounding in my ears, and I was sure he could hear it, too. Every instinct screamed at me to run, to get the hell out of there. But running would only confirm what he already knew.

So I stood there. Still as a fucking statue.

Waiting. Waiting for him to make his move. Waiting for the moment, he decided to end this. Because Joey Romano didn't just let betrayals slide.

His eyes were ice cold. His jaw clenched tightly. His gaze never left mine as he stepped forward. "Why'd you do it?" he asked.

I couldn't find words. My throat felt tight. All I could do was back up and create more space between us.

"And to think, I never thought you'd betray me." His eyes were hard as stone, cold as ice. I felt a sickening twist in my stomach, gnawing at my gut. "I trusted you," he whispered, his gaze glued to me before his eyes fell to the floor. He shook his head, chuckling in disbelief. He lifted his head, cornering me with his eyes. "I treated you like my own flesh and blood, Anto- nio. I gave you my last name. And you tried to kill me. For what?" It was suffocating. The weight of it. The guilt of the trigger I pulled— the betrayal that had shattered everything. Standing in front of him, a man I had once seen as a father. And I had shattered everything we'd built with a pull of the trigger. "You were everything I never had, Antonio." Joey's voice broke the silence again. "You were my chance to make things right. I wanted to give you everything I never had. I can't make sense of this. How could you do something like this?"

"I'm sorry," was all I could manage to say. But it wasn't enough. I knew that. I wasn't sorry enough. Not for everything. Not for the damage I'd done. I didn't know how to make it right. How to take back the mess I'd made. Because there was no undoing what I'd already done. I had pulled that trigger and intended for it to end Joey.

I collapsed onto the sofa, burying my face in my hands. "Why'd you do it?" Joey asked again.

When I finally looked up at him, I didn't see anger. I saw hurt —deep, raw hurt. And somehow, that made it all so much worse.

"I wanted to know if you were in the mafia," I admitted. "I started asking around town, even Mr. Russo. Vincent caught wind of it. One day, he stopped me on my route and said he needed a favor. But it wasn't a normal kind of favor—there was something underneath it, some unspoken threat. He told me I couldn't tell anyone. So I didn't.

"I met him in the park that afternoon, and that's when he told me what he wanted. He wanted me to spy on you and report back on everything I observed. At first, I didn't see anything. Nothing that proved anything. And that pissed him off. One day, he put a gun to my face and threatened me. I guess he thought I was holding out on him and protecting you. So I started watching you more closely."

"That's when I followed you to the warehouse. That's when I saw you kill him. I thought he was dead. I thought Ma had killed him."

Joey let out a deep sigh, collapsing onto the couch beside me.

He buried his face in his hands, mirroring me.

"It's not that I care about him," I continued, my voice breaking. "I don't. You're the only father I've ever really known. And that makes this so much worse. I don't even know what I was thinking. I don't know if I was thinking at all.

"But I started putting two and two together—the only way you could've killed him was if Ma helped you. If she put the gun in your hands and told you to pull the trigger."

"Antonio—" Joey tried to interrupt, but it was like someone had opened a floodgate. I couldn't stop. Months of secrets, of guilt, of doubt spilled out of me all at once.

"I thought you corrupted her. That maybe you were the bad guy, the monster everyone says you are. She was never the kind of person to do something like this. Self-defense? Sure. She did what she had to do to save my life, and I justified it. I let it go. But this? This was premeditated. This was something else. And I blamed you.

"I convinced myself that the only way to end this madness—this never-ending war between you, Vincent, and the mafia running this whole damn town—was to take you out. And to convince Ma to run away again."

My voice trailed off into silence, the weight of my confession settling between us like a storm neither of us knew how to weather.

"Jesus, kid." Joey finally exhaled, running a hand through his slicked-back hair. He looked over at me, but I couldn't bring myself to meet his eyes. All I could do was stare straight ahead. It felt good to finally say it out loud, like shedding ten pounds— but instead of weight, it was guilt. My face was hot and wet, and I hadn't even realized how much I'd been crying until the silence stretched between us.

"Look at me, Antonio."

I forced myself to turn to him. We were sitting almost side by side on the couch, close but miles apart in the ways that mattered. His eyes were watery, too. My lip quivered as I scanned his face— full of sadness, not anger.

"Your mother never asked me to do anything," he said. "It was me. I made that choice. And I'm sorry you had to see it."

He reached for me, gripping my shoulders before pulling me into his arms. I let him. I wanted to.

"I love your mother. And I love you too, Antonio." His voice cracked as he held me, and I clenched my eyes shut, gripping the back of his shirt like I was afraid he'd disappear.

When I finally sat up, I wiped my face, watching Joey do the same.

"Your mother is not some pawn in my game," he continued. "I've done bad things. Things I can't take back. But I never wanted you to see that part of me. Not because I was hiding it. But because I love you too much to put that weight on you. Because you're my son, and I want more for you. I want to be there—front row—for everything you do in life. And I never wanted this world to touch you."

He reached out again, this time placing a firm hand on the back of my neck, grounding me. "We're going to get through this."

Chapter Sixty-Six

JOEY

Antonio and I sat there for a while. The weight of everything he confessed settled between us. He told me how he overheard Vincent talking to Hector—admitting that they were the reason I had been put away. It made sense. I was next in line. Christopher had promised me the position of underboss, but while I was rotting in prison for ten years, that chain of command shifted. Vincent took what should have been mine, and the moment I got out, I was ready to take back what had been stolen from me.

Then Antonio told me something else—something that made my blood run cold. He had heard Vincent and Renee talking. Renee had only been with me to help Vincent find a reason—any reason—to take me down. If I so much as stepped out of line, Vincent would use it against me, eliminate me as a threat, and secure his position for good. That wasn't hard to believe. Not about Vincent. Not about Renee. And oddly enough, not about Hector.

I had suspected Vincent was behind my shooting. That's why I had Ben scope out his place—to prove it. To put an end to it. Turns out I was wrong about that bit.

History has a funny way of repeating itself. In some sick,

twisted way, Antonio and I had been caught in the same cycle. The same betrayals. The same battles. The same war, just with different players.

Even now, when I look at him, it feels like looking into a mirror, staring into the darkest, deepest part of my soul. The tragedy was that I'd been thrust into a life of blood, dirty money, and shadows that haunted me in my sleep. My sins were supposed to end with me—die with me. I was supposed to give Antonio the life I never had, the life I'd always wanted. I wanted him to have more. To be more than me. But instead, I'd tainted his soul. My choices had bled over, staining his hands.

I had never saved Adriana and Antonio. They'd saved me. I bought this house thinking only of myself. I thought I'd suffer alongside Renee long enough to succeed Vincent, then come home to a giant, empty house and fill it with filthy, dirty money. I'd be safe here in my fortress. But that plan shattered as quickly as I'd built it.

I thought I never wanted to be a father—my own father was too shitty, his blood coursing through my veins, writing my fate for me. But that day at the diner when Adriana approached me, it was Antonio behind her that made me want to step in. He was the reason I helped. Because in helping him, I thought I could heal the part of me nobody cared to touch. The part I thought would never have a chance to breathe. Looking over Adriana's shoulder at him, I thought I had a second chance. A chance to rewrite my own destiny. I thought maybe destiny could rewrite itself. I could escape my father's sins and help Antonio escape his, too. The darkness that haunts me was never meant to touch Antonio. The sins of the father were never meant to bleed into the son.

This started with me, and it ends here with us.

My sins will never be his because he's the only son I could ever want. And I'm the only father he's got. His future won't have to be written in the same bloodstained ink as mine.

There was one thing I needed to take care of—confronting

Vincent. I stepped out of the house, ready to get in the car, when Paul's tires screeched into the driveway. He barely put the car in park before throwing the door open and jumping out, rushing toward me like he had just run a marathon.

"Joey!" he called, breathless.

And just like that, history proved once again that it has a way of repeating itself. Karma always comes back around.

Because the next thing out of his mouth was— "Vincent's dead."

For a moment, the words didn't register.

"What do you mean he's dead?" I asked, my throat suddenly dry.

"I mean, they found him face down in his living room. Shot. Point-blank range," Paul said, still catching his breath.

Vincent, the man who had built his reputation on surviving hits that he'd been labeled as "Lucky", hadn't lived up to his nickname this time. Someone had gotten to him first. And this time, he wasn't lucky enough to survive the hit.

I swallowed hard, my plans shifting in real time. There would be no confrontation. No last words. Instead, I had a whole new problem on my hands—figuring out who did it. And why.

"When did this happen?" I asked. "A few hours ago," Paul said.

That meant out of everyone who had a reason to want Vincent dead—and there were plenty—the only ones I could cross off the list were Antonio and myself. We had been at the house for the past few hours.

Which meant the killer was still out there. And I needed to find them.

Continue Reading for
Chapter One of Sinful Oaths

Chapter One: Sinful Oaths

JOEY

The dead don't stay lucky forever.

That was the first thought that hit me when Paul came barreling out of his green Cadillac Series 62 Eldorado towards me. The button to his light gray suit revealed the crisp white dress shirt underneath. His auburn colored businessman hairstyle, which he fluffed to one side, was a mess on top of his head. "Joey!" he called. "Vincent's dead."

I should've felt satisfied. *Relief.*

All I felt was unfinished business.

The sun was a merciless bastard that afternoon, burning down on us as if it knew how hot the streets were about to get. I stood near the driver's door of my black 1959 Ferrari, its polished body baking under the glare. The long driveway stretched out to the street, flanked by sprawling estates similar to ours—Angela's house next door, Lucy's just beyond hers. A few others lined either side, and at the very end of the street, looming like a landmark, stood Staten Island High School.

Paul planted himself in front of me. His eyes pleaded with mine. "You need to lay low because you're gonna be the *first* one they question."

I heard him. He had a valid point. The only trouble was, it

317

wasn't registering. The hatred I carried for Vincent...it drowned out logic. Drowned out common sense. The man had caused more hell than he ever paid for. Now someone had handed him his penance. But it wasn't my hand that did the writing.

"I want to see him," I said with conviction. "I *need* to see it for myself." I stepped towards the driver's side door, but Paul moved faster, blocking me before I could reach it. My brows drew tight, and a knot of irritation formed between them. Heat sparked behind my eyes, as if I could scorch straight through him and the sheer audacity in his gaze.

"You show up at that scene, everyone's gonna know you did it," He warned. "Or at least, think you did. Doesn't matter which one they run with...it's going to be World War Three on the streets."

I knew he was right. The trouble was, I didn't care.

"I was only a few hours late from doing the job myself," I hissed. "If I'd gotten there sooner..." I jabbed a finger into my chest. "...it would've been me pulling the trigger."

Paul's patience shattered like glass. His shoulders stiffened. "Snap out of this!" he barked. He had always been the calm one. In twenty years, I could count on one hand the times he'd raised his voice. "You are going to regret this. You go anywhere near that crime scene, and you'd be better off admitting to the fucking crime yourself."

I stared at him. The words finally sank through, and a strangled chuckle escaped my lips. I dragged in a breath before giving a slow nod. "You're right, Paul."

I glanced behind me. I had everything I ever wanted and more. Adriana had turned our estate into a home, while the entryway leading up to the door boasted a flowerbed that Rosa had planted. I had become Antonio's father in every sense of the word. Adriana was my wife. My health was nearly back to what it had been. My business had grown so much that I was considering specializing in luxury cars—the first luxury car dealership on the East Coast featuring only the finest American and European models. I do have a lot to lose. Or maybe, more accurately, a lot to protect.

I gave his shoulder a quick pat. "If I show up or lay low, it won't matter. I'm already guilty in their eyes. And if that's the case, I'd rather go out with the image of that unlucky bastard *burned* into my head. Let the whole damn world think I was the one who got to him first. I really don't give a fuck, Paul."

Paul blew out a huff through his nose; his lips pulled into a tight line. I had just taken my hand off his shoulder when Adriana's cherry-red 1959 Chevy Impala rolled into the driveway. She glided past Paul's Cadillac and beside my Ferrari, then cut the engine, pushed the door open, and stepped out. Her head peeked over Paul's shoulder. All I could see were her black cat-eyed sunglasses and those perfect victory curls she loved to wear. Her heels clicked against the pavement as she walked toward the hood of the car, coming fully into view as she approached us.

She wore a white A-line dress, narrow at the top and sleeveless, flaring just above her knees. She looked stunning. I hadn't seen her wear it before. It was hard to remember that Paul was furious, trying to convince me not to ruin my life, or that Vincent might have been murdered by someone else. All I could see was her in that dress; everything else faded into the background.

"What's going on?" she asked, suspicion lacing her voice.

Paul got his words out faster than I could. "Could you talk some sense into your husband?" He held my gaze, his green eyes squinting, and lips pressed into a thin line.

Her glare burned into the side of my face as mine locked on Paul's eyes. She wanted an explanation, and I wanted to wrap my hand around Paul's throat for outing me like that. Paul jabbed a finger in my direction.

"Think about what you've got going for you, Joey. Don't throw it all away for your pride. He's dead. Go inside, have a glass of whiskey like the rest of us, and lie low, so you're not the one they suspect."

Adriana crossed her arms over her chest, cocking her hip to

the side as the toe of her heeled foot tapped against the pavement in silent judgment. She tilted her sunglasses down enough for me to see the fierce glint in her dark eyes. "What's he talking about, Joey?"

My mouth went dry, and now it's going to take everything in me to hold myself back from tackling Paul right here in the driveway because the last thing I needed was for Adriana to get caught up in the middle of this. "That's enough from both of you." My voice dropped to a growl.

Paul and I held our standoff a moment longer before he finally let out the breath he'd been holding, turned on his heel, and strode past me to his Cadillac. I felt Adriana's eyes burning into the back of my head as I watched him slam the car into reverse, tires squealing as he backed out and sped off down the street.

The driveway fell quiet again. But only for a second.

Acknowledgments

This story came to life in the summer of 2014 while I was in New York City. It wasn't until many years later that my dearest, most beloved writer and fellow actor friend, Timothy Verrot, pushed me to publish it on Wattpad. We spent countless hours taking up space at every local coffee shop in town, just so he could hold me accountable. Those magical moments of bringing fictional characters to life and making them feel tangible still give me goosebumps. The times we roleplayed as Joey and Adriana—how they would think and act in different situations—made them feel real.

Timothy Verrot, thank you for your invaluable mentorship. Not only did you teach me method acting, but you also introduced me to Jack Grapes' method writing techniques. Your encouragement to create on Wattpad is something I will forever be grateful for. I miss you terribly, my friend, and I'm heartbroken that you can't be here to celebrate this moment with me.

To my husband, the man who blindly supports me every day of my life. The love of my life. The person who makes every day feel like I'm starring in a romcom. The man who fact but you didn't care. And you pushed me to keep going when I thought about giving up.

My sweet children, who screamed at the top of their lungs when I told them I was becoming a "real author." Sorry, you can't read this series right now. Don't worry, I'll publish the other one soon. Just for my boys.

Mom, thank you for spending so much of my youth watching mafia documentaries so we could understand the psychology behind it all. Only you will know the countless Easter eggs hidden within these pages. Your boldness and no-nonsense attitude have always been two of the most admirable things about you, along with your beauty. And all that research really seemed to pay off!

Dad, I wish you were here to see me publish this book. I know how proud you'd be. A man of many layers. The life advice you've given me has brought me here. You always said "can't never could," so I did. I finally did it."

My dearest grandmother, a woman of sheer elegance and charisma, an the inspiration behind Lucy and her dirty martinis. You inspired me to set this story in 1959, a time as glamorous as you and your big personality.

Makayla, my best friend, my closest confidante, and the one person on this planet who knows me better than I know myself. Also, the one who encouraged the banter throughout this series, because if only the world could hear our snarky exchanges, we'd be dubbed a comedic duo. I'm glad they brought you home that day, even though I thought my life as an only child was over. (I know you're laughing, weirdo.)

Julia Kent—thank you for being my first commenter all those years ago on Wattpad. Your encouragement and praise came at a time when I was ready to quit, and you reminded me why I started writing in the first place. You believed in me when I didn't, and I'll be forever grateful for that.

My dearest beta readers who signed up, volunteered their time, and provided feedback as first-time readers. This book wouldn't be what it is without you. Thank you, Emily Noeh, Deseray Messer, Elaine, Bow, Destiny, and Zoe Adams.

Emi at Modern Designs 139—thank you for seeing my vision and turning it into a stunning reality. You truly are a force of nature, and I'm so grateful for your creativity and expertise in bringing this book cover to life. You understood the vision and made it happen!

And last but not least, to everyone who has followed me and believed in me—from my Wattpad days to this very moment, and everything in between—this book is for you. Every ounce of blood, sweat, and tears went into this story, and I hope you read it and lose sleep over it just like I did while writing it.

If you're still reading, congratulations! You've made it to the end, and I hope at least a few of my attempts at humor made you chuckle. It may say I'm the author, but this book wouldn't be possible without the incredible people in this section.

About the Author

Zara's love for storytelling began at the age of nine, when she first plotted a book in a spiral notebook in December 2004. From that moment on, her passion for reading and writing only deepened. With a background in method acting and method writing, she brings emotional depth and authenticity to every story she tells.

Now a wife and mother of three, Zara writes from her home in South Carolina. She is the founder of Olive Press Publishing, a freelance editorial service and independent small press dedicated to supporting authors at every stage of their creative journey. When she isn't crafting stories or working with fellow writers, Zara enjoys spending time with her family, swimming, and traveling the world.

Sign up for her newsletter to stay updated: www.zara-jadeastrid.com

Also by Zara Jade Astrid

Book 2 in the Sins of the Father series, Sinful Oaths.

www.ingramcontent.com/pod-product-compliance
Lightning Source LLC
Chambersburg PA
CBHW050516110726
47899CB00005B/1479